"Brad Thor has mastered the art of the thriller cliffhanger."

—*New York Journal of Books*

"Brad Thor thrills yet again with *Near Dark*."

—*The San Diego Union-Tribune*

Praise for *Backlash*

"As close to perfect as a thriller can be."

—*The Providence Journal*

"*Backlash* is a triumph."

—*Bookreporter*

"*Backlash* is the best thing Thor has ever written."

—*The Real Book Spy*

Praise for *Spymaster*

"A modern Cold War 2.0 thriller . . . impossible to put down."

—*National Review*

"Thor convincingly portrays Russia as a reborn Cold War–era evil empire hell-bent on reconquering its former territory."

—*The Washington Post*

"A master of action and pacing, Thor continues channeling the likes of John le Carré in crafting a thinking-man's thriller packed with as much brains as brawn, making *Spymaster* a must-read for summer."

—*The Providence Journal*

"A terrific, terrific read."

—KKTX

ALSO BY BRAD THOR

The Lions of Lucerne
Path of the Assassin
State of the Union
Blowback
Takedown
The First Commandment
The Last Patriot
The Apostle
Foreign Influence
The Athena Project
Black List
Hidden Order
Act of War
Code of Conduct
Foreign Agent
Use of Force
Spymaster
Backlash
Near Dark
Black Ice

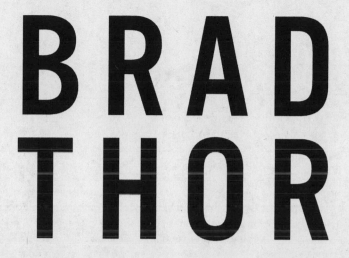

BRAD THOR

FULL BLACK

A THRILLER

EMILY BESTLER BOOKS

ATRIA

New York   London   Toronto   Sydney   New Delhi

EMILY
BESTLER
BOOKS

—

ATRIA

An Imprint of Simon & Schuster, Inc.
1230 Avenue of the Americas
New York, NY 10020

This Emily Bestler Books/Atria Paperback edition August 2021

EMILY BESTLER BOOKS/ATRIA PAPERBACK and colophon
are trademarks of Simon & Schuster, Inc.

For information about special discounts for bulk purchases, please contact Simon & Schuster Special Sales at 1-866-506-1949 or business@simonandschuster.com.

The Simon & Schuster Speakers Bureau can bring authors to your live event.
For more information or to book an event, contact the Simon & Schuster Speakers Bureau at 1-866-248-3049 or visit our website at www.simonspeakers.com.

Interior design by Yvonne Taylor

Manufactured in the United States of America

7   9   10   8   6

Library of Congress Cataloging-in-Publication Data has been applied for.

ISBN 978-1-4165-8661-6
ISBN 978-1-9821-4838-6 (pbk)
ISBN 978-1-4165-8676-0 (ebook)

To the patriots who exist across the political spectrum

To all supporters of freedom and democracy

In the clandestine community, the most sensitive classified assign-ments are referred to as *black operations*.

Few suspect, and even fewer realize, that there is a darker side to black operations. These missions are born in the shadows. They are not classified or recognized. They simply don't exist.

They are Full Black.

The attacks as well as the strategy in this novel are based upon a disturbing blueprint designed to assist in and encourage the destruction of America. This blueprint, entitled *Unrestricted Warfare*, is real.

While this is a work of fiction, specific information was purposely altered in certain sections so as not to enable those who wish to do harm.

Many of the vulnerabilities depicted in this novel continue to exist.

Ex Umbra—From the Shadows

FULL
BLACK

CHAPTER 1

His timing had been perfect. Swerving back into the lane at the last possible second, he watched in his rearview mirror as the white Škoda behind him careened off the road and slammed into a large tree.

Applying his brakes, he pulled off the road and stepped out of his vehicle. The air smelled of spruce and spilled gasoline. The woman from the passenger side joined him. They had to move fast.

Half their work had already been done for them. The terrorist in the Škoda's passenger seat had not been wearing his seat belt. He was already dead.

The driver was trying to unbuckle himself when Scot Harvath arrived at his window. He was cursing at him in Arabic from inside. Harvath removed a spark plug, often referred to as a *ghetto glassbreaker*, from his pocket and used it to smash the window.

Grasping the terrorist's head, Harvath gave a sharp twist and broke his neck. Gently, he guided the dead driver's chin down to his chest.

The final passenger was a young Muslim man seated in the back of the car who was screaming. As Riley Turner opened his door she could see he had wet himself. Painting his chest with the integrated laser sight of her Taser, she pulled the trigger.

The compressed nitrogen propulsion system ejected two barbed probes and embedded them in the young man's flesh. The insulated wires leading back to the weapon delivered a crackling pulse of electricity that incapacitated his neuromuscular capability.

Yanking open the opposite door, Harvath carefully avoided the probes as he pulled the man from the vehicle and laid him on the ground. Once the man's hands were FlexCuff'd behind his back, Harvath removed a roll of duct tape and slapped a piece over his mouth. Producing a pair of pliers, he yanked out the probes. The man winced and emitted a cry of pain from behind his gag. As he did, Harvath looked up and saw a familiar pearl-gray Opel minivan approaching.

The van pulled parallel with the crash scene and slowed to a stop. The sliding door opened and a man in his midtwenties, holding a shopping bag, stepped out into a puddle of radiator fluid and broken glass.

The young operative's name was Sean Chase, and while he wasn't a perfect match, he was the best they had.

Chase was the product of an American father and an Egyptian mother. His features were such that Arabs saw him as Arab and Westerners often took him for one of their own. The question was, would the members of the Uppsala cell accept him?

He was intended to be Harvath's ultimate listening device and was going to switch places with the young Muslim from the backseat of the Škoda, Mansoor Aleem.

Mansoor and the Uppsala cell were the only link the United States had to a string of terrorist attacks that had targeted Americans in Europe and the United States. And as bloody as those attacks had been, they were supposedly nothing, compared to what intelligence reported the plotters were about to unleash.

Subbing Chase for Mansoor was the most crucial and the most dangerous part of the assignment. According to their limited intelligence, only two Uppsala cell members had ever met Mansoor before and actually knew what he looked like. The men were friends of his uncle, a terrorist commander by the name of Aazim Aleem.

The men had been dispatched to Arlanda airport in Stockholm to collect Mansoor and return him to the cell's safe house two hours north. Thanks to Harvath, they were now both dead.

The team had had the men under surveillance since they had arrived at the airport. The driver had made only one phone call after they had picked up Mansoor and left the airport. Harvath felt confident the call had been to the cell in Uppsala confirming the pickup.

Harvath now pulled the young Muslim to his feet and pushed him up against the van. Drawing his Glock pistol, he placed it under the man's chin and pulled the tape from over his mouth. "You saw what I did to your friends?"

Mansoor Aleem was trembling. Slowly, he nodded.

While his uncle was a very, very bad guy, as were the two dead men slumped in the Škoda, Mansoor was on the cyber side of the jihad and hadn't experienced violence or dead bodies firsthand. That didn't mean he wasn't just as guilty as jihadis who pulled triggers, planted bombs, or blew themselves up. He was guilty as hell. He was also a potential treasure trove of information, having run a lot of his uncle's cyber operations. Harvath had no doubt the United States would be able to extract a ton from him. But first, he wanted to be as sure as he could be that he wasn't sending Chase into a trap.

"We know all about the Uppsala cell," said Harvath. "We want you to take us to them."

Mansoor stammered, trying to find his words. "I, I can't."

"What do you mean, you can't?" Harvath demanded.

"I don't know them."

Harvath jabbed the muzzle of his weapon further up into the soft tissue under the man's chin. Mansoor's eyes began to water. "Don't bullshit me, Mansoor. We know everything you're up to."

"But I don't know anything," he said emphatically. "Honestly. I was just supposed to get on the plane. That's all. That's why they picked me up at the airport. I don't know where they were taking me."

Harvath studied the man's face. He was looking for microexpressions, *tells* people often radiate when lying or under stress from an act they are about to commit.

As far as Harvath could surmise, the man wasn't lying. "I want a list of all the cell members. Right now."

"I don't know who you're talking about."

Harvath pushed the gun up harder, causing Mansoor more pain.

"I only knew the two men in the car," he said as his eyes drifted toward the wreck.

"You're lying to me," said Harvath.

"I'm *not* lying to you."

"Describe the other cell members to me. Their ages, backgrounds, I want all of it."

"I don't know!" Mansoor insisted. "You keep asking me questions I can't answer! The only two people I know in this entire country are dead! You killed them!"

With so little time, that was as good as Harvath was going to get. Patting Mansoor down, he located his wallet and tossed it to Chase. He then went through his pockets and removed everything else.

Chase already had a U.K. passport with his picture issued in Mansoor's name. He also had a driving permit, ATM card, two credit cards, and a host of other pocket litter that would make him even more believable.

Chase fished through the handful of items Harvath had taken from his prisoner and pocketed a boarding pass, a London Tube card, and Mansoor's house keys.

Opening the Škoda's trunk, the young operator sifted through Mansoor's suitcase and quickly studied the contents as he replaced the clothing with his own. Knowing everything the cyberjihadist had packed would give him more insight into the identity he was about to assume.

When he was done, he zipped up the case, removed it from the trunk, and closed the lid. Looking at Riley Turner, he said, "Let's get this over with."

Turner approached and unrolled a small surgical kit. She was in her midthirties, tall, fit, and very attractive. Her reddish-brown hair was pulled back in a ponytail. She had blue eyes and a wide, full mouth. Removing a syringe, she began to prep an anesthetic.

Chase shook his head. "I appreciate the thought, but I'll pass on the Botox."

"It's your call," she replied, gesturing for him to sit down on the backseat. "This is going to hurt, though."

The young intelligence operative winked at her. "I can take it."

She swept back his dark hair and abraded his forehead with a piece of sandpaper. To his credit, he sat there stoically, but that was the easy part. Next, Turner removed her scalpel. Placing it at his hairline, she dug in and cut a short, craggy line.

Chase sucked air through his clenched teeth as the blood began to flow down his forehead and into his eyes.

Turner handed him a handkerchief.

"God, that hurts," he said.

"I warned you."

Having secured Mansoor in the van, Harvath now rejoined them. Bending down, he gathered up a handful of broken glass and handed it to Turner, who sprinkled pieces into Chase's hair, as well as the folds of his clothing.

Harvath searched the dead men and recovered their cell phones. After cloning their SIM cards, he reassembled the driver's phone and tossed it to Chase, saying, "Showtime."

CHAPTER 2

Mustafa Karami had not been expecting another call, especially one from Waqar. Waqar was supposed to be driving. *Nafees was to send a text message when they got close to Uppsala.* Something must have gone wrong. Karami answered his phone with trepidation.

"Please, you must help me," said a distraught voice.

"Who is this?"

"Mansoor."

"Why are you calling from this number?"

"There's been an accident. I don't know what to do."

Karami was a thin, middle-aged man with a wispy gray beard. He had been extremely sick as a child growing up in Yemen and had almost died. The sickness had affected his physical development. He appeared frail and much older than he actually was.

Despite his physical limitations his mind was incredibly sharp. He was well suited to the role he had been assigned. Nothing escaped his flinty gaze or his keen intellect.

Having been brutally tortured as a young man by the Yemeni government, he had learned the hard way to place operational security above all else. He didn't like speaking on cell phones. "Where are your traveling companions?"

"I think they're both dead."

"Dead?" Karami demanded.

"A car swerved and we hit a tree."

"What kind of car?"

"I don't know. Who cares what kind of car? *Waqar and Nafees are dead.*"

The young man was borderline hysterical. Karami tried to calm him down. "Are you injured?" he asked calmly.

"No. I mean, I don't know. I hit my head. There's some blood."

Karami needed to bring him in. "Is the vehicle operable?"

"No," replied the young man.

"Were there any witnesses? Have the police been called?"

"I don't know."

"Where are you?"

"I don't know that either. What am I supposed to do? Are you going to come get me or not?"

Karami forgave the boy his insolence. He was scared and very likely in shock. "Tell me what you see around you, so I can discern where you are."

Chase rattled off a few of the landmarks nearby.

"Okay," Karami replied as he removed a map from his desk. "That's good. I believe I know where you are. I will send two of the brothers to pick you up. There's a village less than three kilometers up the road. As you enter it, you'll see a grocery market on your left. Beyond that is a soccer pitch. Wait there and the brothers will come for you."

"Praise be to Allah," said Chase.

Karami gave him a list of things he wanted him to do and then ended the call.

Turning to two of his men, Karami relayed what had happened and dispatched them to pick up the young computer wizard.

When the men had gone, Karami turned to his most devoted acolyte, Sabah. Sabah was a large, battle-hardened Palestinian. In his previous life, before becoming a mujahideen, he had been a corrupt police officer in the West Bank town of Ramallah.

"I want you to find this accident, Sabah, and I want you to make sure that it was in fact an accident. Do you understand?"

Sabah nodded.

"Good," Karami said in response. "Whatever you learn, you tell no one but me. Understood?"

Once again, Sabah nodded.

"We cannot afford accidents. Not with everything that has happened. We can only trust each other. No one else." With a wave of his hand, Karami ordered him out. "Go."

He was paranoid, but he had cause. So many of their plans had been undone that Mustafa Karami was suspicious of everything and *everyone*.

He hoped that Sabah would be able to get to the bottom of it. It was a small country road, after all, and not very often traveled. Karami had selected the route himself. If the accident scene was undisturbed, Sabah would be able to ascertain what had happened. If the police or bystanders were already there, there would be nothing he could do.

If that was the case, Karami would have to conduct his own investigation. It would begin with Mansoor Aleem himself. Until he was satisfied, he could not risk trusting even the nephew of a great man like Aazim Aleem. Anyone could be corrupted. Anyone could be gotten to.

Fulfilling their final obligation was all that mattered now. Karami had sworn an oath. He would stick to that oath and he would not allow anything or anyone to get in his way.

He was reflecting on whether it was a good idea to bring Mansoor to the actual safe house or find somewhere else for him to remain temporarily when the Skype icon on his laptop bounced.

He had been sent a message from the man whom he served—the Sheikh from Qatar.

Everything is in place? asked the Sheikh.

Everything is in place, typed Karami.

Stay ready, replied the Sheikh. **God willing, you will be called to move soon.** And with that, the Sheikh was gone. Karami refocused his mind on Mansoor. For the time being, he would have to be kept elsewhere, away from the safe house and the rest of the cell. There was too much at stake.

• • •

The man who called himself "Sheikh from Qatar" closed his laptop with his liver-spotted hands and looked out the window of his cavernous apartment. He had quite literally a thirty-million-dollar view of the Manhattan skyline. It was stunning. Even at this predawn hour.

He had always made it a policy to be up before the markets. Despite his advancing age, he found he needed less sleep, not more.

As he privately swilled astronomically expensive vitamin cocktails and fed on exotic hormone and stem cell injections, he publicly told people he'd had abundant reserves of energy ever since he was a boy and credited genetics and his impeccable constitution as the source of his vigor.

Such was the Janus-faced character of James Standing. Even his name was a lie.

Born Lev Bronstein to Romanian Jewish parents, he was sent from Europe to live with relatives in Argentina at the outset of World War II.

His parents remained behind, tending their business and hoping things would get better. They never made it out of the death camps.

At thirteen, he ran away from his Argentinean relatives, renounced his Judaism, and changed his name to José Belmonte—an amalgamation of the names of two world-famous Spanish bullfighters at the time—José Gomez Ortega and Juan Belmonte Garcia.

The newly minted Belmonte found his way to Buenos Aires, where he took a job as a bellboy in a high-end hotel. Thanks to his drive and proficiency for languages, he started filling in on the switchboard at night, eventually moving into the position full-time. It was at this point that he began to build his fortune.

Belmonte, née Bronstein, listened in on all of the hotel's telephone conversations, especially those of its wealthy guests. At fifteen, he entered the stock market. By eighteen, he was perfecting his English, and at twenty, he had changed his name yet again and moved to America.

Standing had been the name of a handsome American guest with a gorgeous, buxom, blond American wife who visited the hotel in Buenos Aires every winter. To Belmonte, they looked like movie stars and represented everything he felt the world owed him. Using the first name of one of his favorite American writers, James Fenimore Cooper, he adopted the Standing name as his surname and James Standing was born.

He emigrated to America, where he parlayed his substantial savings and penchant for trading on insider information into one of the greatest financial empires the world had ever seen.

Now, from his gilded perch overlooking the capital of world finance, he read all of the papers every morning before most of the city was even awake.

Regardless of his morning ritual, he would have been up early today anyway. In fact, he hadn't been able to sleep very well. He was waiting for an important phone call.

Someone, to put it in vulgar street terminology, had fucked with the wrong guy. That "wrong guy" being James Standing. And the someone who had fucked with the wrong guy was about to be taught a very painful and very *permanent* lesson.

In fact, it would be the ultimate lesson and would stand as a subtle reminder to the rest of his enemies that there were certain people who were not to be crossed. Not that Standing would take credit for what was going to happen. That would be incredibly foolish. Better to simply let people assume. The mystery of whether he'd been involved or not would only add to the aura of his considerable power.

Though he'd gotten to where he was by breaking all of the rules, he still needed to appear to be playing by them—at least for a little while longer.

Soon, though, like an old hotel on the Las Vegas strip, America was going to be brought down in a controlled demolition. And when that happened, the rules would no longer apply to James Standing.

CHAPTER 3

COLDWATER CANYON
LOS ANGELES, CALIFORNIA

The red Porsche 911 GT3 pulled to the top of the cobblestone driveway and stopped. "Are you going to be okay?"

The man in the passenger seat said nothing. In the middle of the motor court, a verdigris Poseidon watched over a group of nymphs carrying golden seashells. As water tumbled from one shell to another, the sound cascaded through the car's open windows.

The two men sat in silence for several moments. The night air was heavy, damp from the marine layer moving in from the coast. The estate's wrinkled oaks and towering pines swayed like sleeping horses in a neatly manicured pasture.

Behind a long row of brushed aluminum garage doors were several million dollars' worth of high-end luxury automobiles. In the glass-and-steel house next to it were other expensive toys and priceless pieces of art. Behind the home was a hand-laid mosaic swimming pool, a three-hole golf course, and exotic gardens that would have rivaled anything in ancient Babylon. To most outside observers, the man in the passenger seat had it all, and then some.

Larry Salomon, a handsome fifty-two-year-old movie producer, was the man with the Midas touch, or so said those with short memories who seemed not to recall or not to care about how hard he had worked to get to where he was.

Even the politicians Salomon had hosted at his home for fund-raisers, back before he stopped doing fund-raisers, loved to smile and tell him how easy he had it. *Hollywood,* they would say, *is a petting zoo, compared to the jungles of D.C.*

None of them knew what they were talking about. Hollywood was a lot like a Charles Dickens novel. It could be the best of places; it could be the worst of places. Machiavelli, Dante, Shakespeare . . . all would have felt at home here. Tinseltown was a bustling contradiction.

It was a modern-day Zanzibar; a slave market where souls were bartered, sold, and stolen seemingly on the hour, every hour. It was also a place of incredible genius and beauty, where dreams still came true.

Hollywood was where some of man's most endearing and compelling stories were told and retold. It was home to a globe-spanning industry that could frighten and terrify, but more important, could uplift and inspire.

Hollywood was a place where one creative mind could join with others to craft something with the ability to affect the lives of millions upon millions of people. It was a place, for most people, where magic was still alive. Unfortunately, and despite his success, Larry Salomon was no longer one of those people.

In his mind, magic was for the woefully naïve. "Happily ever after" existed only in fairy tales and of course, their modern-day equivalent, the movies. It was smoke and mirrors, and Salomon knew it all too well.

"Larry?" repeated the man who had driven the movie producer home. "I want to make sure you're going to be okay."

"I miss her," said Salomon.

Luke Ralston put his Porsche in neutral and pulled up the parking brake. He had worked on Salomon's past six films, and the two men had developed a very deep bond. With his tall, fit frame, rugged features, whitened teeth, and expensive haircut, Ralston looked like he could have been one of the producer's top actors, if you overlooked the limp that plagued him from time to time.

But Ralston wasn't an actor. He was what was known in Hollywood parlance as a "technical consultant." A former Delta Force operative, Ralston used his extensive military experience to make sure Salomon's actors and actresses looked like they knew what they were doing in their action scenes, especially when those scenes had to do with firearms, hand-to-hand combat, evasive driving, or any number of other tactical situations.

"It's supposed to get easier," Salomon continued, staring into space. "That's what everybody tells you. They tell you to stay strong. But it doesn't get easier."

A mist had begun to build on the windshield. The temperature was dropping.

Ralston pondered raising the car's windows, but decided not to. It would have broken the mood and sent the two men in their separate directions too early. Salomon still needed to talk, so Ralston would sit and listen for as long as it took.

A pronounced silence grew between them. The only sound came from the throb of the GT3's engine and the water cascading in the fountain. Eventually Salomon spoke. "I think I'll go inside."

"Do you want me to come in for a while?"

The older man shook his head. He unlatched his seat belt and searched for the door handle.

Ralston put a hand on his friend's arm. "Skip the nightcap, Larry. Okay?" The movie producer had already consumed enough alcohol.

"Whatever you say," the man replied, waving him off. "The guest-house is free if you want it."

The younger man looked at his watch. They had left Salomon's car at the restaurant when it became apparent he wasn't in a condition to drive. "I've got an early morning run with friends," said Ralston. "I'll call you when I'm done and we'll work out getting your car back."

The producer grasped the handle and opened the door. "Don't bother. I'll figure it out," he said as he climbed out of the car.

There was an edge to Salomon's voice. He was making the alcohol-induced transition from maudlin to angry.

Ralston shook his head. He shouldn't have let his friend consume so much booze. But, at the end of the day, that's what sorrows were meant to be drowned in. "Are you sure you're going to be okay?" he asked as the producer shut the car door and began to walk away.

Salomon didn't bother to turn; he just waved over his shoulder and mounted the steps to the entrance of his home.

Ralston knew him well enough to know that he'd probably go inside and keep drinking. There was little he could do about it. "Try to get some sleep," he recommended as the producer reached the top of the stairs and opened his etched glass front door.

Ralston waited and watched until his friend was safely inside before putting his Porsche in gear and pulling out of the motor court.

On his way down the winding drive, he wondered if he should turn back. Of all the nights of the year, this was the roughest for Salomon.

Had she not been murdered three years ago, it would have been his daughter Rachael's twenty-first birthday. Within a year of Rachael's murder, Larry's marriage had fallen apart. Losing a child was a pain no parent should ever have to bear, having been abandoned by his spouse in the process was almost too much.

When his wife left him and moved back east, Larry never fully recovered. Though actresses, some very well known, threw themselves at him, he hadn't been with another woman since. He had no desire. The only thing that had kept him going was his work.

What if this time he does something stupid? Ralston wondered. Alcohol and depression were a very bad combination.

The thought plagued him all the way down to the gate, and probably would have bothered him all the way home, had something else not captured his attention. *Tire tracks.*

How could there be tire marks on top of his? Ralston slowed down to study the tracks. They were different than those of his Porsche and appeared to have veered off to the left, taking the service drive that led to the rear of the property. Salomon was one of the few wealthy Hollywood people he knew who didn't maintain around-the-clock domestic staff. And while it was well after midnight and therefore technically "morning," it was still too early for landscapers or any of Salomon's other help to have arrived. Someone had to have come in through the gate behind them. Ralston decided to take a look.

Backing up, he killed his lights and turned onto the service drive. In a town like L.A., where you are what you drive, the red 911 had suited him perfectly. Because of distinct engine whine, though, this was the first time Ralston ever wished he was driving a whisper-quiet Prius.

The service road was far less dramatic than the estate's main drive. Instead of a lushly landscaped serpentine approach, it was a boring, blacktopped lane with two switchbacks abutted by cinderblock retaining walls.

After the second switchback, the service road opened up onto a darkened view of the far side of Salomon's house and the silhouettes of outbuildings that supported the estate.

Ralston brought his Porsche to a stop using the parking brake so as not to illuminate his tail lights and watched. A Ford Econoline van was in the process of turning around so that it was facing back down the service road in the direction from which it had come.

Its driver killed the headlamps, but left the marker lights illuminated. Ralston waited, but nothing happened. No one got out. No one got in.

He couldn't help but wonder if he was looking at some sort of getaway vehicle. *Was Larry Salomon's home being burgled?*

It didn't take him long to get tired of waiting. Removing his cell phone, he decided to call Salomon to see if maybe there was some other explanation.

He depressed the speed dial key for Salomon's cell phone, but the call failed to connect. Scrolling through his address book, he tried the number again, but the call still didn't go through. Looking at his signal strength, he saw he wasn't getting any bars at all. He couldn't remember ever having trouble getting reception up here before.

That was all it took. He'd been taught not to believe in coincidences. Releasing the parking brake, he put his car in gear, and as he did, a very bad feeling began to overtake him.

CHAPTER 4

I t was at times like these that Luke Ralston wanted to throttle the State of California for not being more cooperative when it came to the carrying of firearms. Here it was the middle of the night, a strange van had followed his car onto a private gated estate, and he was unarmed. While the van and its driver might have had a completely legitimate reason for being there, he doubted it, and he would have very much appreciated having a weapon right now.

Knowing that if the van and its driver were up to no good they would very likely be armed, Ralston proceeded accordingly.

Speed, surprise, and overwhelming violence of action had been drilled into the very fiber of his DNA in his military career. While he couldn't preemptively attack the van and its driver, he could take immediate control of the situation by using both speed and surprise.

Increasing his speed, he turned on his headlights, engaged the high beams, and raced toward the van.

At that moment, the driver leaped from the van with what appeared to be a shotgun. Ralston pinned the accelerator to the floor.

The weapon exploded with a roar and a round slammed into the front of Ralston's Porsche. The shooter had been aiming at the headlights. Big mistake.

Ralston continued to pick up speed, aiming right for the driver. As the man pumped his weapon to chamber another round, Ralston killed his lights—plunging the man's dilated eyes into darkness.

All the shooter could do was aim for the sound of the car that was barreling down on him, which is exactly what happened.

Whether the driver of the van was just that good, or just that lucky, Ralston had no idea, but his second shot exploded with another booming roar and tore a hole right through the windshield. Buckshot would have deflected off the glass. Whoever was shooting at him must have been using slugs. Ralston didn't need to look over to know that the seat next to him was shredded. A few more inches to the left and he would have been shredded as well.

With the 911's engine screaming, Ralston readied himself for what was about to happen.

Flipping his lights and high beams back on, he once again flooded the shooter's eyes with light. There was the roar of the shotgun once more, but it was the last thing the man did before the right front quarter of Ralston's car struck the man's lower body.

Rather than being thrown clear, the large man was pulled halfway beneath the car. Ralston fought to maintain control. As if guided by some unseen force that wanted to raise the car and snatch the body from underneath the suspension, the Porsche's right side tilted up, and Ralston thought for sure the car was going to flip. But just as it had begun to rise, it slammed back down.

Ralston maintained a death grip on the Porsche's steering wheel as he tried to regain control.

It wasn't until the car spun through the wet grass and slammed into the side of one of the outbuildings that the horror finally came to a stop. But as that horror ended, a new one began.

Unbuckling his seat belt, Ralston struggled to get out of the car. It was a mess. Adrenaline and fear coursed through his body.

What sounded like a muffled gunshot from inside the house suddenly refocused his mind on the threat that still remained.

It was pointless to waste time searching for the driver's shotgun. Without a flashlight the chances of rapidly locating it were slim to none. The odds were the same for finding a secondary weapon somewhere in the van. Ralston took off in a sprint. He had to get up to the house and save Salomon.

Whoever was inside had undoubtedly heard the noise of the melee out on the service road. Whether any neighbors in this remote part of the canyon had heard the shotgun blasts and had called the police didn't matter. By the time they arrived, whatever was happening here would be over. If Salomon was still alive inside, his attackers were going to be doubly determined to complete their objective and to get the hell out. That meant Ralston had to move fast.

Often, high-end home invasions were "inside jobs," where the perpetrators had firsthand knowledge of the layout of the home. They were able to move quickly, knowing where everything and everyone would be. The one thing these home invaders wouldn't be prepared for was Ralston, and Ralston knew the layout of the Salomon home well.

Based on where the van had turned around, it was obvious that whoever was inside had been dropped off at or near the home's service entrance. *Add one more point to the inside job column.* Approaching the door, he saw that it had been propped open. It seemed that not only was this the way in, but it was also going to be the way out.

The good thing about the door having been propped open was that the alarm, which Salomon never bothered to arm, would have already sounded its quick, three-bell chime. No one heard Ralston as he slipped inside the house.

Near the service entrance was a utility room the size of a small family apartment. Here, all of the home's mechanics were housed, including eight panels of circuit breakers.

Ralston cut the power, plunging the house into darkness. Once his eyes adjusted, he went for a weapon.

He could have used a golf club, but he preferred something he was more proficient with. In the kitchen, he found exactly what he wanted. It was the perfect tool—not too long, not too short, and incredibly sharp. He pulled the seven-inch fillet knife from the knife block and moved on.

Coming around the corner of the large island in the kitchen, he found what he assumed to be the victim of the muted shot he had heard from outside. He was relieved to see that it wasn't Salomon.

In his midtwenties, in jeans, a T-shirt, and a pair of Chuck Taylors, he looked like a college kid. Ralston had never seen him before. *Who the hell was he?* he wondered. *A friend? A visiting relative? An employee?*

The boy had been shot through the bridge of his nose, right between his eyes. He was lying in a puddle of milk commingling with his own blood. An upturned bowl of cereal lay nearby. Ralston reached down to double-check him. He had no pulse, but was still warm.

Moving quickly, he crossed the kitchen and moved into the darkened dining room. From what he could tell, nothing was out of place. Salomon's expensive pieces of art still hung on the walls and his box of antique silverware was still proudly displayed on the sideboard. That fact, coupled with the professionalism with which the boy in the kitchen had been dispatched, was making this look less and less like a home invasion and more and more like some sort of hit.

The thought was just solidifying in his mind, when Ralston heard someone step on the warped floorboard that Salomon had never bothered to get fixed.

CHAPTER 5

Ralston's breathing all but stopped. Making sure he didn't bang into any of the dining-room furniture and give himself away, he slipped across the room as fast as he could to the open double doors on the other side. Pressing himself against the wall, he gripped the knife tighter and waited.

He didn't have to wait long. From out in the hallway, he could hear a man's voice. He was whispering and in some sort of a foreign language. It sounded to Ralston like Eastern European, maybe Russian, but he couldn't be sure.

When the man repeated himself, Ralston realized he was speaking over a radio. *Was he trying to raise the driver outside? Or were there more men inside the house?*

Either way, it wasn't good. Ralston needed to get to Salomon. He could hear the man's footfalls upon the wood floor of the hallway growing closer.

Ralston had two choices. He could face the man head-on, or he could wait until the man had passed and take him from behind. Shots had been fired and at least one person inside the house had already been killed. Ralston was literally bringing a knife to a gunfight, so he slipped off his shoes and settled on the latter course of action. Three seconds later, the man moved past the dining room doors.

He was huge—just as the man outside had been—six-foot-three, at least, and well over 250 pounds. He had wide shoulders, draped in what even the home's semidarkness couldn't hide was a very cheap suit. His feet were shod in the long, box-toed dress shoes so popular with Europeans. In one hand he carried a radio and in the other a suppressed pistol.

His hair was crew-cut short and the back of his head looked just like a Russian's. From the base of his neck to the crown of his head, it was flat as a board. It was a cultural attribute that most Russian men, tightly swaddled and picked up seldom by their mothers, shared.

As the Russian passed, Ralston slipped into the hallway behind him. The intruder had no idea he was there until it was too late.

In one fluid motion, Ralston grabbed across the man's forehead, yanked his head to the left, and with his right hand plunged the filleting knife into the anterior triangle between the top of the clavicle and the side of the neck. It severed the man's internal jugular vein and carotid artery. He then swept the blade across, severing the trachea. All that could be heard was a hiss, like air being let out of a tire.

Ralston put all of his weight on the man to prevent him from using his last seconds of life to fight back and rode him down to the floor. Convinced he was no longer a threat, he dragged him off to the side, next to a cupboard, and left him there to bleed out.

It was a black art, the taking of life, and one that Luke Ralston was all too well versed in.

Dropping the knife, he picked up the intruder's suppressed Walther P99 and did a press check. Satisfied that a round was chambered and the weapon was hot, he turned the volume down on the radio, tucked it into his back pocket, and went off in search of Salomon.

The problem, though, was twofold. Were there any more intruders in the house and where should he begin looking for Salomon? He decided to start with the producer's office.

To get there, he had to pass through the entry hall with its wide double staircase. There was nothing for cover and Ralston used the darkness and shadows as best he could. The living room, with its floor-to-ceiling glass windows and ambient moonlight spilling from outside, was even worse, but he made it through both without incident.

The entrance to Larry Salomon's office was down a short hall just past the living room. The hairs on the back of Ralston's neck were standing on end before he even got to the door.

With the weapon up and at the ready, he button-hooked into the room and tried to take it all in.

Everything was different. The office looked as if it had been turned into some sort of war room. Whiteboards and bulletin boards were leaning against the walls and a large, rolling chalkboard was off to one side. Salomon's imposing glass-and-steel desk now sat cheek-by-jowl with two additional, smaller desks, which were topped with high-end Apple computer systems and what Ralston recognized as editing equipment. There were stacks of cardboard filing boxes filled with reams and reams of papers and documents.

There were more pillars of books, some stacked three feet high and surrounded by yellow Post-it notes on a pair of matching drafting tables. And then there was another body.

The man appeared to be in his midforties, doughy, with salt-and-pepper hair and a matching beard. He wore jeans, loafers, and an Oxford cloth shirt. He had been shot in the back of the head execution-style. Ralston rolled him over to see who he was. As with the body in the kitchen, he didn't recognize the man.

Exiting the office, he went down the hall to the back stairs. If Salomon had retained any of the emergency response advice he had dispensed to him dozens of times, perhaps he would have headed straight upstairs. If so, maybe it had bought him some time, especially if he'd heard the shots and had been able to figure out what was going on.

Reaching the top of the stairs, Ralston crouched down and stole a quick peek around the doorframe. The hallway was empty.

Stepping into the hall, he moved as quickly as he could toward Salomon's bedroom. He stopped only for open doors, and even then, it was for just long enough to make sure there were no threats on the other side.

He was fifteen feet away from the master bedroom, when a figure stepped into the hall and fired.

The bullet came so close to the side of Ralston's head that it actually set his right ear ringing. On instinct, having fired hundreds of thousands of rounds during his Spec Ops career, he depressed the trigger of his own weapon twice in quick succession and dropped the shooter onto the carpeted floor of the hallway.

Ralston advanced on the man and kicked the suppressed pistol away before checking to see if he was still alive. One round had entered just below his nose; the other had entered through his throat. He was big and dressed in a cheap suit just like his partner downstairs. The back of his head was flat as well. *What the hell was going on? Who were these people? Why were there Russians in the house?*

Ralston's questions were interrupted by the sound of a sharp crack from inside Salomon's bedroom. It wasn't the crack of a pistol. It was the crack of molding as drywall was being ripped away.

It told him two things. Salomon was still alive, but he had only seconds left to live.

CHAPTER 6

Larry Salomon had expected that a savvy intruder would probably cut his telephone hard line. That was why he always kept a charged cell phone in his panic room. A fixed external antenna had been installed to guarantee reception, but suddenly it wasn't working either. He was panicked. No matter how many times he dialed 911, he couldn't get through.

He'd been around enough weapons, even if only on movie sets where blanks were being fired, to know what real gunshots sounded like. Suppressed gunshots, contrary to what many people thought, were still audible. There was no such thing as completely silenced gunfire.

Having changed out of his evening attire, Salomon had been on his way out of his bedroom and back downstairs for one final drink, when he'd heard the first shot. He'd stood paralyzed, wondering what he'd actually heard. Then the second shot came. That's when he knew.

He had turned and fled back to the master bedroom. He didn't dare waste even a fraction of a second looking over his shoulder to see if he was being followed. He didn't need to. His animal instinct for survival told him that he most definitely had someone pursuing him. He also knew that the two gunshots meant his houseguests were dead.

Charging into his walk-in closet cum panic room, he slammed the heavy metal door shut, threw the bolts home, and hit the panic button for the alarm system. He expected the high-pitched piercing shriek of the alarm to kick in instantly. It didn't, and his fear mounted.

On a small monitor mounted inside the closet, he watched via the hidden bedroom camera as a large man with a gun rushed into the room just behind him. He pressed the panic button again and when the alarm failed to engage, he attempted to call the police, only to discover that neither his landline nor his cell phone were working.

He then watched as the intruder attempted to kick in the closet door. Again and again he kicked, but the steel-reinforced door held. Finally, the man turned and walked out of view. *Had he given up?*

Salomon's question was answered when the man passed back under the camera a moment later with a fireplace tool and disappeared from view once again.

The producer strained to see what the man was up to, but the monitor provided only a very limited field of view. The security system, like the panic room, had come with the house and had been installed by the previous owner. Salomon had never really thought about it much. It was only now that he realized that a pan-and-tilt camera would have been infinitely more useful than a static, fixed lens.

It was at that moment that all the power went out. With the phone line cut and his cell phone signal having somehow been jammed, Salomon wasn't surprised when the emergency generator failed to kick in. Whoever had cut the power knew what he was doing. He was now effectively blind.

He wasn't, however, deaf, and his heart soon choked his throat when he figured out where the intruder was and what he was doing with the fireplace poker.

The first thud had been somewhat displaced, but Salomon locked on to the second swing of the poker like a sonar operator.

The sounds had come from the far end of the closet. On the other side was the master bath. Using the poker, the intruder was clawing his way through the drywall and into what really wasn't a true panic room, but rather just a closet with a very heavy door.

It was a poorly thought out feature that provided a false sense of security and would only slow, but not stop, a determined attacker. It dawned on Salomon how much trouble he was in. He was trapped.

Though he couldn't see the intruder, he could hear huge pieces of drywall being ripped away on the bathroom side of the wall. Any moment now, he feared, the attacker was going to burst through into the closet. Salomon had one ace up his sleeve and he reached for it.

The Mossberg tactical shotgun had been a gift. A friend, moving to New York City, had been afraid to take it with him for fear of running afoul of antigun laws. With its pistol grip, short barrel, and crenelated muzzlebrake Salomon could understand why. He'd kept the weapon around "just in case," figuring if he ever got in trouble for owning it, he could let his lawyers straighten it out. They could simply claim that it had been taken from one of his film sets as a souvenir and that he had no idea it was actually real.

Of course he'd also have to claim that he didn't know it was loaded, but a courtroom appearance was the furthest thing from his mind at this point. All he cared about was staying alive.

Racking the slide, he made ready.

•   •   •

As Ralston charged into the bedroom, he heard the blast of a shotgun, and his heart stopped.

Rushing to the door of the master bath, he saw blood and bits of flesh everywhere. Risking a closer look, he stepped into the bathroom and saw a body on the floor and the distinctive door-breacher muzzlebrake of Salomon's shotgun protruding from the far wall. He leaped out of the bathroom just as the weapon erupted with another roar. Twelve-gauge shot shattered the marble tiles right where he had been standing.

"Damn it, Larry!" Ralston yelled. "Cease fire! It's me! Luke!"

His ears were ringing even harder now, and he wondered if his hearing would ever fully return. "I need to get into the bathroom and see if he's dead. Don't you fucking shoot me," he ordered. "Okay?"

There was a muffled assent from Salomon. Whether it was muffled because his hearing was shot or because it was coming from behind a wall, Ralston couldn't be sure. He peeked back into the bathroom and watched as the shotgun was retracted through the blown-out drywall.

Ralston grabbed two towels and threw them down so he didn't have to walk across the bloody floor in his stocking feet.

The intruder must have been very close when the shotgun went off, as it had blown a huge hole in his chest. Ralston looked for any weapon he might have been carrying and saw another silenced pistol sitting on the edge of the vanity near where the man had been tearing through the wall to get at Salomon.

A good portion of the man's suit coat and the shirt beneath were shredded. Once Ralston had ascertained that he had no pulse, he began peeling the strips of cloth away around his right armpit. He heard the closet door unlock, and seconds later Salomon was behind him.

"Who the hell are they?" he asked.

"Spetsnaz," replied Ralston. "Russian Special Forces, I think."

"How can you tell?"

Ralston lifted the dead man's arm and pointed to the blue-black Cyrillic tattoo. "That's how they mark their blood type."

"What the hell are they doing here? Why would Russian Special Forces soldiers want to kill me?"

"You're not the only one they came for."

"Oh, my God," said Salomon. "Chip and Jeremy. They were downstairs. I heard two shots." His voice trailed off.

"They're both dead. What were they doing here? And what the hell happened to your office?"

"We were working on a film; a documentary," Salomon said, and then changed the subject. "We need to call the police."

"No. We need to get someplace safe," said Ralston. "We've got to think."

"Think?" replied Salomon. "This guy killed Chip and Jeremy and was trying to make me the third. He could be some homicidal maniac, for all we know. We need to call the cops."

Ralston stood up. "This is a professional wet work team. A *Russian* wet work team."

"*Team?*"

"There was a driver outside and at least two others inside the house."

Salomon was trying to piece it all together. "And you killed three of them?"

Ralston nodded.

"How did you know?"

"I saw tire tracks leading up the service road. I tried to call you, but I couldn't get a signal."

"My cell was down, too," said Salomon.

"They must have some sort of jammer. Like I said, these guys were professional." Ralston stepped off the towels and out of the bathroom. Reaching for the shotgun, he repeated, "There may be more of them. We need to get going."

The producer shook his head. "I know how this plays out. If we don't stay here and wait for the cops, we'll look guilty."

"And if we do stay and wait for the cops, we'll both be dead. I'm not going to let that happen. The Russians have infiltrated a lot of police departments across the country."

"Are you serious?"

"Dead serious," said Ralston. "We're not trusting anyone else at this point. When these guys fail to report back in, whoever sent them might send more. They're going to use every contact, every means they have at their disposal. We need to disappear."

Salomon began to object, but Ralston was already making his way across the bedroom. "Are you comfortable using this?" Ralston asked as he handed his friend the suppressed pistol.

"I'd rather have the shotgun."

Ralston nodded and handed it over. Raising the pistol, he prepared to enter the hallway and said, "Stay close. And if you see anything move at all, you pull that trigger. Got it? Don't even worry about aiming."

Salomon nodded and the pair slipped into the hallway and down the back stairs. They stopped at the dining room long enough for Ralston to grab his shoes. He thought about wiping his fingerprints off the handle of the knife that lay only feet away, but decided it wasn't worth the time. They needed to get out of there as quickly as possible. His damaged Porsche was already going to tell the world that he had been there.

In the garage, Ralston grabbed a flashlight and walked over to the key box. He bypassed all of Salomon's luxury automobiles and selected the keys for his vintage navy blue Wagoneer.

Disengaging the overhead opener, he rolled up the garage door and told Salomon to get in the truck. Hopping in beside him, he fired up the Wagoneer and pulled into the motor court.

The gates at the bottom of the drive were on a separate circuit from the house and opened as the Wagoneer rolled over the pressure plates. The marine layer had turned into a thick fog. That would work to their advantage and it helped Ralston decide in which direction to head.

"You're bleeding," said Salomon as they turned out onto the road.

Ralston touched the side of his head and looked at his fingers. The bullet that had whizzed by his ear had actually grazed him. "Don't worry about it," he said.

Salomon *was* worried about it, though. He was worried about all of it. He knew Ralston was right. More men *would* be coming after him. He had uncovered the truth, and the truth made him a liability.

CHAPTER 7

SWEDEN

Harvath had rented a farm on the outskirts of Uppsala for their safe house. It was far enough away from neighbors that they could interrogate their prisoner and come and go without attracting any attention.

In the city of Uppsala itself, he had rented an apartment where he had staged an assault team. Though they were outfitted with gear to look like members of the Swedish Security Service, the government of Sweden had no idea an American operation was taking place on their soil. They were purposely being kept in the dark for the time being. Somewhere in the intelligence community, there was a leak. Because of that leak, one of the highest-value terrorist targets the United States had ever bagged, Aazim Aleem, had been assassinated.

Sitting in the darkened room, Scot Harvath played the entire scene across the panorama of his mind's eye for the millionth time. It was all there—all so vivid—the *boom* of the rocket-propelled grenade leaving its launcher; the *whoosh* as it blistered through the air en route to its target, and finally the deafening explosion as the RPG connected with the trunk and gas tank of his car and the vehicle went up in a billowing fireball.

In a blinding flash, his Yemen operation had gone from a resounding success to a spectacular failure. Aazim, who'd been in the trunk, would have purchased Harvath's group some much-needed goodwill with the CIA, but it was too late for that now.

Staring out the window, he caught a glimpse of his reflection. Although he had crossed the threshold into his forties, he still looked as if he was in his early thirties. His sand-colored hair showed no traces of gray; his handsome, green-eyed face bore few if any lines, and his five-foot-ten body was in better physical shape than those of men half his age. To see the toll the years had taken, one would have to look elsewhere.

By most measures, Harvath was a success. In the immortal words of Mark Twain, he had made his vocation his vacation. He was a man of particular talents who was deeply committed to his country. Those talents and that commitment had propelled him to the pinnacle of his career. The cost to his personal life was something he didn't like to think about.

Nevertheless, ever since Yemen his relationships had been very much at the forefront of his mind. But it wasn't romantic relationships that he had been thinking about. Someone had professionally betrayed him, someone with intimate knowledge of his organization, *someone close.*

It was precisely because of this apparent leak that Harvath had requested permission to run this assignment himself. Somewhere there was a leak, and until that leak was plugged, there was a very short list of people Harvath could trust.

At the top of that list was a thirty-year CIA veteran named Reed Carlton. Carlton had watched as bureaucracy and inertia devoured what had once been the best intelligence agency in the world. As management became more concerned with promotions and covering its tail, and as the Agency's leadership atrophied, Carlton could see the writing on the wall. By the 1990s, when the CIA stopped conducting unilateral espionage operations altogether, he was disappointed, but not at all surprised.

While there were countless patriotic men and women still left at Langley, the institutionalized bureaucracy made it all but impossible for them to effectively do their jobs. The bureaucracy had become risk-averse. Even more troubling was the fact that the CIA now subcontracted its actual spy work to other countries' intelligence services. They happily handed over huge sums of cash in the hopes that other countries would do the dangerous heavy lifting and would share whatever they developed.

It was the biggest open secret in the intelligence world and it was both humiliating and beneath America's dignity.

Once the secret was out that the CIA was no longer truly in the spy business, Carlton knew he had to do something. It was then that he began recruiting former Central Intelligence Agency and Special Operations personnel and stood up his own venture—the Carlton Group. It was modeled upon the World War II intelligence agency known as the Office of Strategic Services, or OSS. It was composed of patriots who wanted one thing and one thing only—to keep Americans safe no matter what the cost.

Frustrated with the CIA's reluctance to do its job, the Department of Defense eventually turned to Carlton to provide private intelligence services in Iraq and Afghanistan. The group's operatives had performed dramatically, developing extensive human networks across both countries. They penetrated multiple terrorist cells and delivered exceptional, A1 intelligence that resulted in huge successes for American forces, not to mention the saving of countless American and coalition lives.

Based upon this success, a key group of DoD insiders decided to bring the Carlton Group all the way inside. They were paid from black budgets and hidden from D.C.'s grandstanding, self-serving politicians. The fact that not one single Central Intelligence Agency employee had lost his or her job after 9/11 told the Pentagon all they needed to know about the broken culture at Langley.

The Carlton Group's mission statement was a testament to their singular focus and consisted of only three simple yet powerful words: *find, fix*, and *finish*.

An exceptional judge of talent, Reed Carlton had studied Harvath for some time before making his first approach. Harvath's background and abilities were a perfect fit for the private intelligence service Carlton had begun to build.

Originally a member of SEAL Team 2, Harvath's language proficiency and desire for more challenging assignments had gotten him recruited to the storied SEAL Team 6. While with Team 6, he caught the eye of the Secret Service and was asked to come help bolster counterterrorism operations at the White House.

Having been trained to take the fight to the enemy, Harvath didn't do well in a defensive role with the Secret Service. Waiting for bad guys to strike was just not his thing. What's more, he lacked diplomacy—a prerequisite when working around politicians. As a result, Harvath pissed a lot of people off, some of them very powerful.

The one person he had managed to keep in his corner was the then-president of the United States, Jack Rutledge. Recognizing that America was faced with a fanatical enemy who refused to play by any rules, Rutledge had taken a significant step toward tilting the playing field back to America's advantage. In short, he had set Harvath loose.

The clandestine program the president had established worked exceedingly well. Harvath did overwhelming damage to the enemies of the United States and continued to do so right up until the end of Rutledge's second term, whereupon a new president entered the Oval Office with a different approach to dealing with America's enemies.

Direct action, political speak for wet work, was replaced with *engagement,* diplomatic speak for capitulation, and Harvath found himself out of a job. As many men of his background do, he moved into the private sector. It wasn't the same, and though Harvath told himself he was still doing good for his country, he was disappointed with the job opportunities. It was then that Reed Carlton had come into his life and had made him an offer he couldn't refuse.

Within twelve months, the "Old Man," as Harvath affectionately referred to Carlton, had drilled thirty years of tradecraft and hard-won espionage experience into him. He had also smoothed out many of his rough edges.

Combined with the deadly skills Harvath had acquired as a SEAL and the exceptional things he had learned in the Secret Service, Harvath's training at the hands of Carlton vaulted him to the top of a very exclusive food chain. He had reached a level many seek, but few ever achieve. He had become an Apex Predator.

The Old Man made the resources available and turned Harvath loose with a simple three-word mandate—*find, fix, finish.* His job was to identify terrorist leaders, track them to a fixed location, and then capture or kill them as necessary, using any information gleaned from the assignment to plan the next operation. The goal was to apply constant pressure on the terrorists and pound them so hard and so relentlessly that they were permanently rocked back on the defensive, if not ground into dust.

In addition to direct-action assignments, Harvath was allowed to stage psychological operations to eat away at the terrorist networks from within, sowing doubt, fear, distrust, and paranoia throughout their ranks. It was everything the United States government should have been doing, but wasn't. At least, it hadn't been until the Carlton Group came on board.

Looking at his watch, Harvath decided Mansoor Aleem had been marinating long enough. It was time to begin the interrogation.

CHAPTER 8

The best interrogators knew that the most effective tool at their disposal was time. Left alone long enough, a prisoner's mind would do half an interrogator's work for him, if not more. No matter what horrors you could conceive of inflicting on a prisoner, the prisoner himself would always conceive of much worse. That was why Harvath liked to leave his interrogation subjects isolated and alone for as long as possible.

Interrogation was a delicate art. The key was getting the subject to tell you what you wanted to know, *not* what he thought you wanted to hear. A good interrogator operated like a surgeon; he wielded a scalpel, not a machete.

Only amateurs and the incredibly desperate actually resorted to true torture. And true torture was not turning up the air-conditioning, putting a subject in a stress posture, shaking him by his shirtfront, or giving him an open-handed slap across the face. Those were harsh interrogation techniques. They were not torture. Harvath knew the difference. He had used harsh interrogation techniques. He had also used torture.

And while he had never taken pleasure in it, it wasn't something he had a moral problem with.

Torture was something he had used only as an absolute last resort. He loved to hear TV pundits and others cite the Geneva and Hague conventions. Putting aside the fact that most of them had never read any of those treaties, the key fact that they all missed was that America's Islamist enemies were not a party to these agreements. What's more, the conventions strictly forbade combatants from hiding and attacking from within civilian populations. Lawful combatants were also required to appear on the battlefield wearing something, whether a uniform or even just an armband, identifying them as combatants—overgrown beards and high-water pants didn't count.

The long and short of it was that if one party refused to sign on and follow the rules, it couldn't expect any sort of protection from those rules. And as far as Harvath was concerned, those who championed the extension of Geneva and Hague to Islamic terrorists were uninformed at best and apologists for terrorists at worst. Believing his country to be made up of good, reasonable people, he preferred to put the terrorist protectors in the former category.

Harvath never allowed himself to underestimate the capabilities or determination of America's enemies. He had looked directly into the eyes of some of the most capable warriors Islam had dispatched, and he saw not only the depth of their conviction, but also the depth of their hate for the West and everything it stood for. There would be no truce with Islam. And while there were indeed good, decent Muslim people around the world, there were not enough of them. They lacked the collective will and desire to not only stand up to the violence being carried out in their name, but to reform the very tenets of their religion that called for that violence.

This was not how Harvath wished the world to be, but the world cared little for what he wanted. It was what it was. Harvath had shouldered a Herculean burden on behalf of his country so that it might remain free and unmolested. Though many others were also responsible for the fact that America remained free, Harvath found particular shame in the fact that it had not remained unmolested.

Attacks on Americans and American interests both at home and abroad had been picking up speed. For every attack that was thwarted and every terrorist taken off the street, ten, twenty, even thirty more popped up in their place. As more attacks had been put in play, some had begun getting through—even to American soil. A handful of those attacks had been Harvath's responsibility to stop. He hadn't always been able to do so. And while the attacks that had slipped through might have been much worse had Harvath not acted, people had still been killed—lots of people. This knowledge followed Harvath like a diseased crow sitting on his shoulder.

The only way to disrupt the enemy, and beat them so far back that they couldn't attack, was to relentlessly hunt them down like the animals they were and unceasingly take the fight to them. That meant the gloves were off. It also meant that certain operations had to be kept secret from grandstanding politicians who would sooner bare America's throat before the pack of wolves outside its door, than summon the fortitude to do the hard work necessary to ensure America's survival.

Though Harvath couldn't pinpoint exactly when it had happened, at some point in the last seventy-or-so years, the political class had become completely disconnected from reality. It was a malady that struck equally on both sides of the aisle. It was evident in every single thing Washington, D.C., did, from its profligate spending, to granting terrorists greater rights and protections than CIA and military interrogators.

Harvath knew what a chilling effect the threat of litigation had created throughout the ranks of American interrogators. It made little difference that the interrogators had gotten real intelligence that had saved lives.

Only a select few of the decent politicians remaining in Washington understood what had to be done and supported it. If the rest of the pols, though, discovered even a fraction of what Harvath had done, he had no doubt they'd drag him to the public pillory and follow that up with a crucifixion upon the Capitol steps with all the media present.

Harvath didn't care very much and he worried about it even less. First they would have to *catch* him. Then they would have to *prove* it. He had no intention of ever allowing either of those things to happen.

In fact, as Harvath opened the weathered barn doors to interrogate his prisoner, consequences were the furthest thing from his mind.

CHAPTER 9

Though no longer part of a working farm, the barn still retained the musty smell of raw earth and animal dung. It was exactly the kind of sensory input a man like Mansoor Aleem would find offensive.

Harvath made a loud show of closing and locking the wide doors behind him as he entered. In the center of the barn, the young jihadist was tied to a wooden chair taken from the farmhouse kitchen. A hood had been placed over his head before they had pulled away from the accident scene.

Though Mansoor had been an unknown up until quite recently, it wasn't hard to work up a profile on him. In fact, by the very nature of what he did, it was quite easy to understand how he thought and thereby select the best approach for his interrogation.

As far as the real world was concerned, the young jihadist was a loser. He was unremarkable in almost every way. With a poor complexion, unappealing features, and a pair of eyes that bulged just enough to suggest he might have a thyroid condition, he was considerably unattractive. He was too skinny and therefore unimpressive physically. Beyond the bulging eyes, he fit the cyber jihadi/hacker mold to a T.

While he was nothing in the real world, in the digital world he could very well be the heat. He might woo the women in the chat rooms as if he were Don Juan incarnate, but he'd never have the courage to approach a member of the opposite sex in the flesh. Cybergeeks like Mansoor were all about control; the control of information. It was the only thing they could have power over. Without it, they were impotent. When you placed them in a situation where they were devoid of any authority, or more precisely devoid of any control, it was tremendously unsettling for them.

They were also completely visual. Depriving them of the ability to see tipped them off-balance and made them more pliant to interrogation.

Harvath knew that the young man would still be in shock over what had happened in the car. That shock would only have been compounded since he had been taken prisoner and kept in the dark. He had been stripped down to his underwear and was shivering in the nighttime cold of the barn.

Harvath walked over and stood just behind the man's left shoulder. He knew Mansoor had heard him enter and he didn't doubt the man could sense his presence directly behind him. Keeping an eye on his watch, he allowed several minutes to pass, adding to the man's discomfort.

Without warning, Harvath drew his hand back and slapped the jihadist hard in the side of his hooded head to make sure he was psychologically off-balance and hadn't manufactured some semblance of resistance or bravado. It was important for the jihadist to understand that he was absolutely helpless.

Harvath stepped back and waited a full three minutes before speaking.

When he broke the silence, he was explicit. "Let me explain to you what is going on," he said. "The only reason you're alive is that until now, I have let you live. I can very easily decide to let you die. The choice is one hundred percent mine. The people I work with couldn't care less what happens to you. Everything that happens from this point forward will depend on whether you cooperate with me. Do you understand?"

Mansoor Aleem nodded.

"Good," replied Harvath. "I also want you to understand this. We know everything. And I mean *everything*. We know who you are. We know why you are here. We know all of it. If you lie to me, even once, I am going to kill you. Do you understand that?"

Once again, Mansoor nodded.

Reaching forward, Harvath ripped off the man's hood. As his eyes were adjusting, Harvath tore the piece of duct tape from his mouth.

"Tell me why you are here," demanded Harvath.

"I'm cold," he said, his teeth chattering.

"Answer my question and I may be able to find you a blanket."

Mansoor tried to lick his lips, but he had trouble creating saliva. "I need something to drink. May I have some water?"

"You're not going to get anything until you answer my questions," said Harvath, raising his voice. "Why are you here?"

"I don't know."

Harvath withdrew his Taser, activated the laser, and pointed it at him.

The jihadist flinched and turned his head away, anticipating another painful jolt of electricity. "I don't know," he repeated.

"You're lying to me, Mansoor," said Harvath. IT people harbored a collective fear of anything that would impair their computer skills. It was almost 100 percent universal. Threatening their eyes, their hands, or the ability of their brains to function was very powerful. "Maybe instead of killing you, I should hit you with so many jolts of electricity that we take that forty-gig brain of yours down to two kilobytes. How about that?"

"They sent me a ticket. That's all I know," he pleaded.

"Who sent it to you?"

"Friends of my uncle."

"Your uncle Aazim?" demanded Harvath.

Mansoor nodded and dropped his gaze to the floor.

"And why would they do that?"

When the young man didn't respond, Harvath put the laser dot on the floor where he knew Mansoor could see it and then traced it up his leg to the yellow stain on his underwear. "Why?"

"Because he had been killed," Mansoor responded as he raised his eyes to lock them on Harvath. "They brought me here to protect me."

Harvath turned off the laser and tucked the Taser back into his coat pocket. "They didn't bring you here to protect you, Mansoor. They brought you here to kill you. Just like they killed your uncle."

The young man didn't know how to respond. He was shocked. He looked away. A full minute passed. Finally, he said, "I don't believe you."

"I don't care what you believe. I'm telling you the truth." Harvath wasn't telling the truth, but that made little difference. If he could convince Mansoor the Uppsala cell had brought him here to execute him, he might be willing to cooperate.

"You think about that for a little bit," said Harvath as he began to replace the hood over the man's head.

"What are you doing?" the jihadist implored, his teeth still chattering, his lips azure.

Harvath didn't reply. Once the hood was in place, he walked over to the doors, unlocked them, and let himself out.

CHAPTER 10

HERMOSA BEACH
CALIFORNIA

"What do you think you're doing?" Luke Ralston asked as he watched Larry Salomon reach for the cordless telephone on the kitchen counter.

"Leaving a message for my office," replied the film producer.

Ralston shook his head. "No calls. No emails. Nothing," he said sternly as he poured a mug of coffee and motioned for his friend to sit down.

They had driven south of L.A. to the quiet coastal community of Hermosa Beach. Ralston had steered clear of the freeways and major arteries in an effort to avoid traffic cameras. He had also disassembled his cell phone so no cellular print could be made of his progress or direction. He didn't need to worry about Salomon's phone, as it had been left behind at the house in Coldwater Canyon.

Ralston knew he needed to get them someplace safe. It had to be somewhere they could lie low and figure out what their next move was going to be. Going to Ralston's apartment was out of the question. Sooner or later it would be crawling with police. The same went for any of the properties Salomon owned in Palm Springs or up near Santa Barbara. For all intents and purposes, they needed to completely drop off the grid. And for that to happen, they were going to need some help.

At just after three in the morning, they pulled into the driveway of a modest stucco house with a Spanish tile roof, two blocks back from the ocean. It belonged to an old friend of Ralston's named Hank McBride.

Hank was a former Navy SEAL in his late sixties who dabbled in a wide field of endeavors, including technical consulting in Hollywood, though he had yet to work on any of Salomon's movies. Despite their age difference, Ralston and Hank McBride had developed a good friendship and shared many of the same friends within the small, tightly knit Special Operations community.

"How long before we see it on the news?" said Hank, who had the TV near the kitchen table turned on, but muted.

Ralston had just come back inside after having parked Salomon's Wagoneer in the garage and covered it with a tarp. "If I had to guess the window on this, I'd say probably not for a few more hours," he replied. The graze on the side of his head had been easily covered with a Band-Aid, but it was a serious reminder of how close he had come to being killed.

Salomon sat down and accepted the mug of coffee. "If I don't get the studio's publicist working on this, it's going to be a nightmare. Just let me make one call so she can get ahead of it."

Once again, Ralston shook his head. "This already is a nightmare, Larry. A grade-A shitstorm."

"I know. I could be tainted by this forever. Look at what happened to Phil Spector. And there'd been only one body in his house. I've got—" Salomon's voice trailed off as he did the math. "Six bodies, if you count what's left of the one outside who you apparently parked on."

Hank let out a low whistle. "Six? That's pretty good."

"Only four of them were bad guys," clarified Ralston. "The other two worked with Larry. Speaking of which—"

Salomon suddenly realized something. "The hard drives. Damn it. We forgot to get them out of the house."

"What hard drives?"

"From the computers in the office."

Ralston needed him to slow down. "Let's take things one step at a time. First, I want to know about the two men who were killed. Jeremy *and*—?"

"Chip," said Salomon.

"Who were they?"

"They were working on a film project with me."

"You said it was a documentary?" asked Ralston.

The movie producer nodded, but didn't elaborate.

"Why was everything set up in your office at home? Why weren't you working at the studio?"

"Because this was a private project."

Ralston's antennae went up. *"Private?"*

"Yeah," said the producer, somewhat absentmindedly, as he stared into his coffee cup. "Personal."

"Larry, we're pretty good friends, wouldn't you say?"

Salomon nodded.

"So why don't you come clean and tell me what you've been up to. Let's start with who Jeremy and Chip are."

The producer took a sip of coffee and set the mug back on the table. He was still very upset. "They were friends of mine. Chip is a blogger and political activist and Jeremy is, or I guess I should be using the past tense, Jeremy *was* a film student who had teamed up with Chip to make a short film."

"A short film about what?"

"Endowments."

Ralston wasn't sure he had heard that correctly. "As in financial endowments? Like at universities?"

Salomon nodded.

"Not exactly the type of summer blockbuster you're known for, but everyone in Hollywood has their pet projects, I guess. What I don't understand is why you were working on this out of your house?"

Hank McBride looked away from the TV and over his shoulder at Salomon. "*Short film* isn't code for porn, is it?"

Ralston held up his hand at the man.

"I'm just saying," replied Hank as he went back to monitoring the television. "Something doesn't sound right. You don't get a visit from a wet work team for making documentaries."

"And you probably don't get it for making porn, either," argued Ralston.

"You do if the Russians are involved somehow," countered Hank.

He had a point. Turning his attention back to Salomon, he said, "Let's back all the way up. Is there any reason someone would want to kill you?"

The producer shrugged.

"That's not a *no,* Larry."

"The film we've been making might not be too popular," Salomon responded.

"Do you think it's something worth killing over?"

"Maybe."

Ralston was taken aback. "Then we really do need to start from the beginning. What's the film called?"

Salomon mumbled his response and Ralston had to ask him to repeat it. *"Well Endowed,"* he said.

"I was right," said Hank without turning away from the TV. "Making skin flicks."

"Do you mind?" asked Ralston.

Hank shrugged and went back to clicking through the muted channels, searching for any stories about what had happened at the producer's home.

Refocusing on Salomon, Ralston said, "Was this project your idea, or did somebody bring it to you?"

"It's a long story."

"Well, it doesn't look like you're going to be going anywhere for a while," said Hank as he stopped on a channel that was streaming helicopter footage from above a hilly, wooded area. "Your house is in Coldwater Canyon, right?"

"Yes," said Salomon.

"Then I'd say the window for when your story would make the news just got slammed shut."

CHAPTER 11

R ealizing he wasn't going to be going back to bed, Hank McBride disengaged from the TV and offered to cook breakfast while his two guests, or the two "fugitives," as he had referred to them until Ralston told him to drop it, continued their conversation at the table.

"It's all very complicated and convoluted," said Salomon as he held his mug out for Ralston to top off. "It's like a shell game the way foundation money gets moved around. In fact, *Shell Game* had been Jeremy and Chip's working title for the project. I thought *Well Endowed* was a little more provocative and would help the film get more attention."

"Sell the sizzle," said Ralston, reflecting on an old advertising adage he had often heard Salomon use, "not the steak."

"Precisely. Documentaries are a tough sell anyway, but a documentary about endowments? Forget it. The only way we were going to get people interested was to sex it up."

Ralston had his reservations about whether a pithy double entendre would make much of a difference, but with the film business, you never knew. "So how did Jeremy and Chip get on your radar screen? Was it at a film festival or was one of them a waiter at one of your favorite dinner spots?"

A fatigued yet knowing look crept across Salomon's face. Hollywood was packed with wannabe actors, wannabe screenwriters, and wannabe directors. Anyone with even a semblance of power who could help get a movie made was under constant assault by those looking to break into the business. Producers, in particular, had pitchman horror stories, including being wooed while in the dentist's chair, as well as the mother of all famous stories, involving a producer being pitched at a rather sensitive moment in her gynecologist's office.

"What difference does it make?"

He was being cagey again and Ralston pressed him on it. "Why do you keep holding out on me?"

The producer looked up from his coffee. "I'm not holding out on you."

"You're not answering my questions and I'm beginning to think maybe Hank was right. Maybe you were making porn. Maybe you ran up a huge drug debt with the Russians too and they came to collect."

"I'm *not* making porn," insisted Salomon, "and you know me. I have *never* touched drugs in my life."

Ralston did know his friend and he didn't believe for a second that Salomon was making porn or into drugs, but he didn't like having his questions parried. "Larry, I'm going to chalk a lot of your current condition up to—"

"My *current condition*?" interrupted the producer. "What are you talking about?"

Ralston held his hand up for him to stop. "What happened tonight would put anyone into shock. Add to it that this would have been Rachael's birthday."

"It *is* Rachael's birthday."

"No, it isn't. It's the *anniversary* of Rachael's birth. She's gone, Larry."

Salomon went off like a flare. "You think I want you to spell it out like that? You think I give a good goddamn about how you see it? She wasn't your daughter, Luke. Don't you *ever* forget that."

The outburst was so intense it froze Hank in mid-scramble over his eggs at the stove.

Ralston motioned for the old SEAL to bring the bottle of Bushmills from next to the fridge.

As Hank placed it on the table and retreated to the stove, Ralston pulled the cork from the bottle and poured a generous amount into each of the coffee cups. He was feeling the effects of everything that had happened as well. A little anesthetic would be good for them.

Salomon took a deep drink of his Irish coffee and said nothing. Ralston respected the silence, just as he had hours earlier in the producer's driveway. Even Hank maintained a respectful distance in the kitchen.

"I'm sorry," the producer eventually said.

Ralston reached out and put his hand on his friend's shoulder. "There's no need to apologize."

"Jeremy and Chip were good people; good filmmakers. I think Rachael would have liked them. And they her."

"She was a wonderful girl, Larry. You have every right to be proud of her."

The producer smiled, taken away for a moment by a thought from a happier time in his life. As his attention returned, his expression became more serious. "I met Jeremy and Chip at a social function."

"If you don't mind my asking," said Hank as he brought over three plates of food and set them down on the table, "how'd you lose your daughter?"

"Let's not go there," Ralston replied, trying to protect Salomon.

"That's okay." Looking up at Hank, the producer said, "My daughter was murdered during a trip to Israel three years ago."

Hank sat his considerable frame down onto a chair. "I'm sorry to hear that. I hope they caught the fuckers and strung them up."

Salomon shook his head. "Unfortunately, they didn't catch them. That's the hardest part for me. How can anyone move on, knowing that person, or persons, is still out there and probably still committing unspeakable acts? How do you even begin to let that wound heal?"

Ralston knew that talking about Rachael would only end up sinking Salomon deeper into depression, so he decided to change the subject. "So you met Jeremy and Chip at some social event, right?"

The filmmaker nodded and scooped up a forkful of eggs. "That's right. I didn't know much about Chip before that. It turns out that he was a real agent provocateur via his blog sites. He'd broken a handful of scandals before the mainstream media even realized what was happening."

"And Jeremy?"

"Jeremy was Chip's protégé. The two of them were looking to broaden their platform beyond the blogs. They saw a potential niche for certain types of documentary films they thought could really do well. Between them, they must have had a hundred different ideas, many of which were very topical and actually quite interesting. To get started, though, they had to narrow it down to just one.

"Some whistleblower had approached Chip with a story for one of his blogs a while back. She worked for the Ford Foundation and had uncovered some unusual activity that she felt should be brought to light."

"What kind of *unusual activity*?" asked Ralston.

"Financial; who the money was being funneled to, how it was being funneled, that kind of thing. But before he could go to press with the story, the woman disappeared. Chip received a note, allegedly from her, saying that she had made it all up."

"Why would she do that?"

Salomon shook his head. "Nobody knew. They figured somebody had gotten to her."

"So what happened?"

"Chip and Jeremy kept after the story. The more they looked into it, the more they uncovered. They started thinking it was too big for the blogs. That's where the idea for the documentary came in. They pieced together a short rough cut, and were screening it for different people who they thought might be interested in helping to get it made. I just happened to be in the right place at the right time."

"Yet you didn't want any of your Hollywood pals to know you were working on it. That's why you were doing it out of your house?" mused Ralston.

The producer nodded and took a bite of his bacon before replying. "With technology these days, especially for a documentary that doesn't require any special effects, we didn't need to be at the studio; we could do it all from home."

"You said you were worried the production was going to ruffle a few feathers. I can see ticking off some foundations by exposing what they might have been up to, but I can't picture them getting together and putting out a hit on you," said Ralston. "That doesn't make sense."

"Not until you understand how much money is involved and what's at stake," Salomon replied. "One hundred years ago, there were only eighteen American tax-exempt private foundations. Today, there are more than sixteen thousand.

"The U.S. not-for-profit sector is the world's seventh-largest economy. The foundations sit on over five hundred billion untaxed and largely unregulated dollars. Some of the biggest foundations give away more in a year than some nations' GDPs. The power of a few of these foundations rival that of our own federal government, as well as the power of countries like Russia, France, and Great Britain. That was the crux of our film—how, where, and why that money and power is being spent.

"We were looking at the foundation world in general, but more specifically at a disturbing ideological agenda shared by many of them. We wanted to know how many of these large foundations, started by successful pro-business Americans, had turned so anti-business and in some cases downright anti-American. Why were environmental organizations lobbying Washington on issues that had nothing to do with the environment? Why were labor organizations lobbying on issues that had nothing to do with workers? Why were foundations funding pro-socialist and pro-communist textbooks and lessons in schools? Why were others supporting the eugenics movement and the works of Josef Mengele from Auschwitz, masquerading under the banner of human genetics? The list went on and on. The key in each instance was in following the money, and the more we followed it, the further down the rabbit hole we went.

"What we discovered was that beginning in the 1940s, radical elements inside the United States had recognized that there were these huge piles of money just sitting inside multiple large foundations and endowments all across the country. These big government collectivists, globalists, socialists, and communists realized that if they could get into positions of power, say on the boards of directors at the foundations or the endowments, they could steer the money any way they wanted. And that was exactly what they did."

"So what you're saying," replied Ralston, "is that they used the money to buy influence."

"Not only to buy influence," the producer continued, "but to develop and push entire agendas. It was like having a tray of financial syringes. Any cause that met their radical agenda received huge injections of cash. Any causes that ran counter to their agenda received huge injections of poison and found themselves beset by opposition groups with bottomless wells of support. They used their money to cozy up to politicians, influence public policy, and elect their own candidates."

"But how could they get away with that?" asked Ralston. "How would nobody raise a fuss or try to expose them?"

Salomon shook his head. "This isn't just a mountain of hush money we're talking about, it's a whole *range* of mountains. This kind of power and influence can purchase a lot of silence."

"And their boards just rubber-stamp anything they do?"

"They don't need a rubber stamp," replied the producer, "when the boards have all been stacked with members who see the world through exactly the same prism. If the people who had started many of these foundations were alive today, they'd be stunned to discover what was going on."

Ralston didn't doubt it, *but so what*? "The more you talk, Larry, the less I think this has anything to do with your documentary. I think we ought to be looking at other possibilities."

"You're wrong," replied Salomon.

"Am I?" asked Ralston. "So lots of foundations and endowments have drifted from their original intent. Big deal. Your documentary might bring some unwanted attention to some in that industry, but as long as they're not breaking any laws, I don't see how anybody is really going to care."

"That's what I thought, too, until I saw what Chip and Jeremy had begun to dig up."

"Which was what?"

"The foundations and the endowments need to make a return on their principal, so they invest in different vehicles. Often times, those vehicles are hedge funds. We discovered that a small group, the most radical, invested with one hedge fund in particular. It's called the Standing Fund and is managed by James Standing."

"The billionaire?"

"The vehemently *anti-American* billionaire," Salomon clarified.

"So what?"

"*So* we discovered that there were some things even the most radical foundations and endowments were afraid to be tied to. What they weren't afraid to do, though, was to use Standing as a cutout. Each of them agreed to allow Standing to retain part of their investment return in order to fund something they referred to as *Project Green Ramp*."

"And what's *Project Green Ramp*?"

Salomon looked Ralston directly in the eyes and stated, "An intricate plan to completely collapse the United States of America."

CHAPTER 12

Harvath was on his way out of the farmhouse with a blanket and a bottle of water, when his cell phone rang. "Go ahead," he said, answering the call and setting the items down.

"We've got a fix on the mobile phone Phoenix Three contacted from the accident site," said Reed Carlton. *Phoenix Three* was the code name that had been given to Sean Chase for the operation. Harvath was Phoenix One and Riley Turner was Phoenix Two.

"We've got an address?" asked Harvath.

"That's affirmative," said the old man. "I'll pass it off to you on the back channel."

The back channel was a reference to the secure network the Carlton Group used to communicate and pass information to each other.

"Roger that," said Harvath.

Using the code name they had created for Mansoor, based on his initials, the old man asked, "Any progress with Massachusetts?"

"Not yet," replied Harvath, "but I think he'll be warming up to us soon."

"Good. I want this op wrapped up and everyone out of there as soon as possible. Understood?"

"Roger that," replied Harvath. He and Carlton spoke at length about how long to give Phoenix Three before launching their takedown of the Uppsala cell. They both understood that the longer Chase was in their midst, the more he might be able to learn. They also understood that the longer he stayed, the greater the odds were that he might be discovered. If he was, they'd kill him on the spot.

The call ended, Harvath gathered up the blanket and the water bottle, and headed outside.

"Anything?" he asked as he approached the operative standing guard at the barn. "Praying? Crying? Anything?" Knowing how their prisoner had spent the time since Harvath had been gone would affect how he decided to continue the interrogation.

"Nothing," replied the operative, an ex-CIA man named Andy Bachmann. He was in his late fifties and built like a drill instructor. The Old Man had suggested him for this operation as they'd known each other in the old days back at Langley, and Bachmann had worked in Sweden before. "Not a sound."

Mansoor Aleem might be tougher than Harvath had thought. Nodding, he walked past Bachmann, unlocked the barn door, and jerked it wide. He stood there with the door open for several seconds to encourage the flow of cold air. The prisoner didn't move.

Considering how he'd been shivering, there was no way that Mansoor could have fallen asleep. *Had he slipped into unconsciousness?* That would be a world record. He hadn't been exposed to the cold *that* long.

For a moment, Harvath wondered if he was being played. "Time to wake up, Mansoor," he said as he walked up to the man and snatched off his hood. There was no reaction.

The man's head was bent forward, his chin resting on his chest. Harvath grabbed a fistful of hair and tilted his head back so he could look at his face. He slapped him, but the man didn't even flinch. He wasn't conscious.

Harvath opened one of his eyelids. The eye failed to dilate. He placed two fingers against the man's carotid and felt for a pulse. *Nothing.*

"Fuck," said Harvath, as he then yelled for the operative outside. "Andy! Andy, damn it!"

Bachmann threw open the door and charged inside, his MP7 drawn from beneath his coat. "What is it?" he said, scanning the barn as he tried to figure out what was happening.

"Get Riley," Harvath ordered. "Now! Tell her Mansoor has flat-lined."

As a medical student and Winter X Games athlete, Turner had been one of the first recruits into a covert Department of Defense program known as the Athena Project. Its goal was to provide women with the same training male Delta Force operatives received, making it possible to send them into the field alone, on all-female teams, or in various mixed assignments such as Harvath's Sweden op. The bad guys could often see the men coming but rarely, if ever, suspected women. He had requested Riley, now a trauma surgeon, personally. Having worked with her before, he knew she was exceedingly capable. There were also personal reasons he wanted her along, but those were far from his mind right now.

As Bachmann took out his radio to raise Riley, Harvath cut his prisoner loose and laid him on the floor. Harvath had killed plenty of people in his career, but they'd all been bad guys who had deserved to die. Harvath had killed each of them intentionally. Mansoor Aleem was definitely a bad guy, but Harvath didn't want him dead. And he definitely didn't want it to happen because he had screwed up.

With him on the floor, Harvath immediately began CPR. The new guidelines called for doubling the number of chest compressions and not worrying about blowing air into the victim's airway. "Don't you die on me, asshole," he said as he rapidly compressed the man's chest. "Don't you die."

"What happened?" Riley shouted as she ran into the barn and saw Harvath on the floor performing CPR.

"I've got no idea," said Harvath, as he kept focused on his prisoner. "When I came back in, he didn't have a pulse."

"Don't BS me," she replied as she rushed to his side. "I can't help him if I don't know what happened."

"I just told you I don't know what happened."

"Did you hit him?"

"No, damn it," Harvath snapped.

"If you struck him," she said, "I need to know exactly where and with how much force."

"For God's sake, Riley. I didn't touch him."

"Fine," she said, reaching out to check Mansoor's pulse. "Stop the compressions for a second."

Harvath did as he was told and watched as she checked for a pulse. "Anything?"

Riley shook her head. Picking up where Harvath had left off, she continued chest compressions with quick, swift pumps. "We're going to need to get him to a hospital."

"The hell we are," replied Harvath. "We do that and we're going to have an international incident on our hands."

"Scot," she said, as she continued the compressions. "He's dead."

"Hypothermia?"

"Hypothermia. Heart attack. What difference does it make?"

Harvath didn't respond.

"If it's hypothermia," Riley added, "that could work in our favor. You're not dead till you're warm and dead, but I don't have the kind of equipment we need to revive him."

Harvath looked at the bag she had run in with and had tossed on the floor. "What about adrenaline? Can you use a syringe and pump it straight into his heart?"

"Intracardial injection?"

"Whatever you call it. Can you do that?" asked Harvath.

"Sure," she replied, "but you need to defibrillate the patient as well. We don't have a defibrillator."

"Prep the adrenaline," said Harvath as he waved Bachmann over. When the ex–CIA operative neared, Harvath told him to take over for Riley and keep giving Mansoor chest compressions.

"What are you going to do?" asked Riley.

"Don't worry. Just hurry up and get that syringe ready."

As Riley opened her bag and prepped the adrenaline, Harvath drew his Taser and pulled out its cartridge. "A Taser won't give him the kind of jolt he needs. They're not built that way," she said.

Harvath didn't care. He'd seen people take punches to the chest and have their hearts restart. If he could put enough juice in Mansoor's body and cause it to convulse violently enough, maybe it would work. Grabbing the Taser from the holster on Bachmann's belt, he removed its cartridge as well.

When Riley had the syringe ready, she nodded, and Harvath told Bachmann to stop the compressions and stand back. Looking at Riley, he said, "Do it."

With no time to swab the man's chest with an alcohol pad, she felt for the fourth intercostal space and pushed the needle through tissue and into his heart. Depressing the plunger, she injected the contents of the syringe into the young man's ventricle.

When she was finished, she withdrew the needle and stood back. "This won't work."

"It has to work," said Harvath as he kneeled over the body. Riley pointed to where defibrillator paddles would normally be placed and then stood back. "Here we go," said Harvath, indicating that he was ready.

When Riley nodded, Harvath counted to three and pulled both the Tasers' triggers at once.

CHAPTER 13

The young Muslim's body went rigid, his head rolled back, and his back arched off the floor.

Harvath withdrew the Tasers and rocked back on his heels as Mansoor's body landed with a thud on the dirt-covered barn floor. Riley reached forward and placed two fingers on his neck to see if he had a pulse.

"Anything?"

Riley shook her head. "Scot, this is not going to work."

Harvath ignored her. "Stand back," he said.

"Scot."

"Stand back," he repeated.

When she was out of the way, Harvath reapplied the Tasers, gave the warning he was about to deploy another charge, and then pulled the triggers.

The prisoner's body went stiff once more and then came to rest on the floor. "Check his pulse," Harvath said.

Riley did as he asked. Feeling nothing, she shook her head and scooted back.

"Damn it," cursed Harvath. "Everybody back up. I'm going to hit him again."

Riley and Bachmann did as they were told. Placing the Tasers against Mansoor's left and right chest walls, Harvath applied yet another stun drive of electricity.

As had happened each time previously, the young man's body convulsed and then dropped back to the dusty barn floor.

"He's gone," said Bachmann.

"He doesn't get to choose when he goes," snapped Harvath. "I'm not done with him."

Without any warning this time, Harvath repositioned the Tasers and pulled the triggers. Mansoor's body stiffened and then dropped back down.

"Check him again," he said.

Riley moved forward and reached out her fingers. "Nothing."

"Fuck!" Harvath yelled.

Abandoning the young man's right and left chest walls, Harvath placed both Tasers directly over Mansoor's heart and pulled the triggers. When the body fell back to the ground, he did it again, and then again once more.

"Scot," Bachmann said, but Harvath ignored him. Angry at the prisoner and even more angry with himself, Harvath pulled the triggers two more times.

Riley said something, but Harvath didn't listen to her either. She put her hand on his shoulder, but he shrugged it off. It wasn't until she grabbed his arm just above his triceps in a viselike pinch that she broke the spell.

"Son of a—" he began, as he turned his anger toward Riley.

"He twitched," she said.

"He what?"

Riley shoved Harvath aside and laid her fingers on Mansoor's carotid. She then leaned her ear over his mouth. "I think I can feel a breath."

Tilting the prisoner's head back, she pinched his nose, placed a CPR barrier over his mouth, and delivered a breath of air. She waited for several seconds and then repeated the process two more times until he began breathing on his own.

"Is he alive?" asked Harvath.

"Barely," replied Riley. "We need to get him warm and get an IV started."

Bachmann wrapped Mansoor with the blanket Harvath had brought with him and then went to the farmhouse to gather more.

Harvath handed Riley the items she requested from her medical bag and then rigged up a makeshift IV stand.

Once she had the fluids running into the young Muslim's arm, Harvath asked, "How long until he's ready to be interrogated again?"

Riley looked up at him. He couldn't tell if what he was seeing on her face was admiration or disgust. He figured it was probably a mixture of both. "You've got to be one of the luckiest people I've ever met. Don't push it."

Harvath had often said it was better to be lucky than good, but he didn't offer that sentiment to her. "I need to know how soon I can start asking him questions again."

Riley shook her head. "First he's got to regain consciousness."

"How long?" Harvath insisted.

"It's indefinite at this point. He probably has some sort of underlying heart condition. I think that's why he coded. He could also have brain damage now. He's going to need some tests; tests we can't conduct where we're supposed to be going. We're going to need access to a friendly hospital."

Harvath knew what she meant by a "friendly" hospital. They had planned for the possibility that Mansoor might get injured in the car crash. Whether that happened or not, he was going to be drugged up and flown out of Sweden on a Sentinel Medevac jet. All the paperwork was in order and an impeccable passport had been created for him. They'd be portraying him as the son of a wealthy Arab who'd had a stroke and was being flown back to the UAE for emergency medical treatment. Not even the most rigorous of authorities would have any reason to suspect the party and their patient were anything other than who they said they were.

By the time Mansoor awoke from his drug-induced stupor, the flight plan would have been refiled for Jordan and he would find himself in one of the multiple "extraordinary rendition" black interrogation/detention sites still in operation despite the U.S. government's public proclamations to the contrary.

Based on the cyber jihadist's enhanced medical needs, though, they were probably going to have to reevaluate which host country's site they were going to use. Carlton and the DoD would make the final call.

The members of the Uppsala cell were another matter. Harvath had decided it would be foolish to put all of his eggs in one basket. He wanted Mansoor out of the country as quickly as possible. He had developed another plan for getting the safe house terrorists out of the country, though he still had no idea at the moment how many there were.

First things first. "How long until he can be ready for transport?" asked Harvath as he gestured at Mansoor.

Riley glanced at her patient and again shook her head. "At this point, I don't even want to try to move him to the farmhouse. That said, the plane has a lot of the medical equipment he's going to need, so as soon as he is ready to be moved, I think we should move him."

Getting Mansoor to the airfield was another shell game, which would be played out via a private ambulance service from Stockholm willing to make the drive up to Uppsala. Looking at the man lying on the floor, Harvath wondered if he'd even survive the trip to the airport. Fortunately, that wasn't his problem. It was Riley's. He had other problems.

The biggest among them was deciding how long to leave Sean Chase in place and when to take down the Uppsala cell. With Riley now tied up with overseeing Mansoor, Harvath was going to have to shift to his contingency plan. He didn't like it, but they had all known that it was a possible outcome. The team, and more important Harvath, would have to do without her.

That meant that things were about to get much more dangerous.

CHAPTER 14

The two brothers who picked Chase up at the soccer field did not speak. They didn't ask about his medical condition, nor did they offer him any food or water. They simply drove him to an abandoned garage on the outskirts of Uppsala and kept an eye on him while they all waited.

What they were waiting for, Chase wasn't exactly sure, but he had an idea. More than likely, the man he had spoken to over the phone, the man he assumed was in charge of the cell, was checking out his story about the accident.

When it was time to pray, the two men let Chase pray alongside them, but he stopped when the wound on his head opened up and started bleeding again.

Fairly confident of how the authentic Mansoor Aleem would behave, he made sure to make a real pain in the ass out of himself. He lectured his two guards about Islamic doctrine and their duty to see to his well-being.

He harangued them so badly that one of the men threatened to kill him. Eventually, he wore them down, and one of them left to purchase some items he had asked for.

The man came back twenty minutes later with energy drinks, candy bars, and first-aid supplies. They allowed Chase to use the garage's filthy, foul-smelling bathroom to clean himself up and tend to his wounds. He did the best he could and then came out and choked down some nourishment. He hated energy drinks and he wasn't all that big on candy bars, but that was the quintessential IT/hacker diet and it was important that he looked the part, right down to the smallest detail, as the smallest details often played the biggest part in making or breaking a cover.

If he had wanted to, Chase could have taken out both in quick succession. There were multiple items lying around the old garage that could have been used as weapons. In the bathroom, he had found a decent strip of metal that he had folded to about four inches long. It was rusting, yet had a sharp enough point that it could be used as a shiv. He wrapped the handle portion of the weapon with plumber's tape he'd found around one of the pipes beneath the sink.

He'd been processing every single nuanced, nonverbal cue the two men had been giving off since they had picked him up. He knew all too well what he could end up having to do and how far he might have to go and he was getting himself all jacked up over it. He had to get it under control.

Taking a look in the mirror, he took a deep breath and told himself to relax, everything was cool. All that nervousness was just his limbic system. A student of Hagakure, he'd meditated extensively on death. He'd done so right before this operation. It was the same before every operation. Death was inevitable. He imagined the worst for himself daily. Whatever was going to happen, was going to happen. That didn't mean, though, that he wouldn't take as many of them with him as possible. Nevertheless, he decided to abandon the homemade weapon.

While he probably could have concealed it in his pocket, if it had been discovered, it would have created no end of problems for him. Even the most paranoid of computer geeks wasn't going to be fashioning his own shivs.

In the gray half-light that spilled in from the dirty glass skylights above, Chase studied the men who'd been charged with babysitting him. If he had to, he could take them, but there was a lot that could go wrong, and if something did go wrong, he had no doubt either of the men would kill him without hesitation.

They were of medium height and solidly built. Their eyes were hard and dark, like pieces of flint, and told him everything he needed to know about them. These men were no strangers to violence.

Despite the men's rough demeanor, Chase kept up the haughty hacker act and repeatedly asked the men how much longer they were going to have to wait until they could leave the garage.

When one of the men retrieved a newspaper from the car and tossed it at him, Chase took a look at it and threw it right back at the man, saying in Arabic, "Do I look like I read Swedish?"

The sooner the men could get rid of him, the happier they were going to be.

Two hours later, one of the men's mobile phones rang and he listened before saying a few words back and hanging up. He then motioned for his colleague to join him at the far end of the garage where they conversed in private. Chase didn't like it. The sudden sequestration made him very apprehensive.

When the men finally returned, he asked them what the call had been about, but they wouldn't say. He was starting to regret having left his shiv in the bathroom. Once again, he took stock of anything in his immediate surroundings that could be used as a weapon.

With nothing to do but wait, he cracked another energy drink and sipped on it as he put together a plan for which of the two men to kill first and how, if he needed to.

He was running through the clever ways he could dispose of the bodies when there was the bleat of a car horn outside and one of the men went to open the garage door.

Once the door was opened wide enough, an anemic-looking Volvo rolled inside. Chase watched as it came to a stop and its engine was turned off. Seconds passed. Through the windshield, the driver appeared to be on his cell phone. When the call was over, the man lowered the phone and stepped out of the car.

He was very large, and judging from the way the other two men reacted to him, someone of stature within the organization. He had a certain presence about him and for a moment, Chase wondered if he was looking at the cell's leader. He was a bit too rough around the edges, though, and Chase pegged him as being somewhere in the command structure, but not at the very top of the pyramid. This was not the kind of man who could blend in and easily remain beneath the radar.

There was also something about his bearing that Chase could not quite place. As he approached, there was a way he walked that he found interesting. He had the bearing of a cop.

His face was a mix of the most exaggerated of Arab features; the long hooked nose, the dark-circled, heavily hooded eyes, thin lips, and dark, weather-beaten skin. His sheer physical size, on the other hand, made him one of the biggest Arabs Chase had ever seen.

"*Salaam alaikum,*" said the man as he approached and kissed Chase on both cheeks.

"*Wa alaikum a salaam,*" replied Chase, returning the greeting. The man's enormous hands gripped Chase by the shoulders.

"Allah has taken two of our brothers today, but you he has spared."

Chase was not sure how to answer. Was the man testing him? "I am undoubtedly unworthy of Allah's favor," he replied.

The large man smiled. "May I?" he asked, indicating he wanted to remove the bandage covering the wound on Chase's head.

Without waiting for permission, the man reached out and peeled the bandage back. Placing his other hand under Chase's chin, he tilted his head back so he could better see the laceration. Even if Chase had wanted to, he couldn't have stopped him. The man was that strong.

Apparently satisfied, he released his chin and gently put the bandage back in place. "Sit down," the man said, pointing to a crate nearby.

Chase did as he was told. The man was speaking to him in English now. It wasn't perfect, but it was quite good. He told the other two men in Arabic to wait outside.

Once they had exited the garage, he turned his attention back to Chase. "Tell me about the accident," he said.

Chase was definitely being tested. "Someone ran us off the road." He made sure there was just enough British in his accent.

"Intentionally run off?"

Chase shrugged.

"What did the car look like?" asked the man.

"It was blue or gray. I can't really remember."

"You didn't see it?"

"Not until it was too late. Nafees and I were talking."

The man studied him. "Talking about what?"

Chase was silent for a moment. Finally, he replied, "About my uncle."

"And what exactly about your uncle were you talking about?"

"I wanted to know what had happened to him; how he had died. I wanted to know who killed him. I wanted to know why."

"What did Nafees tell you?" the man asked.

"He told me the same thing he had at the airport. He told me to wait until we arrived in Uppsala and all would be revealed."

"And what did Waqar say during your drive?"

"Not much, except that I ask too many questions."

The big man smiled, but as quickly as the smile crossed his face, it disappeared. "How did they die?"

Chase had been trained by the best. He knew the man was probing him. The mantra that was drummed into every intelligence operative's head was to deny, deny, deny and launch counter-accusations. The big man had yet to accuse him of anything directly, but the intimations were clear and he needed to go on the offensive. "How do you think they died? I told you, we were in a car accident. You don't believe me? Why don't you go take a look at it yourself? There's blood all over. Nafees was thrown halfway through the windshield."

"But Waqar was still wearing his seat belt," said the man.

"And?"

The man shrugged and said nothing.

"I don't even know who you are," said Chase.

"I am Sabah."

"Your name could be Mickey Mouse for all I care, mate. How do I know you are not a cop?"

The big man smiled again. "I am not a police officer, at least not anymore."

"Well, that's not very reassuring. Waqar and Nafees were friends of my uncle. I don't know the rest of you at all."

"Yet you accepted the plane ticket and came when we asked."

"I came when Waqar and Nafees asked," clarified Chase.

Sabah nodded. "Understood. I only have one more question."

"Only one?"

"What happened to the other car?"

"What other car?" asked Chase, the exasperated, smartass programmer tone fully apparent in his voice.

"The one that ran you off the road?" said Sabah.

"I was in the backseat. I didn't see where it went."

"It didn't stop? The driver didn't offer you aid?"

"I told you, I hit my head."

Sabah smiled. "You told me no such thing."

"Well, whoever I talked to on Waqar's phone, I told him."

"So you were knocked unconscious. When you awoke, the other car that ran you off the road was not there. Is this correct?"

"The more you talk, the more I'm convinced you're a cop," said Chase.

"You're not answering my question."

"I must have blacked out, because the last thing I remember is us rushing headlong into a tree. The next thing I remember was the blood pouring from my head and finding Waqar and Nafees both dead."

"Yet you had the presence of mind to take Waqar's cell phone and call us," replied Sabah.

"Who else would I call? I don't know anyone in this country."

"How did you know to use Waqar's phone to call us?"

"That's a serious question?"

Sabah nodded and Chase rolled his eyes. "Because," Chase said, thankful they'd had the men under surveillance at the airport, "Waqar placed a call when we were walking to his car after I got off the plane. I assume he was calling to tell you I had arrived."

"What did you do with Waqar's cell phone after you made the call?"

"I did exactly as I was told." Chase removed his shoe, pulled out the two SIM cards, and handed them to Sabah. "Just before the village with the soccer pitch, there was a small lake. I took the phones apart and threw the pieces into the water. Anything else you want to ask me?"

Sabah smiled and placed his large hand on the young man's shoulder. "No. I have no more questions," he said. "All that matters is that Allah has delivered you safely to us."

As Sabah motioned to his car, it was obvious to Chase that the man didn't trust him at all. He was beginning to think that leaving the shiv behind had been a very bad idea.

CHAPTER 15

SOUTHERN CALIFORNIA

Ralston wanted to know all about the plot Salomon thought he had uncovered to collapse the United States. "Give me the details on Project Green Ramp."

"To understand it," said the producer, "you have to grasp its underlying principle. It actually boils down to a simple question. If we were in a house and I thought it was burning, but you didn't, would it be okay for me to lie or even use force, to get you out of the house?"

"Hell no."

"Why not?"

"What if you're wrong?"

Salomon smiled. "Bingo."

"What do you mean, *bingo*?"

"Individualism in America is hard-wired into our DNA. We want to make our *own* decisions, even if it means making mistakes. We don't want other people telling us what to do.

"There's a group of people, though, who believe that you and I are too stupid to make our own decisions and that they should do it for us. Despite America being the greatest force for good in the history of the world, they see it as greedy and evil. They've been tearing it apart bit by bit for decades and have become desperate to finish the job. They believe they can *and* should use any means necessary to get across the goal line, no matter what the cost."

"The ends justify the means," said Ralston.

"Exactly," Salomon replied.

"And getting across the goal line means collapsing the United States?"

"According to James Standing, the United States is the only remaining obstacle to a just and stable world."

Ralston shook his head. "That's beyond insane."

"So is sending a Russian wet work team to kill three filmmakers. Standing is a full-on sociopath. Nothing about him makes sense. Despite being born and raised Jewish, he's a rabid anti-Semite. Despite being a billionaire many times over, he's a vehement anticapitalist. Despite having benefitted greatly from everything America has done to empower the individual, he is a vocal proponent of social engineering and the redistribution of wealth.

"One of the best descriptions of him I ever heard was that he was a malignant, messianic narcissist who, left unchecked, would bring about horrors beyond those performed by Hitler, Stalin, Mao, or Pol Pot."

"So who's keeping a check on him?" asked Ralston.

"Nobody."

"Come on."

Salomon held his right hand up and rubbed his thumb and forefinger together. "Money may not be able to buy happiness, but it can buy almost anything else. Even an entire political system."

Ralston looked at him. "*Now* who's insane?"

"I heard a comedian make a pretty good point recently. He said that all members of Congress should be required to wear NASCAR uniforms. You know, the kind with the patches? That way we'd know who was sponsoring each of them. I think he was kidding and we'd never be able to get them to do it, but it's a great idea and would wake people up in this country instantly."

"And Standing would be seen as the root of all evil? That's hard to believe."

"He has a very clear vision as to what he wants to have happen to America. Along with a handful of leaders of other key foundations, he developed a very simple plan to bring it about.

"He started by using his wealth to co-opt anyone who could have any impact on popular culture or public opinion. Newspapers, actors, journalists, publishers, politicians, business people, unions—you name it. The idea was to be able to control the media, as well as any other voices Americans trusted.

"They knew they needed to change the way Americans saw themselves. It's ideological subversion, plain and simple. To get it to take hold, though, they needed to begin planting this new way of thinking in the most fertile minds they could get a hold of."

"Which means kids," said Ralston.

"Precisely," Salomon replied. "That's why Standing and the foundations aligned with him have been such heavy contributors to educational endowments. It's the golden rule. He who controls the gold controls the rules, or in this case, the curricula.

"But it wasn't enough to simply plant this new ideology. For it to blossom, it had to grow without being challenged. Hence the disappearance of civics classes and the portrayal of American history through the lens of imperialism and aggression. Instead of social studies, children were taught studies in social justice with America repeatedly shown as the bad guy."

"How long has this been going on?" Ralston broke in.

"Decades," replied Salomon. "The students subjected to Standing's propaganda are now adults. They're everywhere you look—business, the media, government, even teaching successive generations of kids in our schools."

"Couldn't they be deprogrammed?" asked Ralston. "I'm sure it'd be a monumental task, but—"

The movie producer shook his head. "They're completely immune to anything that deviates from their ideological perception of reality and what they have been taught is the 'real' truth. The lens they look through life at has forever been altered. It's both terrifying and brilliant in its totality."

Ralston nodded. It *was* terrifying.

"On top of indoctrinating kids," said Salomon, "Standing wanted to get as many people dependent upon the government as possible. Government handouts, even for corporations, are like heroin. Most people, once they're hooked, remain hooked and don't even realize it. They rationalize that they're entitled to the handouts.

"And the politicians are just as addicted, except they're addicted to power, and to increase their power, they need to keep doling out more and more handouts. It doesn't matter if we can't afford the handouts. They'll keep borrowing and printing money, running the country deeper into debt in order to keep the heroin flowing. It's a vicious, self-perpetuating cycle.

"In fact, one of the most apropos political observations I have ever read is that a democracy can exist only until the voters discover that they can vote themselves largesse from the public treasury. From the moment that realization takes hold, history shows that the majority of the people will always vote for the candidate promising the most goodies from the public treasury.

"History also shows us that once a democracy goes down this road, things never end well. Each and every single time, the democracy collapses. It always happens. It collapses over loose fiscal policy, and democracy is always followed by dictatorship. And guess what the dictator promises?"

"Utopia?" Ralston replied.

Salomon shook his head. "No. When democracy collapses, fear, violence, and uncertainty fill the void. In essence, it's chaos, and that's what the dictator preys upon. The people are so terrified that they will agree to trade anything, even the most precious possession they have— their liberty—in exchange for a return to order. But when order is restored, freedom is never seen by those citizens again."

"So that's Standing's goal," said Ralston. "But how does he intend to get there? How the hell could he *force* America to collapse?"

"That's the tricky part," Salomon replied. "Historically, when democracies have collapsed it's because they were already unstable to begin with, like us. Then, some sort of crisis, or a group of crises come together in such a way that they push the democracy over the brink. They can come in any form. Often, it's some sort of black swan event."

"Like the earthquake and tsunami that hit Japan," stated Ralston.

"That's a perfect example. The 9/11 attacks were another. Basically, a black swan is something that no one would have ever expected to materialize, which ends up causing massive unforeseen consequences, and after the fact is rationalized as something everyone should have seen coming."

"So Green Ramp is about choreographing a black swan event?"

"That's what we think," Salomon replied.

Ralston shook his head. "Standing manipulates America right up onto the ledge and then shoves. He ought to be tried for treason."

"Now you know why I wanted to make this film. He needs to be exposed."

"What he *needs* is to be swinging from the end of a rope. That's the price you pay for treason."

"Not anymore," Salomon said. "Not in today's America. We don't try people for treason, much less put them to death for it. It's looked upon as an archaic reaction to what should be handled, if at all, as a criminal matter. If we began hanging traitors, we'd lose a good many of our politicians, business and union leaders, even teachers."

Considering some of the crimes that had been committed in the past twenty years in America, Ralston didn't exactly think that would be a bad thing. "Do you have any idea what kind of black swan event they were looking at creating?"

"Unfortunately, no. It's not the kind of thing they put on their website. And it might not be just one black swan, it could be a whole wedge of them."

"But it'll probably have something to do with the economy, right? Some sort of new financial crisis?"

The film producer shrugged. "Considering his expertise, that makes sense, but there are other possibilities. He's stirred revolutions in other countries by creating crises of confidence in government. He'll rig an election and then leak that the election was rigged. But even that might be too pedestrian when it comes to what he has planned for the United States. With his money and demented worldview, anything is possible.

"Remember, no matter what, James Standing feels that the ends justify the means."

"Do you have any idea exactly what his ends are? What is it he has in mind? Some sort of global governance?" asked Ralston.

"Standing is a globalist, all right," replied Salomon. "And he definitely believes he can help usher in some sort of utopia, but there's one final step that would have to be undertaken, and that's the most frightening thing of all about him."

"What is it?"

"Remember what I said about him being worse than Hitler, Stalin, Mao, or Pol Pot if left unchecked?"

Ralston nodded.

"We found an interview he gave on the sidelines of the economic forum in Davos, Switzerland. It was some small European paper and maybe he didn't think it would get any pickup, but he allowed his proverbial mask to slip. In the twentieth century, he said, the world saw the loss of about 225 million people due to war, genocide, and disaster. According to him, the only way mankind can survive the twenty-first century is if the world population is cut by at least five billion. And that will only happen if every industrialized nation is forced into collapse, starting with the United States."

CHAPTER 16

NEW YORK CITY

J ulia Winston crossed her legs in just such a way that James Standing couldn't help but wonder if she was doing it purposely for him. It wouldn't have been the first time a female reporter had done that. It didn't make any difference that he was old enough to be her grandfather. Henry Kissinger had been wrong. Power wasn't the ultimate aphrodisiac, money *and* power were and Standing had more than most could even imagine.

Winston was wearing an A-line skirt, the kind that clung tightly to her upper thighs and showed off her tiny waist. She wore an inexpensive yet chic collared shirt, probably from Brooks Brothers or, God forbid, Banana Republic. Her jewelry consisted of what appeared to be a small pair of diamond stud earrings, but that might have been fake. The only place she seemed to have spent any real money was on her shoes.

Smart girl, thought Standing. While most men wouldn't have made it past her tits, any of the women in the field she was competing with would have checked out her shoes. The difference between *bitch* and *classy bitch* with women always came down to the shoes.

Standing did in fact judge women on their looks and how they dressed, but the make-or-break for him was in the brains department. He didn't have time for unintelligent people. He was too busy and life was too short. Though New York City was filled with gorgeous women, there were few who could keep up with him intellectually. After his penis, there was no greater erogenous zone than his brain. If a woman couldn't stimulate both, he wasn't interested.

The attractive *Financial Times* journalist sitting across from him, though, seemed more than capable of doing both, so he decided to take the provocative way in which she had crossed her legs as just that.

"Let's talk currencies," Winston said as she chewed the top of her pencil and flipped through the pages of the steno pad balanced expertly atop her stockinged knee.

They were seated on low-slung couches in the plush sitting area of his office in Midtown Manhattan. Floor-to-ceiling windows offered a dramatic view of the Empire State Building, and the sheets of polished marble that covered the floors, as well as the walls, gave one the feeling that they had stepped inside some sort of modern Pantheon. It was an aura of grandeur, and it had been created entirely on purpose.

Standing studied the woman. *Who used pencils anymore?* he wondered. He liked it. It was a nice touch that made her stand out, made her different. He liked different.

He also liked how she chewed on the eraser. He was beginning to wonder more and more if she was entertaining the thought of going to bed with him.

While men's sexual energy seemed to ebb as they got older, at seventy-eight, Standing's had increased. He had no idea what those overpriced doctors and high-end nutritionists were crushing up into his so-called vitamin shakes, but he didn't care. Hell, he had half a mind to reverse-engineer the recipe and put it on the market himself. It'd be like fusing Red Bull and Viagra, both multibillion-dollar products.

Julia Winston raised her eyebrows, waiting for a response.

"I'm sorry, my dear," said Standing. His mind had drifted. Only making money could have taken his mind off the prospect of bedding such an incredibly attractive woman. "What was it you were asking?"

The woman repeated herself. "Picking up on your remarks about social justice and social responsibility, we talked about your efforts to get affordable medications to AIDS patients in Africa. We also discussed your belief that America should be just as diligent in providing medical care for everyone in this nation, regardless of immigration status. You have described housing, health care, employment, and fair wages as basic human rights."

"Exactly," said Standing, more focused now.

"Which brings me to currencies; particularly the U.S. dollar. Recently you said you wanted to see a 'managed decline' of the dollar. Can you expound upon that remark?"

"Certainly. The dollar, due to the nation's huge and rapidly expanding deficit, is not a very strong currency, and it has only grown weaker. Normally, in times of crisis, we see flights to safety. Investors seeking safe havens have historically turned to the U.S. dollar—"

"Among other things," the young journalist interrupted.

Standing smiled and nodded. "Of course. But it's important to point out that investors no longer consider the dollar a safe haven. They are fleeing to hard assets, commodities. This demonstrates both a lack of confidence in the dollar, as well as a lack of confidence in currencies overall.

"The system doesn't work. It is broken and needs to be fundamentally transformed. The worldwide distribution of wealth is completely out of balance—a select few get richer while everyone else gets poorer. The only way to correct this is with a new currency system."

"So if the dollar is no longer the world's reserve currency," Winston asked, "what is something like oil bought and sold in?"

"In the beginning, we would use a basket of currencies; special drawing rights, or SDRs, as they're known. Those would give you the makings of a new currency system. And I would add, that the United States' reluctance to consider this move only supports what the rest of the world already knows," said Standing.

"Which is what?"

"That runaway capitalism is a failure."

"Some would say that the *true* failure is too much government regulation; too much intervention in the markets. If you unshackle business, you actually have greater growth. That growth creates a rising tide that lifts all boats."

Standing winked at Winston. "Tell that to the clients of Mr. Bernie Madoff."

The financial reporter made sure she had his remark verbatim.

As she wrote, the billionaire continued. "The use of the SDRs could greatly benefit the United States, but there is an innate parochialism that exists in America, a xenophobia that has been holding this country back for decades. We live in a global society now. Communications are global, corporations are global, trade is global, tourism is global, why not currency?"

The woman looked up at him from her pad. "Some would say that a global currency would put the world just one step away from a global government."

The billionaire shrugged. "Who's to say that's a bad thing? You? Me?"

"I think the American people, for starters, would say it's a bad thing. Maybe even a *very* bad thing."

He leaned forward. "I'll tell you a secret as long as you'll agree it's off the record."

Julia Winston nodded.

"The American people aren't that bright. The entire nation is made up largely of idiots. As long as they have their McDonald's and their sitcom television, they really don't care what happens politically."

The reporter was at a loss for how to respond.

"So back to a global currency," Standing said, as he leaned back in his chair and signaled that they were on the record again. "America can no longer sit on the couch, resting on its status quo. We have always led the world, not lagged behind. America needs to *progress* into the future. It cannot stand still or, heaven forbid, fall behind the other nations of the world. In the short run, there will be difficulties, but what matters is the long run."

"And what if America says *no*?" asked the woman, having regained some of her composure. "What's the downside look like?"

Standing considered his response for a moment and then said, "The U.S.A. will become a nothing, a nobody. We need to realize that the good old days are not ahead of America anymore. They are behind us, and they will continue to be, unless the United States climbs on board with the rest of the world.

"A new system *has* to be created. Part of that system involves shedding our ridiculous reliance on the dollar. America's economy is pulling the rest of the world down."

"You don't believe that the U.S. economy is showing signs of recovery?"

Standing laughed. "Who told you that? A little elf in a little hollow tree? If you see him again, you should make sure to ask for a unicorn ride."

Winston smiled uncomfortably.

"I will tell you this," offered the billionaire. "America must stop seeing itself as the center of the universe. It is not only unhealthy, it's unrealistic. You talked about a rising tide. What does a rising tide do to people who have no boats? It *drowns* them."

"So you no longer have confidence in America?"

"I have confidence that the American model, as we understand it, no longer works. And when something doesn't work, what are your choices? You can either sit and wring your hands, or you can help guide people to something better."

"And what's better than America?"

Standing looked at his watch. "Excellent question," he said with a smile. "And one I'm afraid we will have to save for another time. Perhaps we can have dinner and discuss it?"

The billionaire didn't wait for the reporter to reply. As he stood, the large doors on the other side of the office opened and Standing's assistant walked in to show Julia Winston out.

"It has been an absolute pleasure speaking with you, my dear. I'll make sure my publicist sends you a photo for your piece. Good?"

The woman thanked him and shook his hand. Standing watched her leave. He enjoyed the way her hips moved beneath the tight skirt and the sound of her expensive shoes clicking across his marble floor.

After escorting Winston to the elevator, his assistant returned. "I assume you'd like me to set up a follow-up?"

The financier had removed his suit coat and sat down behind his expansive desk. "Yes. Do it for tonight."

"Tonight?" the assistant said, consulting his iPad. "Tonight you have a cocktail reception for donors to the United Nations' Infinitum Project. It's from seven o'clock to nine."

"Fine," replied Standing. "Set dinner up afterward. Something expensive, but not too à la mode. I don't want to be the oldest person in the room. Le Bernardin or San Pietro."

"Yes, sir. Anything else?"

The billionaire wished he could ask him if he'd received any word on California, but his assistant knew nothing about what was transpiring out there. Standing was very careful about keeping things compartmentalized. "No," he replied. "Nothing else."

"Very good," replied the assistant as he backed out of the office.

The financier waited until he heard the door click shut and then removed the encrypted BlackBerry from his desk. He had waited long enough. He should have heard something by now.

He was about to dial, when one of the multiple flat-screen televisions covering the various cable networks cut to footage of a fancy gated driveway. He searched for the remote so he could turn up the sound. One by one, all of the other networks started running similar footage, including aerial shots.

So, it's done, Standing thought to himself. *Good.* He now had something very much worth celebrating tonight. A thorn had been removed from his paw. The California problem had been taken care of. *Or had it?*

Turning up the volume of the TV tuned to CNBC he caught the

closing remarks of a local reporter throwing back to the studio in New York. "At this point," she stated, "authorities have no idea where Larry Salomon is or what happened to the man seen accompanying him. All that is known, and again, this is still unofficial at this point, is that Hollywood movie mogul Lawrence Salomon is not—I repeat, apparently not—among the dead. Back to you in New York."

CHAPTER 17

THAMES HOUSE
MI5 HEADQUARTERS
LONDON

R obert Ashford sensed his phone was going to ring before it actually did. It wasn't any grand feat of clairvoyance on his part, though. He'd been expecting the call most of the day. In fact, he should have been the one initiating it.

Considering how the Los Angeles operation appeared to have gone sideways, he probably also should have taken the day off to monitor things from a secure location. But that was exactly why he had come in to work. On the remote chance that things went bad in L.A., he needed to be able to maintain as much plausible deniability as possible.

Dismissing his staff from around the small conference table, the barrel-chested man in his early sixties with steel-gray hair and a flat, broad nose unwound the earbuds from around his cell phone. He was one of the deans of British intelligence, and those who worked under Ashford were used to his secretive and sometimes enigmatic nature. They saw him as "old school," an espionage legend who had cut his teeth in the Cold War and who continued to play his cards very close to his vest.

From his perfectly knotted tie, neatly manicured nails, and gleaming cufflinks, to the mirror-fine polish of his shoes and knifelike creases in his trousers, he cut the gallant figure of an aging British gentleman.

He had been with Britain's domestic intelligence service for more than thirty years. MI5 was responsible for national security, counterterrorism, and counterespionage within the United Kingdom. It was similar to America's FBI and was often confused with its sister organization, MI6, which was like the American CIA.

Ashford's staff also knew that he had personal relationships with many in the royal family, as well as leading figures in the British business world. No sooner had they exited and closed the door to his office than the speculation began about what powerful figure he was most likely speaking to. Little would they suspect that he wasn't doing any of the talking.

"What's going on, Robert?" James Standing demanded. "This was supposed to be a simple undertaking. In fact, what was that stupid cockney expression you used with me? *Bright and breezy?*"

Though Standing was speaking on the encrypted phone that Ashford had provided for him, he had been cautioned to speak in code and be as roundabout as possible when discussing things. The United Kingdom hosted two enormous listening posts that fed emails, text messages, and cell phone calls into the Americans' NSA listening program, *Echelon*. Every electronic communication in the United Kingdom, be it over the Internet, a cellular network, or a telephone line, was harvested and a copy kept on permanent storage at one of the NSA's massive server farms. It was always better to be safe than sorry, and Ashford always assumed someone was listening in.

"There has obviously been some sort of hiccup," said the MI5 man.

"Hiccup?" replied Standing back in Manhattan. "You Brits are amazing. I think *fuckup* would be a more apropos term. Wouldn't you?"

Ashford didn't bother responding. There were times when Standing really got under his skin.

"Are you still there?" asked the billionaire.

"Yes. I'm still here."

"Aren't you going to say anything?"

The MI5 man pinched the bridge of his nose. "What do you want me to say?"

"I want you to tell me what happened," replied Standing. "I want to know how we went from *bright and breezy* to all screwed up."

"Unfortunately, I don't have access to that information right now. The sources we'd normally reach out to in a situation like this are not answering their phones."

"Don't give me that *we* bullshit, Robert. You need to get to the bottom of this. Right now. Do you understand me? Only some of the bread got baked. What's more, the bakers seemed to have been very badly burned."

Ashford felt a migraine coming on. Before his staff meeting, he'd been flipping back and forth among several American news feeds. He'd been able to assemble a limited picture of what was happening, but there were still too many blanks that needed to be filled in. He had called his contact in Los Angeles, but the number was no longer in service. He had gone dark. Ashford was not pleased.

The Russians were normally very good at this type of work. In fact, the MI5 man had paid a lot extra to use former Spetsnaz operatives. It was a bit like using a sledgehammer in lieu of a fly swatter, but Standing had a bottomless well of cash, and he wanted the cleanest of clean, the most untraceable of hits.

Each weapon was only to be fired once and then gotten rid of. The hitters were then supposed to be taken to a hotel near LAX to fly back to Russia the next morning. The good thing about hiring Spetsnaz operatives was that on the outside chance something got screwed up and they were caught, they would never, ever speak. Escrow accounts had been set up for each of the hitters, and news of their arrest would trigger an automatic payment to their designated beneficiary and annual payments would continue to be made for every year they remained in prison. It was referred to in Russian as an annuity of silence.

The fact that the operation appeared to have been foiled didn't make any sense. The targets had been three American civilians with no bodyguards or security presence whatsoever. They had neither military nor law enforcement backgrounds. It should have been one of the easiest contracts ever. But somewhere something had gotten screwed up.

"Kitchen fires are very dangerous things," continued Standing. "They have a way of spreading."

Ashford didn't exactly know how to interpret that remark. Was Standing worried about Salomon coming after him? "You've got plenty of fire extinguishers," the MI5 man replied, referring to the billionaire's personal security detail. "I wouldn't worry about it."

"That's the problem with fires. You may think you have it under control, but then suddenly it explodes and it's all around you. Those kinds of fires get lots of news coverage. No one likes fires, but those are the fires I like the least."

"I understand."

"Just in case," Standing asserted, "let me be perfectly clear. If I start smelling smoke, I am going to be very upset."

"Believe me, I'm just as upset as you are."

"Then get this handled. Immediately."

"I'm working on it," replied Ashford.

"You'll want to do better than that," said Standing. "This one could have a very big impact on your career."

"What the hell is that supposed to mean?"

"Check the box," ordered the billionaire who then terminated the call.

The *box* referred to the email account Ashford and Standing shared. It was an additional form of clandestine communication that allowed them to communicate without actually sending any messages over the web. They conversed by leaving messages for each other in the account's draft folder.

Rising up from the conference table, Robert Ashford walked to his desk and sat down in front of his computer to log in through a cleansed, difficult-to-track server on the Isle of Man. He knew that whatever was waiting in the draft folder wouldn't be good news. When he opened the message from Standing he immediately realized how much trouble he was in.

He had been careful, but apparently not careful enough. He scrolled through picture after picture of himself in Yemen. They showed him arriving at the apartment building and then atop the roof unpacking the RPG.

The very last picture in the series turned out not to be a picture at all, but a video. Though he knew what that would show as well, he still clicked on it. Instantly, he was sorry he had.

The video showed Ashford firing the RPG and then leaving the building, but several minutes of footage followed. It focused on the carnage the RPG had wrought: the twisted wreckage of the burning car that had been targeted, as well as the dead, dying, and wounded in the street. Before the video ended, it panned the café across from where the car had been parked. There, Robert Ashford saw a quick glimpse of a non-Arab face and knew exactly who it was.

It was the man who had captured Aazim Aleem, had stuffed him in the trunk of that white Toyota Corolla, and had driven him to the café to be given up to the CIA. The threat from Standing left no room for confusion.

Ashford's migraine flared. He reached into his desk drawer for the bottle of painkillers, but then stopped. He'd have to work through the pain. He couldn't afford to have his brain muddled.

He'd made a mistake trusting Standing. Actually, that wasn't correct. He had never truly trusted the billionaire. He'd trusted their commitment to a shared cause, but he shouldn't have overlooked Standing's self-preservation instinct.

Ashford leaned back in his chair, shut his eyes, and massaged his temples with the heels of his hands. He was in a dangerous box and would have to chart a very careful course. Injecting Scot Harvath, the man from the café, into the game had just raised the stakes to a new level.

CHAPTER 18

Harvath knew the Old Man was right. He was always right. Sightseeing was for tourists, not for counterterrorism operatives. They needed to get off the X, as it was called, as soon as possible.

The operation had been designed to last only a matter of hours, twenty-four, tops, and no more. Because of how vulnerable Chase would be, the insertion had been done completely clean. There were no follow cars and he wasn't carrying any weapons or tracking devices. The assignment was incredibly dangerous. No one wanted to add to the jeopardy he was already in by throwing another ingredient into the mix that could get him killed. If anything happened to him, the Agency would devote its full attention to driving a stake through the Carlton Group's heart.

Ever since the Old Man had started his organization, the powers that be at Langley had wanted it shut down. The Carlton Group was doing everything the Agency claimed couldn't be done, and doing it better, faster, cheaper, and often a lot more quietly.

It upset the CIA to no end that the Old Man had sucked up a lot of their talent and was employing them in a much more streamlined organization that wasn't afraid to take risks. They knew they were too top-heavy. They also knew that they were choking themselves to death on their own red tape. When the next major terrorist attack hit the United States, America was finally going to wake up to how inefficient the Central Intelligence Agency was and call for a stake to be driven through *their* heart. That fact, more than any other, was what kept CIA bureaucrats lying awake in their beds every night. America had been too forgiving after 9/11. It wouldn't make that mistake again.

But instead of fixing its leaking ship, the CIA focused on protecting its turf. The writing was on the wall. Eventually, they were going to be replaced by a leaner, more productive organization. They were in a fight for their very existence and they lashed out accordingly at anyone or anything they saw as a competitor. And that was exactly how the Carlton Group was perceived.

While there was no love lost between the Old Man and Langley, he didn't want to be sucked into their petty games. Already, a handful of stories had been leaked to the *New York Times* about his organization in an effort to discredit it. He had enough sources, both within the paper and back at the Agency, to know who'd been behind it. Though he found it unprofessional, he understood why the CIA was doing it. That's why he'd been intent on mending fences.

Like it or not, his organization was here to stay. No matter how badly the CIA didn't want them around, the Carlton Group now had the top cover and protection of the DoD. That didn't mean, though, that Langley couldn't make it difficult for them. The Old Man had decided the best way to stop the pissing match was to offer an olive branch. That's what the Yemen operation had been all about.

Was it the best idea to swoop into the country and in a matter of days pinpoint and roll up the bad guy that the CIA had been trying to track down for a month? Probably not, but handing him right over and not wanting any credit was a very good idea. Had the attack on Harvath's vehicle not happened and had Aazim been turned over to the Agency, it might have improved the relationship. At least that was what the Old Man had believed. Harvath hadn't been so sure.

Though he had kept them to himself, Harvath had reservations. He thought they might see it as having had their faces rubbed in it. He also doubted they'd share any of the intel they gleaned from wringing Aazim Aleem out like a dishcloth.

Carlton had to be part mind reader. Without Harvath saying anything, the Old Man knew exactly what he was thinking. He was quick to remind Harvath of several things, each of which stung a bit and therefore stuck with him.

The Old Man made it clear that Harvath was an exceptional operative, but not yet as smart or as experienced as he was. He also stated that while one of Harvath's greatest skills was his ability to think and act on his own, it was also one of his greatest flaws.

That last part burned the hottest, most likely because it was right on target. Even in the SEALs, Harvath had danced just on the edge of being a team player. Despite the fact that he was very well liked, his superiors had warned him again and again about his individuality. While there wasn't any one thing they could specifically point to, he was warned that if he wasn't careful he was eventually going to get his teammates killed.

Harvath hadn't liked hearing it then and he certainly didn't like hearing it now from a man he had so much respect for. Under the former president, Harvath had been expected to operate alone and to do things his way. He had excelled, but those days were behind him. For better or worse, Harvath was back on a team again, which required that he perform accordingly. He was determined to make it work.

That was a big reason he was upset to lose Riley Turner to the care of Mansoor Aleem. The very reason the Athena Project had been created by Delta was that an attractive woman's beauty automatically disqualified her as a threat.

Harvath chastised himself for not remembering one of the SEALs' maxims, *Two is one and one is none.* They all knew that Mansoor could have been injured in their manufactured car accident. He should have brought another member from the Athena Project along just in case. But he hadn't, and he knew why.

He'd felt chemistry the moment he met her. He thought she might have felt it, too, but he couldn't be sure. She was very hard to read. He didn't know if that was a good thing or a bad thing.

All he knew was that he thought about her entirely too much. He didn't like that. It meant that something was going on that he couldn't control, and Harvath was *all about* control. It was one of those traits that had interfered with his ability to be a proper team player.

He had avoided bringing another Athena Project member on the assignment because he had wanted her to himself, so to speak. He didn't want to share her. It was stupid, but if given a mulligan he knew he'd do it the same way again.

Harvath was not only exceedingly good at what he did, he was also a fun guy to be around. Nevertheless, the landscape of his personal life was like a tropical beach scattered with the wreckage of broken relationships. As long as you looked at the sand closest to you, it looked pretty good, but the further you glanced down the beach, the more you realized there had to be something out there, just beneath the surface of the water, to have wrecked all those ships.

There was certainly a reef out there, but it was only recently that he had begun to understand what it was made of. The razor-sharp coral that gashed the hull of anyone who got too close to him was in part due to his career. There were very few people whom he could tell exactly what he did. And even fewer who could tolerate his frequent and often unannounced absences.

Like a double helix, the DNA of Harvath's career was entwined with something else—his desire for a family and a stable home life.

The biggest thing people in Harvath's industry had in common was divorce. Disappearing at a moment's notice to go off to some of the darkest corners of the world to do dangerous and unspeakable things wasn't exactly the fertile soil in which happy families grew. You missed anniversaries, birthday parties, holidays, soccer games, school plays, parent–teacher conferences, and on and on. It took an amazingly resilient and unique spouse not only to put up with it, but to keep the family strong and together.

Though Harvath knew a woman like that was next to impossible to find, he specialized in the impossible, and refused to give up looking.

The Old Man must have sensed Harvath's interest in Riley Turner, because he had been reluctant to okay her for this operation. Though Harvath had worked with her once before, his desire to learn more about her had tipped his hand. Nevertheless, Carlton had given in and allowed her to be part of the Uppsala operation. There were no other Athena operatives with her medical skill set. He hadn't needed to overtly remind Harvath to keep it professional. His tone when okaying Riley's participation had said it all.

While he had sons of his own, none of them had gone into his line of work, and the Old Man felt a special affinity for Harvath. That said, he knew Harvath had lost his own father, also a SEAL, just after high school, and he wasn't above manipulating the father-son bond they had developed. It often proved the key to getting through Harvath's headstrong personality and making sure he did the right thing. He suspected something might be materializing between Riley and his operative, but Carlton knew there was little he could do about it. Much like a parent, employers also had to trust that the people they task with difficult jobs will do the right thing and put the successful outcome of the assignment above everything else.

And that's exactly what Harvath did. He had kept things professional, right up until he was ready to leave to join the assault team in Uppsala.

After placing all his gear into his car, he walked back into the barn. Bachmann had helped Riley wrap Mansoor in the blankets he'd brought from the house. He was now standing a respectful distance away while Riley tended to her patient.

Harvath tilted his head toward the door, indicating he wanted the ex-CIA man to wait outside. Bachmann did as Harvath requested.

Once the barn doors were closed, Harvath approached. "How's he doing?"

Riley looked up at him. "His pulse is still thready."

"Will you be able to move him?"

"Probably not for a couple of hours."

"The Old Man says you'll be going to the site in Iceland now. Better medical there."

Riley nodded again.

"He also said he sent a team into Mansoor's apartment outside London. They didn't find much," continued Harvath. "We are assuming he uses a cloud."

Cloud computing referred to virtual networks where data was

stored. It acted as a fail-safe for terrorists in particular, in case they were captured. If they didn't give up their cloud, it was nearly impossible to locate their data. They could also set up their clouds in a way that required them to "touch back" at regularly scheduled intervals or a countdown would be enacted and all of the data on that cloud would be destroyed.

"Don't worry," said Riley. "I'm going to be with him the entire time. As soon as he regains consciousness, I'll press him for the cloud."

"Good," said Harvath. For a moment, he stood there just looking at her. She was, hands-down, one of the best-looking women he'd ever seen.

"The answer's no," she said.

Harvath snapped out of it. "What answer?"

"The answer to whatever it is you're thinking of asking me."

"Who said I was going to ask you anything?" he replied.

Riley shook her head. "I know that look."

"I didn't give you any look."

"Fine," she said. "There was no look."

"You need anything else before I go?" he asked.

"I'm sure if I need anything, Andy will help me."

Harvath shook his head. She was playing with him. He knew she was. Pointing at Mansoor he said, "Stay in touch. I want to be kept up to speed on how he's doing."

"Will do," said Riley as she turned away to prep another IV for her patient.

With nothing else to say, Harvath walked toward the door and exited the barn. But just as he had the first time they had met, he could feel her eyes on him as he walked away. He thought about turning around, but then decided against it. He needed to get his head into the game for what was awaiting him and the rest of the assault team in Uppsala.

The takedown was going to have to happen very fast. In and out in three minutes or less. They had to be gone before the Swedish police arrived at the scene and an international incident was made of the raid.

That meant there was no margin for error. It also meant that there was a very high likelihood that something could go wrong. And as Harvath drove away from the farm toward Uppsala, that was exactly what his gut was telling him was going to happen.

CHAPTER 19

Harvath had wanted to keep the parameters of Chase's operation as limited as possible. This wasn't a long-term, deep-cover operation. He was to be their inside eyes for the takedown.

Chase was to ascertain how many members the cell contained, with whom and how they were communicating, what critical intelligence was being kept at the safe house, and where, as well as what their defensive capabilities were.

At the accident scene, Harvath had cloned the dead terrorists' SIM cards. They also had the mobile number the driver had called after picking up Mansoor Aleem at the Stockholm airport, and Chase had dialed after the accident. Did it belong to the cell leader? Would the Carlton team back in the States be able to track it? As Chase left the accident scene, no one knew. Therefore, Harvath had developed a two-pronged plan.

The most critical information for the assault team, if they could pinpoint the location of the terrorists' safe house, was how many people were inside, whether they were armed, whether there were any explosives present, and what, if anything, had been booby-trapped. Assuming that Chase was not going to have access to a cell phone, and might not have access to a computer, Harvath laid out a simple means of communicating the critical information via whatever window coverings the safe house employed. It was a simple espionage tactic that would draw little to no attention. Blinds, shutters, shades, or curtains, unless the windows had been painted or newspapered over, would communicate the details. Harvath had every confidence that it would work.

To communicate to Chase that they had pinpointed his location, Harvath's car would be parked on the street outside with a book left on the dashboard. This was where Harvath was upset to have lost Riley. If they couldn't get a parking space, they were going to have to create one. Riley could have been used as a diversion, perhaps dropping her purse as her companion, Harvath, got into the car they needed to move. While she was gathering up the contents to place back in her bag, Harvath would work on starting the car. To anyone watching, it would simply appear as if he was waiting for her before starting the vehicle. If he needed extra time, or was having some sort of trouble hotwiring, they could even stage an argument. With Harvath's hands working beneath the dashboard, no one would be able to see what he was really doing.

That option, though, was now off the table.

If Chase didn't see the car with the book on its dash by midnight, he had been told to assume that they hadn't been able to pinpoint his location and that the cavalry wasn't coming. He would be on his own. He was to gather as much intelligence as he could and somehow get himself out. Once out, he was to contact Harvath with details and keep the safe house under surveillance from an optimum distance.

The good news was that they had caught a break. The satellite team back in the United States *had* been able to track the mobile phone of the cell member Chase had spoken with. Now all Harvath had to do was position his vehicle with the book near the safe house where Chase could see it and wait for him to signal.

Southwest of Uppsala, in the low-income suburb of Gottsunda, Scot Harvath began to believe the fates were smiling on him. On a dirty street flanked by rows of drab apartment complexes, he found the perfect parking space.

With the book on the dash, he got out of the car, removed two sacks of groceries from the trunk, armed the alarm, and walked away.

The area was so rough, thanks in part to rampant lawlessness by Muslim youths, that even Swedes hired to pilot Google's "Street View" cars had refused to drive through and map the area. It was yet another in a long and growing list of Europe's sensitive "no go" areas. While Swedish police still responded to calls, they only did so in great numbers because bricks and Molotov cocktails normally greeted them upon their arrival.

There were still ethnic Swedes to be found in the area, though many of the housing complexes were now filled with a mixture of Arab and Somali faces.

As with most of Uppsala's poorer suburbs and neighborhoods, the residents had been co-opted by the hard left political parties. It was one of the few tidbits about Gottsunda that Harvath had found helpful. To help him blend in, he had donned a dirty pair of jeans, tennis shoes, a worn jacket, and a T-shirt with an antiestablishment slogan one of the assault team members had found near the university.

From what they had been told, the immigrants tended to stay away from the ethnic Swedes, who blamed a lot of their problems on the "Muslim invaders." Unless he encountered a group of youths looking to start a fight, Harvath expected to be given a wide berth. His Swedish was limited. The only words he knew were those he had picked up in the SEALs when he had dated a string of SAS flight attendants and earned his call sign, Norseman.

As many people do with foreign languages, he'd learned the bad words first. If anyone did come up to engage him, he could act the part of the surly drunk, toss out a few choice phrases, and keep going. He hoped he wouldn't even need to do that.

Right in front of the safe house and right on cue, the rip Harvath had placed in the bottom of one of his grocery bags tore the rest of the way open and spilled its contents onto the ground. He swore in Swedish and muttered to himself as he bent over to pick everything up. Stealing the occasional glance at the building, he saw that all of the window shades were drawn tight.

Chase wouldn't communicate his message until he saw the car

parked on the street with the book, so Harvath gathered up his groceries and continued down the block.

At the end of the street he turned the corner and walked three blocks. In a weed-choked parking area sat a large panel truck covered with graffiti. Six serious-looking, extremely fit men in matching blue T-shirts and jeans stood talking. Alongside their truck, they looked like a team of movers, which was exactly what Harvath wanted people to believe.

As he got nearer, Harvath could see that though they appeared casual, their eyes were constantly scanning the area, taking nothing for granted. The Old Man had put the assault team together himself and they were true professionals, loaded for bear and ready for anything.

The team leader was a former U.S. Special Forces soldier who then spent several years with the CIA's "Special Activities Division" before being transferred up to the paramilitary "Special Operations Group" composed of ex–DevGru SEALS and CAG operators. He was a tall man with a fishhook-shaped scar on his left cheek. His name was Schiller and he was only a year older than Harvath.

Once the plan for raiding the safe house had been hatched, Schiller had been the one to find the truck. Inside were cardboard boxes filled with the assault team's gear. Posing as a Swedish moving company, they would unload the boxes onto dollies and wheel them into the building. Once inside, they would unpack the weapons, radios, Swedish Security Service uniforms, helmets, and body armor, and suit up.

For a job like this, it was customary to have at least two to three times as many men as they had. Ideally, you'd also have a surveillance team watching the apartment from somewhere close by. One operator would watch the front of the building while another watched the back and a third stayed behind the wheel of the truck. On the perimeter an additional operator would be in charge of communications. Inside, the teams would post men in the stairwells and at the elevator. Finally, there would be the assault team itself, which would be in charge of actually hitting the apartment. That was how it was done on your own turf or in a cooperative assignment with a foreign government. But because the Swedes had no idea that the Americans were operating within their territory, they'd had to remain lean.

As someone who never asked people to do what he wouldn't do, and as someone who always wanted to be the first through the door, Harvath had wanted to lead the team inside. Schiller, though, had been against it.

Harvath was in charge of the operation and thought about pulling rank, but instead he took a deep breath and stood down. The assaulters were Schiller's men. There could be almost a telepathic bond on assault teams. They instinctively knew where each other would be and what each would do at every minute. Harvath understood not to take it personally. He hadn't trained with them. He couldn't blame Schiller or his assaulters for not wanting to compromise the integrity of their team.

Without Riley, they numbered seven, total. Schiller wanted Harvath to stay outside and watch the rear of the building while one of his assaulters stayed with the truck in front. The apartment complex backed up to a large wooded area where a cell member could disappear quickly.

It was a good idea, but it wasn't perfect. None of Schiller's men spoke Swedish—not even any of the bad words. Sitting in the truck might result in some sort of interaction with someone from the neighborhood. Therefore, this time Harvath asserted his authority and stated that he'd remain in front with the truck while one of Schiller's men watched the back and coordinated the radio communications.

Schiller agreed and threw Harvath an extra blue T-shirt. As Harvath changed, Schiller reviewed the rest of the assignments. He would be leading three of the assaulters into the apartment, while a fifth would stay in the hall and cover their six so no one could hit the team from behind.

All of the weapons and radios had been checked before the team had left their temporary apartment in Uppsala. In a sports bag in the cab of the truck was a suppressed MP7 for Harvath along with a radio and a black plate carrier vest emblazoned with the word *Säkerhet-spolisen* across the front and back.

Schiller also handed him a blue baseball cap, since he'd already walked right past the safe house once. To sit outside in the truck, Harvath needed to do everything he could to make sure that he wasn't recognized. The man had raised a good point. That also meant that until they were ready to launch their operation, Harvath couldn't go anywhere near the safe house again. Someone else was going to have to look to see if Chase had raised his signal. In fact, they were probably going to have to take turns. Once again, Harvath wished that Riley was with them.

Each of the assaulters had brought a change of clothes, so Harvath put together a surveillance roster—who would go, when he would go, and what his ruse would be while passing the safe house so that none of them would draw undue attention.

They had an additional vehicle parked a block away from the truck, and Harvath decided they would use it as well, but sparingly. If any of the members of the cell saw the same vehicle go by twice, especially one that wasn't a regular in the neighborhood, they might get spooked and do something stupid.

With all the rotations decided upon, all they could do was wait. The ball was now in Chase's court.

CHAPTER 20

Chase had zeroed in on the cell leader the moment he'd been shown into the apartment. Mustafa Karami was a slight man who looked much older than the other members. He sported a patchy beard, a slim nose, and a pair of deeply set, dark eyes.

He radiated a controlled, simmering anger that seemed ready to erupt at any moment. He was different from most of the jihadists

Chase had come across. Not unique, just different. Most of them were not very bright, and they lacked self-control. That wasn't Karami, though. He was the picture of self-control. He was also very intelligent. Chase could tell that just from one look at his face. That's what made him different.

As the man embraced and kissed him on both cheeks, Chase sensed something else. This was a man who would slash your throat at a moment's notice if he felt it necessary. He would feel no remorse about it either. He'd probably sit there and drink his chai as he watched you bleed out on the floor. Between Karami and Sabah, his number two, Chase had a lot to be concerned about.

The other cell members in the apartment were like the two men who had picked him up at the soccer field and had taken him to the garage. They were either muscle or simply jihadist cannon fodder. None of them were exceptionally intelligent nor were they particularly talented. He doubted they'd be of any intelligence value whatsoever.

After welcoming him, Karami sat Chase down and asked the huge man named Sabah to fetch tea. He made small talk as was customary and when Sabah returned with a tray, he poured the tea and offered Chase a snack. There were bowls of dates, figs, and nuts. Chase thanked him and helped himself.

"Your uncle was a wonderful soldier of Allah. He is in Paradise now."

"Masha'Allah," Chase replied. *God has willed it.*

"It was your uncle's desire that if anything happened to him, we take care of you."

Chase shrugged and took a sip of his tea. It was important that he maintain his aloof, disinterested hacker attitude.

"When was the last time you saw him?"

Karami was testing him as Sabah had. The last time Chase had seen Aazim Aleem was when pieces of him had been blown all over a Yemeni sidewalk, but he couldn't exactly share that. He also couldn't exactly share how he and Aazim had first met.

Chase had spent three years infiltrating Aazim Aleem's terrorist network. He had worked his way right into a position next to a man named Marwan Jarrah, who was helping coordinate Aazim's attack plans for the United States. Then Harvath showed up, Jarrah was gunned down, and Aazim disappeared, but not before several attacks in Chicago were launched and scores of people were killed.

These attacks had come on the heels of a wave of attacks in Europe targeting American tourists. Aazim had built a very sophisticated network. What bothered the CIA was that many of his American cells were believed to still be in place. Nobody knew who they were, much less where they were hiding and what they had planned.

Chase had met with Aazim only twice. He was the only American operative to have ever done so. The first time had been brief and had taken place while Chase and Jarrah were traveling through Pakistan. The second meeting had happened in Chicago and had been much more substantive. Chase had finally put another piece of the puzzle in place as he discovered that Jarrah was working for Aazim, who controlled the network.

The meeting had taken place in Jarrah's office and Chase so impressed Aazim that the terrorist mastermind invited him to help execute a nationwide string of attacks beyond what was planned for Chicago. These attacks, it was alleged, would cause airplanes to rain from the sky, radiation and plague to infect American citizens, and multiple other horrors. Aazim despised America and his goal was for it to know terror like it had never known terror before.

And as that prediction began to unfold, a Mumbai-style siege was launched against three commuter train stations in Chicago and many innocent civilians had been killed.

Jarrah had explained to Chase that Aazim had come to Chicago to check on their final preparations. From there he was going to Los Angeles for the next attack, and he wanted Chase to handle an attack planned for New York City.

When one of the Chicago train station plots was interrupted and Jarrah was murdered, the L.A. and New York attacks never materialized. According to chatter, Aazim had fled the United States. That's when Chase had been charged with hunting him down.

The hunt had led him to Yemen, but Aazim had proven elusive, at least for the CIA. Harvath, somehow, had much better luck. He not only located the terrorist mastermind, he managed to capture him and stuff him in his trunk.

Chase had just been given the keys to Harvath's car when it was struck by an RPG and Aazim was incinerated.

The reason the CIA had allowed Chase to join Harvath's current Uppsala operation was that they were bound and determined to uncover the remainder of Aazim's network, both within the United States and, if possible, the rest of the world.

The powers that be back at Langley didn't much care for Harvath's cowboy reputation. They cared even less for Harvath's boss, Reed Carlton, but they had little choice but to cooperate.

Chase had invested years of his life in infiltrating Aazim's network. He knew more about it than anyone else in the intelligence world, and he made it crystal clear to Agency brass that if they didn't sign off on his joining Harvath's op, he would quit and sign up with the Carlton Group. Either way, he would finish the job he had started.

Chase was a virtual encyclopedia of Aazim Aleem information. British by birth, the terrorist had been a fat man in his late sixties with a long gray beard when he had been shredded in Yemen. But his girth and facial hair were not his most distinguishing features.

That honor belonged to the two stainless steel hooks that he had where his hands should have been. He had traveled to Afghanistan in the eighties to fight in the jihad against the Soviets, and legend had it that Aazim had lost his hands attempting to defuse a land mine near a school. The story was pure propaganda. The jihadist was a bomb maker and had lost them in a premature detonation.

He had been an adept Islamic scholar who had studied at Egypt's prestigious hotbed of Muslim extremism, Al-Azhar University in Cairo. Known only as the "Mufti of Jihad," his anonymous writings and audio sermons on violent jihad were famous throughout the Muslim world. Until Chase, no Western intelligence service had ever been able to uncover the Mufti of Jihad's true identity. Aazim had traveled extensively promoting war against the infidels and the West while collecting a full disability pension back in the United Kingdom.

Since no one really knew who he was until Chase discovered him, the man had traveled freely under his real name. Once he disappeared, Chase went back and studied that travel extensively. It wasn't hard to put together a trail of tickets and every time his U.K. passport had been scanned. It was how he was able to answer Karami's question. "I saw him about three months ago," he replied. "Before he left for Chicago."

"And who was he meeting in Chicago?" asked the leader of the Uppsala cell.

"Marwan Jarrah."

"And then?"

"And then," replied Chase, "New York and Los Angeles, but he left for Yemen and I never saw him again."

Karami studied the young man's face. There was no way he could know these things unless he was exactly who he said he was. Nevertheless, Sabah distrusted the newcomer, and Sabah had excellent instincts. "Tell me about the Sheikh. The Sheikh from Qatar."

Sabah seemed interested in this question and leaned forward.

Chase looked at both men. "What Sheikh?"

"Surely," stated the cell leader, "your uncle confided in you enough to mention the Sheikh."

"Apparently not completely. He never mentioned any Sheikh."

"You never questioned where the funding came from?"

"Why would I care? I'm an IT person," replied Chase. "I had nothing to do with his finances."

Chase's mind was moving like a Rubik's Cube, trying to align the information so that the entire puzzle fell into place. He had never heard about any Sheikh from Qatar. This was completely new to him.

Marwan Jarrah had been near the top of the organization's pyramid, but Chase had always known he was taking his orders from someone above him. That someone had turned out to be Aazim Aleem. The next question was, who had been giving Aazim orders? Was he the ultimate string-puller, or was there someone else? And what was the Uppsala cell's connection to all of this?

At least Harvath had played it smart. Had he thrown a hood over the nephew's head and dragged him off to some black site in Eastern Europe for interrogation the minute they'd uncovered him, instead of surveilling him, the United States might not ever have learned about the Uppsala cell. It had come as a complete surprise even to the real Mansoor Aleem. His uncle Aazim had been smart. The man kept his network compartmentalized. He had to. It was like bulkheads. If one was compromised, it didn't have to mean the entire ship was going down.

Which brought Chase back to the Uppsala cell. Why had Aazim set it up? What was its purpose? Was it an insurance policy of sorts, a guarantee that if he was taken out, their mission would continue? If so, did that mean he had entrusted them with the knowledge of his nephew? There were so many pieces of the puzzle missing.

As Chase spun the blocks of information in his mind, Karami asked him another question. It put him on edge, because it showed the cell leader was not fully convinced he was who he said he was. "Tell me about your uncle's impairment."

"What impairment?" Chase replied. "His hands?"

Karami said nothing. His face was impassive, inscrutable.

"He lost them in Afghanistan," Chase continued. His gaze was locked on Karami. Just out of his field of view, he could feel Sabah's eyes burning a hole right through him.

"How did he lose them?" asked the cell leader.

Chase could sense Sabah was ready to handle any incorrect answer. "Do you want the fable?" replied Chase. "Or the truth?"

"As the prophet, peace be upon him, said, we should appropriate truth for ourselves and avoid lying."

Chase nodded. "It's a shame, as the fable is much more glamorous. He lost his hands when a bomb he was building detonated prematurely. It also resulted in pitted scars around his left eye. This is why he often wore sunglasses, even in the evenings. People mistook him on occasion for being blind, but he had perfect vision."

The answer seemed to satisfy Karami, who smiled. He also sensed Sabah relax slightly, but not much.

The cell leader was about to ask another question when one of the cell members appeared in the doorway and asked if the trio would be joining the others for Asr prayers.

"Do you feel up to it?" Karami asked.

"The key of Paradise is prayer," replied Chase, quoting Mohammed. Apparently the men who had been watching him at the garage had told Karami of his inability to complete the Salah.

The men stood and Chase was directed to a bathroom where he could perform his ritual ablutions. After washing his hands and feet, he joined the others in the apartment's dining room. There was no furniture, only prayer rugs spaced evenly along the floor.

Once all of the men were present, prayers were begun. Chase had been given an extra rug to use and he went through the motions perfectly. No one would have known that he wasn't Muslim.

As he prayed, he was able to take a head count of how many men there were in the apartment. He'd also been able to at least glance into all of the rooms. From what he could tell, there were no booby-traps. He didn't see any explosives or weapons, but that didn't mean that they weren't hidden away somewhere. What it did mean, though, was that there weren't any right at hand. When Harvath and the assault team hit, they would have surprise on their side and therefore the upper hand. That was, *if* they hit.

Chase had still not had a chance to get to one of the windows to look outside for the car with the book on its dash. He had decided he might only get one chance to get near a window and that if he did, he should kill two birds with one stone. If he did get the opportunity, he'd look for the car while positioning the window treatments so that the team outside would have a rough idea of what was waiting for them when they took down the apartment.

Both while moving through the apartment and while at prayer, Chase kept his eyes peeled for objects he could use as weapons. If Harvath and the assaulters didn't succeed in locating the safe house, Chase was going to have to either sneak out or fight his way out. With nine men present, Karami probably ran an around-the-clock guard. Chase slowly began preparing himself for what fighting his way out might look like. Once again he reflected on the lessons of Hagakure.

But try as he might, he couldn't quite focus. Something was bothering him. It took him several minutes to figure it out. There was something missing in the apartment. It wasn't just weapons that were absent. It was computers. There wasn't a single one to be seen. If a raid did take place, they might be able to get to hidden weapons quickly, but computers? Not a chance. Not unless there was a rack of them in one of the closets, all powered up and ready for their hard drives to be wiped clean or blown to kingdom come with the touch of a button.

There weren't many places they could be hidden. He planned on finding out if there were any here or not.

After prayers, he expected Karami to pick back up with his questioning, but the cell leader apparently had other pressing business and disappeared into one of the rooms along with Sabah and two other men and closed the door. This left Chase free to converse with the remaining cell members. It also left him somewhat free to move about the apartment.

CHAPTER 21

In the first room, Chase found multiple mattresses, only one of which was covered by a sheet. There was a milk crate for a nightstand and atop it a table lamp with an exposed bulb and no shade. A small TV, DVD player, and cushions scattered across the floor completed the makeshift dormitory cum rec room. In the corner he noticed a couple of old hookah pipes.

Sitting on cushions in front of the TV were four cannon-fodder cell members—all mouth breathers, as Chase liked to call the IQ-impaired. They were watching footage of American military vehicles being taken out by IEDs in Iraq and Afghanistan. The men found the carnage extremely amusing and were laughing out loud at every explosion.

That's okay, thought Chase. *Yours is coming soon enough. Keep laughing*.

Only one of the men looked up and acknowledged that Chase had walked into the room. The cell members seemed to know that he was related to someone important, which meant he was treated with a certain amount of deference. But he was still a newcomer, so despite that deference, they kept him at arm's length. None of the men invited him to sit.

That was fine by Chase. He had other things on his mind. Pretending to be interested in what they were watching, he made his way across the room. The closet was partially open and he stole a quick glance inside. *Nothing*. Only shirts, trousers, and a row of cheap shoes.

Stepping near the windows, he stopped and leaned against the wall. The view outside would be perfect—right out over the street.

Minutes passed. The explosions on the TV continued, and the four men guffawed right along with them. The joy they took in the killing and maiming of American soldiers spoke to how incredibly sick they were.

As not one of them had given him as much as a second glance, he decided to risk a look through the blinds, which had been drawn tightly shut.

It took him a moment and at first his heart sank as he thought the car wasn't there, but then he saw it—book and all. It was like a shot of caffeine being pumped into his bloodstream. Immediately, his heart raced and he could feel a rush sweep through him. Harvath and the rest of the team knew where he was. This jihadist rats' nest was going to get the shit kicked out of it.

Withdrawing his hand from the aluminum blinds, he forced himself to take a deep breath. *Be cool*, he told himself just as he had back at
the garage. *Everything's cool.*

He ran through his head exactly how he needed to construct his
signal in order to let Harvath know what was going on inside. He
debated whether he should check out the other rooms first. Waiting
was a gamble. What if Karami sent for him or Sabah decided he needed
to be watched more closely? It definitely was a crapshoot.

Chase decided on the bird in the hand. He'd send the signal now.
He could convey the number of men and that he had not seen any
booby-traps, weapons, or explosives. The assaulters would still hit the
safe house just as hard, expecting all of those things to be there. So,
without wasting any more time, Chase got to work.

"What are you doing?" one of the men asked when he heard Chase
monkeying around with the blinds.

"I'm opening the window," he replied in Arabic. "It stinks in here."

It did in fact smell, quite badly, but the man either hadn't noticed
or didn't care. "We were told not to go near the windows."

"I have to get some fresh air," said Chase.

"It is forbidden."

Chase signaled to the man not to worry. "It is my decision, brother.
I will take the responsibility. Enjoy the television."

Used to his place at the bottom of the cell's hierarchy, the man gave
up admonishing the newcomer and he and his associates went back to
watching war porn.

Chase didn't waste any time. He lifted two sets of blinds to the
same height, about a quarter of the way up. He then adjusted the
angle on one set, opened each of the windows differing amounts, and
let the string for the blinds hang out the window on the left. With his
Bat signal blazing, he grabbed a cushion and sat down with the jihadists to watch TV.

By his estimate, the windows had been open for a little more than
ten minutes when Sabah entered the room. "Who touched the windows?" he bellowed in Arabic.

No one answered.

As he repeated his question, he looked directly at Chase. "Who did this?"

"I think the dates don't agree with my stomach," said Chase, fanning the air with his hand.

"What's going on?" said Karami, who suddenly appeared in the doorway.

Sabah gestured toward the windows. "Our guest has been busy creating problems."

"I wasn't creating problems," Chase insisted. "I just opened the window. What's the big deal?"

"The big deal," said Karami as he walked over to the windows, "is that we have certain rules. One of them is that the windows and blinds must remain closed."

Chase didn't like how intently he was studying them. After a moment, he retracted the cord, closed the windows, lowered and shut the blinds.

Turning back to Chase, he said, "The rules were not explained to you, so you will be forgiven your transgression. This time." Gesturing to Sabah, he signaled for him to follow. At the doorway, he beckoned the Palestinian to lower his head and spoke so that only Sabah could hear.

He removed a pen and a small pad from his pocket. Whether what he did next was to sketch or write something down, Chase couldn't tell.

When Karami was finished, he tore off the piece of paper and handed it to the Palestinian, who glared at Chase for a moment and left the room.

Karami then said, "I do not wish for any more problems. Is that understood?"

"I just opened the window—" Chase began, but the cell leader silenced him.

"No more problems. *None.*"

At that moment, Chase heard Sabah bark at one of the other cell members in the hallway. Seconds later, the front door opened and the giant stomped out, slamming the door shut behind.

Chase had no idea if they were on to him or not, but before backing out of the room, Karami forced a smile. It reminded him of the mouth of a shark curling back and revealing its teeth. Every fiber of his being was telling him that he was blown, that he needed to get the hell out of there—now. But he refused to let the fear take hold of him.

Instead, he tried to relax. *Everything's cool,* he told himself. *Everything's cool.* It was a lie of course, and he knew it, but he kept repeating it anyway. Either way, it was all going to be over soon. He just prayed to God that Harvath had seen his signal.

CHAPTER 22

The apartment buildings up and down both sides of the street were nearly identical. It was only by tracking the signal of the phone Chase had called right after the accident that they were able to pinpoint the exact location of the safe house.

Harvath had spaced the trips past it as far apart as he could. They had rotated half of Schiller's men through over the last two hours. They were debating whether they should send the car down the street on the next pass, when one of the assaulters came back to the moving truck and said, "We got it."

Every man who had gone down the street had been carrying the hidden video camera system Riley would have carried in a ruse they had concocted for her had she been able to accompany them. Removing the memory card, Harvath slid it into his computer, pulled up the file, and scrolled through the footage till he got to what they had all been looking for. The resolution of the video of the outside of the safe house was excellent. Freezing the shot he wanted, he zoomed in. There was Chase's signal. No doubt about it.

They were all gathered in the back of the moving truck and Harvath proceeded to decode his fenestral semaphore for the team.

"So, nine tangos total," said Schiller, referring to the number of men Chase had signaled were in the apartment. "Plus, no traps, explosives, or weapons."

"None that we know of," replied Harvath.

Schiller thought about it for a moment and then began sketching out a plan with his assaulters. There had been a lot of talk in the run-up to the operation about use of force. The CIA wanted as many of the cell members taken alive as possible. Though this technically wasn't an Agency assignment and they'd deny any knowledge of it if it became public, both Harvath and the Old Man had been inclined to agree with them. There was no telling who was inside, what they knew, or how valuable any of them could be. Having been on the inside, Chase would have a rough idea of the structural hierarchy and would be able to help interrogators separate the wheat from the chaff pretty quickly, which reminded Harvath of something.

He pulled up two photos of Chase on his computer. He didn't like telling people how to do their job, but he was in charge, and the ultimate responsibility for how things went down rested with him. He showed the photos to the team one last time. They had been taken that morning and showed both a full-length and a tight head-and-shoulders shot of Chase. "Everybody got him committed to memory?"

The team all nodded. "He may still be dressed like this," continued Harvath, "or they might have made him change clothes. Just remember his face."

Once again the team nodded as Harvath added, "And don't forget, you take him down just as hard as you do the others. If you have to Tase him, Tase him. He's a big boy. He can handle it. The other cell members have to believe he's one of them. Got it?"

A chorus of "Roger that" swept through the truck and Harvath turned his computer back around and powered it down.

The team went over their satellite footage of the area once more. They discussed points of ingress and egress, as well as plans B, C, and D.

When they had finished, Schiller opened one of the cardboard boxes. He lifted out what looked like two thin plastic briefcases with a shiny, metal scorpion logo in the middle, and handed them to Harvath.

"What are these?" Harvath asked, opening one of them up.

"Stinger Spike Systems."

It looked like a collapsible metal wall bracket for a makeup mirror, except that it was studded with very sharp, stainless-steel spikes. Harvath had seen law enforcement agencies lay them down across roadways to take out the tires of vehicles in high-speed chases.

"Just in case we need to buy a little more time," Schiller added.

It was a good idea and Harvath was glad the assault team leader had thought to bring them along.

All that was left to do was to launch the assault. Harvath and Schiller had briefly gone back and forth on the timing. They had debated hitting the safe house just after sunset in hopes of catching the cell members in their Maghrib prayers, but it was a very limited five-to-ten-minute window, and there was no telling exactly when they would start their prayers.

There was also the issue of when a moving truck would legitimately show up to unload. Late afternoon was believable, and though early-evening moves did happen from time to time, they were out of the ordinary and would therefore attract attention. Schiller's assaulters were already amped up and pulling on the leash. Harvath decided that the team would move now.

First in would be the assaulter Schiller had assigned to cover the back of the building, a former Green Beret named Pat Murphy. Murphy grabbed a small backpack and hopped out of the truck. He would repark the other car and approach through the wooded area behind the apartment complex where he would take up his position.

As he climbed out of the truck, one of the other assaulters leaned out the window and said, "God help us if there's an Irish bar between here and there."

Murphy flipped the man the finger, shouldered his pack, and began walking. Harvath watched as he crossed the parking area and disappeared around the corner.

Reaching down into the gym bag, Harvath turned on his radio. Twenty-two minutes later, they heard from Murphy. "Phoenix Seven, in place," he stated. "Bang a gong."

That was the all-clear they had been waiting for. It was time to take down the safe house.

CHAPTER 23

D eserted streets always made Harvath nervous. Over his career, he'd been ambushed a handful of times and the scene had always looked the same. People and even animals seemed to be able to sense when something bad was about to happen. More often than not, either the bad guys had told the people to hide inside or the people had noticed the bad guys were up to something and therefore quickly made themselves scarce. Whatever the reason for this block being devoid of any activity, Harvath didn't care. It just gave him a bad feeling.

"Pretty quiet," he said as they neared the apartment complex.

"Too quiet," replied Schiller, who covertly banged on the cabin bulkhead behind him to let his assaulters in back know that they were rolling up on the target.

Harvath scanned the windows and rooftops for any sign of a spotter, but saw nothing. Even so, he felt like there were a thousand sets of eyes on them. "Ten seconds," he said.

Schiller knocked twice on the wall behind him.

When they arrived in front of the apartment complex, Harvath brought the truck to a stop, put it in park, and turned off the ignition. There was no service entrance. Everything went in and out of the building through the front door. It wasn't lost on him how exposed they all were out there in the middle of the street. He wanted to get the assaulters into the building as quickly as possible. Then he'd be the only sitting duck out in the open.

He, Schiller, and one other assaulter climbed out of the cab and got to work. Harvath walked around to the back of the truck, extended the ramp, and rolled up the door. Schiller and his assaulter stepped into the lobby of the building. While Schiller pretended to be buzzing up to someone on the intercom system, his assaulter used a lock-pick gun to open the second set of doors. As soon as they were open, he pulled a rubber wedge from his pocket and propped it open.

Schiller followed him inside and called for the elevator. While he waited for it to come down, he pried the glass cover from the fireman's key box, removed the key, and replaced the cover. When the elevator arrived, he stepped inside and inserted the key. It was now under their control.

The assaulters from the back of the truck had already debused and were stacking boxes on dollies when Schiller and the other man came out to assist them.

Once the dollies were all loaded up, the men disappeared inside with them. Harvath's job now was to stay with the truck and be the team's eyes out on the street. He pulled down the rear door, threw the lock, and then walked back up front and climbed into the cab.

Though he wasn't a smoker, Harvath removed the pack of cigarettes he had purchased, lit one, and hung his arm out the window. It had always been fascinating to him how someone just sitting in a car doing nothing could be suspicious, but the minute you gave him a cigarette and he adopted a casual posture, somehow he became less so. He couldn't explain why that was, but he'd seen it work enough times that it had become a tactic he liked to employ when he had to hide in plain sight.

The truck's side mirrors had been angled outward before they departed the parking area to give them the best possible view of the street and the sidewalks on either side. He could even make out the car with the book on its dashboard several car lengths back. Noticing it, he used his free hand to pull the baseball cap he was wearing down a little tighter.

He pretended to fumble with the truck's radio as he looked out the windshield and studied the windows of the buildings around him. He had yet to shake his feeling that somebody was watching, that something wasn't right.

He also hated just sitting there. It had been the right decision, but it still didn't mean he liked it. He wanted to be where the action was, not sitting in a van waiting for everything to go down. Ultimately, being where he was right now had been his call, and it had been the right call. Leadership was not only about taking charge, it was also about giving your team everything they needed to succeed, and then getting out of their way. It meant knowing when you should be the first person charging through a door and when you should stand down and let someone else do it.

Harvath had the makings of a good leader, and at some point, way in the distant future, that was going to be important, because he couldn't dance on the pointy tip of the spear forever. Eventually, his reaction times were going to slow. When that happened, he was going to have to come to terms with the high-speed life he had lived since his late teens. Time catches up with everyone at some point. The secret lay in knowing when to dial back your lifestyle. Now, though, wasn't the time. Harvath was in the best physical and mental condition of his life and there was no end of bad guys that needed to be dealt with.

As long as he stayed on the right side of his ops and the people he worked for, everything would be fine.

No sooner had that thought entered his mind than the radio in the bag next to him *clicked*. Schiller was indicating that he and his assault team were geared up and ready to breach the apartment.

Murphy clicked back the all-clear from behind the complex and after one last check of the street, Harvath reached his hand into the bag and clicked back his response. *All clear*. It was time to clean out the rats' nest.

As Harvath's hand felt for the butt of his MP7, he could completely visualize what was going on upstairs. With the all-clear having been signaled from outside, Schiller would motion up his breacher, have him pause, and then click his radio one last time before giving the man the command to swing the breaching ram and knock the safe-house door right off its hinges.

Flicking his cigarette into the street, Harvath drew his left hand inside the window and hovered it over the truck's horn. He wanted to give Chase a heads-up, but he knew he couldn't. He needed to appear just as shocked by the entry team as everyone else. If there was a signal before the attack, they could very well cue in on that after the fact. Harvath's plan for leaving Chase under cover with them once they had been transported to a black site for interrogation could all come unraveled.

As Harvath waited on the street below for the assault team to enter the apartment, his heart began to beat faster and the hairs on the back of his neck suddenly stood on end as if the air was charged with electricity. It was a way his gut had of signaling him that something wasn't right.

CHAPTER 24

Having seen the book on the dashboard of the car outside, Chase knew the assault team would hit the apartment before nightfall. There was no way of knowing if they had seen his signal. He hoped so, because he couldn't do it a second time. There was a very bad vibe in the safe house. If he got caught opening the blinds or any of the windows again, he had no doubt there'd be hell to pay.

Sabah had returned, and he and Karami had shut themselves up in one of the rooms at the end of the hall. Chase wondered if there were any computers or weapons hidden away in that room. He also wondered where Sabah had gone in such a hurry and what he and Karami were now talking about.

Chase was certain that the Uppsala cell was in the final stages of something. What it was, he had no idea, but it sure felt as if they were about to go operational on something. Was the Uppsala cell Aazim's *dead man switch*? Had he provided Karami with a target deck and a way to activate the network's sleepers in the United States and elsewhere upon his death?

These were all questions Chase couldn't wait to start asking. He also wanted to know why it had been so important for the Uppsala cell to bring Aazim's nephew in. Was the uncle just that overprotective, or did Mansoor know something or have access to something of value? They'd be getting to the bottom of all of it soon enough.

In the meantime, Chase stayed with the cell's cannon fodder and watched war porn. One of the jihadists got up at one point to get tea and actually brought back an extra glass for the newcomer. It was a good sign; a sign of respect. Quietly, Chase hoped that it meant that they had begun to accept him. Their willingness to believe he was one of them would affect how successful the interrogations would be once they had been deposited in whatever black site Harvath had arranged for them.

Chase knew exactly what was in store for him. Very likely, he was going to get Tasered when the assault team hit the safe house. He'd be FlexCuff'd and hooded. If he resisted, which he planned on doing quite vehemently, he'd get a tune-up, which meant he'd be slapped around.

After they were tossed in the truck with the other cell members and spirited back to the farm, Harvath would line them up in the barn and have their clothes cut away from their bodies with EMT shears. They'd then receive the same "packaging" all extraordinary rendition prisoners had been receiving since 9/11.

After being fitted with suppositories containing a psychotropic drug to make them more compliant and to disorient their comprehension of time and space, they'd be fitted with diapers for the long plane ride, dressed in matching coveralls, shackled, and with their heads still hooded with bags that allowed for no light to get in, they'd have sensory deprivation headsets fitted over their ears.

From there, they'd be placed in a different windowless vehicle from the moving van that had been used in the raid. Harvath's clever plan for getting them out of the country, with the Swedish government none the wiser, would be put into effect.

Chase wasn't looking forward to any of it, but no one had forced him to take this assignment. He had agreed to it because he knew that until they had hunted down every last member of Aazim Aleem's network, America wouldn't be safe. You couldn't just cut out part of this kind of cancer and hope that it never came back. You had to get all of it. Any cells left behind were guaranteed to metastasize.

There were many ways of going after the cancer of Islamic terrorism. There was the radiation of interrupting terrorist financing, the chemotherapy of denying havens from within which to train and operate, and the most delicate and most efficient method, which was also the most dangerous and time-consuming, was to go in with a scalpel and carve up every single cell. Only through the last and most extreme method could you be absolutely sure that no cancer remained behind. It was in this particular area that men like Sean Chase and Scot Harvath were particularly skilled.

But unlike Harvath, because of his background Chase could be injected right into the Muslim corpus. He could drift through the Islamic bloodstream, seeking out the most radical, the most deadly cancer cells without ever being seen as foreign and eliciting any sort of immune response. Once in, he could mount his own T-cell response, calling in highly efficient killer cells, run by men like Scot Harvath, to attack the cancer and permanently purge it from the body.

Harvath liked Chase's no-BS attitude and ability to cut through red tape to get the job done. Though he had been trained for long-term deep-cover assignments with little to no contact with his handlers, when he did have to deal with day-to-day operations at the CIA, the bureaucracy bothered him. It had chewed up and spat out a lot of good operatives. A handful of them had written books about how broken Agency culture was. Much to Langley's displeasure, one of the most insightful, *The Human Factor*, had become a huge favorite among CIA employees and a de facto field manual for those who wanted to keep America safe. Chase had read *The Human Factor* so many times the cover had fallen off.

And while he hadn't been at the Agency long enough yet to become completely jaded, the lessons he learned from the book informed everything he did. That was part of the growing appreciation he had for Harvath. Mission success was everything to a guy like that. If Harvath broke some of the crockery along the way, that was the cost of doing business. He'd worry about the Krazy Glue later. Though it would drive his bosses nuts, that was exactly how Chase thought the war on terror, or whatever politically correct term the Seventh Floor was using these days, ought to be fought.

As the thought drifted from his mind, Chase watched one of the jihadists lean over and grab a hookah pipe from the corner. Standing up, he took it into the bathroom and filled it with cold water.

"Do you smoke?" he asked when he returned and began packing the bowl while another man pulled out a pair of tongs and a lighter.

Chase hated tobacco, flavorful or otherwise. But the men were making a new overture toward him and he was determined to take advantage of it. "Of course," he said.

The man with the tongs used them to withdraw a small piece of coal from a paper bag near the TV. Holding his lighter underneath, he heated the coal until it began to glow and then placed it on the screen above the fruit-flavored tobacco, or *shisha*. Chase was offered the honor of smoking first.

The hose was covered in brightly colored braided silk. Chase placed the plastic tip between his lips and breathed in. The water inside the pipe gurgled as the smoke was cooled and fed into the hose.

Chase took a deep drag and allowed the smoke to completely fill his lungs. He held it for a moment and then, instead of allowing it to slowly escape through his mouth or nostrils, he encouraged his cough-ing response and began hacking.

The four jihadists roared with laughter. The newcomer was obvi-ously a neophyte and had no experience with a hookah. Instead of telling the truth, he had lied to protect his manliness.

Still hacking, Chase struggled to stand. He continued coughing as he placed his hands on his thighs and fought to breathe. The cannon fodder laughed as if they were watching the funniest thing they'd ever seen.

Being the butt of the joke didn't bother Chase. In fact, that's exactly why he'd spurred on the coughing fit. Shuffling toward the window, he kept coughing as the men kept laughing. In fact, it wasn't until he had his hand on the blinds that they realized what he was up to.

"Don't," said one of the men who could barely stop laughing long enough to get the word out.

"Karami will cut your hands off," said another.

A third added, "He'll cut all our hands off," as the men began laugh-ing even harder.

"I can't breathe," said Chase, who was pretending to be in between coughing fits. He knew the men were serious about his not opening the window and would probably try to physically restrain him if they had to. But he had no intention of opening it. He just wanted a peek outside and would then immediately abandon the window, appearing to heed his colleagues' warnings.

As he pulled back the edge of the blinds, Chase's cough immedi-ately stopped. The moving van was already outside, but it wasn't in the right place. Harvath and the assault team had made a mistake. They were hitting the building across the street.

And though it was difficult to tell for sure, it looked as if someone had adjusted the windows and blinds of an apartment across the street, exactly the way he had.

CHAPTER 25

As Harvath was envisioning the assault team entering the safe house, the entire third floor of the apartment complex exploded. The shock wave tilted the moving truck up onto two wheels and almost knocked it completely over onto its side. Shards of glass rained down on the street as columns of boiling fire leaped out of the third-story windows and rolled up into the sky.

Stunned, Harvath snatched up his radio and tried to hail the members of the team, but his ears were ringing so badly that, even with the volume all the way up, he wouldn't have been able to hear anything. It was as if Yemen were replaying itself all over again. The terrorists must have had the whole third floor wired with explosives.

Pulling his plate carrier from the bag, he threw it over his head and then snatched up his MP7. Opening the door, Harvath leaped out of the truck and bolted into the building. It was exactly what he had been trained not to do. Even if the explosion was a booby-trap rigged to the front door, or had been set off by the terrorists inside when they realized they had been compromised, there could still be a secondary device, a device meant to kill any rescuers who then rushed into the building. That was all true, but Harvath didn't care. Those were his men up there. If any of them were alive, he was going to get them out.

As Harvath charged up the stairs three at a time, the temperature soared and thick, black smoke filled the air. It was nearly impossible to breathe. Pulling his T-shirt up from beneath the vest and over his mouth and nose, he exposed the flesh of his midsection. It felt as if the surface of his skin was being blasted with a blowtorch. He was starting to burn, but he pushed it from his mind.

The deafening roar of the fire grew as he neared the third floor. Coming up to the last flight of stairs, he saw that the blast had blown the metal fire door completely off its hinges and it was now blocking the stairwell.

Harvath reached for the railing to leap over it, but the railing was so hot that he snatched his hand right back.

Striking out with the heel of his boot, Harvath kicked at the door until it dislodged and he shoved it down the stairs behind him. He tried to crouch beneath the smoke, but it was so heavy, so thick, and so voluminous that there was just no bottom to it. Hoping to get some sort of break once he actually got into the hallway, he bent his head and charged the rest of the way up to the landing.

He could feel the hair being singed off his arms as he lunged through the empty door frame and into the hall. There was debris everywhere. Harvath was going to shout, to see if there were any survivors and if they could hear him, but he couldn't get enough oxygen into his lungs. The heat was unbearable.

The bright orange blaze burned hotter and the flames leaped higher. Harvath knew he should get out. There was no way that anyone could have survived that explosion. But Chase and Schiller and the rest of the team were his responsibility. If only one of them was still alive, Harvath needed to find him, so he pushed deeper into the burning hallway.

He had gone no further than a few steps when there was an ear-splitting crack as a larger section of the floor above came pancaking down.

With visibility next to zero, Harvath would have been crushed had it not been for a hand that reached out, grabbed him by the drag handle of his plate carrier, and yanked him into the stairwell.

"We've got to get out!" yelled Pat Murphy who had burst into the building from the back.

"No," Harvath shot back.

"They're all dead. Let's go."

"We don't know they're dead."

"They're dead," Murphy insisted as he dragged Harvath away from the landing.

After the first couple of steps, Harvath began moving on his own. When they hit the ground floor and exited the lobby, a crowd had already formed in the street. The people blanched when they saw the two ash- and-soot-covered men exit the building carrying weapons.

Someone noticed that they were wearing Swedish Security Service plate carriers and started to ask Murphy questions in Swedish. The ex–Green Beret ignored him.

"The other car is about two hundred meters behind the woods," said Murphy, leaning in so Harvath could hear him, but keeping his voice low enough that the onlookers couldn't discern that he was speaking English. "Let's get the hell out of here."

Harvath had no choice but to agree. There was nothing they could do here. If they stayed, they'd be arrested and an already tragic situation would be made much worse.

Harvath nodded at Murphy, and the two set off for the back of the building, the woods, and the car parked just beyond. Neither the truck nor the car with the book on the dashboard could be traced back to them, so Harvath didn't think twice about abandoning them. The key now was to get out of the country as quickly as possible.

They were about to swing around the side of the burning apartment complex and disappear, when there was the sound of breaking glass and screams from the crowd of onlookers.

Harvath spun just in time to see a man falling backward out of a fourth-story window of a building across the street.

CHAPTER 26

Chase now knew that Karami had been sketching the windows. Somehow he had figured out the signal he had created with the blinds. Karami had either known or suspected an attack was coming and he'd set up an ambush across the street, duplicating Chase's entire signal. And if he had done all that, then he had to know Chase was not who he said he was. Therefore, the young operative wasted no time.

He was dramatically outnumbered and the only thing he had on his side was surprise. *Surprise,* and the shock the men in the room around him were in due to the explosion from across the street.

As soon as he knew he would have to fight his way out, he again wished he'd brought the shiv he'd made.

The hookah was the nearest and best weapon he had available and it broke over the head of the first jihadist he struck with it. Unconscious or dead, Chase didn't care. The man dropped to the floor and that left three.

Chase slashed the second Islamist's throat with the jagged, broken glass base of the hookah as the two remaining men turned on him.

They charged in unison. Chase caught the first man with a low thrust kick to the knee and the other with a foreknuckle strike to the throat.

The man who received the kick to his knee fell to the floor screaming in pain. The other man, who had been struck in the throat, was a different story. His windpipe should have been crushed, but Chase had failed to grab his hair or his clothing and pull him into the strike. The man had recoiled just as the punch came in, lessening its severity. Like an enraged bull, he gathered himself and charged again. This time, Chase would not screw it up.

As the man came in, he bent his head and ran at Chase with his fingers spread and his hands outstretched like claws. Wherever he had grown up, apparently it was his mother who had taught him to fight.

Chase slipped between the man's arms and caught him right beneath the chin with a perfectly placed uppercut. Chase drove him backward with two jabs to his face.

The man swung wildly and got lucky, punching Chase in the side of the head. The blow hurt like hell and immediately his ear felt as if it was on fire. Chase let his anger get the better of him.

Spinning, he kicked the man directly in the center of his chest, sending him out through the glass window down to the street below.

Chase knew he couldn't have survived the fall and didn't bother to look to see if he had. There were five men left in the apartment and he moved quickly. He wasn't about to wait for them to come find him.

He had made it almost all the way to the doorway when he saw the barrel of the rifle. He wasn't surprised that the terrorists had had guns hidden away. Grabbing the weapon, he tried to twist it away from his attacker.

There was a rapid burst of fire as the rifle erupted. Where all of the rounds went, he had no idea. All he knew was that one had torn right through his right bicep and hit the bone. The pain was excruciating, and he immediately lost the use of his arm.

Sweeping his left arm, he came up underneath the barrel and knocked it off him just as another volley of shots was fired. The noise at such close range was deafening.

By moving the weapon, Chase had his opponent off-balance. Finding the weapon's upper handguard, he pushed down with all his might, forcing the man to lean forward. As he did, Chase snapped his head forward. There was a spray of blood and a sickening crack as Chase connected with the bridge of the man's nose.

It was game over. Chase snatched the rifle away from him. Balancing the buttstock against his left shoulder, he depressed the trigger and put a three-round burst right through the man's chest.

He then spun and capped the jihadist with the blown-out knee who was coming back at him from behind. *Five down, four to go.*

He could sense movement from out in the hallway and didn't bother looking to see who it was. Propping the gun up against his shoulder once more, he fired a burst directly through the wall.

There was a scream and the sound of a weapon clattering to the floor. Shooting without identifying the target was usually a bad thing, but Chase didn't give a damn. Even if he had capped Karami, this was kill or be killed.

He doubted Karami would have come down the hallway himself. That's what cannon fodder was for. He hoped he'd just nailed Sabah, but he doubted it. It was probably one of the two goons from the garage.

Bending his left arm into an L shape, he positioned the stock in the crook of his elbow, up against his good bicep. Popping the weapon around the edge of the door frame, he sprayed the hall with another burst.

He waited for any return fire, and when none came, he risked a quick look. His guess had been right. Lying facedown on the floor in a pool of blood was the man from the garage who had gone out and bought him the bandages and energy drinks. *Six down.*

Chase now had a decision to make. Duck back inside the room and wait the other three out, or take the fight to them. Neither option was that appealing. In a matter of seconds, the street outside was going to be filled with police and other first responders. He needed to capture Karami and Sabah if he could, do a quick sweep of the apartment, and then get the hell out of there. He had no choice but to step out into the hallway and risk exposure.

Wedging the rifle against his shoulder again, he took a deep breath and swung into the hall. His right arm hung limp at his side. Blood was rolling down his hand and dripping off the tips of his fingers.

With his heart thudding in his chest, Chase moved forward as quietly as he could. His senses were hyperalert, attuned for any sudden movement or noise he might hear above the ringing that might give his remaining attackers away. The apartment, though, was quiet. *Too quiet.*

As he moved, he was plagued by the thought that the technique he had used would be used against him, and any moment now he would be shot through the drywall. *Hagakure,* he reminded himself. *Hagakure.*

He carefully peeked into the first room he came upon. It was empty. After a quick scan, he turned his attention back to the hallway. The rifle was growing heavy in his left arm.

The next room was a bathroom, which was empty as well. He stopped repeatedly and strained his ears for any sign of where the others might be hiding. There was nothing. Growing ever closer to the room that Karami and Sabah had disappeared into earlier, he had a good idea of where the remaining three men were. Sure enough, the door to that room was closed.

Chase was a risk-taker, but he wasn't an idiot. There was every reason to believe that kicking the door in could only result in all sorts of bad news for him. There could be three heavily armed men waiting for him on the other side, or the door itself could be booby-trapped.

Stepping into the bathroom, which had only a shower, no tub, Chase crouched behind the toilet and balanced the rifle's magazine on the seat. At this angle, he could see only a very narrow sliver of the door he was shooting at. Taking aim, he squeezed the trigger and let another hail of lead fly.

The rounds chewed up the left side of the door, splintering the frame. Chase waited for a response, but none came.

Picking up his weapon, he walked into the hall and put another burst through the door as well as through the drywall. No response.

Against his better judgment, he decided to kick the door open. He counted to three and let his foot fly.

The moment his shoe connected, he heard a roaring barrage of gunfire.

CHAPTER 27

Harvath ran across the street and charged directly into the building he'd seen the man fall from. He didn't know if his mind was playing tricks on him or if he'd actually caught a glimpse of Chase in the upper window.

Murphy was right behind Harvath, and they ignored the elevator and headed right for the stairs. They were halfway up to the fourth floor when some Islamist skidded to a halt on the landing above them and tried to bring his weapon up to fire. The man never had a chance.

Harvath and Murphy both drilled him with suppressed rounds to his chest and face. The man's finger pulled down on the trigger in spasm and his weapon discharged wildly. Rounds ricocheted through the stairwell, sending Harvath and Murphy diving for what little cover there was.

When the dead terrorist's weapon fell silent, Harvath double-tapped him with two quick shots to the head just to make sure. After kicking his weapon away, they resumed their charge up the stairs.

When they got to the fourth floor, Murphy covered Harvath as he stepped into the hall. There were only four apartments per floor, and based on the window the body had come out of, Harvath knew exactly which one they were looking for. He just prayed that Chase was inside and that he was still alive.

Covering the apartment door with his weapon, he signaled for Murphy to come forward and join him.

Harvath studied the door frame for any sign that it was wired. He didn't see anything, but that by no means meant it was safe. Schiller and his team hadn't seen anything either, and the entire third floor of the building across the street had been incinerated. This apartment could be rigged to explode as well.

If it wasn't rigged, and they did have Chase inside, was he sitting there with a gun to his head? Would they shoot him if Harvath kicked open the door and rushed in? Without knowing how many there were, could he and Murphy take them out before they did anything to Chase?

It was a big gamble. Five men on his team were already dead. Whatever Harvath decided to do, he'd better be sure he was absolutely certain about it. He already had gallons of blood on his hands. He needed more information.

Taking a deep breath, he placed his ear against the door and listened. He heard a noise from inside. It was faint at first, but the longer he listened the louder it grew.

It sounded like a scuffle. Then Harvath realized it wasn't a scuffle at all, but rather the sound of somebody turning the place inside out.

He signaled Murphy to be ready, and then, taking a step back, Harvath raised his boot and kicked the door in.

Nothing exploded, except the door off its hinges from the force of Harvath's kick. He figured he had a fifty-fifty chance of being right. If someone was turning the place over, it meant he was looking for something. And you don't bother looking for something if you're about to blow yourself up. At least that was what Harvath hoped. Lucky for them, he'd been right.

Harvath moved quickly inside, his weapon up and at the ready. Murphy was right behind him. They hadn't even made it through the living room when there was a burst of automatic weapons fire and rounds came slamming through the wall at the other end of the room. Harvath and Murphy hit the floor.

The Green Beret came up onto his elbows and prepared to return fire, but Harvath waved him off. They had no idea where Chase was. They couldn't just fire blindly through the walls.

"Phoenix Three!" Harvath yelled. "Are you in here?"

"Harvath?" came the reply.

"Roger that."

"I'm coming out. Don't shoot."

Chase stepped out into the hallway and walked toward them. His arm was covered with blood.

"Is there anyone else here?"

Chase shook his head. As Murphy swept the rest of the apartment, Harvath ripped open Chase's sleeve and checked his wound.

"Does it hurt?"

"A lot. It hit bone."

"We'll get you taken care of," replied Harvath. "Right now we've got to get out of here. Is there anything worth gathering up?"

"Maybe. I turned the place upside down fast and dirty, but couldn't find anything. If we had more time—"

"We don't." Already the sounds of approaching emergency vehicles could be heard in the distance.

"The apartment is clean," said Murphy as he rejoined them. "What do you want to do?"

Harvath knew what he didn't want to do. He didn't want to walk through the throngs of people out on the street, around behind the burning building and off into the woods to pick up Murphy's car. Too much could go wrong. His car, the one with the book on the dashboard, though, was parked right outside. It didn't matter if people saw it or gave a description to police. They wouldn't be using it long enough to make a difference. All they needed to be able to do was make it back to the barn.

With Murphy on point, the three men exited the apartment and quickly made their way down the stairs. They laid Chase down on the backseat. Murphy rode shotgun and Harvath slid behind the wheel.

The onlookers stared, their mouths agape. They didn't know what to make of any of it. The last thing the trio heard as they sped off were the cries of revulsion from the crowd as Harvath drove over the body of the dead terrorist still lying sprawled in the middle of the street.

CHAPTER 28

Two extensive medical kits had been allotted for the operation. One was with Riley Turner and Mansoor, who, along with Andy Bachmann, had already left for the airport near Stockholm. The other belonged to the assault team and was sitting in the back of the moving truck that had been abandoned at the scene of the failed safe house raid.

Harvath, though, had a couple of items in his bag of tricks that he never traveled without. As he debriefed Chase and cleaned up his wound, he unwrapped a tampon, cut off about an inch, and packed it into the hole. He then wrapped Chase's arm with duct tape. It would do for now, but Chase was going to need professional medical help.

Riley had arranged to delay the flight until they could get there. It was a big enough aircraft and the three additional passengers would be posing as the security detail for the wealthy Arab patient. As long as Chase didn't start bleeding, they should be okay. Just to be sure, Harvath wrapped a few more pieces of duct tape around his arm. It was going to be a pain in the ass to get off, but that was a problem for later.

Murphy sanitized the barn and the farmhouse as Harvath helped Chase put on his suit.

"He must have left the phone in there, knowing we'd be tracking it," said Chase as he winced, sliding his arm into his jacket.

"Karami definitely knew something was up," stated Harvath. "He reproduced your signal perfectly."

Chase felt terrible. "I got those men killed."

"No, you didn't."

"If I'd just found a way to look back out the window sooner, maybe I could have warned you."

Harvath shook his head and the two men fell silent.

"You didn't see Karami or Sabah leave the building?" asked Chase.

"No, but I wasn't looking. If it wasn't for the guy that came through the window, I never would have known there was a second apartment. I thought you were dead."

Chase let that sink in for a moment before saying, "How about the Sheikh from Qatar? Any idea who he is?"

"No," replied Harvath, "but that'll be one of the first questions Mansoor is going to get asked."

"I don't know how we'll get access to any of the forensics, but I'll bet the Swedes find fried computer parts in at least one of those apartments that got blown up."

Harvath nodded. "I agree."

"They were getting ready to go operational," Chase said. "I'm telling you. We need to hunt them down and we need to stop them."

"First things first," replied Harvath. "You need to get your arm taken care of."

"Don't worry about my arm," Chase said as he tried to move it and failed. "As soon as we get this redneck bandage off and let a real doctor have a look, I'll be fine."

Harvath doubted it. Chase was going to be out of the game for months, if not longer. "Whatever you say, boss."

"Don't patronize me, Harvath," he shot back. "I want you to promise me that you'll wait."

"For what?"

"For taking out Karami and Sabah," said Chase. "I want to be there."

Harvath understood the man's desire for revenge. Harvath felt it just as intensely, if not more so. He had learned, though, to keep such things to himself. "Let's figure out what kind of shape your arm's in and then we'll talk."

Chase held up his left index finger and pointed at Harvath. "I want us to do it together."

Harvath smiled. The kid was a liar. He just wanted to do it. It had nothing to do with Harvath. He just didn't want to be left out. "I'm going to go make sure everything is ready. We shove off in five. Okay?"

"Roger that," replied Chase as he turned to the mirror and tried, with one hand, to straighten the knot Harvath had tied in his tie. Staring at his reflection as he struggled, he couldn't help but wonder if this was what so many of America's disabled vets went through. He didn't like needing somebody else's help getting dressed.

In fact, it pissed him off and reminded him of the IED videos the jihadists had been laughing at back at their safe house. That only made him angrier.

• • •

The Swedish airport authorities stamped the group's passports and waved them out toward the tarmac where they boarded their waiting aircraft.

Sentinel Medevac was a private company the Carlton Group hired jets from on occasion. Their normal clientele were humanitarian groups and international NGOs. Sentinel was viewed as something akin to the Red Cross, and that was why the Old Man liked working with them. Their planes were an excellent means of covertly moving personnel and equipment in and out of foreign countries.

What Harvath liked about them was that in addition to their fleet of extensive, high-end aircraft, Sentinel's owner—a successful young doctor out of North Carolina—was a patriot who was more than happy to assist the Old Man and his operators. The doctor always sent the best jets and the galleys were always well stocked.

Normally, Harvath waited until the plane had taken off before fixing himself a drink. Not this time. Losing all those men had been devastating. He walked straight to the back of the plane, dropped a handful of ice cubes into a glass, and poured several fingers of Maker's Mark.

He was halfway finished with his first drink before the plane had even been cleared for takeoff. When its wheels finally left the ground, he settled back in his seat and tried to make sense of what had happened.

Operationally, they had played their cards very close to their vest. The Old Man had kept the need-to-know circle tight, working long hours and doing several jobs himself. Nevertheless, the operation had been a total failure, worse than Yemen. In Yemen all they had lost was a high-value target. In Uppsala, a high-value target and his second in command had gotten away and five members of the operation's assault team had been killed.

From a straight scorecard perspective, it had been very, very bad. Coming on the heels of the failed Yemen op only made it worse.

Karami, the cell leader, was a serious player who truly knew what he was doing. Requiring his safe-house to be completely sterile while cell phones were left in a secondary operations center of some sort across the street showed both discipline and intelligence. Picking up on Chase's signal via the windows and blinds showed an amazing attention to detail. Having prewired the secondary location to detonate showed an ability to think several steps ahead. Harvath and his team had been incredibly lucky to have gotten as close to Karami as they had. It would be very difficult to do so again.

But Uppsala didn't appear to have failed for the same reason Yemen had. Did Yemen happen because of a leak or was there another reason? Despite how careful he had been, could Harvath have been followed by Aazim Aleem's people? Would they kill their own man by blowing up the car he was in via an RPG rather than let him be extradited and interrogated by the Americans? *It was possible. Anything was possible.* Harvath made a mental note to be even more diligent in the future.

It made him think about the whirlwind of events that had just occurred. Technically, as badly as the Uppsala operation had gone, it hadn't been a total failure. They had Mansoor Aleem in custody and they had successfully inserted Chase into the cell long enough for him to ID its leader and pick up some minor intelligence on some supposed Sheikh from Qatar.

Their newest problem was Chase's certainty that Karami was about to activate some sort of attack. Harvath had witnessed firsthand Aazim's previous attacks by his European and Chicago cells. Very few nights went by that Harvath didn't picture the faces of the screaming children in the Chicago train station who had come so close to being killed. After that kind of trauma, he had no idea how they could ever grow up to lead normal lives. It was incredibly sad.

Sadder still was the number of innocent people who had been killed around the world by Muslim terrorists. People who had been doing nothing more than going about their daily lives. The majority of these victims had been Muslims themselves. In fact, for all the propaganda to the contrary, the biggest killers of Muslims were other Muslims.

If it were up to Harvath, he'd drop all the supporters of a worldwide Islamic caliphate onto an island and let them battle it out. He'd also include all those who supported Islamic charities knowing full well their money was going to finance terrorism. That you weren't blowing yourself up or hijacking aircraft didn't mean you weren't participating in the jihad. There was jihad of the pocketbook as well.

There was also public relations jihad. It was active daily in the American press. Either media figures denied entirely that there was a Muslim terrorism problem, or they tried to play the false moral equivalency card and paint Christian fundamentalists as equally dangerous and prolific in their violence. When asked for examples, they often cite the Oklahoma City bomber, Timothy McVeigh, though McVeigh never claimed to be a Christian and never cited the Bible, or any other religious text, for that matter, as his reason for carrying out his horrific act of terrorism. It was amazing how many people believed the disinformation.

Then there were those media figures who actually tried to put a happy face on Muslim extremism and Sharia law under the banner of cultural diversity. Surely the victims of honor killings, and those beaten and killed for not wearing headscarves, for dating men from outside their faith, or for trying to convert to another religion would strongly disagree.

Harvath was stunned at times by how uncommon common sense was. As far as he was concerned, all of the media figures *and* the politicians who enabled that kind of barbarism could go to the island, too. Better yet, he would have loved to have flown them all over to Waziristan and dropped them off. Anyone who made it back alive could then spout off about anything they wanted. Until they had seen the evil done in the name of that religion and how good Muslims were brutalized by the people of their own faith, he'd rather not hear them opine on the subject.

He'd seen the worst of what was being done in the name of Islam and it needed more attention, not less. For good Muslims to be able to reform their faith and live peacefully with the rest of the world, they needed American media and politicians on *their* side, not the side of their enemies.

There were times when Harvath wondered why he continued to do what he did. Why defend a country that included many who thought their nation was arrogant and deserved to be humbled and brought low? Why defend these people? Better yet, agree or disagree, why risk everything, including your life, over and over again, for over 300 million people you would never meet?

These were good questions and went to the core of who he was and why he did what he did.

Harvath had become a SEAL after his father had died in part because he felt guilty about how rocky their relationship had been at the end. But making your dead father somehow happy, or proud of you, wasn't enough fuel to have propelled a career like Harvath's. There had to be something deeper, and there was.

Harvath had no brothers or sisters. Because of his career, his father had spent a lot of time on assignments in places he couldn't talk about. He often left without even being able to say good-bye. Though his mother tried to compensate for his father's lengthy absences, he carried an emptiness that he had never been able to fill. He always wanted to feel needed, that he was worth coming home to, or better yet, was worth never leaving.

Growing up on Coronado Island, his best friend had been his next-door neighbor, a developmentally delayed boy with an enlarged head, named Fred. Other children taunted him mercilessly and called him "egghead." Though not particularly big, Harvath stood toe to toe with all comers to defend his best friend. Without his father around to teach him to fight and his father's pals stopping by only occasionally to take him fishing and check up on his mom, he had to learn how to defend himself and Fred. He became street-tough real fast, often fighting several other children at the same time. Never once was he afraid to do what had to be done to defend his friend. He was the boy's ever-present protector, a role nobody played in his own life.

It was a void Harvath wouldn't have filled until he joined the SEALs and had teammates, comrades in arms, to whom he would entrust his life on a regular basis and who always had his back.

Was there a need in Harvath to take risks and would that need have been there regardless of the amount of time his father spent deployed? Most likely. That need to take risks in order to feel alive, to do the impossible, to face one's fears and not back down, was present in every single warrior he'd ever met. They also shared a sense of honor in being chosen to stand and defend the country and people they held dear. Protecting them and protecting America, making sure no harm came to either, meant they were defending that which they cherished more than their very lives.

Harvath willingly defended those he didn't agree with, even those who loathed the very existence of men like him, because as Americans or allies, he believed passionately in their rights as individuals to think and do what they wished. It didn't matter how he might disagree with them or vice versa. He felt it made him stronger to defend their rights—without any expectation, any recognition, or any reward.

In part, he and other warriors like him did it for themselves, to have a better sense of self-worth. It was who they were and what they did best. They did it for the man next to them, the men who had come before them, and the men who had been taken from them on dangerous missions in dirty little places no one would ever hear about. It was simple and it was complicated all at the same time, much like Harvath himself.

Harvath lived by the adage that the measure of a man was what he did when no one else was looking. He also knew, having learned it with Fred, that very few people will stand up and put themselves in harm's way to protect those who cannot protect themselves. At its root, protecting people was his calling in life. It was something he couldn't ignore. His honor wouldn't let him. And in a sense, it was because he had devoted himself to protecting the American dream for others, that he had never been able to fully enjoy it for himself.

Harvath couldn't stop thinking about the assaulters who had been killed. He wondered how many of them had families. Most likely several of them. Maybe even all of them. How many wives were they leaving behind? How many children? What kind of impact would losing their fathers have on them? The stories that would never be read. The hugs that would never be given. The right piece of fatherly advice at the right time that now wouldn't be offered. The impact was incalculable.

Opening his eyes, Harvath lifted his head and looked toward the rear of the aircraft. Riley was trying to remove the hillbilly Band-Aid from around Chase's arm. It wasn't going well. Almost as if she knew he was watching her, she glanced up, shook her head, and went back to what she was doing.

Harvath had no idea what that was supposed to mean and at this moment, he didn't care. He tried to focus his mind on rolling up the rest of Aazim's network before they could carry out any further attacks.

To stop them, though, Harvath was going to have to predict where lightning was going to strike. He was going to have to be in the right place at the right time, or as the father of hockey great Wayne Gretsky taught his son, skate to where the puck is going to be, not where it has been.

The puck had been in Sweden. Was it still there, or had it moved someplace else? If it had moved, where would it be next? Those questions were still at the forefront of Harvath's mind as he closed his eyes once more and his exhausted body slipped off into the regenerative unconsciousness of a deep, black sleep.

•   •   •

The flight from Stockholm to the former United States Naval Air Station in Keflavik, Iceland, took just more than three hours. Harvath was still asleep when the wheels of the private jet touched down and jolted him awake.

Though on paper the Naval Air Station had been turned over to the Icelandic Defense Agency in 2008, there was still a heavy American presence at the facility.

The aircraft taxied into a large hangar where an ambulance was waiting to take Mansoor to the base's hospital. Riley had insisted that Chase, his arm in a sling, come along as well so that they could take a better look at him.

Chase could have hopped a flight back home if he had wanted to and gotten patched up back there. Riley had already irrigated the wound, redressed it, and started him on a course of antibiotics. It hurt like hell, though, and he figured the sooner he knew the extent of the damage the sooner he'd know how soon he could get back in the fight.

He also didn't want to go anywhere until he knew what Mansoor's prognosis was. If the guy was going to be ready for interrogation again soon, Chase wanted to be there for it. He knew the most about the network and he wanted to help guide some of the questions, if not do a portion of the interrogation himself. Riley was going to stick around and wait for the prognosis as well. Even though she'd be handing him over to a new doctor, she still felt responsible for him.

Harvath was the only one without a reason to stay in Iceland. The only thing he could think of was that if Karami or Sabah popped up somewhere in Europe, he'd be a lot closer and get to them a lot faster from Iceland than he would from D.C.

Something told him that Europe was where the puck had been. America was where he needed to skate to now. That's where the puck was going to be. He couldn't help but think that if Aazim Aleem had come to Chicago in advance of those attacks, and had planned on sending Chase to New York while he went to L.A. to oversee additional strikes, the Uppsala cell leader would have to do the same thing. He had nothing to back that up, though. It was just a gut feeling.

His gut also told him that despite what she had said in the barn back in Sweden, he shouldn't give up on Riley Turner. It could take days for them to run the battery of tests on Mansoor. This could turn out to be the perfect window he'd been looking for to get to know her better and for her to get to know him.

Coming off the deaths of the assault team, though, the timing wasn't right. Men had died on their operation. She hadn't been at the scene, but she was part of the team. It was a loss for all of them.

It was also probably just as well. The Old Man was going to want Harvath to render a full debrief. There was also the issue of monitoring the Swedish investigation. Knowing the Old Man, he'd already reached out to the authorities in Sweden with a piece of intelligence that pointed the finger of responsibility for what had happened at a completely different foreign intelligence service. Whatever service he chose to implicate, he would do so in such a way as to not be airtight, but to be enough to convince the Swedes there was little doubt. It also probably served one of the many other ops the Old Man was running at the moment. He often likened running an intelligence service to dropping pebbles in a still pool. You had to know not only how far out every ripple would radiate, but which ones would intersect and with how much force. The man was truly a savant.

Was it the best way to treat an aligned nation like Sweden? No, but it was unfortunately the way the game had to be played. In the world of three-dimensional chess, checkers players found themselves swept from the board pretty fast. You were either steps ahead of everyone, even your allies, or they were steps ahead of you. The Carlton Group had been created to help catapult America back into the lead.

Considering the Old Man's attention to detail, Harvath wasn't surprised when moments after stepping off the jet his cell phone rang.

"Yes, sir," he said, moving aside for the ambulance team that was transporting Mansoor and his stretcher down the stairs.

The Old Man's voice was as clear as if he were standing right next to Harvath. "What's the situation there?" he asked.

"They're transferring Massachusetts to the ambulance now," Harvath replied, referring to Mansoor Aleem by his operational code name.

"Any change in his condition?"

"Negative."

"Are you sure he's not faking it? That's textbook for these guys, you know."

Harvath was well aware that they were taught to feign illness, severe if possible, to avoid interrogation for as long as possible. They were also taught to inflict physical harm on themselves and to blame it on their captors in hopes of having their interrogations suspended altogether.

Three SEALs Harvath knew had been accused of abusing a prisoner in Iraq after the guy had thrown himself out of the back of their truck and smashed his own head against his cell wall. The SEALs were eventually exonerated, but not until after being put through a ridiculous trial and having grandstanding members of Congress suggest that all terrorist captures be videotaped via helmet cams and that they remain under video surveillance 24/7.

Harvath had a better idea. Seeing as how most of them were of little to no intelligence value, he figured he could save the U.S. government a lot of money. The United States should simply adopt a policy of no longer capturing terrorists. If we find you, you're dead. No Gitmo. No nothing. Just dead. It would be interesting to see what ran out first—virgins in Paradise or Muslims down on earth willing to martyr themselves.

"His heart stopped, so I don't think he's faking it," replied Harvath.

"Whatever it is, there's plenty of people there who can handle it," said the Old Man. "I need you back here double-time."

"What's going on?"

"Your little friend, Moonracer, has been breaking a lot of eggs."

Harvath knew immediately who he was talking about. His little friend was a dwarf named Nicholas, who until recently had been better known to Western intelligence agencies as the Troll. He dealt in the purchase and sale of highly sensitive and often classified information used to blackmail governments and powerful individuals.

Nicholas had a way with data—both analyzing and accessing it. He had crafted countless algorithms, and one of his trading programs had been purchased by a major international financial institution. None of his legitimate clients knew his true identity. If they had, none of them would have done business with him, rightly assuming that his products contained countless trap doors.

Harvath had crossed paths with Nicholas on multiple occasions, and their relationship had moved from one of hostility to détente to friendship. Despite his stature and various peccadilloes, he was a man of amazing abilities—abilities that Harvath recognized could be of incredible value to the United States.

Nicholas had discovered Aazim's nephew, Mansoor, and the young man's connection to the terrorist network. Harvath wanted Nicholas to be brought inside the Carlton Group, and the Old Man had been dead set against it. He had even threatened to terminate

Harvath's contract over the issue if Harvath didn't drop it. Harvath didn't drop it. Nicholas was an asset and either he could be their asset, or he could be someone else's—or worse, continue to work on his own account.

For his role in stealing classified American intelligence, Nicholas had been made an enemy of the state. The Old Man had constructed multiple conditions before he would accept Nicholas's involvement with the Group, of which the highest and hardest was getting Nicholas pardoned.

Presented with information on Nicholas's valuable skills and repeated cooperation with previous clandestine assignments, a closed-door meeting of the Senate Select Committee on Intelligence decided to make a recommendation in favor of his pardon to the president. The president accepted their recommendation, but the pardon came with multiple strings attached, including the surrender of certain patents and trademarks Nicholas held, the money from which would be accepted in lieu of prison time.

While Nicholas complained that "Uncle Sugar," as he liked to call the U.S. government, was bleeding him dry, he was happy to join the Carlton Group. Because of his size, he had spent most of his life alone. He felt ennobled to be part of something bigger than himself. *Moonracer* was the Group call sign he'd been issued.

When the Old Man said that Nicholas was "breaking a lot of eggs," Harvath remembered Nicholas's warning when he had joined the Group. His type of work wasn't pretty. Much of it was also illegal. Breaking a lot of eggs meant he was going to have to do a lot of things Reed Carlton wouldn't like. He promised to insulate him from as much of it as possible. That said, he was going to continue breaking eggs.

"Well, sir," replied Harvath, "some organizations need leg breakers and some need egg breakers. At least we've got the best."

"We can debate that later. I want you back here because he's apparently broken enough eggs to put together an omelet."

Harvath gripped his phone a bit tighter and lowered his voice. "Did we get a lead on something?"

"You'll see when you get here. Now get that jet refueled and get moving."

Harvath had no idea what Nicholas had uncovered, but he quietly prayed that it was something they could use to stop Karami and the other cells before they could strike again.

CHAPTER 29

L arry Salomon had finally hit the wall and asked if there was someplace he could lie down. Hank McBride showed him to the guest room. Luke Ralston, though, was too amped up to sleep. There were too many unanswered questions moving around in his head. He stayed in the kitchen, poured himself another cup of coffee, and turned the volume on the TV back up.

Helicopter footage was being broadcast on all the local channels split-screened with live shots of reporters speaking outside the gates to Larry Salomon's home. Comparisons to the Tate-LaBianca murders, Phil Spector, and even Nicole Simpson were being made, though none of those murders were directly comparable to what had happened.

The only thing they had in common was that celebrity was involved, and that was all that the Los Angeles newscasters needed. As macabre as it was, people loved stories like these and it was where the phrase "If it bleeds, it leads" came from. Toss in a ton of money and more than a little dash of Hollywood, and the story was destined to bust out as a national news phenomenon.

The reporters still had very little to go on. They knew that there were multiple fatalities inside the house and that the residence belonged to legendary movie producer Lawrence Salomon. There was no mention of Russian Spetsnaz. There was no mention of the two dead documentary filmmakers. And there was no mention of a search under way for either Salomon or Ralston. Ralston had no doubt, though, that it was on. *Big-time.*

In fact, there were probably police officers going through his house right now. More officers would be talking to his neighbors. Detectives would be pulling his phone records as well as Salomon's to see who each had been talking to in the hours leading up to the events at Salomon's house. When the restaurant where Larry had left his car opened up, they'd be calling the authorities and more officers would swoop down on the restaurant, the vehicle would be impounded, and staff would be questioned, all in the hope of uncovering even the smallest detail that might explain what had happened.

Even though the murders had happened further up in Coldwater Canyon, it would still be in the LAPD's jurisdiction. That meant that some of the best detectives in the country would be working the case. Ralston wondered how long it would take for them to uncover his background. *Probably a while.* The Army was very protective of the identity of its Special Operations Forces, especially Tier One Delta operators. Considering the magnitude of what had happened, though, his background wouldn't stay hidden forever.

In the meantime, he had to hope that the LAPD detectives working the case were going to look at the size of those Russians and start putting things together. What worried Ralston, though, was that without anyone to explain who the bad guys were, the Russians might be viewed as Salomon's security, who'd all been taken out in an attempt to kidnap the famous film producer.

The more Ralston thought of it, the more he started to worry that that might end up being the working hypothesis. Salomon didn't have lots of people up to his house. Ever since Rachael had been murdered he hadn't been the same, and his friends and colleagues would tell the police as much. Hell, even Ralston's visits to the house seemed to be happening less often. He hadn't even known about the documentary Salomon had been putting together right in his home office.

As good as the LAPD detectives were, they would still be tempted to take the path of least resistance. Too often in law enforcement, investigations could be more about closing the file than about solving the case.

Without any witnesses, the police would be operating in a vacuum. They'd be going strictly on the forensics. Ralston went through in his mind what they'd probably already assembled.

Outside the home, they had his wrecked 911, a Ford Econoline van, and one very mangled body. Maybe they had found the getaway driver's shotgun. Inside the house, the man named Jeremy lay dead in the kitchen and Chip in the home office. One dead Russian lay near the dining room, and two more lay upstairs, one having been shot from inside Salomon's closet cum safe room. Finally, two of Salomon's vehicles were not in the garage. No jewelry, cash, artwork, or other valuables were apparently missing.

Ralston asked himself what he'd be thinking right now if he was an LAPD detective.

The Russian on the first floor with his throat cut would be one of his primary focal points. The body of the young filmmaker, Jeremy, would be the other. One had been killed with a gun, the other a knife. In fact, Ralston had left the fillet knife right there on the floor next to the first Russian he had killed. Though no law enforcement agency had his fingerprints on file, once the prints were lifted off the knife they'd be sent for verification to the Army and that's where the unraveling of his background would begin.

Even someone who wasn't a detective would be able to figure out that the fillet knife had come from the block in the kitchen. It meant that whoever had cut the throat of the man outside the dining room hadn't come to the house prepared. That said a lot about motive.

What he also hoped would be apparent was the chronology of events on the first floor. Killing the man outside the dining room with a knife meant that Ralston didn't have a gun at the time. Jeremy had been killed in the kitchen while eating a bowl of cereal. Only an idiot would assume that Ralston had breezed through the kitchen, grabbed a knife, moved on and sliced the throat of the man outside the dining room, only to return to the kitchen and shoot Jeremy. That would just be stupid.

And while all of this seemed obvious to Ralston, he realized he had the benefit of knowing everything that had happened. He couldn't trust that the police would put things together the same way.

Retracing his steps in his mind's eye, he went through Salomon's office and up the back stairs. On the floor of the hallway was another very large and very dead man. The more he thought of it, the more he realized how their look screamed "private security."

What didn't scream private security and should be a dead giveaway to the cops was the fact that none of them was carrying an ID. Ralston had patted two of them down and had not been able to find anything. That was a pretty strong calling card for contract killers.

Eventually, he assumed, ballistics would show that Jeremy and the man lying in the hallway upstairs had been killed with the same weapon. Would they figure out that Ralston had taken it from the dead Russian downstairs after cutting his throat?

Then there was the man in the bathroom whom Salomon had blown a hole through with his shotgun. With the fireplace tool nearby on the bathroom floor and the ripped-up drywall, even a neophyte would have been able to tell what happened there.

That being the case, Ralston still tried to imagine any other way it could have been interpreted. He couldn't come up with anything. It was just too obvious that the dead man in the bathroom was trying to tear his way into the safe room and that someone, presumably Salomon, had blown him away. Tests for gunpowder residue inside the closet would confirm that.

Based on the wounds the man in the hallway had received, one round beneath the nose and another through the throat, what conclusions would the police draw? Ralston wondered. That kind of shot placement coupled with the knife work he'd done downstairs would signal a high degree of skill. They'd know Salomon didn't do those things. Those things had to have been done by a professional.

Firing from inside the closet with a shotgun, though, in their minds would be consistent with something Salomon would do. The question was, would the detectives put it all together this way?

It seemed to Ralston that the evidence should be crystal clear. Salomon had been under siege and Ralston had rescued him. There was only one problem, and the movie producer had called it right at the crime scene—innocent people don't flee.

That would be the one glaring thing that didn't make sense. No matter how clear the evidence was, there could only be one reason in a detective's mind for why Salomon and Ralston had fled—they were guilty of something.

From there it was only one step to any number of harebrained motives the cops might come up with. *Ralston and Salomon had had an argument. Ralston had kidnapped Salomon. Ralston intended to do away with Salomon, but decided to finish the job somewhere else.*

It didn't matter whether it made sense or not. Ralston had been around long enough to know that with a big enough hammer and the right amount of force, a square peg could be pounded through a round hole.

The longer it took for the police to find them, the more they were going to believe that at least one of them was guilty of something. Ralston didn't have to wonder which one of them that would be. He knew all too well.

He also knew how his military background would be used as an excuse to allocate significant and extraordinary resources to the investigation. That was something he hadn't thought of at first. The LAPD had a very deep bench, but when it came to hunting a guy like him, they would not be shy about asking for help. Very soon, they were going to have a former operator, if not a team of them, out looking for him. As soon as that happened, it was going to be nearly impossible for him to get to the bottom of what had happened. Every time he thought he understood his window of opportunity, it was suddenly slammed shut.

There was too much at stake, though, to let that deter him. If there was one thing he had learned early on at Delta it was that when God closes a window, it just means you need to kick open a door.

Whoever had sent that wet work team to Larry Salomon's house was going to learn what a mistake it was to fuck with a Tier 1 door kicker.

But first he was going to need to figure out exactly who had sent that wet work team. For that to happen, he was going to need access to very special information—information that would not be easy to come by.

He knew who he had to call. He also knew that person had promised to kill him if and when he ever did.

CHAPTER 30

"Not only do you have a lot of nerve, calling me," said the voice on the other end of the line, "but you lied to my assistant, *lied to her about one of my kids,* to pull me out of a meeting?"

"I'm sorry," replied Ralston. "I knew you wouldn't take the call unless—"

"You're damn right I wouldn't have taken your call. In fact, I have no idea why I'm even still talking to you."

Ralston knew why she was still talking to him, but he kept his mouth shut. They both knew. His giving voice to it would have only made her angrier, though, and that would have guaranteed the end of the conversation. Hot tempers ran in their family.

"Ali, listen," he began.

"You don't get to call me Ali."

"Okay. Alisa," said Ralston, relenting. He'd burned this bridge and he'd have to eat as much crow as she chose to dish out in order to be able to get across this river.

"In fact," the woman plowed on, "the last time we spoke, I told you *never* to call me again."

"I know you did. I wouldn't call you unless it was important."

"*Important?* You want to talk about *important?* My sister's trial. *That* was important."

Ralston had known, before even dialing her number, that she would go there. She still resented him. He didn't blame her. Had their roles been reversed, he might have felt the same way.

"You were the only one," she said. "The only one."

She took a breath and Ralston didn't attempt to fill the silence. She needed to vent, to be angry.

"Everyone testified against those two monsters," she began again. "Everyone but *you.* And it's because of *you* that those bastards never went to prison. They never served a single, solitary day for what they did to my sister. So fuck you, Luke. *Fuck you.*"

Ralston had met Alisa Sevan's younger sister, Ava, not long after arriving in Los Angeles. He had been invited to his first "Hollywood" party, a Saturday afternoon barbecue at a director's home in Malibu.

He saw Ava chatting with a group of friends out by the pool. She was stunning. She was wearing a bikini with a brightly colored sarong tied provocatively around her hips. Her thick black hair spilled over her shoulders. Ralston had never seen a more gorgeous woman in his life.

When he introduced himself, her friends found it cute that he had no idea who the twenty-five-year-old soap-opera actress was. She found him fascinating. Unlike the pretend bad-boy actors and models she had dated, he was the real deal. He was also in Hollywood, but not "of" Hollywood, which made him refreshing and quite a find. Even more important, he made her feel safe.

Their relationship was very passionate right from the start. Ava was a party girl and liked to have a good time. She drank, dabbled in drugs, and was an absolute tigress in the bedroom. Though Ralston could have done without the drugs part, everything else about her was spectacular and he chalked it up to being young, sexy, and successful in Hollywood. Doing coke or dropping some ecstasy from time to time was nothing more than a way to accessorize her lifestyle. Ralston, though, kept his recreational pursuits to cocktails. His motto was *You always know what comes out of a bottle.*

Not long after they began dating, Ava brought him to meet her family. Her father, one of L.A.'s premier criminal defense attorneys, lived in Pacific Palisades with Ava's mother and her two Yorkshire terriers. That first dinner was also when Ralston met her older sister, Alisa. She was equally attractive, if not more so, but that's where their similarities ended.

While Ava was wild and devil-may-care, Alisa was focused and traditional. She had gone to law school and had become a successful entertainment attorney, choosing to trade on her smarts instead of her looks. She had married an investment banker in her late twenties and they had three children. Though skeptical of Ralston at first, the family had come to appreciate him as a solid man who truly cared for Ava. Their hope was that he'd be a good influence on her. She needed to grow up, and everyone had been concerned about her substance-abuse problems.

As levelheaded as Ralston was, though, he'd fallen completely under Ava's spell. Though he was tough as hell, he was entranced by her, and that led to making excuses for her behavior. He loved the merry-go-round they were on and he had no desire to get off. *Was Ava a drinker?* Sure, but she never missed a day of work and always delivered her lines perfectly. *Drugs?* Yes, she did drugs, but not enough to be worried about. Or so he had thought.

Ava actually had a bad addiction problem that was getting progressively worse. She tried to hide it from Ralston and the rest of the people who cared for her, but soon no one could deny it.

She and Ralston broke up three times and each time he took her back, thinking he could "fix" her. Finally, he insisted she get into some sort of rehabilitation program. Ava reluctantly agreed and enrolled in one not far from where they had first met. It was supposed to last for weeks. Within days, she was home, proclaiming herself "cured." It was one of the saddest things Ralston had ever seen.

Ava held out for seven days, not even having so much as a sip of wine with dinner, then she fell right off a cliff. She not only began using again, it also became apparent that she had run up some pretty big debts.

Her jewelry went first. Then she traded in her leased Mercedes for a much cheaper hybrid vehicle. She could claim all she wanted that she was trying to "give the earth a hug," but Ralston knew why she'd made the switch.

Ava's father called him a week later and told him that Ava had reached out for a sizable loan. He wanted to confirm what it was for and Ralston told him the truth. Ava's drug problem was completely out of hand. The soap opera had placed her on a leave of absence. Even their makeup artists couldn't hide what Ava was doing to herself.

Though Ralston probably should have left her for real and allowed her to hit bottom, he couldn't. He stayed with her, but to his credit, he never gave her a single cent. Neither would her father, as it turned out, but Ralston didn't learn that until later.

Ava's family—her mother, father, and Alisa—had joined in a united front. They would pay for rehab, if she would fully commit to it, but other than that, she was on her own.

Alisa kept in contact with Ralston from that point forward. Ava was so angry with her family for not "helping her out" that she stopped speaking to them.

When Ava finally lost her apartment, Ralston knew that if he didn't let her move in with him, some opportunist would take her in and get her to do God only knew what. As screwed up as she was, he loved her. He wasn't a complete idiot, though. He still had to work during the day and so cleared all of the booze out of his house, along with anything of value she might be tempted to steal and pawn for drugs. He also quit drinking, hoping that by setting a good example, he could help her get clean. It didn't work.

Ava used the brains her family was renowned for, and what little of her looks she had left, to get what her addiction-riddled body needed. Bad people reentered her life from an earlier time, before Ralston. Alisa, though, did know them, and she warned him to keep them away from her. Ava was circling the drain. There was little Ralston could do, short of kidnapping her and taking her deep into the mountains somewhere to go completely cold turkey.

He decided that there was no other option. If she kept going like this, she was going to kill herself. He began looking for a cabin to rent and started studying the phases of detoxification and what to expect.

Alisa bought a stack of nutritional books aimed at rebalancing the body and had them sent over to his apartment. She also offered to pay for half of the expenses for renting the cabin. Ralston appreciated her offer. He wasn't exactly rolling in money.

He was wrapping up a project with a studio and figured he could be on the road to the cabin with Ava in two weeks. Ava had even mentioned that if they could "just get away," she thought she could hit the reset button on her life. It made him feel better about his plan. Maybe there was hope after all.

That hope faded after about two days. Ava's hybrid was repossessed, and at first Ralston thought that might be a good thing. It was better that she wasn't driving. Then she took another turn for the worse.

She disappeared for three days and came back with needle marks in her arms. When Ralston asked her where she had been, she told him she didn't want to talk about it. She pushed past him and went into the bathroom to take a shower. She was in there for hours, and Ralston could hear her crying the entire time. He needed to get her the hell out of L.A.

He called the producer he was working for at the time and asked to be let go early. The producer said that they couldn't afford to replace him at the moment and said that he was sorry, but Ralston would have to stay.

Ralston went in to work the next day and when he came home, Ava was gone again.

At two in the morning, she called him crying. She was incoherent, but he managed to get her to tell him where she was.

The abandoned house was near Crenshaw Boulevard in L.A.'s dangerous Hyde Park area. Ralston kicked in the door. There were empty liquor bottles, beer cans, and cigarette butts, but no Ava.

In the back portion of the house, he found a filthy mattress lying in the middle of the floor. A couple of portable lamps were positioned on each side. They had been switched off, but were still warm to the touch. Nearby was the plastic packaging for a particularly vile sex toy. Ralston's heart sank. He'd been on enough movie sets to know what he was looking at. He needed to find her.

As he stepped into the kitchen, he heard a noise from outside. It sounded like the lid of a dumpster had been dropped. When he made it to the alley, he saw two men in the distance, running away. He also found a dumpster. Without opening its lid, he knew what he was going to find inside.

Praying to God, Ralston eventually found the strength to lift the lid. What he saw broke his heart wide open. By the time he dialed 9-1-1, the men he'd seen running from the alley were long gone.

In the days that followed, the cops asked him a lot about Ava's drug use. They wanted to know who she bought from. Ralston couldn't help them. He had no idea. Alisa provided the police with a ton of information. Ava had met her dealer through one of the soap opera's crew members. Alisa even knew the identity of the next person up who supplied her dealer.

The detectives found her depth of knowledge interesting, to say the least, and wanted to know how she knew as much as she did. Alisa was no fool. She was an attorney, after all, and never answered the officer's questions, at least not truthfully. That didn't come out until the trial.

Alisa and her father had paid off both the dealer and the supplier to not provide Ava with any more drugs. Both of the subhumans had agreed at first and then tried to extort more money out of the family, threatening to hook Ava on even worse substances. When they refused, the drug pushers had made good on their threat.

Both Alisa and her father were convinced it was the same two men who had been responsible for Ava's death. Putting them at the scene of the crime would have been all that was necessary to secure a conviction. But as much as Ralston wanted to see the people responsible for Ava's death pay, he hadn't seen the faces of the men in the alley. He couldn't ID the two drug dealers as the figures he'd seen running away from the dumpster.

Even the district attorney tried privately to convince Ralston to testify against the two men. They were career criminals with horrific records. It didn't matter if they were really the ones who were responsible. They had been responsible for untold suffering, and if they didn't kill Ava, they were going to wind up killing someone else's son or daughter.

The arguments were not lost on Ralston. At the very least, these were the men who had gotten Ava hooked on drugs and continued to feed her addiction. But Ralston had only one thing that truly belonged to him in life: his honor. As much as he wanted to kill both the pushers with his bare hands, he couldn't lie. He could not positively identify them as the two men from the scene.

Without his testimony, the case had fallen apart and so had his relationship with Ava's family. They had needed him, and in their minds, he had let them down.

Now, several years later, he needed them. "I understand why you're still angry," he said.

"Are you patronizing me? Boy, do you have balls. You know, I should have had you drummed out of the business."

"Alisa, I need your help."

The woman laughed. "You want *my* help with something? Let me rephrase my prior statement. You have *colossal* balls."

Ralston considered telling her that not a day went by that he didn't think about Ava; that he didn't wish for some sort of penance he could perform for letting Ava down. Though he knew Ava's addiction was just that—Ava's addiction—he still felt incredibly guilty for her death. He tortured himself wondering whether, if he had quit the movie he'd been working on, he could have gotten Ava up to that cabin and gotten her sober. He wondered what would have happened if he'd chased those men down the alley. *Would he have been able to ID them in court? Would he have even survived the altercation?* All he had was the tire iron from his car. *What if they'd been carrying firearms?*

"I never wanted Ava to die," he said. "Please."

There was silence, several moments of it.

"Please," he repeated. "I need your help."

Alisa knew that Ralston was a good man. She also knew that the men accused of Ava's death were the ones who were responsible. She was one hundred percent sure about that. Ralston had allowed Ava's killers to go free. It made it very difficult to hear from him now, much less be asked to help him.

"If this is about cozying you up to one of my firm's clients to help you get some movie deal, I swear to God I'll make good on my promise to kill you. Do you understand that?"

"It's not about business. I'm in trouble."

"If you need a lawyer, you've come to the wrong place," replied Alisa. "You'll have to find somebody else."

"No," said Ralston. "I don't need a lawyer. At least not yet."

She had no idea what was going on, but he definitely had her attention. "What have you done?"

"I'll explain it when I see you."

"Oh? Just like that we're having a meeting?" she replied. "Sorry, I'm booked."

"Damn it, Ali. This is serious."

"What this is, Luke, is my time, which gets billed at eight hundred and seventy-five dollars an hour. At least, that's what I get paid when I am working, which is what I was doing before you called pretending to be from my children's school and pulled me away from my client and a very important negotiation I'm trying to hammer out for her."

Ralston decided he was going to have to give her something to get her to meet with him. And as strained as their relationship had been, she was the closest thing to family he had. "Did you hear what happened at Larry Salomon's house?"

"Did I hear about it? Everyone's heard about it. It's all people in this town are talking about this morning. Why would you ask me," she said, her voice suddenly trailing off. "Tell me you had nothing to do with what took place at Salomon's house."

"I need to see you. I need a favor."

"Oh, my God."

"Ali, please," he said. "I need to see you."

"Did you kill those people?"

"No comment."

"No comment?" she replied. "Oh, my God."

"Ali, come on."

"What happened to Salomon?"

"He's fine," said Ralston. "He's with me. He can vouch for everything."

"Then I suggest you two turn yourselves in to the police. Pronto."

"We can't. At least not yet. That's what I need to talk to you about."

Alisa was quiet as she thought about how to handle it.

"Are you still there?" Ralston asked.

"Quiet," she replied. "I'm thinking."

Ralston remained quiet.

"Where are you?" she finally asked. "Are you somewhere in L.A.?"

Ralston was hesitant about answering, but realized he was going to have to trust her. "We're south."

"How far south? San Diego? Mexico City?"

He decided that for the time being it was better for all involved if he didn't give her too much information. Until he knew for sure that she was on his side, he was going to be very careful. After all, she had promised to kill him. And though he doubted that she really meant it, there was still part of him that knew better than to cross her, or her father. "Can you get down to Manhattan Beach?" he asked, picking a quiet beach community just north of where he was.

"Well, you certainly can't come up and meet me in my office, can you?"

It was a rhetorical question that Ralston didn't need to answer. "How soon can you be there?"

Alisa checked her watch. "I'll have to figure out what to tell my client and cancel the rest of my appointments. Depending on traffic, I can probably be there in about an hour."

They picked a place to meet and Ralston said, "Thank you. I really appreciate your doing this for me."

"Don't thank me just yet. Wait till you get my bill. I charge double for travel."

CHAPTER 31

Ralston printed Alisa's picture from her law firm's website and gave it to Hank, who made the short hop up to Manhattan Beach to make sure she wasn't being followed.

He sat across the street from a small shop on Manhattan Beach Boulevard called Barbie K. Wearing what he referred to as his retired man's formal attire—flip-flops, T-shirt, and a pair of board shorts—he fit right in with the rest of the locals.

Ralston had picked the small boutique off the Internet and told Alisa that there would be an envelope waiting for her when she got there. She wasn't crazy about all the cloak-and-dagger, but she had agreed.

Ralston figured his picture had to already be circulating with the police. It was only a matter of time before it wound up on the news and he was named as a "person of interest." The last thing he wanted was to meet Alisa anywhere near a television set or where a police car might roll by. Fortunately, California offered the perfect place for them to meet and talk without being disturbed.

Knowing what a fashionista Alisa was, especially when it came to her shoes, Ralston had written a note telling her what to buy and where to meet him, and then had Hank leave it with one of the sales-girls at the boutique. Forty-five minutes later, Alisa showed up.

Fifteen minutes after that, she exited the store wearing a new, much more casual outfit and a sensible pair of shoes. Hank followed her from across the street and watched as she walked back to her car, popped the trunk, and deposited the shopping bag with the business attire and high-heeled shoes she had driven down from L.A. in.

To her credit, she didn't pull the note back out of her pocket. She knew where she was supposed to go next.

The street ran downhill toward the ocean, and it was easy for Hank to hang back and watch. Convinced that she was not being followed, he pulled out his cell phone when she got to the little restaurant and called his house. Ralston answered on the first ring.

"She's clean," he said. "I'll see you in five."

Ralston had not wanted to leave Salomon alone. He was still sleeping, but Ralston was afraid of what he might do if he woke up and no one was there. He might rationalize a quick call or email to his office and then all hell would break loose.

When Hank got back, he described what Alisa was wearing and then handed over the keys to his car. Ralston had borrowed a change of clothes from his friend, plus a baseball cap and sunglasses.

Hank gave him ten minutes and then picked up his phone. Dialing ⋆67 to block caller ID, he described Alisa to the hostess and asked if she could bring her to the phone. As it was midafternoon, it didn't take long to track her down.

"The beach should be very nice right now," he said, "especially south of the pier." Then he hung up.

Alisa went back to her table, paid for her Diet Coke, and left the restaurant. She walked the block and a half down to the beach and stepped onto the sand. The weather had been nice for several days. It was sunny and the sand was warm. She didn't visit the beach normally at this time of year. In fact, she didn't visit the beach much at all. Between the kids and work, she didn't seem to have much time.

Owing to the unusually nice weather, there were more people out than she would have expected. *Only in California*, she thought, *could this many people avoid work in the middle of the week.* She looked around for Luke, but she didn't see him, so she continued walking toward the water.

The waves were a decent size and there were dozens of surfers bobbing up and down in the ocean, waiting for the next one to carry them in.

At the water's edge, she removed her sandals. It felt good to be barefoot. She watched as a nice wave began to form and the surfers paddled hard to catch it. Tilting up her face, she stood for a moment, enjoying the warmth of the sun.

She had no idea Ralston was standing behind her until he spoke. "Hello, Ali."

Alisa didn't turn around. She wasn't ready yet. She stayed where she was, her face upturned to the sun. "When you close your eyes and listen to the sound of the ocean, it's hard to imagine there's anything wrong in the world."

Ralston let her have a few more seconds of soaking up the sun. The years had been kind to her. Being a mother, a wife, a successful attorney, it all seemed to agree with her. She was even more beautiful than he remembered. She had long, black hair and green eyes just like Ava and the same long, dark eyelashes. She kept herself in very good shape, but the sex appeal she radiated was different than her sister's had been. Alisa's sex appeal came not so much from her looks, but from her self-confidence. "How about a walk?" he finally said.

She nodded and they walked along the water's edge, away from the pier. Ralston seemed to have trouble deciding what to say, and it was Alisa who broke the silence. "I'm billing you for the new clothes, as well as my travel time."

Ralston smiled. "Fair enough."

"You want to tell me what happened?"

He did. He wanted to tell her all of it, but he needed to be careful. "Last night would have been Rachael Salomon's twenty-first birthday. Rachael was Larry's daughter."

"Wasn't she killed on a trip to Israel or Egypt?"

Ralston nodded. "Israel."

"Did they ever catch who did it?"

"The Israelis had their suspicions, but no, they never did catch who did it."

"That must have been very painful for him."

The irony of the two situations wasn't lost on him. "Rachael was the Salomons' only child, and it ended up destroying their marriage. Elizabeth left Larry and moved back to Manhattan."

"That's very sad," said Alisa.

"I don't think she liked L.A. and the movie business much anyway," replied Ralston. "But it is sad."

"As my father says, *The truest test of gold is fire.*"

"How's he doing?"

"He's fine. Still practicing law."

Ralston smiled again. "I know. I see his name in the papers all the time."

"*Without promotion,*" Alisa said with a smile as she quoted him again, "*something terrible happens . . . nothing!*"

Ralston chuckled. "Your father has always been a smart guy and he makes sure everyone knows it. I remember that joke he told me the first night I came to the house."

Alisa rolled her eyes. "The whole *It takes at least two Jews to outsmart an Armenian?*"

"He's definitely proud of his heritage."

"My mother's Jewish and she absolutely hates that joke."

"I know," said Ralston. "Ava told me after we left that night. Your mom puts up with a lot, but deep down she loves your father's big personality."

The mention of Ava brought a lull to their conversation. A wave broke and washed up onto the beach. Neither of them moved out of its path. The wet sand was heavy and difficult to walk through.

"You know, my parents liked you a lot," Alisa said.

"I liked them, too."

"You were the first person that Ava brought home that my dad didn't complain about as soon as you were out the door. Everybody else tried to impress him. You didn't. He liked that."

"He wasn't crazy about me being older than Ava, though," said Ralston.

"True, until my mom reminded him that they had the same age difference."

Even though it was small talk, the conversation was good for both of them. They both needed to heal. As Ava's older sister, Alisa had felt partly to blame for Ava's death. That guilt had been projected onto Ralston for not testifying. She needed to stop blaming him for the pain she felt over Ava's death, and Ralston needed to stop blaming himself. They both needed to let go and to be let go.

"How's Brent?" Ralston said, changing the subject to Alisa's husband.

"He's fine."

"The kids?"

"They're good too," she replied, "but we could have done the whole *How's your family* thing over the phone."

Ralston knew that wasn't true. They needed to see each other. They needed to acknowledge together that Ava was gone. They needed to close that chapter and, as painful as it was, put it behind them. It was the only way they could move forward. It was the only way that he could be sure that she would help him.

Alisa noticed that Ralston was limping. "Are you okay?" she asked. "What about Larry? Is he okay?"

"We're both fine," he replied.

"But you're limping."

Ralston waved it off. "My hip acts up from time to time. Don't worry about it."

"What happened?"

"It's a long story."

Alisa pointed down the coastline. "It's a long beach."

Ralston looked at the ocean and then back at her. As they walked, he told her everything that had happened.

"Why haven't you called the police?" she asked once he had finished. "No district attorney, no matter how publicity hungry, would bring charges in this case. You need to turn yourselves in."

"We can't. Not yet at least. And that's why I need your help," said Ralston.

Alisa looked at him. "I don't understand why you can't turn yourselves in."

"Because the men who came to kill Larry were professionals. Whoever hired them not only can afford to send more, he probably will."

"You know who sent them?"

"We have an idea," said Ralston.

"Then tell the police. Tell the district attorney. They can help protect you."

As another wave rolled up onto the sand, Ralston stopped and turned to look at her. "The men who came to kill Larry were Russian Special Forces—Spetsnaz. I don't need to tell you how influential the Russians are in Los Angeles."

No, he didn't need to tell her. There was a large Russian community in L.A., and a part of it was composed of Russian Armenians. Because of her father's heritage, he'd attracted a lot of their business. His reputation as the toughest criminal defense attorney in Los Angeles attracted the rest of the Russians, especially many of the most colorful and less than virtuous.

"You don't think the police can protect you, do you?" she said.

"I know they can't. There are just too many foxes in the henhouse."

"So what are you going to do?"

Ralston didn't need to think about his answer. "For starters, I'm going to find out who sent that team to kill Larry."

"And let me guess," she said. "That's where I come in."

Ralston nodded. "Those three hitters inside Larry's house were fresh off the boat. Somebody local had to set it all up. They needed to be met at the airport, given their weapons, driven to Salomon's. That's the way these things normally work."

"What do you want me to do?" she asked. "Take out an ad in the Russian *Kurier* newspaper?"

"I'd like you to talk to your father. I'm guessing that there's only a handful of people in L.A. who could have put this together. Most likely, it's someone who worked for the Russian FSB or its predecessor, the KGB."

"Hold it," said Alisa. "That my dad has represented some unsavory people from that community doesn't mean he knows who to go to for contract killings."

"I'm not saying he does," replied Ralston. "What I need is for you to ask him. He knows enough people. One of them is going to know who could have put something like this together."

"And what happens when word gets back to this person that my father is asking questions? What's to say they're not going to come after him? Or my mother?"

Ralston tried to set her mind at ease. "Your father's well-respected in that community. Nothing is going to happen to him and nothing is going to happen to your mom."

"I'm glad you're so confident."

"Ali, your dad's a smart guy. We both know that. He knows how to ask questions without getting himself in trouble. There are probably a hundred people who can tell him what I need to know, and very likely, they all owe your dad a favor. I'm just asking for him to cash one in for me."

"And why would he want to do that?" she asked.

Ralston looked at her. The attraction he'd never acted upon, but had always felt slightly guilty about while dating Ava, was still there. He tried to put it out of his mind. He knew she had felt it, and fought it, as well. That was the reason she hadn't hung up on him when he called. It was why she was standing here on the beach with him now. It was why she wanted to help him. She just needed a reason to, something other than the feelings she'd always harbored for her sister's boyfriend.

"Your father won't need a reason," said Ralston. "And he won't ask you for one. I was good to Ava. He knows that. I tried to help her. That's all that should matter."

"And if he says *no*?"

"He won't," replied Ralston.

"You're pretty sure of yourself, aren't you?" said Alisa.

"No. What I'm sure of, is you. You won't let him say no."

Before she could respond, he removed a small piece of paper from his pocket and handed it to her. "Memorize this and then burn it."

"What is it?" she asked.

"It's an email account I want you to use, so we can communicate. The instructions are there. I've left a signed agreement in the draft folder retaining you as my attorney. I've also left a letter clearly stating that you have directed me to turn myself in to the police and that I intend to do so once Larry's safety can be guaranteed," he replied.

"What about *your* safety?"

Ralston closed her hand over the piece of paper and let his hand linger atop hers. "I can take care of myself."

Alisa thought about drawing her hand back, but didn't. "Why won't you tell me who's behind all of this?"

"I can't," he said as he let go of her hand. "Not yet. Please just talk to your father for me."

With that, he turned and walked away. Alisa watched him go, her mind filled with questions about what kind of trouble he was in as well as what kind of person would send a Russian hit team after one of the most popular producers in Hollywood.

CHAPTER 32

"Do you always travel with security?" Julia Winston asked as she took another sip of the 1992 DRC Montrachet that James Standing had ordered.

They were sitting at a corner table in New York's famed Le Bernardin restaurant. The billionaire's protective detail occupied two additional tables a respectable distance away.

"Unfortunately, the world can be a dangerous place," he replied, lowering his glass back to the table.

The reporter still had many more questions she wanted to ask him and she wasted no time. Picking up her pad and pencil, she said, "That's a perfect place for us to pick back up. Let's talk about the world as you see it, or more precisely how you'd like to see it."

"I'd like to see us all get along."

"Meaning?"

"Meaning, we're all citizens of the world. What happens in one nation can affect another and because of that, we need a better collaborative decision-making process. It must be something that allows for more intelligent decisions to be made and for those decisions to be made faster, with less bickering and foot-dragging. We share a planet where a volcano that erupts in Iceland can disrupt flights in Europe. An earthquake and tsunami that sweep Japan can destroy nuclear reactors, causing radiation to drift across the Pacific to the U.S. These are all things of *collective* interest and affect more than just one nation, agreed?"

Julia nodded.

"Where these items of collective interest exist, where multiple nations have skin in the game, as it were, it is my opinion that the only way to get the right things done is by subordinating state sovereignty in favor of international law."

"And for international organizations as well?"

Standing smiled. "Yes, in fact I just came from a reception at the U.N. You see, it's all about clarity of purpose. If we can come together with a shared set of values and a shared sense of purpose, we can make the world a much better place.

"Let's take economics, for instance, a subject I know you and I are both interested in. We cannot continue the failed economic policies of the last thirty years. Our planet is dying and we have more people than ever before in poverty. The only way to bring about reform is for the pendulum to swing from the market toward the state."

Julia looked up from her pad. "But hasn't the free market actually lifted hundreds of millions of people out of poverty?"

Standing shook his head. "The capitalistic system is morally bankrupt."

"What about India and China? Average incomes there have skyrocketed over the last thirty years."

"I'm glad you mentioned China. China is a perfect example of what state-run capitalism can achieve. It proves that capitalism doesn't require democracy. In fact, it operates better without it. And as far as India is concerned, it is home to a third of the poorest people on the planet. I'd think twice about using India as an example of the benefits of capitalism."

"So we should ignore that the 1980s and 1990s, often known as the new golden age of capitalism, saw the proportion of the world's population living on a dollar a day or less drop so dramatically that it was enough to offset rising populations in developing countries?" she asked.

"Not at all," replied Standing. "Life has, in fact, gotten better for people around the world. That is thanks to globalization. But quality of life is nowhere near as good as it should be. The planet is possessed of abundant resources and wealth, yet—"

"*Yet* you think that wealth should be spread around, correct?"

"I think that if it is in our power to make the lives of our fellow human beings better, we should do everything we can to make that happen."

"Would that include transferring America's wealth, let's say, to citizens in poorer nations?"

Standing laughed. "What wealth? America is bankrupt. In fact, if we had a global reset, America would be much better off."

"Better off how?"

He thought about it for a moment and then said, "This is oversimplifying it, but picture a homeowners' association somewhere in America. Let's say there are fifty homes. The spectrum of the owners' indebtedness will run from no debt and healthy bank balances to one, maybe two families who are hanging on by their fingernails, not sure how they'll afford their next bag of groceries, much less their next mortgage payment."

Julia looked at him. "You're saying the family who has worked hard, paid off their mortgage, and has saved their money should bail out the family who can't afford their house, much less groceries?"

"It's not that simple," cautioned Standing. "What happens if the poor family defaults on their mortgage?"

"Why don't we examine why they can't afford their house and groceries? Did they bite off more than they could chew?"

"Who knows? Maybe Mom and Dad just had a run of bad luck. Maybe they both got laid off. That these people have financial problems doesn't mean they deserve them."

"I'm not saying they do, but—"

"Answer my question," said Standing. "What happens if this family goes under and defaults on their mortgage?"

"I assume they'll be foreclosed on and eventually evicted."

"Correct," replied Standing. "And what happens to the house, then?"

"It goes on the market."

"At what price?"

"At whatever the market will bear," said Julia. "That's the way markets work."

"Not in this case. You see, the bank doesn't just have one house, it has thousands; hundreds of thousands. It doesn't want to be in the home ownership business, it wants to be in the money-lending business. Its motivation is not to hang around and wait for the free market system to work. It wants to dump that house as quickly as possible, and to do that, it's going to dramatically mark down the price. What would that do to the values of the other properties in the homeowners' association?"

"It would effectively lower them."

"Which means, through no fault of your own, the equity in your home has been diminished. So, what would make more sense? Losing your equity? Or everyone chipping in together to make sure everyone succeeds?"

The woman looked at him. "You're offering a false choice."

"No, I'm not."

"Of course you are, Mr. Standing. If I have worked hard, saved my money, and paid off my mortgage, I shouldn't have to bail out another homeowner."

"Not even if they have fallen on hard times?" he asked. "Imagine if you were in their shoes."

"I have no doubt that it would be terrible, but it isn't the government's job to take money from one group and give it to another."

Standing smiled again. "Really? What do you call taxes, then?"

"I disagree with a lot of how the U.S. government spends my money, but we're not talking about taxes."

"In a way, we are. What happens when the family in our scenario doesn't pay their share of the fees and assessments of the homeowners' association?"

"I would imagine that their property would end up getting a lien placed on it," she replied.

"But in the meantime, the association's expenses still need to be paid for, and that burden falls more heavily on the other owners. They have to dip into their reserves, or if the reserves are too thin, they have to pay more in order to cover those who can't. We can push those who have the most to give more, but as increasing numbers of homeowners go under, sooner or later the burden to make up what they cannot contribute will be overwhelming. We won't be able to collect enough from the wealthiest homeowners to make up for it.

"Wouldn't it be better, not to mention easier, to simply rebalance the scales? The sooner you can get that family who is in default back into a job and working, the better it is for everyone. The prosperity effect, as I like to call it, inures to everyone's benefit. This is about recognizing people's dignity."

"And in no place on earth," she said, "have the freedom and dignity of the individual been more available and assured than in America."

"Human dignity is a *global* concern," replied Standing. "There can't be social cohesion as long as there is such a vast chasm between rich and poor in the world."

"And you see dismantling capitalism as the answer?" she asked.

"I see *unfettered* capitalism as the reason the chasm exists. Human dignity cannot be realized without equitable income distribution. Because human dignity and social cohesion matter to all of us, this is an issue that transcends national sovereignty."

"Therefore it should be dealt with by international law and international governing bodies," she replied, repeating his earlier statement.

"Exactly," said Standing. "This is why a global reset would be so good for so many nations, including the United States. As with the homeowners' association, everyone would benefit. It would give every nation the chance to be rid of its debts and to start fresh."

"But what you fail to realize is that one person's debt is another person's asset. I look at my mortgage much differently than my bank does. To me it's a debt, one that I took on willingly, by the way, and one that I'm morally obligated to pay back. To the bank it's a business transaction, which it took on willingly, and from which it rightly expects to profit, thereby serving the interests of its shareholders. No one put a gun to either of our heads."

"So the housing bubble all happened by accident?" asked Standing.

"No," Julia replied. "The housing bubble happened for a multitude of reasons. One of the biggest was the government strong-arming banks into providing mortgages to people who didn't qualify."

"People have a right to a place to live."

"You'll forgive me, Mr. Standing, but I think you and I have a very different view of what *rights* are."

"Rights should be what an enlightened government decides is best for everyone."

The reporter shook her head. "As Americans, we hold that we have been endowed by our creator with our rights. These rights cannot be taken away or limited by any government. We have the right to—"

"Life, liberty, and the pursuit of happiness," Standing said with a wave of his hand. "I know, but tell me how anyone can be happy without a place to live?"

"There's nothing in the founding documents that says the government owes you a house. There's also nothing in there that says the government owes you a job, an education, or medical care."

"Those documents you love so much were written over two hundred years ago," he replied. "There is no possible way America's founding fathers could have seen how complex society would become."

"And if they had been able to see into the future, you think they would have felt it best for people to be ruled over by an elite group?"

"Government should provide opportunity."

"I agree, but government isn't the solution to our problems," Julia stated. "Government *is* the problem."

"I wouldn't have figured you for a radical, Ms. Winston."

"I'm not."

"Really? It sounds to me as if you'd like to do away with government."

"I don't want to do away with government," she replied. "I want to make it work."

"So do I," said Standing. "And if we all started over together, the global economy would instantly rebound."

"But once we start over, how would you prevent disparities from growing again? It's a fact of life that some people will work harder than others. Some people even will choose not to work."

"We'd need a universal set of rules applied to everyone equally."

"These rules would also govern capitalism?"

"Absolutely," he replied. "Capitalism is the source of all that's wrong in the world. It has become too big for any one nation to regulate. People are hurting and it is within our power to stop that hurt. We are a noble species. It is our duty to lift people out of despair. The only way to do that, though, is to challenge global capitalism head-on, with redesigned international institutions and far more encompassing international laws."

"All overseen by a global governing body," she said.

"For collective issues like human dignity and things that affect it? Of course. Individual rights have to take a backseat for the good of everyone's collective rights."

"Is there anything this global governing body wouldn't have control over? It seems that almost anything could be placed beneath the umbrella of *human dignity* and *collective rights.*"

"I see what you're doing," replied Standing with a wry grin. "You're trying to box me in."

The journalist shook her head. "I just find it interesting that a billionaire, someone who has so benefited from capitalism, should be such an outspoken proponent of socialism."

Standing bristled at the remark. "You're an attractive woman, my dear, but you had better wise up. Big tits and a pretty smile are only going to get you so far."

Julia was stunned by his vulgarity. "Excuse me?"

"You have no idea how offensive I find that remark. Do you have any clue, any clue at all how fatiguing it is to be committed to doing good, only to be hammered for it day in and day out by people like you?"

"People like *me*?"

"Yes, you free-market zombies. All you do is complain about government intervention. You lie to anyone who will read your columns, listen to your radio programs, or watch your TV shows. You tell them we need less government regulation. You tell people that capitalism works precisely because people pursue their own self-interest. You don't want any checks on that self-interest at all. Every man and woman for him- or herself. No accountability."

Leading financial figure or not, Julia had no intention of letting his remarks go unanswered. "Your tasteless comment about my breasts aside, Mr. Standing, I never said people in the free market should not be held accountable. I think they should. But the answer isn't adding more rules, it's to enforce the ones we already have. If our lazy, inept bureaucrats had been doing their jobs, Bernie Madoff would have been caught. What's more, the thousands of Wall Street bankers who bundled lousy loans in collateralized debt obligations they knew would tank would also be locked up.

"And while we're on housing, as far as your HOA analogy goes, I wouldn't want the value of my home to drop for any reason. If it did drop, then I'd lose equity, but I should decide if I help neighbors in their time of need. The government shouldn't make that decision for me. Sometimes, it's not a handout that people need, it's a kick in the rear.

"If a family has honestly fallen on hard times, then I believe good neighbors would pull together to help them. That's what we do in this country and we do it because it's right.

"You, though, don't want to address how that family fell upon hard times. In your mind, they're automatically victims. Their situation could never possibly be their fault. If they're poor, or in financial straits, that's because somebody else put them there. Somebody stole what was rightly theirs or prevented them from achieving. You'd never think to ask if maybe they purchased a home they couldn't afford. Did they purchase expensive vacations and flat-screen TVs instead of laying away emergency funds for a rainy day?

"And while you see these people as victims, I and the other *free-market zombies*, as you put it, see these people as *individuals*. Individuals empowered to make their own decisions. Neither you, the government, nor anyone else has the right to be in the business of trying to regulate outcomes. You can call it social cohesion, income equality, or social justice. It doesn't matter. Despite whether the term offends you or not, what you are advocating is pure socialism."

Standing gripped his butter knife and tried to keep his temper in check. "If asking society to invest in its citizens in order to make life better for them is socialism, then I guess I'm guilty as charged."

"But you're not asking society to do these things. You're trying to force it. You want to subvert the power of nations to decide their own destinies in order to impose a global system of laws overseen by a global system of governance. You're not only a socialist, Mr. Standing, you're a socialist who has not only benefited greatly from capitalism, but one who then wants to use those gains to utterly destroy capitalism and replace it with your vision of what will bring about some sort of perfect world where an omnipotent government provides everything people could ever want or need."

"Socialism and communism are simply terms meant to demonize. I don't even think you know the difference between them."

Julia Winston nodded vehemently. "I most certainly do. They both seek public control of the production and distribution of wealth and while many believe they mean the same thing, they don't. One is voluntary and the other is involuntary."

Standing rolled his eyes. "Yes, yes, yes. Evil communism forces everyone into what the state wants and socialism is elective."

"Wrong," she replied. "Communism is the end game of socialism. Communism is the theoretical, stateless utopia where mankind has been perfected to the point where government is no longer needed.

"A completely voluntary communist society stems from the Marxist theory of evolution. For the Marxists, the communist utopia is the apex of human development—a time at which man has genetically evolved out of his selfish ways and consistently acts toward the common good, completely of his own volition. To get from capitalism to the hypothetical utopia of pure communism, society must be subjected to the tyranny of socialism. That's where people make their mistake in describing the two philosophies. They think socialism is voluntary and communism is involuntary when actually the reverse is true.

"So in the interim phase between *selfish* capitalism and *selfless* communism we have socialism. Under socialism, mankind, for its own supposed good, is subjected to the authority of dictatorship, an enlightened ruling class of elites who control the human environment in egalitarian terms in order that they may steer the proper genetic evolution of mankind."

Standing looked at her. "You are such an attractive woman, I could almost believe anything you say. I think that's why FOX News has been so successful."

"You are changing the subject, Mr. Standing," said Julia.

"I haven't changed it, my dear. You have. Don't you believe in justice? Don't you believe in people not being allowed to game the system?"

"Of course I do."

"Then why are you so against making the world a better, more equitable place for all of us?" Standing asked. "You have given me the usual shallow, shopworn defense of capitalism, but you haven't given me one *concrete* reason why my ideas are so unreasonable."

"*One concrete reason?*" the reporter replied. "I can actually give you four. First, it is morally wrong to take anything that doesn't belong to you and having the state do the taking doesn't magically make it okay or right. Second, socialism has been tried repeatedly and has never worked, *anywhere*. Yet each new crop of elites think they can enact socialism and this time it will be different. They stick the socialist fork back in the electrical outlet expecting a totally different outcome, but it always ends up the same.

"Third, when people become reliant on the state, that reliance erodes their self-respect, their sense of self-worth, their work ethic, and their independence. Finally, socialism promotes class envy and class warfare. The makers resent the takers for draining their resources and the takers resent the makers because no matter how much the takers take, they always want more. They erroneously believe that the makers have an abundant supply from which they should be continuously compelled to give. But, as Maggie Thatcher so aptly put it, the problem with socialism is that eventually you run out of other people's money."

Standing shook his head. "I'm afraid you have misunderstood me, my dear."

"You know what, Mr. Standing? At first calling me *my dear* was cute. You reminded me of my grandfather, but now I find it patronizing."

The billionaire liked that he had gotten under her skin, but he didn't like being compared to her grandfather.

"And as far as misunderstanding you," she continued, "I haven't. I understand you all too well. Listening to you speak, I keep remembering that old Chinese proverb. *Give a person a fish, and he'll eat for a day. Teach a person to fish, and he'll eat for a lifetime.* Your problem is that you want to give everyone fish. If you really cared about human dignity, you'd be giving everyone fishing lessons."

Standing shook his head once more. *Why was this so hard for these flat-earth types to understand?* "Despite everything we've talked about, despite the disproportionate number of *haves* versus *have nots,* the inequitable distribution of wealth, all of it, you've never had one doubt about capitalism? You can look me in the eye and tell me that somehow greed and self-interest are good things?"

"All I know, Mr. Standing, is that there is no perfect place where greed doesn't exist. In fact, the greater the government control, the more greed there is. The people who are the worst off in our world don't live under capitalism, they live in societies that have turned away from or are prevented from embracing capitalism and free trade. So you'll pardon me for saying so, but what you're proposing isn't going to make the world a better place. If you were successful at doing what you say you'd like to do, it would make the world a much, much worse place, and I pray to God it never happens."

"*God,*" said Standing with a derisive sniff. "You see the state our planet is in and you still believe in God. You really aren't very bright, are you?" It wasn't a question. It was a statement.

"I'm bright enough to realize that now that you've made your money and are one of the wealthiest people in the world, you've abandoned the ideas that got you here and have replaced them with fantasies of a classless utopia," said the reporter as she stood up.

The billionaire was taken by surprise. "What's going on?"

"Thank you for the wine."

Was she leaving? "Where do you think you're going?"

"Back to my office to finish writing my article."

"I asked you to dinner and expect you to stay for all of it," he replied, his eyes narrowing as he took hold of her arm. "Sit down."

"You've got less than two seconds to take your hand off of me, Mr. Standing. I promise you that I'll snap your wrist before your security team even knows what has happened. I can only imagine that bones break very easily in a man of your age and take very long to heal."

How dare she? Standing was enraged, yet he forced a smile onto his face and removed his hand from her arm. People in the crowded restaurant were watching. "Let's not embarrass ourselves. I'm sure we can find something else to talk about."

Sliding out of her chair, Julia Winston forced her own smile. "Good night, Mr. Standing."

As she walked away, Standing got in the last word, uttering it loud enough for her to hear. "*Bitch.*"

He snapped his fingers to get the attention of his security detail and indicated that he was ready to leave. He'd be damned if he would suffer the additional embarrassment of sitting at his table and dining by himself like some lonely old man.

His waiter rushed over. "Is everything all right, Mr. Standing?"

"Everything is fine, Jeffery," he said, a less-than-convincing smile upon his lips. "Something has come up and we won't be able to dine with you tonight."

"I'm sorry to hear that, sir." Looking at the three-thousand-dollar bottle of wine, he added, "What would you like to do with the Montrachet?"

Though he would only pour it down the drain once he got home, Standing certainly wasn't going to gift such an expensive bottle of wine to a mere waiter. "Put a cork in it and give it to Max," he said, gesturing over his shoulder at the head of his security detail. He then stood up from the table and headed for the front of the restaurant. He had no idea that his evening was about to go from bad to worse.

As he climbed into his armored Denali, Standing's encrypted cell phone rang.

CHAPTER 33

Standing told his driver and security team to stand on the sidewalk while he sat in the Denali and took the call. He didn't want anyone to listen to him speaking to Robert Ashford.

"I'm afraid I have bad news," said the MI5 operative.

"You seem to be in the bad-news business a lot lately, Robert," replied Standing. "It's starting to become a habit I don't care for."

And Ashford didn't care for the rebuke, but he held his tongue. Standing had too much incriminating leverage stacked against him. He decided to get right to the point. "I've received word that the rabbit hutch was compromised."

Standing had expected the conversation to be about what had happened in L.A., not about Mustafa Karami and the terror cell in Sweden. *Rabbit hutch* was the code name it had been given. "How was it compromised?"

"Local authorities are being very tight-lipped. They suspect a foreign intelligence agency had targeted the cell."

Standing's blood pressure was starting to rise. "Which intelligence agency?"

"They believe it was the French."

"The French? How the hell would they have been involved?"

"They have some sort of evidence pointing to the DGSE's Action Division. They seem pretty convinced it was them. The French, of course, are denying it."

"Of course they're denying it," snapped Standing. "There's no way the French could have put any of this together."

"Well, someone did."

Ashford was right. "Tell me what happened."

"The hutch operated two apartments, one across the street from the other. One was where operations were handled. The other was a completely sterile safe house. All computers, cell phones, and what-have-you were kept in the operations apartment.

"Somehow the location of the apartments was uncovered. An assault team outfitted to look like the Swedish Security Service attempted to take them down."

"*Attempted?* Meaning they didn't succeed?"

"The operations apartment was rigged to explode, and when the assault team hit, it did."

"What about the safe house apartment?" asked Standing.

"Two of the faux Swedish Security operatives were seen going into that building as well. One man from the hutch was thrown from the window and killed. There was also gunfire. According to witnesses, when the phony Security Services men exited the building, they had another man with them. He was bleeding. They had a car parked outside. They laid him on the backseat and then the three of them drove away."

Standing's heart suddenly stopped beating. "Was it Westminster?"

All of the terrorist network's commanders and lieutenants had been named after locations in the United Kingdom. The head of the network, Aaazim Aleem, was Oxford, Mustafa Karami, Westminster.

"No. He was much younger," said Ashford.

"Was he from the hutch?"

"Some said he looked Arab, some said Italian, but I think we should assume he was one of ours."

"Okay, but why only take him?" asked Standing. "What happened to the rest of them? Where's Westminster?"

"Including the man who had been thrown out the window, they have found seven bodies at the safe house apartment. They were all younger men in their twenties and early thirties."

"So no sign of Westminster. What about Cardiff?" he asked, referring to Sabah.

"Based on what I have been able to glean," replied Ashford, "they are not among the dead at the safe house, which means—"

"Either they were in the operations apartment when it blew, or they managed to escape altogether."

"Correct."

Standing worked to keep his anger in check. First they had gotten to Aazim and now they had tracked down Karami. He needed to think. "Could the Americans be behind this?" he asked.

"Carlton and his group? I don't know how they could have located the hutch, but they were the ones who tracked down Oxford, so we should probably put them at the top of our list."

"I don't want to hear 'probably.' I want to hear 'for certain.' You have a relationship with them. Use it."

Ashford was getting angry again. "And just what am I supposed to do? Ring them up and ask if they happened to have anything to do with hitting a terror cell in Sweden? We were lucky to have taken care of Oxford before they could turn him over. If I start asking questions about Sweden, they're going to get suspicious."

"Then you'd better see to it that they don't. You're the spook, you figure it out," said Standing, adding, "If Westminster did manage to get away, how long until he makes contact?"

"It depends on how long it takes him to get to the alternate safe house. Once he's in place, we'll hear from him."

"If you don't hear from him in the next eight hours, cut him out of the loop and promote the next commander."

"That would be Birmingham."

"Fine," replied Standing.

"And if Westminster does make contact, what do you want me to tell him?"

Standing thought about it for a moment. Whether it was the Americans or not, someone had managed to track down the Uppsala cell. Whom they had taken out of the safe house and driven away with was anyone's guess. Someone was way too close. They needed to step up their plans. All of the attacks had been color-coded. "The silver- and goldsmiths have already received the newsletter, correct?"

"Yes," said Ashford, using the code words for the next attacks. "Silver and gold are ready to go, but do you really want to jump that far ahead?"

"We don't have much choice, do we? Somehow, trade secrets have been compromised. I want silver tomorrow and gold the day after."

"I'll handle it. Anything else?" asked Ashford.

"Have you cleaned up your mess in Los Angeles?"

"I'm still working on it."

"Well, work faster," said Standing. "Your ass is on the line."

Ashford was about to reply, when Standing disconnected the call and the line went dead. *Arsehole,* he thought to himself. His dislike for the man was growing by the hour.

Nevertheless, Standing had every right to be angry over what had happened in Los Angeles. The fact that Ashford couldn't reach his contact only made him look more unprofessional. He was going to locate him soon, or else come up with some sort of Plan B. As soon as silver and gold were unleashed, the United States was going to be locked up tighter than a drum.

CHAPTER 34

The Carlton Group's offices were located in a nondescript glass office building ten minutes from Washington Dulles International Airport.

Pat Murphy, the surviving assaulter from the Uppsala operation, and Andy Bachmann, the former CIA man, had hitched a ride home on the jet with Harvath. Murphy kept to himself in the back of the plane. He'd lost his entire team, and Harvath knew there was nothing he could do to help assuage what the man was feeling. Harvath had simply thanked him again for pulling him out of the building, handed him the bottle of Maker's Mark, and left him alone.

After the post-landing formalities at Dulles, a team met Murphy to accompany him home. It was standard operating procedure. The man had been through too much to just be sent off on his own. Bachmann offered to go along, too.

Harvath extended the assaulter his condolences once more and told him that he'd be in touch. Before climbing into one of the black Suburbans the Old Man had sent to the airport for them, he thanked Bachmann and asked him to make sure Murphy had anything he needed.

When the vehicle pulled out onto the Dulles Toll Road, it was just after midnight. It took them eight minutes to get to the office.

They pulled into the underground parking structure and Harvath was let out near a service door. He punched a code into a pad at the wall, the lock released, and Harvath entered a short maintenance corridor. At the end was a service elevator. He looked up at the surveillance camera in the corner and then waited for the elevator to be sent down. When it arrived and the doors opened, Harvath stepped inside.

The building was twenty-five stories tall and the Carlton Group's offices were on the top floor. The main elevators that served the building proper and all its tenants had buttons from L to 25, but no 13, which meant those elevators technically only went to the twenty-fourth floor. As a precaution, the Group also controlled the entire twenty-fourth floor, which supposedly included a collection of unoccupied offices. Should anyone ever manage to get a peek at the twenty-fourth floor, it wouldn't appear unusual at all.

The special service elevator Harvath was in went only to the twenty-fifth floor. When the doors opened, he stepped out into a carpeted foyer area. Sitting behind a desk were two large men dressed in suits and ties. They nodded to Harvath and buzzed him in.

Passing through a heavy blast door hidden behind panels of mahogany, he entered the headquarters of the Carlton Group.

The entire space had been built to the strictest TEMPEST specifications. Though the Carlton Group was a private organization, they were contracted to the DoD and handled classified information. Every step was taken to safeguard against what was referred to in intel-speak as "compromising emanations," or CE. CE was any electrical, mechanical, or acoustical signal from equipment that was transmitting, receiving, processing, analyzing, encrypting, or decrypting classified information that could be intentionally or accidentally intercepted. It was a sophisticated science that looked at everything from magnetic field radiation and line conduction all the way to how window blinds can vibrate and give away conversations held in offices and what is being typed on a keyboard feet away from a window.

The antieavesdropping measures aside, the Carlton Group's offices resembled a large, successful law firm. There were private offices, conference rooms, and multiple cubicle areas that had been collectively nicknamed Kubistan by staff.

As in the CIA's counterterrorism center, employees were grouped according to the regions and areas in which they possessed expertise. Taking a page out of Silicon Valley's handbook, they were encouraged to move when assignments dictated via mobile workstations that looked as if they came straight out of an IKEA catalog. The Group's director of operations referred to it as "clustering" and had found that often the personnel themselves formed more effective and productive teams than when management assigned specific people to specific projects.

One of the nation's longest-serving and most revered spymasters, the Old Man was not a management guru. He believed in simply hiring the best people possible and then trusting them to do their jobs. He'd watched how too much management and bureaucracy had choked the life out of the CIA, and he had sworn he'd never let it happen at his organization.

That said, he'd drawn a few lines in the sand with his management team. Employees were expected to dress like business professionals. There were no casual-dress Fridays. He expected people to comport themselves with dignity. They were the best and he expected them to look like it.

He was particular about facial hair. Unless you were going into the field and it was a part of your cover, male employees were expected to be clean-shaven. He didn't want to see any piercings other than earrings, and then only two, on female employees only—one in each ear. If you had a tattoo, it had better not be visible. There were also strict rules about physical conditioning, grooming, and hygiene.

There were only two exceptions to "Reed's Rules of Order," as they were known. The first had to do with smoking. As a relapsed smoker himself, he allowed people to smoke, but they couldn't go outside to do it. Smokers had a habit of getting too chummy and chatty with strangers and other tenants in a building. They milled around outside and lingered over cigarettes, wasting productive time. They also made themselves vulnerable to surveillance and approach.

To cater to the smokers, he'd built what became known as "the coffin"—a small glass booth, barely big enough for two people, at the far end of the office. It had an intense air-purification system that roared so loudly you could barely hear yourself think.

It wasn't supposed to be comfortable. There wasn't even a place to sit down inside. You went in, got your fix, and got out. Strangely enough, no one ever saw the Old Man using the coffin, and it was widely suspected he had had an equally efficient, though much quieter, system placed in his office allowing him to smoke whenever he wanted to.

The other exception to Reed's Rules of Order had to do with his newest employee, Moonracer. He was an eccentric little man who was also particularly cunning. The Old Man didn't trust him a single bit.

When it came to bringing Nicholas on board, Carlton had been one hundred percent against it, but Harvath had made a very compelling case and he'd eventually relented once the man had been able to secure his presidential pardon. That didn't mean that he had changed any of his ways. The Old Man had created a secure area within which Nicholas operated, and within which he could constantly be monitored.

Nicholas had refused to shave his beard and had also insisted that the two enormous white Russian Ovcharkas, or Caucasian Sheepdogs, he owned, which were never away from his side, be allowed to come to work with him. Though Reed Carlton loved dogs, he had refused the request. The little man then claimed they were service animals and hinted at bringing a suit against him for violating the Americans with Disabilities act. The Old Man didn't know if Nicholas was pulling his leg or if he was actually serious.

Once again, Harvath had stepped in and had lobbied for the dogs, explaining that the Group wouldn't secure Nicholas's cooperation unless the dogs were part of the deal. Carlton relented once more. It was obvious that Harvath had appointed himself the little man's guardian. That point was driven home shortly after Nicholas's first day on the job.

Because of the man's physical limitations, a special Sensitive Compartmented Information Facility, SCIF for short, had been built for him. A SCIF was an enclosed area within a building used for processing sensitive information. Nicholas's SCIF was built to his specifications on a raised floor and stuffed full of all the computer equipment and data links he had asked for. As with the other sections of the Carlton Group, Nicholas's SCIF had been assigned a title based on its function. A white sheet of paper with the words *Digital Ops* had been printed out and taped to the door.

The next day it had been taken down and replaced with another sign: The Lollipop Guild. When Harvath heard about it, he had hit the roof.

It took him less than fifteen minutes to track down who had done it. And cornering him in the men's room, it took every ounce of restraint he had for Harvath not to punch the man's lights out. To his credit, the man didn't deny that he had posted the sign. In fact, he owned right up to it and launched into what a mistake he felt it was having brought a criminal like Nicholas into their operation.

Harvath didn't care what the man thought. He told him that if he didn't stay away from Nicholas, he would put a bullet in his head and dump his body where his family would never find it. Five minutes later, the man was in his supervisor's office registering a complaint against Harvath. To the supervisor's credit, he had backed up Harvath and told the man that if he didn't close his mouth and get back to work, Harvath wouldn't have a chance to shoot him because he was going to do the job himself. That seemed to put an end to things. Word quickly got around that anybody who screwed with Moonracer was going to get a visit from his big brother, Norseman, and that Harvath had carte blanche to do whatever he wanted and management would turn a blind eye.

• • •

Arriving at the SCIF, Harvath punched in his code, waited for the green light to come on, and listened for the locks to slide back and the hiss of air as the door was released.

CHAPTER 35

The growling of Nicholas's two dogs, Argos and Draco, ceased as soon as they saw who it was. Both of them stood up from their beds and trotted over to see Harvath.

"Hello, boys," he said, patting them on the head. "Hello, Nicholas."

The little man was typing away at his keyboard. He quickly raised his left index finger, indicating he'd be with Harvath in a second, and then returned to typing.

In the eerie lighting of the SCIF, Harvath studied Nicholas's face. He had been attacked over the summer with a razor. It had happened in a remote mountainous region of Spain. There wasn't a hospital, or even a clinic, for over a hundred miles. One of the monks who found him had some medical experience and had sewn him up. All things considered, Nicholas was lucky to have received any stitches at all. In fact, he was just lucky to be alive.

He had since undergone two procedures to help improve his appearance and reduce scarring. From what Harvath could see, Nicholas was almost back to normal.

As soon as the little man was finished with what he was typing, he hit the Enter key, saying, "And a Dolly for Sue."

Nicholas needed an extraordinary amount of computing power to do what the Carlton Group had brought him on board to do. When the NSA categorically denied him access to their massive data centers, he turned to the next best thing and hacked into Google's.

Google had dozens of data centers around the world and more than a million servers, from right there in Reston, to places like São Paulo, Moscow, Milan, Tokyo, and Hong Kong. Nicholas had given the ones he used most often nicknames—Spotted Elephant, Bird Fish, Charlie-in-the-Box, Ostrich Cowboy, Scooter for Jimmy, and a Dolly for Sue.

Harvath had chalked it up to eccentricity until someone in the Group had asked him if he knew the significance of Nicholas's code name. The little man had chosen it for himself and it had been approved. Harvath figured it had some poetic meaning for him until he learned that Moonracer was the name of the winged lion that ruled the Island of Misfit Toys. He was responsible for flying around the world each night in search of unwanted toys. It was a fitting moniker.

When it became obvious that Nicholas was not going to grow any bigger, his godless Soviet Georgian parents had decided he was an embarrassment and would forever be like a stone around their necks. They no longer wanted their son and decided to get rid of him.

They made no attempt to find him a suitable, loving home. They didn't even try to place him in an orphanage. Instead, they abandoned the boy, selling him to a brothel on the outskirts of the Black Sea resort of Sochi. There, Nicholas was starved, beaten, and made to participate in unutterable acts no child should ever be subjected to.

It was there that Nicholas learned the true value of information. Pillow talk from the alcohol-loosened lips of the brothel's powerful clients proved to be a gold mine, once he knew what to listen for and how to turn it to his advantage.

The women who worked in the brothel were society's castoffs, just like Nicholas, and they took pity on him. Those ladies of the night were the first to ever treat Nicholas with respect. They became the only family he had ever known, and he repaid their kindness one day by securing their freedom. He had the madam who ran the brothel, along with her husband, dispatched for the inhuman cruelty he had suffered at their hands.

Though he moved beyond the horrors of his youth, he never forgot them. He carried with him a tremendous burden of shame. He was no angel. He had done many bad things since leaving the brothel in Sochi. He had done many good things as well, particularly with the vast amount of money he had made and lost over the years. He wanted to cleanse himself. Whether that was possible, only time would tell. Agreeing to come to work with Harvath was a step in that direction.

Pushing his chair back from the desk, he reached his tiny arms into the air and arched his back. Lowering them, he turned to face his friend. "I'm sorry about Uppsala," he said.

"Me, too," replied Harvath, nodding toward the minifridge on the opposite wall.

Nicholas nodded. "Help yourself."

Crossing over to it, he opened the door and peered inside. "Does the Old Man know you've got a bottle of wine in here?"

"What he doesn't know won't hurt him. Besides, with the hours I've been putting in, I deserve a drink now and again."

"Do you have any beer?" asked Harvath.

"Do I look like I've suddenly turned into a beer drinker?"

Though a man of diminutive stature, Nicholas had perhaps the best taste of anyone Harvath had ever met. From clothes to wine and food, Nicholas was a connoisseur of all the good things life had to offer—and that included beer. Harvath had sat and drunk with him before. "Seriously, you don't have any beer?" Harvath asked.

"It was hard enough getting the wine in here without Carlton knowing. Five percent per volume versus twelve. You do the math."

Wine packed a stronger punch than beer. Harvath got it. He settled on a Red Bull instead and closed the fridge door.

"I thought you didn't drink that stuff anymore," said Nicholas.

"Only in emergencies," he said, popping the lid and rolling a chair over. "Like when there's no beer."

Nicholas smiled and made room for him. "How's Chase? I heard he got shot in the shoulder."

"Bicep," Harvath corrected, pointing at his own. "I think it hit the bone. He'll be riding the bench for a while. So," he continued, changing the subject, "the Old Man says you've made some progress?"

"I have," replied Nicholas, as he pulled up an instant message screen and typed a note to the Old Man that Harvath had arrived.

"Is he still in the office?"

"Yeah. He wanted me to let him know when you got here so we could go over everything together."

"While we're waiting for him, why don't you give me the thirty-thousand-foot view of the situation?"

Nicholas nodded and turned back to his computers. Moving his little fingers across the keyboard, he brought up a series of images on the screens around the SCIF. "In the early 1990s, the Chinese watched in utter fascination at how rapidly the United States defeated Saddam Hussein in the first Gulf War.

"They realized that there was absolutely no way they could ever meet the technologically advanced American military on the conventional battlefield and win. They also realized something else. As they studied how the United States had waged its wars, they saw that leaps in technological innovation drove innovation in American military tactics. Not the other way around.

"The Chinese considered this quite a profound discovery and began to embrace the idea that in a China-versus-America conflict, the inferior China could beat the superior United States. In fact, China's defense minister, General Chi Haotian, even stated that war with the U.S. was inevitable and that China would not be able to avoid it. He posited that the key issue for the Chinese armed forces was going to be controlling the initiative, or how the war would be fought. It would all come down to how each side approached waging war. China knew exactly what their plan would be. Their blueprint became known as *unrestricted warfare*.

"The first and most important rule of unrestricted warfare is that there are no rules. Nothing is forbidden. The plan calls for merciless, unconventional out-of-the-box thinking. The key is asymmetrical attacks on every sphere of American life—political, economic, and social.

"Using the ancient martial doctrines of leaders like Sun Tzu, they focused on the time-proven methods of surprise and deception, particularly by weaponizing civilian technologies and employing them without morality, mercy, or limit in order to crush American society."

"What do you mean by *weaponizing* civilian technologies?" asked Harvath.

"What is one of the most important technologies that touches every single home and business in America?" said Nicholas.

Harvath thought about it for a moment and replied, "The Internet."

"You are correct, but the Internet is the second most important. The first is electricity. If electricity were weaponized, meaning an opponent had found a way to use it against the United States, America would be devastated. Without electricity, fuel doesn't get pumped, trucks don't move, food and drugs don't get delivered, the economy comes to a grinding halt. As the economy grinds to a halt, society starts to break apart. Fires don't get extinguished, looting and crime doesn't get stopped, you pick up the phone to dial 911 and there is no dial tone. Soon there are no police, there are no firemen. All there is, is chaos.

"With power grids and power stations so dependent on the Internet, I would argue that losing the Internet to an army of hackers would have the same effect as an enemy turning off our electricity, either through widespread sabotage or with an electromagnetic pulse weapon.

"The Chinese military leaders who developed the unrestricted warfare plan explained that in the realm of low-intensity conflict, the vulnerabilities of the United States actually become exponentially more pronounced. In essence, there are multitudes of things that U.S. citizens believe are harmless that a clever enemy could turn against them and use to cripple them in a heartbeat.

"The blackout of 2003 hit eight U.S. states and parts of Canada. Not only was power generation and delivery affected, but so were the water supply, transportation, communication, industry, and the overall economy. There was also looting. The overall cost was estimated at between seven and ten billion dollars.

"The outage affected more than fifty-five million people and was the second most-widespread electrical blackout in history. And I'll give you one guess who was behind it."

"The Chinese," said Harvath.

Nicholas nodded. "Forensic investigations showed that PLA-sponsored Chinese hackers, or *crackers* as they're referred to, had hacked into a U.S. electrical power system network that controlled distribution to the Northeast and were mapping it. It has been privately alleged that they were leaving behind hidden, malicious software, known as Trojan horses, that could be activated at a later date, specifically in a time of unrestricted warfare, in order to knock American power systems offline. Where it went wrong, supposedly, was that while leaving the Trojans, some cracker or group of crackers accidentally activated theirs, causing the blackout."

"You don't believe that?"

"It's possible that the crackers made a mistake. Subsequent investigations of networks across the United States showed widespread compromise of the nationwide electrical system by the Chinese. Trojans had been planted everywhere."

"If that's true, why didn't the U.S. confront China over it?"

"These kinds of things are very difficult to prove. Senior government and intelligence officials didn't want to rock the boat with China unless they could prove it beyond a doubt."

Harvath shook his head. "People have no idea how dangerous that country is—our politicians included."

"I agree," replied Nicholas. "At least eleven people died because of the blackout, and it contributed to the fall of the Ontario government in a provincial election. And it only lasted a couple of days.

"The impact on national security was just as serious. Without power, critical systems used by the United States to detect illegal border crossings, port landings, and breaches of sensitive sites were all compromised. Even more disturbing was that the blackout was a neon sign for terrorists, if you will, pointing right at one of America's greatest Achilles' heels."

"Makes me wonder if it really was a mistake by the Chinese, or a dry run."

"Indeed. The only way to be sure of your hypothesis is to test it. If the 2003 blackout was a test, it was successful, but it exposed all the Trojans they had planted throughout the U.S. electrical system."

"Unless that was intentional," said Harvath. "If they triggered the 2003 blackout on purpose to see what would happen and how we would respond, they had to have known we'd do a comprehensive analysis of all of our networks to see how badly we'd been penetrated. Maybe they intended for us to find all of those other Trojans. We find them, clean them out, and thank God we got them before they could be activated as well."

Nicholas smiled. "Only what the U.S. discovered and cleaned out was exactly what the Chinese wanted them to discover and clean out. The United States pats itself on the back, stopping its search right there."

"You think there are more?"

"Deeper Trojans in the U.S. electrical network? I think it's a virtual guarantee," said the little man. "In fact, I wouldn't be surprised if the Chinese had actually written programs intended to piggyback off American efforts to rid their power networks of the surface Trojans. The U.S. may very well have unwittingly helped the Chinese burrow deeper, providing China greater access than they could have ever achieved on their own.

"That's the driving philosophy behind unrestricted warfare. It is all about positioning yourself for victory. Why meet your enemy sword to sword, where he is strongest, when you can force him to expose his side, where he is weakest, and strike at him there?"

"Besides weaponizing civilian technologies, what else does the plan call for?" asked Harvath.

Nicholas ran his hand through his short, dark hair. "Slowly influencing the culture with their values via cultural warfare. Influencing American media. Cornering and rigging the markets for things America needs, such as oil and rare earth minerals, through resource warfare. Joining international bodies like the U.N. Security Council and voting against American resolutions and interests as part of international law warfare. Manipulating the value of the dollar and subverting the banking and stock markets via financial warfare. The list is multifaceted and it goes on and on."

"And it includes terrorism."

"Most definitely. You see, while they watched America's mighty military deal with Saddam in the first Gulf War, they also noted the severe difficulties that the same mighty military had in dealing with a low-intensity conflict like Somalia. They noted how effective the U.S. embassy bombings were in Beirut, Kenya, and Tanzania. They noted as well the havoc caused by terrorists in the first World Trade Center bombing in 1993. They noted how Chechen terrorists were able to plague the Russians as Northern Ireland guerillas had done to the British.

"For the Chinese, terrorism became seen as an exceptional weapon to wield against the United States. It can not only cause great physical and economic damage, but it delivers a severe psychological shock to the citizens of the country it is visited upon. If you could somehow harness and focus Islamic terrorism, it would give you a great battlefield advantage. It would also provide camouflage, as you would be using foreign nationals to do your bidding.

"There's an interesting tidbit many people aren't aware of. When the 9/11 attacks happened, we all saw dancing in the streets of the Muslim world. What we didn't see, though, was the sheer exuberance displayed by state-controlled Chinese media. They produced video games, books, and documentaries glorifying the violence and calling it a 'humbling' blow against an arrogant nation.

"Many people also don't know that the Chinese predicted that bin Laden would hit the World Trade Center and that they predicted it three years before it happened. U.S. intelligence also learned that before 9/11, the Chinese military had been providing training to the Afghan Taliban and al Qaeda. The American intelligence apparatus was stunned by this revelation and couldn't figure out why the Chinese were mixing with Islamic terrorists. It all had to do with unrestricted warfare.

"The Chinese wanted to build their own worldwide Islamic terror network that they could unleash against their enemies, particularly the United States, at will. They developed deep ties with the Taliban in order to develop even deeper ties with al Qaeda. Much as they had mapped U.S. electrical networks, they wanted to map existing Islamic terror networks, particularly AQ.

"The Chinese are brilliant students. They have an almost superhuman ability to sublimate their arrogance and approach subjects with a completely open mind. They assume nothing and feel no embarrassment at their lack of knowledge. Not that it would make too much difference if they did. It wouldn't last long. The Chinese are incredibly fast learners.

"Taking their new knowledge, they compare it against what they know of the world and what they have learned from thousands of years of history. Then they slowly begin to put it into play. This is how the Chinese were able to build a terrorism network rivaling al Qaeda."

"Which was headed by Aazim Aleem," said Harvath. "Correct?"

"Exactly. Aazim headed the entire network, but he had no idea that he was working for the Chinese. He believed he was running a branch of al Qaeda, with al Qaeda's full knowledge and support. He had no idea that he was a tool in the unrestricted warfare toolbox."

"But the Chinese lost control of the network."

Nicholas held up his tiny index finger to make a point. "Technically, they didn't lose it. It was *stolen* from them. This is the big mystery we've been dealing with. Who stole the network, and why?"

Harvath was about to pose a new question, when a chime rang and the green light at the SCIF door illuminated. A fraction of a second later there was the hiss of air as the locks released, the door was opened, and in stepped the Old Man.

CHAPTER 36

Reed Carlton walked into the SCIF. He was a tall, fit man in his midsixties with a prominent chin and silver hair.

Harvath stood up and greeted him.

"We got our asses handed to us in Sweden," the Old Man said as he grabbed a chair and wheeled it over. It was late, and he was tired and not in a good mood. "I don't care what it takes. We're going to nuke these bastards. That's the word from on high at DoD as well."

Harvath knew the Old Man was speaking figuratively about nuking the terrorists. It was his term for complete and total victory. *Nuke 'em,* he would often say before Harvath left on assignment.

There were times, though, in anger over the loss of lives, he would suggest nuking the entire Middle East region. The Arabs, he'd rant, were ungovernable and immune to civilization. As international terrorism sprang almost exclusively from the Middle East, and the Middle East refused to curtail it, why not put an end to it once and for all? Why allow a single additional American to be killed by the fanatics? "The last time I checked," he would say, as people who didn't know he was exaggerating listened aghast, "we can still drill through glass."

He didn't mince words, and Harvath admired that about him. He had the type of take-no-prisoners, get-the-job-done, and to-hell-with-political-correctness attitude that the United States needed a lot more of.

Nicholas had a mug in front of him. Picking it up, he looked at Carlton and offered, "Coffee?"

"It's a little late for coffee," the Old Man replied. "Why don't you pour me a glass of wine?"

"Wine?"

"Son, I know every single thing that goes on here," Carlton said.

Nicholas liked being called "son." He turned his eyes to Harvath, who was the closest to the fridge.

Harvath rolled over to it in his chair and withdrew the bottle. Grabbing three cups, he rolled back.

"I thought you didn't want any," said Nicholas, as Harvath poured what was left in the bottle into the three cups.

"Changed my mind," he replied, as he passed out the cups. "It wouldn't be right to let you two drink alone."

Carlton accepted his cup and held it up. "To those who have fallen."

Harvath and Nicholas repeated the toast together and drank from their cups. They then waited for the Old Man to take charge.

"This isn't a book club," he finally said. "You don't need me to kick things off. Just pick up from wherever you were when I walked in."

"Yes, sir," replied Nicholas as he set down his cup and pulled up another image on the closest screen. "As I was explaining, the Chinese had created a sophisticated Islamic terror network as part of their unrestricted warfare plan for the United States, but this network was stolen from them.

"In fact, as best we can tell, it wasn't just the network that was stolen, it was everything."

"Everything? What do you mean, *everything*?" asked Harvath.

Nicholas brought up a satellite photo. "The Chinese military's unrestricted warfare planning took place exclusively at this outpost in Mongolia. The project was so classified, the base didn't even have a name. They referred to it with a three-digit number, *Site 243*.

"As we've learned, the sole purpose of this base was to allow the Chinese to study America and plan their unrestricted warfare package. The operatives there spoke only English, ate only American foods, read American books, watched American TV, played American video games, studied American politics and financial markets, and surfed nothing but American and Western websites. It was as close to America as you could be without leaving China's umbrella.

"The operatives there were steeped in American culture and the American way of thinking. Most of them had previously worked or studied abroad in the U.S. Their job at Site 243 was to study America and to find its weaknesses. Under the supervision of their military handlers, they were then charged with developing the most unusual and devastating attacks they could come up with."

"Attacks from the side," said Harvath.

"Yes," replied Nicholas as he put up another image. "Someone discovered what the Chinese were up to and hired an extremely adept hacker to steal the unrestricted warfare plans. Then they launched an attack on Site 243, making sure no one was left alive and no copy of the plans was left behind. But they didn't stop there.

"Any Chinese military or intelligence officer who had any knowledge of the program, regardless of where he was, was hunted down and killed. Whoever stole the plans wanted to make sure that they had the only copy and that they were the only ones who could activate it."

"But we don't have any idea who stole it or why, do we?" asked Harvath.

Nicholas shook his head. "At this point, no. We have the hacker who helped steal the unrestricted warfare plans. She has been interrogated and is still being held at an offshore site. She claims she never knew the identity of the person or persons who hired her. The interrogators believe she is telling the truth.

"What we were able to get from her, though, is that despite her clients' warning against it, she opened the package she stole. What's more, she copied some of the data onto a separate drive."

"Which you were able to recover," said Harvath.

"And which you tried to sell back to the United States government rather than doing the right thing and turning it over," added Carlton.

Nicholas put up his hands. "I eventually saw the error of my ways and delivered the drive to this organization."

"What was on it?" asked Harvath.

"As you'll recall, you and I spoke while you were in Yemen. Just before—"

Harvath held up his hand. He didn't need to be reminded. The call had come in just before his car and Aazim Aleem had been hit by the RPG.

"What I had shared with you," continued Nicholas, "was that there was some pretty interesting information on that drive. That was how we learned that Aazim had a nephew in London who was a digital courier for him. I also discovered that the drive held some highly encrypted data. From it, we began to get a better handle on what unrestricted warfare was. The problem, though, was there weren't any specifics. I was able to figure out that the recent attacks we had seen in Europe and in Chicago were only a small wave preceding a giant tsunami, and that the tsunami was meant to crush the United States, but that was all. At least I thought it was all, until I came at the encryption from a different angle and found this."

Harvath watched as Nicholas pushed a key and all the screens showed the same image, a map of the United States. A black dot popped up in Chicago, followed by one in New York and one in Los Angeles.

"What are we looking at?"

"Based on what Chase learned inside Aazim's network, we believe we are looking at—"

"Target cities?" interrupted Harvath.

"Exactly. We know Aazim had been in Chicago and that he wanted Chase to handle an attack in New York while he went to oversee one in L.A. We think these represented the first wave."

"First out of how many?"

Nicholas looked at Carlton, who nodded. "See for yourself," said the little man as he pressed another button on his keyboard.

Instantly a dot appeared in Dallas, followed by Houston and Miami. Then Philadelphia had a dot and then Newark and San Francisco. Next came Atlanta, Phoenix, Seattle, and Denver. The dots were multiplying so fast, Harvath couldn't keep track. Some cities had more than one dot.

In addition to major American cities, there were smaller ones, ones not immediately thought of when considering potential terrorist targets. There were dots next to Madison, Wisconsin; Casper, Wyoming; and Wichita, Kansas. Bloomington, Indiana; Hartford, Connecticut; Johnson City, Tennessee; Springfield, Missouri; and Billings, Montana, had also been marked.

"My God," Harvath said. "How many are there?"

"Over two hundred," replied Nicholas.

"Cells?"

"That's what we think. The scope is amazing. But now watch this."

Nicholas pressed another button and Harvath watched as all of the dots changed color.

"Why are they doing that?"

"We think the colors represent the style of attack," said the little man. "You can see Chicago is lit up red, blue, orange, silver, and brown."

"You mean there may have been five different kinds of attacks planned for Chicago?"

"Yes."

"And we only disrupted two?"

"Unfortunately."

Harvath studied the map, looking at the different colors. "Chase was inside the Chicago cell and he only uncovered the suicide bomb and active shooter plots. You think they kept things that compartmentalized? Aazim Aleem had three other types of attack planned for Chicago that Chase never learned about?"

"It's very possible," replied Carlton. "Especially if the actors were working alone and didn't need the support of the overall network. It's the way I'd do it."

Five different attacks was a large number to throw at one city like Chicago, but there were plenty of cities on the map that appeared to have been targeted for multiple attacks. Harvath was looking for some sort of pattern. "Orange dots seem to be pretty randomly dispersed. Any idea what those represent?"

Nicholas leaned back in his chair, took a sip from his cup, and studied the map. "No idea."

"Not even a guess?"

"Guesses are something I've got plenty of. Honestly, orange could be anything. There are orange dots in New York City, San Jose, Dallas, Atlanta, Cincinnati, and a bunch of other locations. Silver and gold seem to be just as random."

"What about purple? I'm only seeing those in a few places. All of them port cities. New York again, Los Angeles, Houston, Seattle."

"We noticed that, too," replied Nicholas, "but those are also major urban centers with large populations, and there might be another factor they have in common that we're not seeing. That's the problem. There's just so much we don't know."

Harvath looked back at the Old Man. "Any other thoughts, if you were behind this?"

Carlton was studying the monitors. "I've been looking at this map until my eyes bleed. Without some additional piece of information, it's nearly impossible to unlock."

"What kind of warning are you giving the cities that do have the dots?"

Carlton shrugged. "The FBI will quietly inform local and state law enforcement of a nonspecific terrorism threat to their jurisdictions and they'll raise their internal alert levels accordingly."

"No mention of this to the public, then?" asked Harvath.

"Not right now. We don't want to tip our hand. If we go public with this, it could speed the attacks up. Whoever is pulling the strings could give the cells the green light."

The Old Man was right, but they couldn't just sit and do nothing. "If this map is accurate," said Harvath, "at least we know the cities where they're planning to strike. How do we filter it down even more?"

Nicholas waved at all of his computer equipment. "I'm doing everything humanly possible. I'm looking for any data points I can find, no matter how small. I'm turning over every single digital rock you can imagine. We're leaving nothing unturned. The ops tempo was already very hot, but with Chase saying he felt something was about to kick off, we've kicked everything on our end into overdrive."

"What about the names Chase gave us? Karami? Sabah? Some Sheikh from Qatar?"

"It's all in the blender. We just have to see what we get out."

Harvath turned to Carlton. "How about any IDs of the cell members Chase took out in the safe house?"

"We're working on that," said the Old Man. "We're also working on seeing if their forensics teams uncovered anything from the apartment building across the street where the explosion happened. For the moment, the Swedes are being very tight-lipped. They suspect the involvement of a foreign intelligence service and until they feel they've figured out who it was, they're not talking with anyone."

"I assumed you would have already helped them out with that."

"It's in the works. Trust me. Subtlety is a delicate art. It requires patience."

"These guys, though, could begin lighting up American cities this morning," replied Harvath. "There's got to be something else we can do."

"What you can do is go home and get some rest," said the Old Man. "I want you ready to move as soon as we do hear something."

Harvath was wiped out. He knew he needed sleep. Draining what was left of his cup, he stood up. "As soon as we hear from Iceland with the medical assessment on Mansoor, I want somebody to call me. They need to start interrogating him as quickly as possible. We have to access his cloud."

"In the meantime," said Carlton, "we're working every other angle we have."

"We still don't have anything on who targeted my car in Yemen with that RPG, though, do we?"

The Old Man shook his head. "No. Not yet."

"Obviously," interjected Nicholas, "someone didn't want the U.S. interrogating Aazim Aleem."

"Obviously," replied Harvath. "Whoever was responsible for having Aazim killed didn't want him revealing either who he worked for or what the scope of his operation was."

"There's one thing that bothers me about all that. Whoever hijacked the unrestricted-warfare plan was running Aazim via whatever cutout the Chinese had established, ostensibly the Sheikh from Qatar. We don't know if the Sheikh is a real person that members of the network have ever met with, or if he's some disembodied figure who only communicates through emails or telephone calls."

"What are you getting at?" asked Harvath.

"I don't think Aazim was taken out to prevent him from revealing who gave him his marching orders. He couldn't give away intelligence he didn't actually possess."

"So then he was targeted to prevent revealing the scope of his operation."

"That's what bothers me," said Nicholas. "You and Chase were sitting at an outdoor café within sight of your car when it exploded. You said the RPG came from a rooftop a block or two away?"

Harvath nodded.

"Why silence Aazim? Why not simply aim the RPG a couple of degrees in the other direction and take out you and Chase at the café? In the ensuing chaos, Aazim could have been released from the trunk and then spirited away, disappearing yet again."

Both Harvath and the Old Man looked at Nicholas. He had made an excellent point. "Don't get me wrong," he added. "I'm sure whoever was running Aazim didn't want him interrogated. But it would have made more sense to kill you. The fact that he's dead means that he either made someone very angry or had outlived his usefulness."

"Or both," said Carlton.

"*Or both,*" agreed Nicholas. "But with Aazim gone, there's definitely tension and uncertainty within the network. I think that's why this Karami character wanted Mansoor brought to Sweden. Maybe he doesn't trust the Sheikh from Qatar. Maybe he wanted to pump Mansoor for as much information as possible. If that's true, then maybe we can find a way to exploit the upheaval and use it to our advantage."

"That's a good idea," replied Harvath as he said good-bye to both of the dogs. "But we're going to need a hell of a lot more intelligence before we can even think of launching an operation like that."

Carlton stood up, placed his hand atop Harvath's shoulder, and guided him toward the door. "Go home and get some rest," he repeated. "I'll call you if anything breaks."

Harvath did as he was told. Retrieving his personal vehicle from the garage, he headed south on I-495 toward home. By the time he hit US-1, all he could think about was a hot shower and falling into bed.

He let the water pound on his body for a good five minutes before turning it off and reaching for a towel. He was too tired to shave.

After cracking the bedroom window, he lay down and closed his eyes. Sleep should have come quickly, but it didn't. Instead, his mind took over and replayed everything that had happened in Sweden, over and over again.

He couldn't escape his feelings of responsibility, the guilt he felt over the deaths of the assaulters. He tried to focus on something else, something positive. He thought about Riley Turner and what she might be doing at the moment.

It worked for a while, but then he was back on the mental rack, his mind torturing him with what-ifs and second-guessing over what had happened. He thought about pouring himself a stiff drink and numbing it all away, but chose instead to lie there and take it.

Finally, two hours later, he drifted off into a fitful sleep. In it, he was haunted by visions of a larger, more gruesome attack he felt sure was about to hit the United States.

CHAPTER 37

Robert Ashford possessed one of the key character flaws necessary to a traitor. He thought he was smarter than everyone else. This allowed the overeducated career bureaucrat to sell out his own country, because he believed he knew what was best for his nation and its people.

Of course, he was being well-paid for his treason, but he rationalized the money away by telling himself that it wasn't about money. This was about right and wrong, and if only England and the rest of the West had stood up and done the right thing, none of what he was doing would have been necessary.

It was this deep-seated belief and growing disenchantment with the direction of the world that had drawn him to James Standing.

Ashford had read all of the billionaire's books. Never had one person been able to put what he was feeling so succinctly into words. Standing was the high priest of a glorious new truth. A majestic ship was about to sail and there would be only so many seats on board. Ashford had no desire to be left behind. In fact, he thought he could be very helpful in bringing about the new dawn that James Standing was going to usher in.

The two had been introduced at a cocktail party given by a mutual acquaintance, an influential member of Parliament. Standing was impressed not only with Ashford's thorough reading of his books, but also with his dedication to his vision of a new world. Slowly, the men's relationship built.

Ashford was a confirmed bachelor and the billionaire had originally thought him gay until he realized the MI5 man was simply a careerist. Entanglements, familial and otherwise, were seen as something that could only slow him down. Without wife, children, or girlfriend, Ashford could work any and all hours without fear of recrimination. With both military and intelligence training, he was the perfect man for the job Standing was creating.

When the billionaire had assured himself that Ashford's loyalty could indeed be purchased and assured, he parted the curtains and drew the man inside. Now, Ashford was trapped. Standing had him and he could never go back.

And despite most of his colleagues' having already retired, Ashford was still in the game. It was all that mattered to him, and he was damn good at it. At least he had been. All of a sudden, though, too many things were not working the way they should.

While he still had no idea what had happened to the sanction of the Hollywood producer, the source of the rest of his operational headaches was easy to pinpoint—*Arabs*.

Ashford was an unrepentant bigot of the highest order. He didn't just dislike, he actually *detested* working with Muslims. In his opinion, Muslims—Arab Muslims in particular—were some of the laziest and most uncreative people he had ever come across. Their zealotry bred myopia and an inability to think for themselves. In his experience, the only thing they were good for was blowing themselves up. He had yet to meet enough clever members of the faith to believe that those possessed of even average intelligence were anything more than an aberration.

He was putting the finishing touches on elevating the next commander in the Aleem network, when Mustafa Karami finally made contact.

He found the email in the draft folder of the account he was about to delete. He quickly copied it into a translation program, and when the Arabic had been translated to English, he read the man's brief account of what had transpired in Uppsala.

Both the safe house and the apartment used for their ops center across the street had been compromised. According to Karami, a team of men posing as professional movers had been behind the attack. The ops center had been detonated, but two men survived. They were both dressed as Swedish Security Service agents.

Karami reported that both he and Sabah had been able to escape to the emergency retreat location, but that he had no idea what had become of the rest of the cell members. At this point, he was standing by, awaiting further instruction.

Ashford took several minutes to compose his reply. He front-loaded the email with what he referred to as "Muslim Mumbo Jumbo"—the blessings of Allah and all of that antiquated nonsense that he felt was a complete and utter waste of time, but was important to maintain the charade of his being the number two to the man who financed the entire network, the mysterious Sheikh from Qatar.

The Chinese had established the fictitious Sheikh as the network's financial benefactor and ultimate authority, who allegedly took his orders directly from the al Qaeda leadership. The mistake the Chinese had made, though, was that they had not perpetrated the myth of the Sheikh much past Aazim Aleem, the operational director of the network. When Ashford had been forced to kill Aazim before he could be interrogated, there was reluctance on the part of Mustafa Karami to take over.

Karami was used to taking orders from Aazim. He had never met the Sheikh and therefore didn't trust him. Ashford had been tempted to cut Karami out of the picture right then and there and simply move to the next commander in the network's hierarchy, but Standing had told him to have patience. Karami had been Aazim's designated successor for a reason. He trusted Karami and recognized him as the most able to take over, should anything ever happen to him. And it had.

Ashford had been extremely fortunate to get to Aazim before Scot Harvath and the Carlton Group could hand him over to the CIA.

As Aazim was a British citizen and Ashford had worked with Harvath and the Carlton Group to stop an Aazim cell from carrying out attacks in London, Carlton had kept him abreast of what was happening, including reading him in on the operation to apprehend Aazim and turn him over to the CIA in Yemen.

But as soon as Aazim had been killed, the information flow stopped. Ashford knew better than to be paranoid. They were closing their ranks and being much tighter with their compartmentalization. It just meant information would be harder to get. They had to believe he had something of value to trade, and an idea had already begun to form in his mind about how to get Reed Carlton to let down his guard and show his cards.

For the time being, though, he needed to focus on Karami. James Standing wanted the silver and gold attacks launched.

Carefully, he typed out the appropriate activation message, translated it, and placed it in the draft folder for Karami.

Logging out of the account, he scrubbed his back trail and shut down his computer.

He did the math in his head and computed when news of the first attacks would hit the wires. At best, there were about sixteen hours before all hell broke loose in the United States.

CHAPTER 38

SOUTHERN CALIFORNIA

Like most in the Special Operations community, retired or otherwise, Hank McBride was incredibly resourceful. He had managed to track down everything on Luke Ralston's list. With Southern California the home to SEAL Teams 1, 3, 5, and 7 under Naval Special Warfare Group One, Hank had probably done it with one phone call, two at the most.

The motorcycle was a red 2007 Yamaha YZF. It was a bit much for

Ralston's taste, but no one gave flashy street bikes a second look in Southern Cal. It was fast and maneuverable, which was what he had asked for. If he needed to weave through traffic or outrun the police, the Yamaha would do the job perfectly. Using a motorcycle also meant that he could wear a full-face helmet and be able to better conceal his identity.

The pistol was a cold "drop piece" that one of Hank's buddies always took with him when he drove down to Mexico. It was a Colt Anaconda with a four-inch barrel, chambered in .44 Magnum. Ralston hadn't expected a revolver, especially from a SEAL, but he was happy to have a firearm, any kind of firearm, and he tucked it into the backpack Hank had given him, along with the other items.

It had been a big gamble meeting Alisa in Manhattan Beach the day before. It was an even bigger gamble traveling up to L.A. now. Broad daylight was not the environment Ralston wanted to operate in, but he'd been given no choice.

Alisa's father had refused to help her unless she told him who the favor was for. She was asking for a very dangerous introduction—one incongruous with the legal dealings of an entertainment attorney. He'd already lost one daughter because he wasn't able to protect her from violent criminal elements. He'd be damned if he was going to lose another.

With no choice, Alisa had filled her father in on the entire meeting she'd had with Ralston. Martin Sevan wasn't happy. He told her he'd have to think about the favor Ralston wanted the Sevan family to do for him.

Two hours later, Martin called Alisa back and told her to have Ralston come and see him the next day at noon. Ralston had no idea if the man was going to help him or not, but the fact that he had asked him to come to the house and not the office was a good sign, and Ralston had decided to go prepared.

He arrived two hours early. After driving by the front of the house and not seeing anything that gave him cause for concern, he found a place to park his bike and then secreted himself in a ravine along the side of the house. He had a perfect vantage point from which to surveil Martin's property as well as that of his immediate neighbors.

Ralston didn't know how much animosity, if any, Ava's father harbored toward him over her death. For all he knew, the man despised him and was planning to set him up and hand him over to the police. He had to accept that as a possibility. He could very well be walking into a trap. From his vantage point, though, the only people he had seen in or near the house were the gardener and the housekeeper, both of whom he had met before. That was it.

At a quarter to twelve, a black Aston Martin Rapide pulled into the driveway and stopped near the entrance to the house. Ralston watched as Martin Sevan exited the vehicle, retrieved his briefcase from the backseat, and walked inside. His movements were calm and unhurried. He didn't glance around furtively as if trying to pick out nearby police spotters who might be poorly hidden and who could give the entire sting away. He looked like any businessman who might have come home for lunch. *So far, so good*, thought Ralston.

He decided to remain in the ravine a little while longer. Five minutes later, a white Acura pulled into the driveway and parked right behind Martin's Aston Martin.

From behind the wheel, a heavyset, middle-aged man wearing a dark suit climbed out of the car. Unlike Sevan, this man was a bundle of nervous energy. He was visibly uncomfortable. He took a long, slow glance around his immediate area before turning toward the house. Walking up to the front door, he depressed the button for the bell and waited to be admitted. Ralston didn't know what to make of the man. He was definitely jumpy about something.

At five minutes after twelve, having seen no further activity, Ralston decided he needed to make a decision. Actually, he needed to make a move. The decision had already been made. He hadn't come all this way just to turn around and leave. He had no idea who the second man in the house was, but he assumed he would soon find out. With no police surveillance that he could detect, he had no choice but to make his way inside.

He looped around the back of the house. Skirting the swimming pool, he found the patio doors unlocked. Martin Sevan and the man in the dark suit were sitting in Sevan's home office waiting for him.

"Hello, Marty," Ralston said as he stepped into the room.

Sevan was in his late fifties. He was short, but powerfully built. His black hair was slicked back and he had the same penetrating green eyes as his daughters. He had removed his suit coat and his shirtsleeves were rolled halfway up his thick forearms. It was the first time the two men had seen each other since the trial. "Hello, Luke," Sevan responded. "How've you been?"

"I've been better," he replied, knowing that lawyers never asked a question they didn't know the answer to.

Sevan didn't bother responding. Instead, he introduced the man in the dark suit. "Luke, I'd like you to meet Aleksey Lavrov. Aleksey, this is Luke."

Ralston shook the man's hand and Sevan invited them to sit. "Anybody need a drink?" he asked as he poured himself one.

"Yes, please," said Lavrov. His English was heavily accented. The collar of his shirt was too tight and fleshy rolls of fat spilled over the top. Despite having put on a suit, presumably for the meeting, he hadn't managed to get the knot of his tie all the way up and his top button showed by about a half-inch. He was sweating and his narrow eyes purposefully avoided Ralston's gaze.

"Luke?" Sevan asked. "Something for you?"

"No thanks, Marty."

Sevan poured a drink for himself and one for Lavrov and then took a seat behind his large desk while the other two men sat in upholstered chairs on the other side facing him. "So?" he said, drawing the word out.

Ralston remained quiet. This was Marty's show and he was going to run it any way he saw fit. Ralston just hoped that having Lavrov present meant that he had the information he needed.

"I made a couple of phone calls on your behalf, Luke," Sevan stated. "The LAPD are very interested in speaking with you."

"We'll get around to talking sooner or later."

"I'm sure you will. What about Mr. Salomon?"

"What about him?" asked Ralston.

"Is he okay? Unharmed?"

"He's a little shaken up, as you might imagine, but he's doing okay, all things considered. Why?"

Sevan pursed his lower lip as he shook his head. "Just making sure, that's all."

"I told Alisa he was okay."

"She told me you did."

"So why are you asking?"

"Because, Luke, I'm a litigator. A big part of what I do is reading people. I wanted to hear you say it. Or more important, *see* you say it."

Ralston didn't like being put under the microscope, but it was he who had come asking for the favor, so he bit his tongue. "Larry Salomon is alive and well."

"You know one of the theories that the LAPD detectives are pursuing is that you kidnapped Salomon," stated Sevan.

"Well, that's a pretty stupid theory."

"Is it?"

"For crying out loud, Marty. If I was going to kidnap Larry Salomon, I would have been a lot more creative and wouldn't have left calling cards with my name on them all over his house and property," replied Ralston.

"Reasonable or not, it's one of their theories. They definitely have you pegged as the person who did all of the killing."

"*All* the killing? Two of Larry Salomon's associates were already dead when I entered the house. If I hadn't done what I had, Larry would have been killed as well."

Sevan put up his hands and with a wry smile said, "Don't shoot. I'm just the messenger."

Ralston wondered if he was being played with and decided to get to the point. "Alisa tells me you can help."

"Interesting. All I told her was that you shouldn't have asked her for that kind of favor. I explained that if you wanted something like that, you'd have to come to me."

Sevan *was* playing with him. "Well, here I am, Marty. You didn't need me to come all the way up here, especially with the police and God knows who else looking for me. You could have told Alisa to tell me to go to hell. But you didn't. You wanted me to come see you. Therefore, I can only assume you wanted to tell me to go to hell in person, or you want to help me. Which one is it? Are you going to help me?"

"Let me ask you a question instead," replied the attorney. "What would you have done if you knew, beyond a shadow of a doubt, that those two scumbag drug dealers were the ones in the alley that night. What if you knew beyond a shadow of a doubt that they had been the ones who had killed Ava. Would you have testified then?"

"No."

Sevan arched his eyebrows. "*No?* Why not?"

"If I could have positively identified the people in that alley, they never would have made it to trial. I would have killed them both myself," said Ralston.

The attorney smiled at the man in the dark suit, Lavrov, as if to say, *Be careful with me, I know dangerous people.* He then turned his focus back to Ralston. "You still sound very passionate. Almost genuine."

"Fuck you, Marty. I didn't come here to take your crap. If you want to hold me responsible for what happened to Ava, if you want to blame me—after all you know I tried to do for her—then at least have the guts to say so. But don't you dare impugn my integrity and question how I felt about her and still feel about the people who did that to her. Don't you fucking do that."

Sevan sat quietly, as did Lavrov, who was being made very uncomfortable by what he was hearing. Finally, Sevan said, "What if I told you, you were right?"

"Right about what?"

"Right about the men in the alley that night. What if I told you that I had tracked down the men responsible for murdering Ava?"

"I'd say you're lying."

"Why would you say that?"

"Because," replied Ralston, "if you'd found them, you'd have already turned them in to the police."

Sevan opened the drawer in front of him and removed an envelope. Slowly, he slid it halfway across the desk.

"What's this?"

"The names and addresses of the two men who murdered Ava."

Ralston looked at him. "And you've just been sitting on this information?"

"Let's say I've been trying to decide what the *right* thing is to do with it."

Was Sevan nuts? Talking about taking out Ava's killers in front of Lavrov?

The attorney seemed to be reading his mind. "Mr. Lavrov is trustworthy. Don't worry about him."

"You don't want this on your conscience, Marty. Give whatever you have to the police."

"Even if it means Ava's killers only get life in prison, or worse, walk free?"

"Marty, you're an attorney, for God's sake. You'd throw that all out the window for revenge? All of this?" Ralston asked, looking around the luxuriously appointed office. "Your family already lost Ava; they couldn't stand to lose you, too. Don't be a fucking idiot, Marty. Whoever's names are in that envelope, give them to the cops. You may hate my guts, but one day you'll thank me. Sometimes, revenge is a dish that's better never served."

Sevan looked at Lavrov. "I told you, didn't I?"

"Told him what?" said Ralston.

Sevan shoved the envelope the rest of the way across the desk so that it came to rest in front of Ralston. "Open it."

Ralston was tempted, but at the same time he knew that if he read what was inside that envelope and those people ended up dead, he'd be one of the prime suspects. Having Lavrov witness the entire thing just gave him a bad feeling. "Not interested."

Sevan's eyebrows arched again. "I think you should open it."

Ralston leaned back in his chair. His body language was answer enough.

The attorney looked at Lavrov and said, "You open it."

Lavrov glanced at Ralston and then leaned forward and timidly retrieved the envelope.

The man's fat fingers approached the flap of the envelope as if he were handling the repository of some historic document.

"Hurry up, already," Sevan prodded.

Lavrov did as he was told. He removed a single, folded sheet of paper. Setting the envelope on the desk, he unfolded the page and turned it around so Ralston could see.

CHAPTER 39

Any question that Martin Sevan had called him to the house to do anything but mess with him was immediately put to rest. The piece of paper Lavrov held up was completely blank.

"Fuck you, Marty," Ralston said as he grabbed his backpack and stood up.

He was halfway to the door before he heard Sevan say, "Get back in here. You passed."

"I what?" he said, turning angrily to face the attorney.

"You heard me. I said, *passed*. Now get back over here and sit down."

"Up yours, Marty."

Sevan nodded. "Yeah, you're pissed off. I get it. Now stop acting like a little girl and sit down. We've got a lot to go over."

"Is this some big game to you, Marty?"

The attorney's face was as serious as Ralston could ever remember having seen it. "This is *not* a game. This is my career. Hell, this is my life and my family's lives. You think I'm just going to hand over the kind of information you asked for without knowing if I can trust you?"

"What does trusting me have to do with anything?"

"Luke, do I look like I'm stupid? Larry Salomon is your meal ticket in this town. Nobody likes when somebody messes with their rice bowl. Understand?"

Ralston was following him, but didn't know exactly where he was trying to go with it.

Sevan shook his head. "This town robs people of their souls. I needed to know that you hadn't sold yours. I needed to know that you were still the kind of guy who would do the right thing."

Now Ralston really was confused. "Wait a second," he said. "That's what I did at the trial and you hate my guts for it."

"*Hate*'s a very strong word."

"Don't bullshit me, Marty. Your entire family wrote me off after I refused to testify against those two guys."

"It was a tough time for our family."

Ralston looked right into the man's eyes. "Yeah? Well, at least you all had each other. I had nobody. I loved Ava and still miss her to the point that it hurts. Worse than that, I have to live with always wondering what would have happened if I had only gotten to her faster. Or what would have happened if I had told the producer I was working with at the time that he could fire me, but I had to take Ava away for her own good?"

"What do you want me to say?" asked Sevan.

"Frankly, Marty, I don't give a damn. I loved Ava. I know you did, too, but your family circled the wagons and I was left out in the cold. I get it. I was just Ava's boyfriend. You didn't owe me anything and I didn't expect anything."

The attorney looked at him. "We could have handled things better. I'm sorry that we didn't."

An apology? That had been the last thing Ralston had been expecting. He didn't know how to respond, and Sevan seemed to sense that.

"It wasn't right. We wanted, no strike that, we *needed* someone to blame for Ava's death, and when those two animals walked free from that courtroom, we focused our anger on you. I think all of us in time realized that was the wrong thing to do, but you were essentially out of our lives and our pride kept us from seeking you out."

"L.A.'s a pretty small town, Marty."

"We just wanted to put all of it behind us. It was easier to just let it go. Picking at a scab doesn't help it heal."

Ralston shook his head. "Scab. Nice analogy."

Sevan tilted his head to the side and raised his palms. "The fact is that I have a chance to try to make things right and that's why I've asked you here." Gesturing to Lavrov, he added, "That's why I've asked both of you here."

Ralston retook his seat and turned his attention to the overweight man in the dark suit. He didn't say a word. He simply set his backpack down at his feet, kept one eye on the window, and waited for the man to speak.

Lavrov looked at Sevan. When the attorney nodded, Lavrov turned his eyes back to Ralston and said clearly and evenly, "I think I know who sent the Spetsnaz soldiers to kill your friend."

CHAPTER 40

Ralston didn't know Aleksey Lavrov from a hole in the ground. Informants could be notoriously unreliable, especially somebody else's. They liked settling scores by turning parties against each other. That Marty Sevan vouched for the guy didn't mean Lavrov was without an alternative agenda. Until he was sure, Ralston knew enough to play his cards close to his vest.

Ever the exceptional reader of people, Sevan noted Ralston's reticence and said, "Before we proceed, it would probably be helpful if Aleksey gave you a bit of background on himself."

"Yes, that would be helpful," Ralston replied.

The attorney gestured to Lavrov, as if he were coaching him for trial, and nodded for him to speak.

The husky man reached for his cocktail and took a long sip before setting it back on the coaster. After drying his mouth with the back of his meaty hand, he cleared his throat and said, "I work with the FBI's Los Angeles field office. I am a naturalized American citizen, but Russian by birth. I work in the office's Russian organized crime task force."

Ralston's eyes flicked to Sevan. What was he getting him into?

"Don't worry," the attorney said. "Aleksey is an *informant* for the task force. He's not an agent."

"I am one of the FBI's sources within the Russian community," Lavrov clarified.

"And what's your connection to Mr. Lavrov?" asked Ralston.

"I'm his attorney," said Sevan. "I actually arranged his relationship with the FBI's Los Angeles field office, in exchange for dropping certain charges that had been brought against Aleksey."

"And he owed you a favor."

"Aleksey is a very smart man who realizes that it pays to have a good lawyer. Right, Aleksey?"

The heavyset man nodded.

Ralston looked at the Russian warily. "So what do you have for me, Aleksey?"

"Mr. Sevan explained to me that you think the men who tried to kill your friend, Mr. Salomon, were Russian. More specifically, Russian Spetsnaz. Correct?"

"Correct."

Lavrov rubbed his chin. "Please. I am not being disrespectful, but many American people watch movies and think every Russian is Spetsnaz."

Ralston looked at him. "Mr. Sevan did not explain to you who I am, did he?"

"He told me you work in movies. That you make sure people

understand how to shoot guns and drive cars. I assume then that you are a stuntman. Correct?"

"You're partially correct," Ralston replied, glad Sevan had not told the man everything about his past. "I am a technical consultant on films. Before that, I was in the U.S. military. I have worked with Russian Spetsnaz before."

"Then you must have been someone very important in the military. Russian Spetsnaz are not easy to kill. They are very difficult to kill. Even regular Russians are not easy to kill, but you killed four Spetsnaz?"

Ralston didn't want to get into details with Lavrov. "You will have to take my word for it, Aleksey."

"You are sure that these men were not Russian mafia, maybe?"

"One of the men had a tattoo right here," he said, pointing under his arm. "It was his blood type, in Cyrillic."

"This is Spetsnaz," Lavrov relented. "You are correct."

"So who in Los Angeles would have been able to coordinate a Spetsnaz hit team?"

The Russian thought about the question for a moment. "You would be looking at someone with experience within the Russian intelligence services. The FSB, or what used to be called KGB. Same people, same mentality, same game plan. Only the name is different. I can think of three men."

Three? Ralston thought. He was going to have his work cut out for him. "I'll need names, addresses, and what kind of security they may have."

Lavrov held up his hand. "One of the men has been in Russia visiting family since the beginning of the summer. Another man is very old and lives in a nursing home. I don't think these are the men you want."

"Why not?"

"Besides one being out of the country and the other needing a nurse to feed him?"

Ralston knew that the Italian Mafia often ran operations long-distance and that some of their most senior members were also their most dangerous. The line about old age and treachery popped into his mind. "Yes," he said. "Besides age and proximity, why should I discount those two?"

"The first man, the one who is on vacation in Russia, he was KGB Ninth Directorate. He operated the Moscow VIP subway. The man in the nursing home was in the Fifth Directorate. He dealt with censorship of writers and filmmakers. I still find it ironic that he ended up retiring in Hollywood."

Lavrov raised good points. "Tell me about the third man," said Ralston.

"His name is Yaroslav Yatsko. Former Russian FSB and current Russian organized crime figure here in Los Angeles."

"What was his position with the FSB?"

"He was with the First Chief Directorate of the KGB, actually. He specialized in foreign espionage and stayed on through the transition from KGB to FSB. From what I understand, he continued with foreign espionage activities before moving to California."

Ralston had to wonder what the hell was wrong with the American government that they let these kinds of people into the United States. "What's he doing now? What kinds of things is he involved with?"

Lavrov shrugged. "Extortion, stock fraud, antiquities scams, identity theft, credit card fraud, money laundering, counterfeiting, human trafficking from Mexico, arms dealing, and film piracy. Take your pick."

"What about murder for hire?"

"Violence and murder are the *sine quibus non* of Russian organized crime," offered Sevan. "Without those two ingredients, there would be no Russian organized crime."

"Yaroslav Yatsko," said Lavrov, "keeps a very quiet, low profile. He hides behind multiple legitimate businesses in order to justify his income and comfortable lifestyle."

"But is he known to carry out murders for hire?" repeated Ralston.

"Specifically? No. But it is rumored throughout the community that he has facilitated several high-profile assassinations in Mexico. Allegedly, he has carried these attacks out on behalf of warring cartels, politicians, and business leaders."

"That's Mexico. I'm talking about here. What about in the U.S.?"

Lavrov shook his head.

"Then I'll want the address of that nursing home, too. It looks like I'm going to be busy."

"That might not be necessary," replied Sevan.

"Why not?"

"Because of the Mexico rumors," said Lavrov.

"What about them?"

"Most of the victims had exceptional security. They had bodyguards, alarm systems, dogs; all of the things you would expect of the wealthy and powerful, especially in a Third World country like Mexico. Supposedly, that is Yaroslav Yatsko's claim to fame. He can get around anyone's security."

"And how did he do that?"

"By eschewing local talent and bringing in his own people from Russia," said Lavrov. "He is known for only using the best. He only hires Spetsnaz."

CHAPTER 41

NORTHERN VIRGINIA

If his cell phone hadn't rung, Harvath could have easily slept another several hours. Fumbling for the device on his nightstand, he activated the call and brought the phone to his ear. "Harvath," he said, looking for his watch to see what time it was.

"Scot?" asked a woman's voice on the other end. "It's Riley. Did I wake you up?"

"No," he lied, sitting up in bed and trying to focus. "I'm still trying to beat back the jet lag. What's up?"

"I owe you an apology."

"For what?"

"For Massachusetts."

Harvath knew who she was talking about, but not what. "I don't understand."

"His condition. Remember when I told you the Tasers weren't designed for what you wanted to do?" she said.

"But it worked."

"It did, but I thought it was just dumb luck, or maybe the hand of God, I don't know, but I wasn't ready to believe you could restart someone's heart with a Taser—no matter how many times you zapped him. Well, we've been running tests here and it turns out that our patient has something called WPW or Wolff-Parkinson-White syndrome. It has to do with having an extra, abnormal electrical pathway in the heart. Symptoms often don't appear until people are in their teens or early twenties. It can cause rapid heartbeat and in more serious cases sudden death."

"So what's his prognosis?"

"We've performed a catheter-based procedure known as ablation. It should correct the problem."

"That's great news," said Harvath, and he meant it. They were overdue. "Does he have any brain damage?"

"Not so far as we can tell."

"When will you be able to restart the interrogations?"

"Soon," she replied.

"How's Chase?"

"All things considered, pretty good. The bullet did chip his humerus, though."

"Impossible, Chase doesn't have a humorous bone in his body."

"Very funny."

Harvath liked flirting with her and could picture her rolling her eyes. "He's going to live, though, right?"

"First, this wasn't a life-threatening injury," said Riley. "In fact, I think your duct tape field dressing posed more of a risk to him than anything else."

"Most doctors think my duct tape bandages are cool."

"Those doctors probably had nurses to assist them. Your duct tape idea may be clever, but it's a pain to remove, especially for the patient."

"He's a big boy, trust me. He tells me all the time. You didn't hurt him."

"You asked about his injury," she replied, trying to steer the conversation back to where it had been. "There appears to be a little wrist drop due to some radial nerve injury, but if he does the requisite physical therapy, everything should be fine."

"What do you mean by *wrist drop*?"

Riley took a breath and then said, "He's a bit limp-wristed."

Harvath laughed. "Please tell me that's how you'll write it up for his medical file."

"It's not funny."

"Yeah, it is. That file follows you for life."

She ignored him. "Anyway, I thought you'd want the update."

"I appreciate it. Thank you."

"I guess that's it, then."

Harvath was picturing her in his mind and didn't want to let her go just yet. He liked the sound of her voice. "Who's going to head up the interrogation once it gets started?" he asked, hoping to extend their conversation a little bit longer.

"I haven't seen them yet," said Riley, "but apparently the Agency flew in a couple of specialists last night. They're ready to go as soon as the medical team gives the all-clear."

"They're good people. Some of the best. They'll do a good job."

"They couldn't be any worse," she said.

"Than who?" asked Harvath.

"Chase."

"*Chase?* What are you talking about?" asked Harvath. "He tried to start the interrogation already?"

"No, but he asked if I had access to ketamine."

"Horse tranquilizer?"

"That's one of its uses. In humans it's highly hallucinogenic. Chase showed me a pair of special-effects contact lenses he had with him that could make a person's eyes look like the devil. He wanted to pump the patient full of ketamine and freak the hell out of him in hopes of getting him to talk."

Harvath laughed again. "I guess that's one way of doing it."

"You would actually endorse that kind of thing?"

"For some backwater Taliban member living in a cave in Waziristan, maybe, but not for this patient. I think Chase was just pulling your leg."

"I might be inclined to believe you if he didn't actually own a pair of those contacts," replied Riley.

"He's young and aggressive. He'll learn."

"In the meantime, I'm not letting him near the ketamine."

"Probably a good idea," said Harvath, who sensed their conversation was winding down.

"I've got to get back. I'll call you if I learn anything new."

"I appreciate it. Thanks for keeping me in the loop."

"Sure thing," she replied. "Stay safe."

"You, too," he answered and then disconnected the call and set the phone back on his nightstand.

She didn't have to call him. She could have had the Old Man or even Chase do it. He was glad that she had contacted him personally.

Harvath sat there propped up in bed and debated whether he should try to grab some more sleep. Though the quality of what he'd been able to get so far was marginal at best, he'd still been out for ten hours. What he needed now was some exercise.

Getting out of bed, he got dressed in a pair of shorts and an Atomic Dog T-shirt. A creature of habit, he tucked a loaded Taurus 9mm Slim semiautomatic into a belly band and headed downstairs.

He bypassed the coffeemaker and grabbed a bottle of water from the fridge. After hydrating, he pulled on his running shoes and stepped outside. It was a perfect day, sunny and with a light breeze.

His house was a small, renovated eighteenth-century stone church known as Bishop's Gate that stood on several acres of land overlooking the Potomac River, just south of George Washington's Mount Vernon estate. During the Revolutionary War, the Anglican reverend of Bishop's Gate had been an outspoken loyalist who had provided sanctuary and aid to British spies. As a result, the colonial army had attacked the church, inflicting grave damage.

It lay in ruins until 1882, when the Office of Naval Intelligence, or ONI, was established to seek out and report on the enormous post–Civil War explosion in technological capabilities of other foreign navies. Several covert ONI agent training centers were established up and down the eastern seaboard to instruct Naval attachés and military affairs officers on the collection of intelligence and the finer aspects of espionage.

Because of its isolated yet prime location not far from Washington, D.C., Bishop's Gate was secretly rebuilt and became the ONI's first covert officer training school. As the oldest continuously operating intelligence service in the nation, the ONI eventually outgrew Bishop's Gate. The stubby yet elegant church with its stone rectory was relegated to "mothball" status.

The Navy had many such properties in its inventory, but the majority of those suitable for use as dwellings were reserved for high-level defectors and other displaced political personages the United States government found itself responsible for.

Regardless of a property's status, if it fell within the U.S. Navy's portfolio, the U.S. Navy was responsible for maintaining it. With so many properties to look after, maintenance and carrying costs were quite high. This, coupled with the fact that Harvath, a U.S. Navy SEAL, had shown exemplary service to the nation, played a large role in the secretary of the Navy's agreeing to a special arrangement suggested by the former president of the United States.

The church building and the attached rectory, which had been converted into a nice-sized house, came to more than four thousand square feet of living space. Those structures, along with a garage, an outbuilding, and the extensive grounds of Bishop's Gate, had been deeded to Harvath in a ninety-nine-year lease. Per the lease he was to pay a token rent of one U.S. dollar per annum. All that was required of him was that he maintain the property in a manner befitting its historic status and that he vacate the premises within twenty-four hours if ever given notice, with or without cause, by the United States Navy.

While Harvath had gone above and beyond for the president, he had still been stunned to be extended such a generous offer.

On his first visit, while exploring the rectory attic, he found a beautifully hand-carved piece of wood. Upon it was the motto of the Anglican missionaries. It seemed strangely fitting for the career Harvath had pursued. TRANSIENS ADIUVANOS, it read. *I go overseas to give help.* At that moment, he had known he was home.

That was several years ago, and now he couldn't imagine living anywhere else.

Standing on his front steps, he stretched each of his legs. He had decided on a short run, just up to Mount Vernon and back. Once his muscles were warm, he started his jog.

Exercise always had a way of clearing his head and making him feel more energized. Today was no exception. He didn't think about work at all. He thought about the things he needed to get done around his house. He thought about getting out on the Potomac and doing a little sailing. He also thought about what kind of ruse he could run to get Riley Turner to D.C. for a visit.

A few miles later, at the entrance to Mount Vernon, he turned around, picked up his pace, and ran back. When he returned to the bottom of his driveway, he stopped and walked the rest of the way to the house, allowing his body to cool down. It had been a good workout and the endorphins were racing through his body.

Passing through the kitchen, he ignored the coffee machine again and headed upstairs for a quick shower. When he was finished, he threw the temperature selector to the coldest setting and forced himself to remain under the ice-cold water for a full thirty seconds. It was better than three shots of espresso.

He toweled off and shaved at the sink. When he was done shaving, he walked into his bedroom and grabbed a pair of jeans and a shirt from his closet. It had been a while since he'd had time all to himself to do whatever he wanted. The last couple of months had been a blur.

Because it was Saturday, there were plenty of people Harvath could have called to meet for drinks, but traffic in and out of D.C. would be a nightmare. He also had a policy of not going out for the first couple of nights after getting back from an operation. He knew himself well enough to know that he might feel good now, but in an hour or two he could be ready to crash again. He'd be better company on another night. Besides, sometimes he enjoyed spending the evening alone.

With his fridge all but empty, cooking wasn't an option. Grabbing his keys, he headed outside and hopped into his truck.

Twenty minutes and two stops later, he had returned with a six-pack of beer and a bag of barbecue from Johnny Mac's Rib Shack.

Parking the car, he breezed through the house long enough to drop four of the beers in the fridge, kick off his shoes, and grab a roll of paper towels before heading down to his dock.

It was officially fall, but northern Virginia was enjoying a nice Indian summer. Having been on the road so much, Harvath was grateful to be enjoying at least a small piece of it.

Walking to the end of his pier, he sat down and leaned against one of the posts. Out on the water, there were plenty of boaters getting a head start on their weekend and enjoying what was left of the quickly fading daylight.

Harvath opened one of the beers and took a long sip. He'd made the right choice by staying in tonight. Right now, there wasn't any place he'd rather be than sitting right there looking out over the Potomac. No matter how often he traveled or how long he was gone, when he thought about home, this was what he thought about, a couple of beers and his pier. This was the one place in the world where he always felt the most relaxed. It was the one place where he seemed to be able to leave his problems, at least most of them, back on the shore.

Taking another drink, he watched as a boat passed by, pulling a young skier in a wetsuit. Inside the boat, Mom, Dad, and a sibling cheered. Harvath smiled. It reminded him not only of why he did what he did, but also of what he hoped to have for himself at some point in time.

Reaching into his bag from Johnny Mac's, he pulled out a barbecued pork sandwich and tore a paper towel from the roll. As he watched the sky begin to turn orange, he figured the evening was just about perfect. The only thing that could have made it better was having someone else there to share it with him. For the moment, he was happy to take what he had been given. He knew all too well that perfect moments had a way of getting shattered.

CHAPTER 42

DES MOINES, IOWA

The Century Theater multiplex in Jordan Creek was the perfect place to see your very first movie. They had twenty screens, stadium seating, an arcade area, and even ice cream at the concession counter. Mike Bentley smiled at his wife, Shannon, as their five-year-old twins grabbed their hands and pulled them through the parking lot in hopes of speeding up their parents' pace.

"Mom, you're too slow," complained Trevor.

"C'mon, Dad," said Tyler. "C'mon!"

Just to drive the boys nuts, Mike pretended he had pulled a hamstring and began to limp. The twins cried out in protest. Mike teased them a moment more and then gave in and the family increased their pace.

The closest the twins had ever been to a movie theater was the DVD player in the back of Shannon's minivan. Tonight would be their first real movie theater experience.

It was opening weekend for a new animated family movie that Mike and Shannon had heard great things about. They had read all of the books in the series to the boys and decided this would be the perfect first film experience for them. Mike, an Iowa state trooper, had even arranged to have the night off so they could all go together. Shannon had suggested that maybe an afternoon matinee would be better, but the boys had insisted that *nobody* goes to movies in the daytime. "If you want to see a real movie," they had said, "you have to go when it's dark." In the face of such wonderful child logic, Shannon found she couldn't say no.

The boys had taken a nap that afternoon, and when they came down from their room, their mother and father were bowled over to see that they had dressed up for their evening out. They wore matching khaki trousers, blue blazers, white button-down shirts, and matching, striped clip-on ties. It was so incredibly sweet that Shannon had trouble keeping herself together. Even sweeter was that the boys insisted that their parents get dressed up for the big event as well.

Mike and Shannon complied. When everyone was ready to go, they piled into the minivan and drove to Pizza Hut, the boys' favorite restaurant, for dinner. Everyone commented on how handsome the boys looked. Mike and Shannon were very proud. According to his wife, Mike was actually beaming at one point.

Trevor and Tyler did a great job of not spilling anything on their nice outfits and actually passed on dessert in order to save room for popcorn at the theater.

After paying for the tickets, Mike handed one to each of their sons and allowed them to hand them to the ticket taker, who tore them in half and guided the family to theater number six.

"Anybody want to play some video games before the movie starts?" Mike asked.

Trevor looked at him. "Dad, first we've got to get our popcorn and then we have to get our seats."

"Yeah," said Tyler. "If you don't get your seats early, you have to sit in the front row and you end up with a whole creek in your neck."

"Who told you that?"

"Grandpa," the boys said in unison.

Mike looked at his wife and shook his head. Shannon's father lived with them and the boys never made a move without conferring with him. They'd wanted him to come along with them tonight, but his emphysema had been bugging him and he didn't have the strength to drag his oxygen around with him. Mike loved the man like he was his own father, but he was enjoying its just being the four of them tonight.

"Well, I don't want anybody getting a crick in their neck," he said, winking at Shannon, "so I guess we'd better get our popcorn and hurry up to our seats."

When asked by the concession stand attendant what size popcorn they wanted, the boys each requested an extra-large. Shannon tried to talk them out of it, but they had brought money along from their piggybanks, wanting to help pay for the evening, and they insisted.

"If they don't finish them, they don't finish them," Mike whispered to his wife.

"And if they get sick in the car on the ride home," she replied, "Daddy gets to clean it up."

Mike smiled and gave Shannon a pinch right in the spot that always made her yelp. She laughed and slapped his hand away, then told the boys they could each have their own popcorn bag if they ordered the small. Negotiations began in earnest and Shannon caved, allowing each of the boys to have a medium.

Popcorn and drinks in hand, Mike Bentley led his family toward theater number six. As they walked in, the boys' eyes widened at the enormous space. Despite what Grandpa had said, both of the boys said they wanted to sit in the front row. Though there was no such thing as a bad seat in a modern theater like the Century, Mike was happy when Tyler spotted a group of four seats about halfway up and close to the middle. When it came to seats, he'd always been a middle/middle kind of guy, and he was pleased to see that it was obviously a characteristic passed down on the Y chromosome.

A lot of families had turned out for the movie. The theater was quickly filling up and more families were still pouring in.

The Bentleys settled into their seats and Mike began fielding questions from the boys about all the pre-movie ads playing on the screen. During a lull while something onscreen had captured the boys' attention, he leaned over to Shannon and kissed her. As far as he was concerned, this was just about the perfect evening.

When the lights began to dim, the boys nearly leaped out of their seats, they were so excited. Mike was so focused on his family that he never noticed a North African man carrying a backpack who walked into the darkened theater all by himself and sat four seats away.

CHAPTER 43

Qusay Ali Atwa had been waiting for this moment for years. There were times when he thought he had been forgotten about, but they had told him that that would never happen. He had been instructed to blend into American society as best he could and to wait. He was to pray and maintain his faith. Above all, he was never to reveal, and also never to forget, why he had been sent to America.

In exchange, Qusay's family in Sudan had been well looked after. They received monthly payments that allowed them a much better standard of living than they ever could have realized had he stayed behind in their village. Qusay's standard of living had been considerably improved as well. Even the poorest of the poor in the United

States lived better than the majority of the Islamic world. They had cell phones, air conditioning, flat-screen TVs, satellite service, food, clothing, cars, and shoes. It was all the more reason to hate America. They hoarded the world's wealth and placed man-made law above God's divine law. Qusay had to work every day to conceal his hatred for them.

Des Moines had not been his choice. It had been chosen for him. The winters were unbearably cold. No matter how many layers he wore, he spent nearly half the year chilled to the bone. He was an extremely slim man in his thirties whose appearance reflected the effects of starvation and malnourishment in his youth. His eyes were sunk deep into their sockets and his cheekbones were severely pronounced. The brown skin across his face was drawn taut. His skull appeared misshapen and his twiglike limbs appeared impossibly thin, as if they were ready to snap at any moment.

But despite his outwardly frail appearance, inside Qusay Ali Atwa beat the heart of a warrior. He believed deeply in Allah and the messages he had conveyed through the prophet Mohammed.

As the holy Qur'an instructed, Qusay took neither Jews nor Christians as his friends. He had been taught since childhood that they were perverted transgressors. They were unbelievers, and unbelievers were like panting dogs. They were the vilest of creatures and it was his duty to fight them.

Sometimes, he had to work extra hard to remind himself of these facts. At the poultry-processing plant where he worked, he saw incredible acts of kindness and even love between his coworkers. Such acts had even been directed at him. In inclement weather, he had been offered rides. At holidays, though they knew he was a Muslim, they had invited him to their homes. On one occasion when he had been very sick, several of the women had cooked for him and had dropped the food off at his home. They had even included lists of ingredients for each dish in order to demonstrate that the meals had been prepared with his halal dietary restrictions. He threw all of the food into the garbage.

Qusay consoled himself with multiple verses from the Qur'an that clearly stated that good deeds by unbelievers made no difference in the eyes of Allah. If they refused to submit to Islam, they were destined for the fires of hell. There was no redemption for them.

The Qur'an was also clear that people of religions other than Islam were to be violently punished not only in the afterlife, but in the here and now. Non-Muslims were to be fought with every tool available until there was no other religion but Islam. It was Qusay's duty to pursue the unbelievers, to seize them wherever they could be found and slay them. Allah was strict in his punishment and Qusay accepted willingly his fate in carrying it out.

When he received the phone call, he was very excited. He was told to put his affairs in order. He was told how soon before the attack to make his martyrdom video and what to do with it. His handler cautioned him not to speak about his assignment with anyone, lest the infidels discover their plan. Qusay took every word seriously and followed the instructions to the letter.

He selected the materials just as he had been taught, breaking up the purchases among several stores so as not to attract attention. They were readily available, everyday items, and no one gave any of them, or him, a second thought.

Back in his apartment, Qusay combined the ingredients and assembled his package just as he had been shown. He had been told to start detaching himself from this world and to begin thinking of what awaited him in Paradise. Two days before he was to carry out his assignment, he received a package in the mail. It was a small vial of pills sent from a supposed Internet pharmacy. He was instructed how and when to take the pills and was told they would help make his assignment easier, as he would be more relaxed.

Finally, it was explained to Qusay one last time what would happen to his family if he did not successfully carry out his operation. He understood, and he vowed that he would not fail. The only thing he wished was that he could have contacted them one last time. He would have liked to have spoken with his father and his two brothers. To his disappointment, it was strictly forbidden. Qusay could only hope that they would be proud of him.

He prayed and took strength reading from the holy Qur'an before leaving. In the theater parking lot, he removed the orange vial from his pocket and consumed the last of the pills. Twenty minutes later, he purchased his ticket and entered the multiplex.

The lights had already been dimmed when he entered the extremely crowded theater number six and took one of the last remaining seats. To his relief, no one seemed to notice him, or the backpack he was carrying. Placing it at his feet, he sat back and silently prayed, trying to remember not to nod or move his lips, as he had been told law enforcement officers had been trained to look for such cues, as they indicated that a shahid was about to martyr himself.

As far as Qusay could tell, though, there were no police officers present in the theater. It was nothing but families; mostly mothers with young children, though there were a handful of fathers scattered about. One in particular, with two blond boys, had turned several minutes into the film and looked at him. He had then turned and looked at him twice more.

Despite the calming effect the drugs were supposed to have, Qusay grew more apprehensive each time the man turned and looked at him. He was worried that somehow, the man had divined his intent. But if that was so, why hadn't the man done anything? Qusay decided it was foolish to wait any longer.

He readied his package just as the man looked at him a fourth time and stood up from his seat. "Mike, what are you doing?" a woman said, but the man ignored her.

Moving to the end of his row and stepping out into the aisle, the man pointed at Qusay and gestured for him to get up. Qusay stared at him, his heart racing.

The man removed a badge of some sort, held it up, and gestured once more for him to get up and step into the aisle. All around them, people were beginning to pay attention to the unfolding spectacle rather than the movie.

"You," ordered the man, as he swept his sport coat back and placed his right hand on the butt of a pistol holstered at his hip. "Iowa state trooper. Put your hands where I can see them."

At this point, Qusay could feel all eyes in the theater on him. He thought of his family and smiled.

As Mike Bentley drew his pistol, Qusay Ali Atwa detonated his backpack.

CHAPTER 44

NORTHERN VIRGINIA

W hen the light had completely gone and Harvath had finished his meal, he left the dock and headed back up to his house. Sooner or later, the Old Man was going to want his written report. Tonight seemed as good a time as any.

Grabbing his laptop from the safe in his office, Harvath powered it up and made himself comfortable at his desk. Normally, his dog would have been sitting right underneath his feet, but he'd been away so much he'd left him with friends.

Harvath spent the next several hours working on his report. Reed Carlton was a detail person and never complained that Harvath's summaries were too long. That was fine by Harvath, he was a detail guy as well and he found that the deeper into detail he went, the better he was able to wrap his head around what had gone right, what had gone wrong, and what needed to happen going forward.

He had begun his narrative in the aftermath of the Yemen operation and moved forward. Halfway through, he knew he wasn't going to be able to sleep until he had written everything down, so he got up and went into the kitchen to brew a pot of coffee. Carrying an extra-large mug back to his desk, he sat down at his laptop and picked up right where he had left off.

As he wrote, he became increasingly confident that Karami, the Uppsala cell leader, was still in Sweden. Leaving the country after what had happened would have been too risky. His network might be able to get him out by boat, but they'd have to wait until the heat died down. Harvath made note of it in his report and also made a mental note to bring it up with the Old Man.

From there, Harvath moved on to a moment-by-moment breakdown of everything that had happened leading up to the explosion. Chase was undoubtedly working on a similar report for his superiors, and Harvath made an additional note to get a copy of it to see if it would help fill in any of his blanks.

Soon, he found himself speculating about what had gone wrong. It wasn't easy reliving the blast and envisioning the deaths of Schiller and his team, but it was necessary. Harvath put his ego aside and was completely candid about where he felt he had failed and how he believed the terrorists had been able to gain the upper hand.

Harvath was focused on being brutally honest regarding his possible failings in the assignment. Men under his command had died and he owed it to them and their families to try to ferret out every single detail, no matter how damaging it might be to him, in order to make sure that such a thing never happened again.

He was so focused on this part of his report that he didn't at first hear his cell phone vibrating on the credenza behind him. When he did finally notice it, he reached for it without looking and raised the device to his ear.

"Harvath," he said absentmindedly, as he finished typing his sentence with his free hand.

"Do you have the TV on?" asked the Old Man.

Harvath was no longer focused on his report. "No. Why?" he asked, reaching for the remote and turning on the TV in his office. "What's going on?"

"We just got hit. Simultaneous attacks in multiple cities across the country."

"What were the targets?" he asked as he flipped to the channel he wanted.

"Movie theaters. Multiple bombings in at least twenty of them."

Harvath had one of the cable news networks up on his TV and he could see live footage of fire trucks and ambulances outside a theater complex in Oregon.

"The death toll is predicted to be in the thousands."

Harvath feared the Old Man was right. On a Saturday night, many theaters would be packed. "Do we know anything about the bombers?"

"The FBI has taken the lead and they're already on the ground at several of the sites. I've got a call in to a contact there and he's going to share whatever they find."

Harvath watched as footage from other movie theater bombings was fed onto the screen. There was no one word to describe the feeling that was rushing through him. It was eerily reminiscent of how he had felt on 9/11. It was a mixture of pure rage and a haunting, guilt-ridden feeling of responsibility. It was his job and the job of others like him to stop things like this. It was their job as sheepdogs to keep the wolves away from the flock. They had failed. Though they needed to be right 24/7, 365 days a year, the terrorists had to be right only once. It was only a matter of time.

Nevertheless, that didn't make Harvath feel any better about what was unfolding right now on TV screens across the country. Somehow the wolves had snuck one past—a big one. Thousands of people were dead. There was no telling at this point how many more were injured. The sheepdogs had just chalked up a major loss.

"Do we have any idea who was behind this?" he asked.

"Not at this point," said Carlton, "but I think we should assume it's our network."

If that turned out to be true, then Chase was spot-on about their going operational. "What can I do?"

"Moonracer thinks he may have something. How soon can you get to the office?"

Harvath looked at his watch. "I can be there in an hour."

"Hurry up," replied the Old Man. "If this is our network, this is just a warm-up. They're going to try to hit us again and I want to make sure they don't succeed."

CHAPTER 45

Even though he was contracted to the DoD, Harvath and his organization technically didn't exist. That meant he couldn't barrel up to Reston under lights and klaxon. He didn't even have them.

Instead, he had to apply a lead foot and hope he didn't get pulled over along the way.

The traffic wasn't as heavy as it would have been only an hour before, but it was still rough. Harvath shot from lane to lane, ticking off a lot of other drivers, many of whom leaned on their horns and gave him the finger. The fact that he was driving a brand-new black Chevy Tahoe made no difference. If you didn't have lights or a klaxon, you were the same as everybody else. He tried to not let his own stress and animosity get the better of him. Nobody knew who he was. To them he was an overly aggressive driver.

As he tore his way up to Reston, Harvath listened to the reports of death and destruction coming in on his satellite radio. It was horrific. One thing was for sure, Mansoor Aleem's interrogation would be kicking off momentarily. There was no way the CIA was going to allow this attack to stand. The president and the director of national intelligence were probably already rattling the cage of the director of central intelligence. Every single law enforcement and intelligence agency was calling its personnel in right now. It was all hands on deck.

Just then, Harvath saw a set of red and blue flashing lights racing up behind him. He cursed out loud as he prepared to be pulled over. But as the lights grew closer, they suddenly swung over onto the shoulder.

Harvath had no idea to whom the blacked-out Suburban belonged. It was probably some Fed racing back to D.C. in response to the attack. Harvath decided to take advantage of his lead, and he swung onto the shoulder as well and slammed down his accelerator in order to catch up and ride his bumper.

At Springfield, the Suburban took the Capital Beltway toward D.C. and Harvath weaved back into traffic as he kept going toward Reston.

In the twenty minutes it took him to make it the rest of the way to the office, he counted no fewer than seventeen vehicles, complete with flashing lights, headed in the opposite direction toward D.C.

Pulling into the garage, he grabbed the first parking space he could find and made his way to the service door and the private freight elevator beyond.

The first thing he noticed when he stepped onto the twenty-fifth floor was that the guards at the entrance to the Carlton Group had been doubled and they were no longer in suits. They were outfitted in full tactical gear, with knee-to-cranium Crye Precision level IV ballistic protection, and toting MP7s. The company's security protocols were very specific. A terrorist attack on U.S. soil automatically kicked their alert level up several notches.

Harvath was buzzed in and was told the Old Man was in the Tactical Operations Center, also known as the TOC.

It was a high-tech command post outfitted with computers and video monitors used for guiding tactical teams during an operation. Right now, all of the monitors were tuned to different news channels. Each screen showcased the carnage from the bombings across the country.

"The death toll is already over three thousand," said Carlton as Harvath entered the TOC. Shaking his head, he motioned for Harvath to follow.

They left the TOC and joined Nicholas in his SCIF. The dogs barely stirred as the two men entered. There'd probably been a lot of activity over the last couple of hours and they were growing used to people coming and going.

"We should have been able to stop this," said Nicholas. "We weren't fast enough."

"Even if we had known about this specific attack, there's no guarantee we could have stopped it in time," said Carlton.

Harvath reached into Nicholas's fridge and pulled out an energy drink. "How does this stack up against your map of dots?"

Nicholas made a couple of clicks with his mouse and brought up a map of the United States. "These are the cities and towns where theater attacks have been confirmed," he said, as the locations popped up from coast to coast. He next overlaid the terrorist map with different-colored dots all around the country.

He then deactivated all of the dots except for one color and said, "We now know what kind of attack silver represents."

"Silver screens," replied Harvath. "How many years have we been worrying about an attack like this?"

"Too many," said the Old Man.

"Wait a second," interjected Nicholas. "You knew an attack like this was coming?"

Harvath shook his head. "Al Qaeda in particular likes symbolic targets. The film industry has always been a deep concern for the United States."

"So why didn't the government do anything?"

"Like what? Ring every theater with tanks?"

"Why not search people as they go in?"

"If we did that, where would it end?" said Harvath. "Grocery stores? Buses? Libraries?"

"It would be better than nothing."

"The government didn't just sit by," Carlton explained. "They've been working closely with the movie industry for years. The last thing Hollywood wanted to do was suggest that theaters were unsafe."

"But they *were* unsafe."

"Up till now, they were completely safe."

"Now, they'll be completely out of business," said Harvath. "The quintessential American experience of sitting with strangers in the dark watching a story unfold on the big screen is over. Nobody will go back to a theater after this."

"People went back to flying after 9/11."

"Largely because they had to," said Carlton. "I agree with Scot. This will be different."

"If you own any stock in Netflix," replied Harvath, "it just went through the roof."

They all studied the map up on the monitor in silence for a moment.

"What do we know about the identities of the bombers?" Harvath asked. "Anything?"

"The FBI has already pulled the security footage from all of the theaters that had cameras," said Carlton. "It appears to have been a mix of Middle Eastern men, eighteen to thirty-five, and Africans of the same age range from Somalia or possibly Sudan. All of them carried backpacks into the theaters."

"Any names? Anything we can cross-reference?"

"One. Ayman Hasan Shafik. Police in Albuquerque were reviewing CCTV footage with the FBI from their theater that got bombed and they recognized him immediately. Apparently, he had been involved in several domestic-abuse calls. Each time, though, his wife refused to press charges."

Harvath shook his head.

"Shafik was a naturalized U.S. citizen. Originally from Egypt," said Carlton. "I'll let Nicholas fill you in on the rest."

The little man turned halfway around in his chair to look at Harvath. "Ever heard of TIP?"

Harvath shook his head.

"TIP," continued Nicholas, "is short for Total Intelligence Paradigm. It's something a Finnish company has built and it's absolutely amazing. Not only can it search any database, but it looks for patterns, and as it does, it actually learns and thinks, using artificial intelligence. It searches medical records, military records, utility bills, phone traffic patterns, bank accounts, Facebook usage, Twitter, emails, online purchases, credit card usage, voter registration, you name it. It is so sophisticated, it can access much older, antiquated databases without having to write new programming to access it. Essentially it can read blind, out-of-date data.

"The most amazing part is that it doesn't just spit out a list of items attached to the name you give it. It develops an entire profile and from there builds a relationship tree of the people associated with your subject."

"And the Finns gave you access to this?"

"Not exactly," said Nicholas. "But that's beside the point. What's important is that we were able to enter Ayman Hasan Shafik's name and then watch what TIP came back with."

"Which was what?" said Harvath.

"Fifteen years ago, Shafik arrived in the United States on the same Egypt Air flight as a man named Mohammed Fahad Nazif."

"That thing pulls up fifteen-year-old flight manifests?"

Nicholas nodded.

"So who's Nazif?"

"According to TIP, Nazif is a suspect in a highly classified FBI investigation."

"Wait a second," replied Harvath. "How does TIP know about a highly classified FBI investigation?"

Nicholas exhaled the air from his lungs and shook his head. He glanced at Carlton before responding. When the Old Man signaled his approval, the little man began to speak. What he had to say wasn't good. In fact, it was very, very bad.

CHAPTER 46

"Up until TIP," said Nicholas, "the gold standard in intelligence software belonged to the United States. An American company called Inslaw manufactured the premier collection, case management, and analysis system, called PROMIS, Prosecutor's Management Information System.

"It was the precursor to TIP and operated 24/7 looking for nexuses and correlations between people, places, and organizations. It's brilliantly adept at accessing proprietary corporate databases like those of banks, credit card companies, and electric, water, and gas utilities. Running complex algorithms, it built amazing relationship trees outlining exactly who knows or who interacts with whom.

"For example, if you were the subject of an investigation and you started using more water or electricity, it would suspect you had people staying with you. It would then search through all your phone records and emails, looking for any of your contacts that had suddenly stopped or reduced their usage of specific utilities, and suggest that they might be the ones at your house. This would be backed up with credit card transactions showing train or plane ticket purchases, gasoline, et cetera.

"PROMIS would then focus on these people and pull up all of their records, searching for any criminal history, mentions of them in previous investigations, and any and all hints of a conspiracy that might exist between you two and what it might entail. It was like the Terminator. It never slept. It never stopped. And the U.S. was all too happy to share this software with its allied intelligence partners.

"I say *all too happy*, because the U.S. had built a backdoor into the system. This door allowed the U.S. to monitor everything the other intelligence agencies were doing with the program and provided Uncle Sam with the same data that foreign intelligence agencies were accumulating.

"Interestingly enough, the Israelis—who conduct relentless espionage against their supposed ally and benefactor, the United States—had also been able to build a trapdoor into the system before America offered it to its intelligence partners. The trapdoor provided the Mossad with a treasure trove of information on Jordanian intelligence operations, in particular their vast dossiers on problematic Palestinians.

"Copies of PROMIS wound up on the black market, and intelligence agencies and governments around the world began using it to track and kill dissidents. The system was incredibly effective and became known as the *perfect* killing machine.

"PROMIS could tell an intelligence officer or a military commander that a certain dissident had been spotted in a particular part of the country and had taken a bus or train to another location where the dissident spent the night at a particular person's house. It didn't matter if that person traveled under a false name or not; age, height, hair, eye color, and any other distinguishing features could be fed into PROMIS and it would search until it found the person. It succeeded in getting tens of thousands of dissidents killed around the globe.

"In fact, there's an infamous story about an impending miners' strike in South Africa back in the apartheid days. PROMIS helped track down the instigators, all of whom then 'disappeared.' The strike never took place.

"It is easily one of the most incredible and most incredibly dangerous pieces of software ever constructed. At least it was.

"When the Finns discovered the trapdoors in PROMIS, they realized they needed their own system, not one provided by a foreign government with potentially ulterior motives. That's when they started working on TIP and took the process to an entirely new level.

"They kept all the features of PROMIS and then, via true artificial intelligence, went supernova by giving it a fully functioning brain. TIP not only can think, it can *anticipate*. The U.S. is going crazy trying to catch up. That's one of the reasons NSA has partnered with Google. And if you think TIP is scary, wait'll you see what Google is building with all they're learning about human behavior from the millions of Google search queries logged on their system every day."

Harvath didn't doubt it. And while he appreciated any edge he could get in the fight against America's enemies, the damage programs like PROMIS and TIP could wreak in the wrong hands was obvious. "There's really no such thing as privacy anymore, is there?" he said.

"Not in the United States," replied Nicholas. "At some point, remind me to explain the Narus technology to you and the electronic driftnet the NSA has strung out across cyberspace. Suffice it to say that every single email, text message, fax, and phone conversation is being recorded and stored. The problem for the NSA is sifting all that data for what they want. It's like trying to drink from a fire hose. It's one of the big reasons the terrorists are going low-tech. As the Chinese recognized when assembling their unrestricted warfare plans, the U.S. is overdependent on technology. Outwit that technology and you can flummox the world's sole superpower.

"That's what the Finns have done with TIP. The system is so amazing, it has been able to double back on America."

"How many U.S. intelligence agencies has it compromised?" asked Harvath.

"We don't know yet," said Carlton, "but we've alerted the appropriate people on our end."

"Was our group penetrated?"

"Not that we can tell," said Nicholas. "They seemed more interested in the FBI, CIA, NSA, DIA, and other, more high-profile places."

"How long have you had access to TIP?"

"Not long enough."

"Okay, so what's the connection with this guy Shafik in Albuquerque?" asked Harvath, changing gears. "You ran his name through TIP and you came up with the Egypt Air flight manifest. He arrived in the U.S. with another Egyptian named Mohammed Fahad Nazif. Nazif is the subject of an FBI investigation, correct?"

"Correct."

"Why is the FBI interested in Nazif?"

Nicholas clicked his mouse and zoomed in on the map. "Three weeks ago, Mohammed Fahad Nazif blew himself up while rigging the support columns of a downtown Chicago office building with military-grade explosives."

"What?" replied Harvath.

"The building is known as 100 North Riverside Plaza. We believe it was selected as another transportation target because it was built suspended over the Amtrak train tracks."

"So at least one of the dot colors represents transportation?"

"That's what we now think."

"How come we didn't hear about this?" asked Harvath.

"The FBI used local media to put out a cover story about a gas rupture and a minor explosion," said Nicholas. "It happened in the business district late on a Sunday evening. No one, other than Nazif, was injured or killed."

"Even so, we should have been read in."

Carlton shook his head. "You keep forgetting that you're in the private sector. The FBI doesn't have to tell us anything."

It was true. A decade past 9/11, the FBI and the CIA still barely shared any intelligence. To expect either of them to share with a private organization was crazy. "We've got two dead Egyptians, then," said Harvath. "They both originally came into the country on the same flight fifteen years ago and both attempted to carry out terrorist attacks with explosives a few weeks apart. One succeeded and one didn't. Does that about sum it up?"

"Almost," said Nicholas. "They both came into the country on what is known as dual intent visas. One came in on an L-1, the other an H1-B. The exact type of visa isn't important. What is important is that because it was a dual intent visa, they were allowed to apply for a green card while they were working here. Both requests were granted."

"Tell me they were both sponsored by the same employer," said Harvath.

Nicholas shook his head. "Unfortunately, no. They were sponsored by two different companies. What's interesting, though, is that by accessing the Department of State database, we discovered that both men applied for their visas at the U.S. consular office in Cairo within weeks of each other."

"Okay," said Harvath, sensing there was something else.

"After accessing the Immigration and Naturalization Service database, we learned that both men, though living in different parts of the country and working for different companies, used the same law firm to process their green card applications."

"Dual intent visas with an American sponsor would have meant a lot less scrutiny upon arriving in the United States," said Harvath.

"It also meant that they could come and go back to their country of origin if they wanted, without raising significant attention. Essentially, they had a corporation standing behind them, vouching for their authenticity. And because of their visas, they were recognized as aliens of extraordinary ability."

"How many dual intent visa holders were on that flight?"

"Including Shafik and Nazif?" replied Nicholas. "Eight."

"So besides our bombers, there were six others," said Harvath, hopeful that they might be on to something. "How many of the six ended up applying for and being granted a green card or U.S. citizenship?"

Nicholas held up his left index finger. "Only one."

"Another Egyptian?"

Nicholas nodded. "Want to venture a guess about when and where his original visa application was made?"

"Same U.S. consular office and within the same time frame as Shafik and Nazif?"

"He also used the same law firm to apply for his green card."

"That's it," said Harvath. "What do we know about the law firm? Did the same lawyer handle all three green card applications?"

"The firm is based in New York," replied Nicholas. "Though it could be the same attorney farming out the work to associates, a different lawyer was listed on each application. We're trying to get hold of their billing records to see if there is some similarity in how the legal fees were paid."

"Where is our third Egyptian now?"

"Los Angeles. His name is Tariq Sarhan."

"I want everything you can find on him," said Harvath.

"I've already started," said Nicholas as he selected one of his monitors and brought up a multicolored graph.

"What's that?"

"A quick snapshot of utility usage at the home registered to a Mr. Tariq Hafiz Sarhan. According to TIP, he's taken on several houseguests in the last thirty-six hours. Which means either he's got relatives who just dropped in—"

"Or he's planning something," replied Harvath, who then turned to Carlton. "We need to handle this. Just us."

"Meaning?"

"No Feds. No local law enforcement."

"That's not going to sit well. Especially not in the wake of what just happened. We could get our asses handed to us."

"We already have," said Harvath. "Two of our operations have already gone sideways."

Carlton knew he was right. "What do you want to do?"

"Until we know what's going on, we need to be totally off everyone's radar. We limit everything to just you, me, and Nicholas. The operation can't leave this room. We don't even tell DoD if we don't have to. We go Full Black."

The Old Man looked at Nicholas and then back at Harvath. "Okay," he finally said. "Tell us what you're going to need."

CHAPTER 47

The home of Yaroslav Yatsko, the ex-FSB agent, sat in the Hollywood Hills above Sunset Boulevard. It was pink stucco with a small, mosaic-studded swimming pool and hot tub that spilled its warm water into the pool like a waterfall. The landscaping was lush and thick. It was early evening and no one saw Luke Ralston when he magnetized an alarm contact point, jimmied a window in the back, and let himself in.

The house was empty, yet the smell of sour Russian cigarette smoke lingered in the air. Yatsko had been here and, judging by the packed bag sitting at the foot of the bed in the master bedroom, he was planning to come back.

Ralston searched the bag. It included some clothes and a few toiletry items, but that was all. Yatsko appeared to be getting ready to go to ground. There was probably a safe or a cache of some sort in the house with money, a weapon, and maybe even a few fake IDs with matching credit cards. Ralston was going to need some extra cash and he had no problem taking it from some two-bit Russian hood.

Lavrov had made some phone calls, trying to quietly pin down Yatsko's whereabouts. The former FSB man had been seen briefly at several of his businesses, before disappearing for the rest of the afternoon. The man probably had a bunch of loose ends to tie up before falling off the grid. Ralston was glad he had managed to get to the house before the Russian disappeared for good. Now, all he had to do was wait.

After selecting an item from Yatsko's impressive baseball memorabilia collection, Ralston found a seat and made himself comfortable.

Less than two hours later, he heard a car enter the drive and pull around to the garage at the side of the house.

As the garage door went up, Ralston made his way to the window and watched as a black BMW turned around and backed into the garage. Yatsko was alone. That he was backing into his garage made no sense unless it was a security measure of some sort. Ralston stepped into the hallway off the kitchen near the door that led into the garage and made ready to welcome the Russian home.

The BMW rolled into the garage and its ignition was turned off as the garage door descended. Moments later, Ralston heard a door slam shut, followed by footfalls and then a code being punched into an alarm panel in the garage. When the door into the house opened, Ralston waited until the Russian had stepped all the way inside before swinging the bat.

It connected squarely with the Russian's knees, and he screamed in agony as he collapsed to the floor.

Ralston pulled out a pair of plastic restraints from his pocket and quickly zip-tied the man's hands behind his back.

"You're dead," Yatsko yelled through his clenched teeth. He had a thick accent. "I don't know who you are, but you are *dead*!"

"That's right," Ralston said. "You don't know who I am and *you're* the one who's going to be dead if you don't shut your fucking mouth. Where's the safe?"

"That's what this is?" he groaned. "A robbery?"

Ralston kicked him hard in the side. "Where's the safe, asshole?"

"Bedroom."

Despite the man's size, Ralston grabbed him by the collar and dragged him across the wooden floor to a hallway on the other side of the living room.

"Which one?"

"The last one," said Yatsko. "On the left."

Ralston dragged him into the bedroom and let go of him. The walls of the room were lined with fabric-covered panels. An ugly, overly large four-poster bed took up way too much space.

"Where?" demanded Ralston.

"Wherever you go, I'll find you," said the mobster. "I promise you."

"The only thing I want to hear out of you," said Ralston as he cranked the bat back and swung it hard at the man's broken right kneecap, "is where the safe is and how to get into it."

The Russian cried out once more and tears again poured out of his eyes and streamed down his face.

"How about the other knee? Should I hit that one again, too?"

"Behind the wardrobe," the man stammered.

"What's that?"

"The wardrobe," he repeated, his voice quavering. "The safe is behind it."

Ralston pushed the chest out of the way. All that was behind it was one of the ugly fabric panels. Gently, he pushed on it and it popped open upon a set of hidden hinges.

"What's the combination?"

Yatsko gave it to him.

Inside, Ralston found multiple stacks of currency, passports, a portable computer drive, and some jewelry. Pulling a pillowcase off one of the pillows on the bed, he crossed back over to the safe and took everything but the jewelry.

Grabbing Yatsko by the collar again, he dragged him out of the bedroom.

"But I don't have anything else worth stealing!" he implored.

"Shut up."

Ralston dragged the Russian back across the house and into the hallway near the kitchen. He dropped him near the door to the garage.

"Do you want my car?" the mobster asked. "Take it. The keys are in it."

He was trying to negotiate, to offer the intruder something, anything. He had to have sensed that the man had not come just for a robbery.

"Is there fuel in the car?" Ralston asked.

"Yes," Yatsko replied, hopeful.

"Good," replied Ralston as he pulled a roll of duct tape from his backpack, tore off a piece, and placed it over the Russian's mouth. "Because we're going to take a little ride."

Ralston kicked open the garage door and dragged Yatsko over to the rear of the BMW. Popping the trunk, he noticed the mobster's eyes widen. Then he figured out why. Inside was something wrapped in several garbage bags and taped up in the shape of a mummy.

Ralston looked at the Russian lying on the garage floor. "Yaroslav, you piece of shit. What did you do?"

Pulling a knife from his pocket, Ralston sliced through the tape and garbage bags. What he found was what appeared to be a homeless man around Yatsko's height and age. Upon closer inspection, he saw that all of the man's teeth had recently been pulled out and his fingertips had been cut off.

There were several gas cans in the trunk as well. Ralston lifted one and sloshed it around. *Full.*

"Yaroslav," he said, "were you going to set your house or your car on fire with this poor guy's body in it? With no teeth and no fingertips, no one could ever say it wasn't you. In fact, it'd probably look like you got whacked by some competing faction, eh? You are one slippery motherfucker, aren't you?"

Ralston bent over and wrapped the Russian's ankles with duct tape. Pulling him to his feet, he pushed the mobster backward into the trunk, where Yatsko whacked his head against the lid and landed atop the corpse.

Ralston looked down at him and smiled. "At least you'll have company for our ride out to the desert."

After wiping the house clean of his fingerprints, Ralston returned to the garage, climbed into the BMW, and turned the key in the ignition. He'd have to work fast. He had only so many hours of darkness.

CHAPTER 48

T he Pearblossom Highway was an old, undivided two-lane blacktop interspersed with remote homesteads and dirt roads that led out into the Mojave Desert toward Las Vegas. Ralston had worked on a small, independent film in the Mojave years ago and almost missed the turnoff.

The dusty road wasn't marked by anything more than a twisted Joshua tree and a large rock formation that looked like the side of an Indian's face.

The heavy BMW sedan bumped and jolted as it hit numerous potholes and washouts along the way.

Finally, Ralston pulled off the access road into a small clearing ringed by sagebrush and turned off the ignition. Stepping out of the vehicle, he stretched his arms overhead and then leaned from side to side in order to stretch out his sore back.

When he was done, he grabbed his backpack from the backseat, fished out a flashlight, and walked around to the trunk. It was a clear night and the stars in the desert sky were fairly bright, but there were several different species of things Ralston didn't want to step on if he could avoid it.

Popping the lid of the trunk, he clicked on the flashlight and shined it in Yatsko's face. He had a small laceration on his forehead, probably from getting bumped around in the trunk.

"We're here," said Ralston as he pulled the Russian out and let him drop onto the dusty ground.

Yatsko was somewhere in his late sixties or early seventies. He had a broad, flat face that looked as if it had been hit with a shovel. His greasy hair was dyed unnaturally black.

Ralston used the flashlight to get his bearings. Once he figured out where he was going, he propped the Russian against the car and then flipped him over his shoulder. He weighed a ton.

Despite the pain radiating up his spine from his hip, Ralston kept going. He didn't have far to go. The wash was just through the brush beyond the clearing.

When he got there, he set Yatsko on the ground, propping him up in a sitting position. He could see, even through his trousers, that his knees had swollen up like basketballs. He'd thought about bringing the baseball bat along, but had decided against it. He wouldn't need it. All he had to do was tap the guy in the knee with the toe of his shoe and the man would be sent into fits of agony.

The question was, considering the pain he was suffering, would he cooperate? He'd worked with Russians before and had watched them take amazing amounts of punishment. They could be like plow animals.

It was time to find out if Yatsko was going to play ball. Reaching down, Ralston ripped the piece of duct tape from his mouth.

He expected a string of invective to start immediately. It didn't. The Russian was trapped. He knew it and was sizing up his captor.

"You already have the money from my house," he eventually said. "I can get you more. Much more."

"This isn't about money," replied Ralston.

Despite the pain, the former FSB man smiled. "It is always about money."

"How many people during your career in Russia offered you money? Deep in the bowels of the Lubyanka I'll bet there were many."

"Who are you?"

"I'm nobody. Just someone who happened to be in the right place at the wrong time."

Yatsko looked at him, a slow trickle of blood running down the side of his face. "Do I know you?"

"No. You don't know me."

"Then I must know the man who sent you."

Ralston shook his head slowly. "No one sent me."

"Then who are you, damn it," he spat. "Why did you bring me here?"

"First, tell me who the man is in your trunk."

"Who cares? It's none of your business."

Ralston took his flashlight and swung it at the side of the Russian's face. It connected with a sharp crack.

Yatsko saw stars and when the pain receded and his vision returned, he looked up at Ralston and spat two teeth out at him. "Fuck you."

Ralston hit him again, harder. "I've got all night and no place to be."

He waited for the mobster to recover and then repeated his question.

"He's a vagabond," the Russian yelled. "Nothing. No one. Trash."

"Did you kill him?"

"Yes, I killed him."

"Why?" asked Ralston.

"You already know why."

"So you could burn the body and disappear."

Yatsko didn't answer. He didn't need to.

"Tell me who hired you," demanded Ralston.

"Hired me for what?"

Ralston brought his foot down hard on the man's left knee.

"Hired me for what, damn it," the Russian cried out.

"You sent a team of men to kill a friend of mine."

"I don't do killings."

"Bullshit."

"I do lots of other things, but never killings," said Yatsko.

"What the fuck do you call the dead guy in your trunk?"

"That's different."

"Tell me who hired you."

The Russian looked up at him and with a straight face said, "I can't tell you what I don't know."

Ralston was now at the end of his rope. This guy was one of the worst liars he had ever met. It was going to take him all night to beat the truth out of him. He decided to speed things up.

"Don't move," he said, knowing the man couldn't, even if he had wanted to. "I'll be right back."

Leaving Yatsko alone in the wash, he trudged through the sage-brush back to the car.

Moving the corpse out of the way, he removed one of the cans of gasoline and shut the lid of the trunk. Walking around the edge of the clearing, he played his light over the ground. There were empty beer cans and wine bottles, but that wasn't what Ralston was hoping to find. Then, several feet away, he saw it.

Returning to Yatsko, he dropped the tire on the ground next to him and opened the gas can. "I wish I could tell you that I was a patient guy, Yaroslav, but I'm not."

The mobster looked at him, trying to figure out what he was doing.

"I'll bet you've done a lot of bad things in your time, haven't you?"

Yatsko didn't reply.

"Have you ever *necklaced* anybody?"

Ralston waited for the man to respond, but he remained quiet.

"It's a terrible way to die," he said, standing the tire up on its side and filling it with gasoline. He then rolled it forward several feet and back again in order to evenly coat the inside.

Yatsko looked away.

"Legend has it that it began in Africa, but there are some who say it started in Haiti. The Brazilians also lay claim to it—they call it *microon-das*—a play on the word *microwave*. Apparently, it gets pretty hot. But not so hot that you die right away. They say it can take up to twenty minutes."

"Go to hell," said Yatsko.

"I'll let you go first and do some reconnaissance for me," replied Ralston as he lifted the tire.

The Russian squirmed and tried to avoid being ringed, but sitting on his ass with two broken knees in front of him and his arms lashed behind his back, there wasn't much he could do.

The pungent odor of the gasoline filled his nostrils as his captor forced the tire down over his shoulders.

"You sent a team to kill my friend, Yaroslav. Now we're alone in the desert. No one's coming to rescue you. This is going to end very badly. It's up to you."

"I told you to go to hell," he repeated.

Fucking Russians, Ralston thought to himself. "It's certainly not the way I'd want to go," he said, producing a book of matches he'd found back at Yatsko's house. Removing one from the pack, he struck it and leaned forward.

Yatsko turned to face the match and with a puff, blew it out.

Ralston grinned. "You're a funny guy. Last chance," he said as he struck another match and used it to light the entire pack on fire.

He held the flaming pack just above the tire. The Russian could huff and puff all he wanted, but he wouldn't be able to blow them all out. What's more, they were soon going to be too hot to hold on to and Ralston would drop them right onto the gasoline-soaked tire.

The former FSB agent seemed to realize he had no choice. "His name is Ashford," he offered suddenly. "Robert Ashford. He's a British Intelligence officer for MI5."

"MI5?"

"Yes."

It didn't make any sense. Ralston figured the Russian was making it up to save his own skin. He wanted to make sure the man was telling the truth.

He dropped the flaming matchbook into the sand and crushed out the flames with his shoe. "Who were you hired to kill?"

Yatsko looked right at him and without hesitating said, "Larry Salomon, the movie producer, and two other men he was working with."

"Why were you hired?"

"They don't tell me and I don't ask."

"How many men did you send?"

"Four," said the Russian. "One of my men was the driver. He was supposed to wait outside. Three others were brought in from Russia to do the job."

"Brought in by you."

"Yes. Brought in by me."

"And you were hired by someone named Robert Ashford who works for MI5?" said Ralston.

"That's what I told you."

"Why would MI5 want to kill Larry Salomon and a couple of documentary filmmakers?"

"I told you, they don't tell me and I don't ask."

Ralston found the man awfully flip for someone who still might very well get roasted alive. "You didn't think the job was a little strange?"

"You could never do what I do," stated the Russian.

Ralston looked at him.

"You ask too many questions."

Yatsko was really pissing him off. "I believe that you sent that team to Salomon's house," said Ralston. "But I don't believe this has anything to do with MI5."

"I can prove it."

He was negotiating again, but Ralston listened anyway. "How?"

"The portable drive you took from my safe."

"What about it?"

"It has copies of my communications with him," said the Russian.

"Really?" Ralston said sarcastically. "An MI5 operative was that careless. What do you have? Copies of the personal check he scribbled out for the hit?"

"Everyone slips up. Everyone makes mistakes at some point."

"My mistake has been listening to you. I think you're full of shit."

Yatsko shook his head. "When you've been at this game as long as I have, you learn to protect yourself. Listen, you don't want me. I'm just the middleman in all of this. You want Ashford. But to get him, you need what's on that drive. The file is encrypted, though. If you want access to it, you'll need a password."

"Give it to me."

The Russian smiled. "Once I'm safe and away from you, I'll provide you with it."

Ralston turned and began walking back to the car.

"Where are you going?" asked the mobster.

"To find some more matches."

"Cobb 2-2-4-6."

"Say that again," Ralston instructed as he turned and came back.

"Cobb 2-2-4-6. *Cobb* has two b's, as in *Ty Cobb.*"

Without a computer, Ralston had no way to know if the man was telling the truth or not. Bending down, he pried off the tire.

Once it came free, he gave it a shove and rolled it the rest of the way down into the wash.

"So what happens now?" asked Yatsko. "You take my car and make me crawl? I'll eventually need some of that money you took from me."

This guy really did have balls. Ralston looked at him and shook his head. "There's still the matter of the two filmmakers at Salomon's house who your Spetsnaz guys whacked."

The Russian looked at him. "You."

"What about me?"

"You're the one Salomon was at the restaurant with. You drove him home. Who are you?"

"I told you," replied Ralston. "I'm nobody."

"You killed them. Didn't you?"

Ralston didn't respond.

"You're not going to let me walk away from here, are you?"

"You couldn't walk if you wanted to."

"You know what I mean," said the Russian.

"Yeah," said Ralston, pulling out his revolver.

Yatsko's face changed. There was nothing but hate in his eyes. "Fuck you," he yelled. "Fuck you!"

He was about to yell it again, but the sound of Ralston's weapon discharging drowned it out.

Ralston pulled the trigger once for each of the murdered filmmakers, Chip and Jeremy. He then fired a third time for the homeless man in the trunk of the car and kept pulling the trigger until the weapon was empty.

The Russian deserved much worse. He deserved to have been necklaced. Ralston, though, wasn't the kind of man who could torture another man to death, not even one as evil as Yaroslav Yatsko. Ralston was, after all, still a man of principle.

CHAPTER 49

T he house Nicholas had found for Harvath had been fore-closed on and would be going to auction at the end of the month. "It should be coming up on your right," he said over Harvath's earbud.

"I see it," Harvath replied as he rolled past. The house was located in Monterey Park, just east of downtown Los Angeles.

"How's the line of sight?" Nicholas asked from back in Reston.

"I'll let you know in a minute."

Harvath maintained his speed as he passed Tariq Sarhan's house. It was three houses up on the left. Harvath had seen it before arriving by using Google Street View. It was a single-story ranch with a high wooden privacy fence that ran the length of the front. There was no light from inside.

"It's going to be tough," he said to Nicholas once he had driven past. "We're not going to see anything over that fence. Not unless I can plant one of the remote cameras somewhere."

"You've got two with you. You could put one on the front and another on the back."

Harvath looked at his watch. It was already after 4:00 A.M. The sun would be coming up in less than three hours. He didn't want to get near the target house until he had had a chance to study it better. "I think I'd better get set up at my new digs first."

Making a right turn at the end of the street, Harvath drove several blocks over and then doubled back.

Parking around the corner from the house he was going to occupy, he popped his trunk and removed a heavy backpack. Closing the lid, he locked the car and got ready for the hardest part of his entry. He was going to approach the foreclosed property from behind, but to do so he was going to have to cut through four backyards. He prayed none of the homes had dogs.

Slinging the pack over his shoulders, he stepped onto the sidewalk and cut across the lawn of the first house.

There were motion lights near the garage, so he chose to go around the other side. At the gate to the backyard, he stopped and readied his Taser. The last thing he wanted to do was to Tase some poor dog that was just doing its job and protecting its territory, but there was no other way for him to get where he needed to go undetected.

After looking over the fence for any telltale signs of animals, he quietly rattled the gate and waited. Nothing happened. Lifting the latch, he pushed the gate partway open and slipped into the yard. He stayed away from the house, hugging the property line, and moved quickly.

In the far corner, he crouched low, scratched at the fence, and waited. When no dog came to investigate, he boosted himself up and over. He repeated the process two more times until he reached the final fence separating him from the foreclosed property. Fortunately, he hadn't encountered any dogs.

Leaping the final fence, he landed in a backyard untended and overgrown with weeds. He moved rapidly to the rear of the house and peered through a kitchen window. All of the appliances were gone and there was garbage strewn across the floor. At the back door, he removed a lock-pick gun and a thin, spring steel tensioning wrench.

Sliding the tensioning wrench into the lock, he applied pressure and then inserted the pick gun. As he clicked the gun, the pick struck the pins inside the lock and knocked them upward. With each click, he applied a little more pressure to the wrench, causing the plug to catch the top pins. Seconds later, the door was unlocked and Harvath slipped inside.

He did a quick sweep of the first floor. Unoccupied homes that had gone into foreclosure had become frequent targets of squatters.

Looking around, he saw that the house had been absolutely trashed. There were large holes punched through the walls, most of the fix-tures had been stripped out, and it looked as if even the copper pipes had been taken.

Once he was confident that the first floor was clean, he retraced his steps and set up a battery-powered MSensor wireless perimeter security system. If anyone else entered the house, he'd be alerted instantly.

Moving back to the stairs, he headed up to the second floor. There was a small room above the garage that promised to provide the best view of Sarhan's.

The upstairs was in an even worse state of disrepair than the first floor. As Harvath quickly checked out each room to make sure it was unoccupied, he marveled at the damage. He couldn't begin to understand the mind of someone who would strip a house bare and vandalize it so totally on his way out. It was just something he could never picture himself doing.

At the end of the hall, he found the room he was looking for and stepped inside. It wasn't any better than the other rooms on that floor, but it wasn't any worse, and compared to a lot of the hides he had holed up in around the world to do surveillance, this one was pretty nice. It wasn't the Ritz, but there were no bugs and no snakes. Plus, he had a roof over his head. All things considered, he had it pretty good.

Removing the clean cell phone he had brought with him, he texted a quick message back to Nicholas and the Old Man: *I'm in.*

He then took a small headlamp from his pack, affixed a red filter, and slipped it on. The lamp provided just enough light to see by, but not enough to be noticed by anyone from outside.

Unpacking his equipment, he laid it all out methodically on the floor. He had brought everything he thought he might need that would fit in his pack. In addition to the perimeter security system and the two wireless cameras Nicholas had mentioned, there was an infrared-capable digital video camera, infrared-capable still digital camera, a laser microphone, lightweight tripods, a night vision monocular, and several other small pieces of equipment.

He was also carrying a laptop with a filtered screen so it wouldn't give off too much light in the darkened house. It was set up to stream the feeds back to Nicholas's SCIF via cellular network or satellite. Harvath powered it up and was pleased to see the signal was quite good.

The home's previous residents had destroyed everything except the window treatments. Though the ones in this room were old and soiled, Harvath was happy to have them. After turning on his monocular, he balanced it on the base of the window frame and pulled back the curtain partway.

He could see Sarhan's home, but in addition to the privacy fence there was a tree, which blocked a significant portion of the sight line. The laser mic worked by being beamed through a window at something inside, such as a picture on a wall, that would vibrate as people spoke. Harvath could already tell they weren't going to get any audio. And until he figured out whether it was worth the risk to get close enough to the house to plant his two remote cameras, he wasn't going to be getting any decent video either. The only things he had a halfway decent view of were the street and Sarhan's driveway.

Pulling back from the window, he turned off his monocular and assembled the equipment. After everything had been camouflaged and positioned in the window just the way he wanted it, he checked the image quality on his laptop and then began streaming the feeds back to Reston.

He had worked out a shift schedule with Nicholas so that there would always be a set of eyes on the house. In the morning, the little man would covertly reestablish the home's power. They had decided to wait until daylight in case any of the lights had been left on. The last thing they wanted to do was advertise that the home was suddenly occupied.

Sliding a Cliff Bar from his pack, Harvath leaned back against the wall and tried to make himself comfortable. There was no telling how long he would be here.

CHAPTER 50

While it was Nicholas's shift, Harvath closed his eyes and allowed himself to drift off. It was morning and he had been asleep for several hours when his cell phone began vibrating and woke him up.

He popped the earbud in, and his eyes were drawn to the laptop as he activated the call.

"Do you see what I see?" asked Nicholas from the SCIF back in Reston.

"I do now," replied Harvath as he grabbed a pair of binoculars and crawled over to the window. A white passenger van had pulled up in front of Sarhan's house. He read off the license plate number.

"I'm running it now."

Harvath readjusted the laser mic and also activated a small parabolic he had pointed toward the driveway.

Nicholas had an update for him momentarily. "The van is registered to a cardboard box manufacturer in Torrance, California."

"Throw it into the TIP program and see if it connects any dots."

"Roger that."

Harvath had moved to the still camera and was taking pictures of the van. It was hard to make out the driver from this angle. He appeared to be waiting for someone.

Two minutes later, the microphones picked up the sound of Sarhan's door opening. Muted good-byes were exchanged in Arabic before two young Middle Eastern men appeared towing wheely bags.

Harvath snapped several wide shots and then got close-ups of their faces. "Let's run these right away."

"I'm already on it," replied Nicholas.

They were dressed in casual business attire. It reminded him of the airport security footage of the 9/11 attacker Mohammed Atta. He suddenly had a very bad feeling about what he was seeing. "Where are you two girls going?"

The two men placed their heavy bags in the van's cargo area and climbed inside. The driver then pulled away from the curb.

"Can you follow them in the traffic cam system?" asked Harvath.

"Yes."

"You should ping the Old Man and let him know what's going on."

"Already did."

"Good," said Harvath as he watched the van disappear at the end of the street. *What is going on inside that house?* he wondered. Had they just wrapped up some sort of meeting and these two guys were heading home, or was something else going down?

Ten minutes later, the mystery deepened as two more men with luggage exited the house and climbed into a taxi that had just arrived.

Once again, Harvath snapped pictures, and everything was beamed back to Nicholas in Reston.

"We need to follow that taxicab as well. Make sure you get all the information about the cab company and the driver and put it all into TIP."

There was a delay in Nicholas's response as he clicked away at his keyboard. Finally he said, "Scot, I can't sweep data and follow two vehicles."

"Get the Old Man to help you."

"I already am," said Carlton, who had joined Nicholas in the SCIF and had plugged into the call. "We're going to have to open this up a bit."

"No, we've got to keep it contained."

"Scot, I'm making the call. Nicholas will remain in charge on this end, but I'm going to open this up to the personnel in the TOC. We need the manpower."

Harvath knew better than to argue. "Just tell them these are people of interest. They don't need the big picture."

"Agreed," replied the Old Man as he clicked off to activate the office's Tactical Operations Center.

"So far," said Nicholas, "the two vehicles appear to be headed in opposite directions. Maybe they're going to different airports. Or maybe one pair is going to catch a plane and the other a train."

"Or maybe they're doing SDRs," stated Harvath, referring to the surveillance detection routes one used in order to ascertain whether one was being followed. "Just stay on them. They look like they're headed out of town. As soon as we know where, we need to have teams waiting to put them under surveillance."

"The Old Man already has teams standing by."

Harvath was about to say something, when another taxi pulled up and two more men exited the house.

"Are you getting all of this?" asked Harvath as he took still more photographs.

"Yes," replied Nicholas.

The driver popped the trunk, the men placed their wheely bags inside, and after shutting the lid, slid into the backseat, and the vehicle pulled away.

"That makes three two-man teams in less than half an hour," said Harvath, adding, "you still have nothing back on the photographs or the vehicles?"

"All of the vehicles check out. This cab, too."

"Do we have any idea yet where the other two are headed?"

"No," said Nicholas. "I'm starting to believe you may be right about the SDRs."

"Whatever you do, don't lose them," replied Harvath.

Harvath glanced for the thousandth time at the dated picture of Tariq Sarhan he had been issued. All of the men who had left the house were too young to have been him. He still had to be inside, and at this point, there was no question that he was definitely up to something. Harvath decided he couldn't wait any longer to find out what.

He grabbed several extra mags for his compact .45 caliber H&K USP Tactical pistol along with its suppressor. He tucked the pistol into a holster at the small of his back and the rest of the gear into the pockets of his coat.

"I'm going to zero comms," he stated. "I want a closer look at the target."

"A closer look?" replied Nicholas, "or are you going over to take him?"

"If the Old Man asks, tell him you can't raise me. Understood?"

"I don't think that's the right thing to do."

"Lucky for me that—" Harvath cut himself off midsentence.

"Repeat, please," said Nicholas.

"Hold on."

"What's up?"

"I've now got a black Lincoln Town Car approaching," said Harvath, who was at the camera as two more young Middle Eastern men exited the house with wheely bags. They were soon followed, though, by a third.

"Zoom in on the third man, please," said Nicholas.

Harvath didn't need to be told. He zoomed in and began snapping pictures of Tariq Sarhan. "That's our guy," he stated.

"Is he going to get in the car with them?"

"Negative," replied Harvath as he watched Sarhan kiss both of the young men on the cheeks and remain in front of the house as they walked down to the curb.

"I'm running the plates on the Town Car, now."

"Roger that," said Harvath as he watched Sarhan through the camera. "I hope you saved a little cake for me, Tariq, because you and I are going to have a little party of our own."

"The Town Car looks clean. It's registered to a Los Angeles limousine company. Wow, that makes eight guys. He really did have a lot of people in there."

"Now we're going to find out exactly what the hell he's up to," said Harvath. "I'll call you back."

Harvath disconnected the call and stayed at the window. He watched as the Town Car pulled away and Sarhan turned and went back into his house.

After grabbing a roll of duct tape and his Taser, Harvath exited the little room and headed for the stairs. He had no idea if Sarhan was alone or not now, but he had a pretty good feeling that he was.

The man had aged a lot since his photograph had been taken. He was still very thin, but his face was drawn. His hair had gone gray and he wore glasses. He looked more like a university professor than a terrorist, but that didn't mean anything. Harvath would know soon enough what the man's game was.

Having disabled the perimeter security system, he was halfway to the back door when his cell phone vibrated. Unwinding the earbud and placing it in his ear, he activated the call and said, "I told you we were going to zero comms."

"Sarhan's on the move," stated Nicholas.

"What?" replied Harvath. He stopped and thought about returning upstairs to see for himself.

"He just came back out wearing a jacket and opened his garage door."

"Is he alone?"

"As far as I can tell."

Harvath turned around and headed for the front door. "Tell me when you can see his car."

"He's backing out now," said Nicholas. "It looks like a blue Nissan Sentra." He read Harvath the license plate.

"Tell me which direction he goes when he pulls out of the driveway."

"Roger that."

Seconds ticked by. Finally, Nicholas said, "He's coming south. He's going to go right past you."

With the tall hedges in front of the downstairs windows, Harvath knew he'd have a hard time seeing the street. "Let me know when he does."

"Fifteen seconds."

Harvath waited.

"He should be passing you now."

Harvath unlocked and cracked the front door. Sure enough, he heard the sound of Sarhan's car as it passed. He figured it would take him at least ten seconds to get to the end of the street.

Fishing the car keys from his pocket, he said to Nicholas, "You let the TOC handle the other cars. I want you personally tracking Sarhan for me. Got it?"

"I got it," said the little man as he began clicking once again at his keyboard back in Virginia. "What are you going to do?"

There were only two things Harvath could do. He could break into Tariq Sarhan's house, tear it apart, turn it upside down, and see what he found, or he could go after the man himself.

As far as Harvath was concerned, there was only one move that made any sense.

CHAPTER 51

"Come on, Nicholas," Harvath said over his phone. "That car has to be somewhere. It didn't just vanish."

Harvath had stepped out of the house and looked down the street just as Tariq Sarhan had applied his turn indicator and made a right turn. As soon as the car had disappeared from sight, Harvath had taken off running. He reached his rental car about a minute and a half later.

Jumping inside, he started it up and pulled out into the street. At the end of the block, he came to a four-way stop. Nicholas had yet to pick up the blue Sentra on any of the traffic cams.

"I'm still searching," said Nicholas.

Having grown up in Southern California, Harvath knew its freeway systems intimately. Right now, he was inside a sort of rectangle made up of four different freeways—the San Bernardino to his north, the Pomona to his south, the Long Beach Freeway to his west, and the

San Gabriel River Freeway to the east. Sarhan could be headed toward any of them.

"How about the other four vehicles?" he asked, trying to figure out what was going on. "Do we know anything yet about where they're headed?"

"Negative," said Nicholas. "The TOC is tracking them, but they're all headed in different directions."

The longer Harvath sat at the stop sign, the more rapidly his heart began to beat. He tightened his hands around the steering wheel. "Come on, Nicholas," he said again. "Where is he?"

There were several agonizing moments of silence before the little man responded, "Got him. He just made a left turn four blocks in front of you."

"Good job," said Harvath as he stepped on the gas. "Don't lose him."

Sarhan looped around, doubled back, and changed direction multiple times. He even stopped twice for gas. There was absolutely no question that he was trying to figure out if he was being followed. This went on for more than forty-five minutes before it appeared he had finally committed to wherever it was that he was going.

He followed the Pomona to the Santa Monica Freeway and continued west toward the ocean. As Harvath saw signs indicating the intersection for the 405, or the San Diego Freeway as it was known, he wondered if Sarhan would alter his course or keep going toward the ocean. He was staying as far behind the blue Sentra as possible and was forced to endure long stretches where he couldn't even see the vehicle. Fortunately, he hadn't exited and Nicholas had been able to keep relatively good track of him.

The same couldn't be said for the other vehicles. They had lost two out of the four and were scrambling to find them.

"He's changing lanes," Nicholas said over Harvath's cell phone.

They were coming up on a series of choices. Sarhan could remain on the Santa Monica Freeway, or the 10 as it was known, or he could head north or south on the 405. The first ramp was for the 405 south toward San Diego.

"He's in the far left-hand lane now. He's not getting on the 405. At least not southbound."

"Are you sure?" asked Harvath.

"So far. Stand by."

Harvath watched as the exit for the 405 interchange got closer. "What's he doing?"

"He's still in the far left lane. No change. Stand by."

"Standing by."

"It looks like we can safely say—" began Nicholas, who then stopped midsentence and shouted, "South! He just swung across four lanes of traffic. He's taking the 405 south."

"Son of a—" Harvath cursed beneath his breath as he tried to maneuver. He was boxed in and had to slow down dramatically in order to find a gap and change lanes. The traffic was so tight that he almost missed the exit.

Once he had fully merged onto the 405, Sarhan parked himself in the far right-hand lane, and despite how fast the other cars were going, he kept his vehicle at fifty miles an hour.

Harvath was about to ask what the hell the guy was up to, when Nicholas reported that Sarhan was apparently preparing to exit for the Howard Hughes Parkway. Harvath continued to follow at a safe distance.

Moments later, Nicholas said, "The TOC has relocated the two missing vehicles."

"Good," replied Harvath. "Where?"

"Surface streets fifteen and twenty-two miles away, respectively."

"What about the other two?"

"One of them is on the Century Freeway headed west and the other one looks set to join it. It's merging onto the Century from the Harbor Freeway."

Harvath could picture the entire map in his mind's eye and he now knew where they were headed. "Get the Old Man on the line right now."

It was only a matter of seconds, but it felt like minutes to Harvath. Finally Carlton clicked in and said, "What do you have?"

"I know where they're headed."

"Where?"

"LAX," replied Harvath.

The Old Man snapped his fingers at someone, probably indicating he wanted a map of some sort, and said, "Los Angeles International? Are you sure?"

"Unless they're all meeting up for a fishing charter out of Marina Del Rey, that's where they're headed. Sarhan has already gotten off the 405 and any moment is going to start doing his final SDRs on the surface streets that lead to the airport."

"We've got vehicle descriptions, plates, even eyes on. Do you want to alert LAPD and have them stopped before they can get too close to the airport?"

It was a very tough call and one Harvath didn't completely want the responsibility of making. If LAX was a target, the sooner they were stopped, the better. But if it wasn't, if these men were doing nothing more than returning to their cities of operation, then pulling them over would ruin everything. They would know they'd been blown and the one and only lead Harvath and his team had would be lost.

"Scot," the Old Man repeated. "It's up to you. If you want to pull the trigger on these guys, I'll make the call to the LAPD myself."

Harvath knew what they had to do. "No," he replied. "We need to let them go."

"And if the airport is the target?"

"Then they need to be ready. Call DHS and tell them they need to conduct an immediate shift change."

The Old Man understood what Harvath was calling for. When credible threats to U.S. airports were raised, the Department of Homeland Security swapped out regular TSA employees with specially trained, former military Special Operations personnel. They would be dressed exactly the same as the TSA agents, but that's where any similarities ended.

Realizing that air marshals should only handle planes and not airports, a highly secretive and secure training facility had been established near Harper's Ferry, West Virginia. There, counterterrorism exercises were run against a host of realistic airport structures—terminals, baggage claim areas, even an airport hotel. In addition to operators posing as uniformed TSA agents, there was also a highly lethal plainclothes contingent dressed to look like passengers.

When the government wanted to be ready for a threat, but not to broadcast it to the public, and especially not to the bad guys, this was how it was handled. The only problem in this case, though, was the timing.

"There's no way DHS can do a shift change in time," said Carlton.

Harvath caught a glimpse of Sarhan's car as it turned a block ahead of him and replied, "Tell them they don't have a choice."

CHAPTER 52

Harvath's assumption that Sarhan was headed for LAX was confirmed when the man's circuitous route ended with his pulling into the parking structure adjacent to Terminal One.

"Can you tap into any of the garage cameras?" asked Harvath as he sped up.

"It'll take a few minutes," said Nicholas.

"Hurry up," replied Harvath as he swerved around the car in front of him and pinned the accelerator. "I need to know where he is and what he's doing. For all we know, he's going to switch vehicles."

"I'm going as fast as I can."

Instead of entering the parking structure on the upper-deck depar-
tures level like Sarhan, Harvath chose one of the arrival-level entrances.
Snatching his ticket from the dispenser, he pulled in and began
scanning for the blue Nissan.

"Where is he, Nicholas?"

"Stand by. Still waiting for access to the camera system."

Human nature being what it was, most people wanted to park close
to the terminal and have less distance to walk. Harvath easily found a
parking space near the garage exit and parked there. If Sarhan was
planning on driving out of the terminal, he'd have to drive right by
Harvath's vehicle.

No sooner had that thought entered Harvath's mind than he realized
that if Sarhan did have a backup vehicle, it didn't necessarily have to be
in this parking structure. He could easily walk out, hop on the shuttle,
and head to the long-term lot, where he could have another car waiting.
It seemed a bit far-fetched to Harvath, but anything was possible.

"We've got garage video," Nicholas said, interrupting his thoughts.

"Do you see his car?"

"Negative. He may have already parked."

"Are you scanning the parked cars or just the ones that are moving?" asked Harvath.

"Both, but there are only so many cameras. You can't get a perfect
view of every single vehicle."

"Have DHS make sure Sarhan's picture gets to all of the parking lot
attendants at the airport. If anyone sees him, make sure they call it in.
Tell them not to do anything else, but call it in."

"Got it," said Nicholas, whose voice trailed off for a moment as
something caught his eye. "I've also got a blue Nissan Sentra."

"Where?"

"Second floor."

Harvath was already out of his car and heading for the nearest stairwell as Nicholas gave him the precise location of the car.

"Is the license plate a match?" he asked as he opened the stairwell
door.

"I can't see it. I can't even get a partial."

"Is he in the car or has he already gotten out?"

Nicholas took a moment and then replied. "Unless he's taking a nap, the car appears to be empty."

"Find him. Check all the other cameras. Roll back the footage. Do whatever you have to do."

"We're working on accessing the recorded footage now."

"And make sure nobody moves in on Sarhan or any of his people unless I say so," said Harvath.

"That may be a problem."

Harvath was about to open the door to the second level. "What do you mean, *that may be a problem*?"

"DHS told Carlton that they appreciate the tip, but that this is their jurisdiction and we don't have any authority."

"Damn it," he replied. "They're going to mess this whole thing up. Do they know I'm the person in the field?"

"No. Carlton didn't want to reveal that."

Harvath didn't know that it would make any difference. It had been over two years since he'd worked for DHS and there was a completely new secretary in place now. He wouldn't care that some former DHS employee was tracking a team of would-be terrorists. If his people could pinch them before anything happened, he'd rack up truckloads of brownie points with the press, the public, and especially the White House. Harvath should have seen that coming. In the wake of so many successful attacks on U.S. soil, DHS needed a win. Though he wanted to believe they'd do the right thing, too often it was the political thing, the thing that would play well for public relations, that was chosen.

"Did they tell you where they were on the shift change?"

"Negative," said Nicholas.

"Damn it," Harvath repeated as he got ready to open the door. "Tell the Old Man that he needs to find a way to work this out. Somebody, somewhere, owes him a favor. If DHS jumps the gun, they could blow this entire operation."

"I'm sure he's doing everything he can."

Harvath opened the door and stepped onto the second level. "Where are the other vehicles?" he said quietly.

"The first one is about two blocks away."

"Okay, let's keep chatter to a minimum until—"

"Got him," interrupted Nicholas.

"Sarhan? Where?"

"He got out of his vehicle, all right, but he didn't walk toward any of the exits. He walked to the northeast corner of the structure."

"Did he get in another car?" asked Harvath.

"Negative."

"Do you have him on any of the cameras?"

"Negative," replied Nicholas. "Not at present."

"Roger that," said Harvath as he approached the parking stall with the blue Nissan. Checking the plate, he relayed the numbers back to Nicholas.

"That's it."

Harvath slipped his hand into his pocket and withdrew what looked like a threaded screw. It was a tool a spook buddy of his had designed and had given away to his friends in the community as a Christmas present. Foreign intelligence agents overseas had long been known to drive nails or screws into the tires of Americans they suspected of conducting espionage. Harvath's buddy had seen it happen on more than one occasion and had decided to take the tactic to the next level. Employing a pal who was a machinist, he had him fabricate a screw with a hollow shaft and a small opening at the top and the bottom. In essence, it was an inch-long spike that relieved a tire of its air very quickly.

He eyeballed the interior of the vehicle, scanning for any sign of what Sarhan might be up to. "Did he have any bags with him?" he asked.

"Negative," Nicholas replied. "Just what looked like a zippered case for a small laptop or an iPad maybe."

"Keep looking for him."

Choosing the tire he wanted, Harvath leaned over, jabbed in the screw, and kept walking.

If Sarhan hadn't come to catch a flight or to switch vehicles, there was only one other reason, based on what Harvath had seen, for the man to be here. LAX had to be the target.

Four two-man teams had left Sarhan's house and, via intricate SDRs, had taken great pains to make sure they weren't being followed. Despite leaving before Sarhan, he had beaten them to the airport. Any doubt about what was about to happen was fading from Harvath's mind.

Sarhan was the cell controller. He had picked the parking garage at Terminal One as an overwatch position. From the northeast corner of the garage, he could watch as all four teams drove past.

The fact that the men were traveling in pairs also made sense now. It was an insurance policy. Each was there to keep the other committed to the operation. With a two-man team, cowardice could be minimized, if not completely eradicated. If one of the men chickened out, the other would take care of the situation. It was a growing trend in terrorist operations.

Sarhan was there to make sure everything went off as planned. Very likely, he had been instructed to film as much of the carnage as possible so that it could be fed to Al Jazeera, which, in turn, would joyfully broadcast it to the Muslim world. Harvath, though, was determined that none of that was going to happen.

Holding his keys in his hand, he moved past the rows of cars pretending he was looking for his.

"The first of the vehicles just entered the airport," said Nicholas.

"Understood," Harvath replied as he kept walking.

"Did you notice anything off about any of the vehicles?"

"Negative. Why?"

"One of the guys in the TOC thinks that the cab that just pulled in is riding too low."

Harvath had been so preoccupied with Sarhan and the men coming out of his house that he hadn't paid nearly enough attention to the vehicles. "Nobody got out," he said into his earbud's microphone.

"Excuse me?" replied Nicholas.

"The van driver. The taxicab drivers. Even the driver of the Town Car. None of them got out when they picked the men up at Sarhan's."

"So?"

"So it doesn't make sense," said Harvath. "Why didn't they get out and help with the bags?"

"Maybe they were told not to."

"Why?"

Nicholas thought a moment. "Because they don't want anyone else handling the bags?"

"Bingo."

"I just got another IM from the guy in TOC. He really doesn't like that first vehicle. He says it reminds him of VBIEDs he saw in Iraq."

Harvath had seen his share of vehicle-borne improvised explosive devices as well. "Watch where it goes, and tell him to look at the other vehicles. I want to know if he thinks the same thing."

"What are you thinking?" Nicholas asked.

"I'm thinking those guys with the bags go in, explosions happen, and when survivors rush out of the terminals, if those four vehicles are VBIEDs, the survivors get taken out in a secondary attack that's even worse than the first."

"What should we tell DHS?"

It was the right question, but not the one Harvath wanted to have to answer. If they told DHS that they now believed they had four teams of suicide bombers being dropped off by vehicles loaded with explosives, it was game over. They wouldn't wait to see what happened. They'd shut the entire airport down. If Harvath was right, DHS would succeed in saving countless lives. If he was wrong, Sarhan and his men, who could very well be controllers of other cells scattered across the country, would know they had been blown and all those potential leads would evaporate.

The FBI would get involved, but even if they used CIA interrogators, they'd never be able to lean on Sarhan and his men hard enough to get any actionable intelligence out of them. And once the FBI was involved, they'd see to it that the men were afforded every single protection under the law. Nobody would be putting bags over their heads and transporting them to Iceland or one of the other black sites.

Caught on American soil, they'd be handled under criminal court rules and proceedings—that is, if the FBI could come up with enough to even hold them.

It wasn't that Harvath didn't respect the Bureau, he did. It was just better that they didn't get mixed up in this. It was also better, at least at this moment, that DHS not be given any encouragement to pull the trigger prematurely. "Don't tell them anything," he said.

"And if those are VBIEDs?" asked Nicholas.

Harvath could now make out the silhouette of someone standing in the northeast corner. Ducking into a row of parked cars, he crouched and adjusted the side mirror of the vehicle he was leaning against. "Contact," he said quietly into his microphone.

CHAPTER 53

"What's he doing?" asked Nicholas. Watching in a sideview mirror through multiple layers of autoglass, Harvath had a pretty lousy view. "He's leaning against the concrete half-wall with a laptop open."

"What's he doing on the laptop?"

"I think it's a ruse. He's trying to look busy while he watches his teams arrive at the airport."

"Now what?" asked Nicholas.

Harvath knew that the only way anyone was going to get any answers out of Tariq Sarhan, especially quick ones, was if he was asking the questions. The problem was, how the hell would he interrogate him in the middle of a parking garage?

Two vehicles away from Sarhan was a brand-new, white Cadillac Escalade. Harvath described it, gave Nicholas the license number, and said, "How long?"

"Give me three minutes," he replied.

Harvath looked at his watch. "You've got two. Make it happen."

Ninety seconds later, Nicholas said, "The OnStar folks are very sorry to hear you've lost your keys, Mr. Chaffee. Let me know when you want it opened."

"Stand by," said Harvath, as he stepped out from the row of parked cars. Holding the key fob for the vehicle he'd parked downstairs, he proceeded forward.

Sarhan had a pad, pen, and a few papers set up next to his laptop. If anyone had wondered what he was up to, he could have argued that he had just dropped someone off and was filing a quick sales report or was trying to be productive while waiting to pick someone up. What none of them would suspect was that from this vantage point, he was taking advantage of a perfect view of all the traffic coming into the airport.

"Unlock it now," said Harvath as he closed within fifteen feet of Sarhan.

The lights on the Escalade flashed and the locks *thumped* as they popped up. The Egyptian turned, looked at Harvath briefly, and went back to what he was doing.

Harvath ignored him. Walking around to the driver's side, he opened the door and climbed in. Had there been space enough to maneuver, there was nothing he would have rather done than to drive the Escalade right into Sarhan and pin him against the concrete wall. It would have saved him a lot of time.

He listened as Nicholas updated him that the first vehicle had dropped its passengers at the Tom Bradley International Terminal and that two more were also just pulling in. It was time to crash Sarhan's party.

Grabbing the latch, Harvath popped the Escalade's hood and stepped out of the car. As he raised the hood, he looked around to see if anyone other than Sarhan was in the immediate area. Satisfied the coast was momentarily clear, he fiddled with the vehicle's engine and cursed. The Egyptian glanced at him again and then went back to what he was doing. The fact that the Escalade had likely been there before Sarhan arrived ruled Harvath out as a threat to him. There was no way anyone could have known he would set up there.

Harvath stepped away from the truck and closed the distance with the Egyptian so rapidly that he didn't realize what was happening until Harvath was almost on top of him.

Pulling his Taser out of his pocket, Harvath hit the trigger and watched as the expression on Sarhan's face went from surprise to shock to agony—all in a matter of a few seconds. The man's muscles seized and he fell forward.

Harvath worked quickly. After zip-tying Sarhan's hands behind his back, he gathered up his belongings and dragged him back to the Escalade. The rear windows were tinted and that's where Harvath had decided to conduct his interrogation.

Shoving the Egyptian inside, Harvath climbed in behind and told Nicholas to remote-start the vehicle.

He buckled Sarhan into his seat belt, zip-tied his ankles, and then took the seat next to him. When the vehicle started, Harvath reached for the rear seat audio controls and dialed in a local funk radio station. The Escalade was well insulated. In fact, it was built like a bank vault, but Harvath turned up the volume of "Too Hot to Stop" by the Bar-Kays just in case the Egyptian began to scream.

Sarhan didn't, not at first. He also didn't demand to know who Harvath was and what he was doing to him. The first thing he did was spit in Harvath's face. That was all Harvath needed. *Sarhan was guilty*.

Harvath brought his elbow around and smashed the Egyptian's nose. A gush of blood sprayed and Sarhan cried out. Harvath turned up the volume on the radio.

"We know everything, Tariq. *All of it.* I'm only going to give you one chance. How do we recall your men?"

"You can't," the man said with a smile.

Harvath gave him another burst from the Taser.

The Egyptian howled this time as the electricity coursed through his body.

"Tell me, Tariq. The pain only gets worse from here."

"Fuck you," he hissed.

Harvath raised the Taser to give him another jolt. The man's body stiffened in anticipation. Harvath, though, had a better idea. Reaching back down, he depressed the rear cigarette lighter. He saw a flash of fear cut across Sarhan's face. But as quickly as it had appeared, it was gone.

"The fourth vehicle has entered the airport," Nicholas said. "Vehicles two and three have dropped off their passengers at Terminals Two and Four."

"Roger that," replied Harvath.

"I'm not afraid to die," said Sarhan.

Harvath smiled. "I wish I was allowed to kill you. Unfortunately, I can't."

"You can't do anything."

"I wouldn't go that far," he said as the cigarette lighter popped.

"I have rights," the Egyptian stated arrogantly.

"And if I was a policeman I might care. But today isn't your lucky day. You see, I'm not a policeman. Technically, I don't even exist. I promise, though, you're never going to forget who I am." Snatching out the glowing cigarette lighter, Harvath brought it close enough to Sarhan's face to feel the heat radiating off it. "How do we recall your men?"

The Egyptian tried to spit at him again, but Harvath moved out of the way. The projectile of blood and saliva hit the window behind him and rolled down. Harvath was done playing games. Grabbing the man's face in a vise grip, he drove the lighter right into the man's upper lip.

Sarhan screamed bloody murder, but Harvath didn't let go until the smoke stopped rising from the man's seared lip. The smell of burnt flesh filled the SUV.

Dropping the lighter to the floor, he reached under his coat and drew his pistol. He then pulled the suppressor from his coat pocket and began spinning it onto the threaded barrel.

He didn't even give Sarhan a moment to think. Placing the weapon against his knee, he pulled the trigger.

There was a crack as the weapon discharged, and Sarhan set off into a fresh chorus of screams and curses. Harvath brought his elbow up again and slammed it into the man's jaw, causing the Egyptian to bite down on his own tongue.

Reed Carlton's voice suddenly came over Harvath's earbud. "All of the teams are now inside the terminals. What's our play?"

Harvath snatched up Sarhan's cell phone. It had been set to silent and he had received four text messages, each one saying the same thing: *We are in line.*

"Shit," he said aloud as he raised his pistol and placed it right against Sarhan's temple. "I've changed my mind. Tell me how to recall your men, or I am going to kill you."

The Egyptian looked at him and smiled before muttering a final, defiant "Fuck you."

Harvath pulled the weapon back and then brought it crashing down into the side of his head. "Fuck you, too."

"What do we tell DHS?"

Harvath was out of time. They couldn't risk it any further. "Tell them to take them all down."

"Roger that," replied Carlton.

The Old Man's voice was then replaced by Nicholas's. "The Lincoln Town Car just pulled in one floor below you. Our man in the TOC says all of the vehicles are overloaded. He's positive now that they're VBIEDs."

CHAPTER 54

Christie Jacobson wasn't a big fan of flying. It wasn't that she was afraid to fly, she just hated all of the hassles.

Her mother had worked as a TWA stewardess back in the glamour days of airline travel in the 1960s. She could still remember how elegant it was. You always got dressed up to fly. You even got dressed up just to go out to the airport to pick people up.

When she was a little girl, all of the stewardesses had looked to her like princesses or fashion models. They wore tiny hats, white gloves, and perfectly tailored uniforms. They even took your picture with a Polaroid camera and gave it to you as a souvenir. That's how special airline travel was. Things certainly had changed.

Now, airline travel was like bus travel. No one dressed up, the service was lousy, and the entire air of elegance was gone.

Before Christie had changed positions within her company, the experience used to be a bit better. Up until last year, she'd been a very frequent flyer, which meant she was normally upgraded to first class and could check in at the premier counter. She didn't have to stand in an insufferably long line like the one she was in now.

Glancing at her watch, she wondered if she was going to make her flight. There had to be at least sixty people in line in front of her, and only a handful of agents. Despite the automated check-in kiosks, everyone seemed to be having problems and needing help.

Christie looked behind her and saw that the line stretched past the retracta-belts and stanchions and into the terminal. There had to be several hundred travelers. She didn't even want to think about what the security line was going to be like. That was the one thing she hated the most about flying. As a breast cancer survivor, she'd had more than enough radiation to last for two lifetimes. She despised the full-body scanners the TSA had introduced and how when she politely opted out of a scan, she had to be subjected to a full-body pat-down. If the scanners wouldn't have stopped either the shoe bomber or the underwear bomber, she didn't really see the point.

She liked to joke that the friendly skies would be a lot more friendly if everyone was required to fly naked. It was a cute joke; at least she thought so. During pat-downs, though, she'd been warned that joking wasn't such a good idea.

She didn't blame the TSA agents for the security measures. They didn't make policy. They were there to carry it out, and Christie made it a point to thank them every time for working so hard to keep all travelers safe. Like it or not, life had changed because of 9/11.

Considering what had just happened in all those movie theaters across the country, she figured life was about to change again. Would there be pat-downs and screenings at the local multiplex now? Probably. Something would have to be done to demonstrate that America was serious about never letting such an attack happen again.

Christie had stayed up most of the night watching the news coverage in her hotel room. It was incredibly tragic, but she couldn't turn it off. The entire nation was grieving. She'd felt very alone in her hotel as she watched and had called her husband. They'd turned to the same cable channel and had watched the coverage together, though they were thousands of miles apart. She was glad to be going home the next day.

She wanted to hug her husband and her children. She wanted to hold on to them for a long, long time. They were big moviegoers. They loved seeing films the weekend they came out, and as far as they were concerned, there was nothing like the experience of the big screen.

Their theater could have easily been targeted by the terrorists. That seemed to be the message of the attacks. No one was safe. Theaters in big towns and small towns alike had been struck.

And before the news had even confirmed it, she knew who had been behind the attacks. She knew it was al Qaeda. They had promised to return and they had. First it was the train stations in Chicago and now movie theaters. *What was next?* she wondered.

Was she even safe in the airport? She'd noticed the two Middle Eastern businessmen standing several people in front of her. *Could they be terrorists?* She supposed they could, but it just seemed so farfetched. What were the odds she'd get into a line with two terrorists?

Christie chastised herself for having those thoughts. She refused to allow herself to look at every Muslim person as a potential terrorist. They were regular people until shown to be otherwise.

She wondered how many others were having the same thoughts she was having. Muslims of good conscience were going to have to stand and denounce the violence. If they did that, Christie Jacobson would be proud to stand with them.

She tried not to look at the two businessmen. Plenty of other people were probably staring at them and she didn't want to add to their number. In fact, if she were going to look at them at all, it would be with a smile. No matter how many accusatory looks they received today, they'd remember the kind one.

The line shuffled forward and Christie found herself in a position to deliver her encouraging smile. Catching the eyes of one of the men, she smiled and nodded. Immediately, the man's face darkened and he turned his head away.

His friend, though, saw Christie's gesture and nodded curtly. He then turned to the other man and began speaking to him quietly. The man didn't seem to care. He was concentrating on thumbing out a text or an email on his BlackBerry. Christie felt foolish.

She tried to console herself with the notion that maybe it was a cultural difference. Maybe where these men came from, women didn't directly engage them and smile at them. She decided to leave them alone. They didn't have to acknowledge her kindness.

To take her mind off the interminably long and slow-moving line, she scanned the other faces in the crowd. She enjoyed people watching. It was fun imagining people's backgrounds and what their professions might be.

There were plenty who might have been incredibly interesting, but most just kind of looked *blah* and unkempt. The game was more fun to play with unusual-looking people. Though she'd never confess it to her husband, Christie found the game the most fun with unusually *good*-looking people, like the man who was standing several steps back from her.

Because of the way the line wrapped around, they were now facing each other. She tried not to stare, but it was hard. He was *really* good-looking. The man was over six feet with bright blue eyes and one of those taut jawlines that screamed physically fit.

Studying the man, she tried to imagine what his profession might be. He was big enough to have been a professional athlete of some sort. He was probably in his early to mid forties. Bush pilot had a nice ring to it and seemed a good fit.

Not wanting to stare, she had averted her gaze, but as she now risked a glance back at him, she noticed his expression had changed. There was suddenly an intensity to his face that was very unsettling. He was moving away from her. That's when she saw him draw the gun.

"Show me your hands!" he yelled. "Open palms! Away from your body! Do it now!"

It took Christie a moment to realize that he wasn't talking to her, but rather the two Middle Eastern men. Half the people standing in line had dropped to the floor, while the other half were quickly backing away, knocking over the retracta-belts and stanchions.

Intuitively sensing she was in the way, Christie dropped to the floor. No sooner had she hit than she heard the earsplitting thunder of the man's weapon going off.

She looked up to see the head of the man she had smiled at snap backward as a pink mist materialized in the air. All around people were screaming.

She looked at the other Middle Eastern man. His hand looked to be wrapped in a death grip around the handle of his rolling bag.

As the man plunged the handle down, she was reminded of an old-fashioned dynamite detonator box.

If there was any consolation, it was that the explosion was so intense that Christie Jacobson and the others in the terminal never felt any pain.

CHAPTER 55

Harvath had hopped into the Escalade's driver's seat and was halfway down to the ground floor when he heard the explosion. "What the hell just happened?" he demanded.

"One of the bombers detonated," replied Nicholas. "Terminal Two."

"Damn it," he shouted.

"The Lincoln Town Car is on the move."

Harvath accelerated.

"Stop. Stop. Stop," Nicholas ordered. "He's going up."

"Up? Why the hell would he be going up?"

"I don't know."

Harvath threw the big SUV into reverse and stepped on the accelerator. He only made it thirty feet before a car suddenly appeared in his rearview mirror. Slamming on his brakes, he threw the Escalade into drive and raced down the ramp. "I can't get back up this way," he said as Sarhan bounced around in back. "I have to use the up ramp. Watch that Town Car and tell me what he does."

"Will do."

Racing onto the up ramp, Harvath backed off the gas just a bit. If the Town Car was a VBIED as they believed, rolling up on him way too quickly was only going to spook the driver into detonating in the garage. Surely he had heard the explosion as well, and knew that the attack was on. That meant Harvath needed to be doubly careful. One wrong move and it was all over.

"He's just exited the ramp on the third floor," said Nicholas.

Why the third floor? Harvath wondered.

Nicholas had the answer seconds later. "He's going to try to exit onto the upper-deck roadway through the entrance."

"Doesn't it have spikes?"

"If it does, he doesn't seem to care."

Harvath pushed the Escalade faster. He pulled the wheel hard to the side, popped up onto the third floor, and raced for the upper-deck roadway.

Nicholas's voice came over his earbud. "He jumped the curb and took out the ticket machine! The far left lane!"

"Which way did he turn?"

"To the right. He's headed toward Terminal Two!"

Harvath pinned the gas pedal to the floor. "Have all the other bombers in the other terminals been interdicted?"

"Affirmative."

"What about the other VBIEDs?"

"LAPD is trying to move in on them now."

The entire upper deck was going to be crowded with people, especially outside Terminal Two, where the explosion had happened. "Tell LAPD that they can't ram the vehicles," Harvath insisted. "They have to shoot the drivers. Tell TSA to try to get everyone off the sidewalks. Now!"

Harvath had no idea if the other three vehicles had started their run or not. All he knew was that his best option was to get the Town Car. The LAPD would have to get the others. He just hoped they'd all be able to do their jobs on time.

Racing toward the entrance, Harvath could see where the Town Car had made its exit. Hitting the curb at over sixty miles an hour, he applied his brakes and pulled the wheel hard to the right as he shot out of the parking structure.

He came barreling out in the wrong direction and sideswiped two oncoming vehicles. It was a lucky break. If they hadn't been there, he might very well have flipped the Escalade as he spun out of the garage and pulled hard to his right.

Punching the accelerator again, he raced ahead. There was no need to ask Nicholas where the Town Car was headed. It had to be Terminal Two. That was where it was going to do the most damage.

Seconds later, he veered onto the main upper-deck roadway that circled the airport. He could see Terminal Two dead ahead. He could also see the Town Car. There was no way he was going to catch it in time.

He heard the rapid crack of weapons fire as law enforcement officers engaged the Town Car, and Harvath watched in horror as the vehicle headed right for them.

Terrified civilians ran in multiple directions, some even right out into the street, all trying to get away from the danger. Harvath had to swerve to avoid hitting a large group.

No sooner had he regained control of his vehicle than he saw the

Town Car plow into two patrol cars and the team of LAPD officers who had bravely stood their ground firing.

Harvath brought his Escalade to a screeching halt and leaped out. Holding his wallet in the air half-opened, so as not to be mistaken as a threat and shot, Harvath blatantly misrepresented himself. "FBI!" he yelled, and advanced on the twisted mass of vehicles. They had all been pushed up onto the sidewalk. Harvath couldn't see any of the officers.

He was less than ten feet away when the door of the Town Car was thrown open. Dropping his wallet, Harvath raised his pistol in both hands.

The driver swung out one leg and then the other. Harvath shot him in each knee and raced forward. The driver raised a pistol and began firing wildly.

Harvath dropped to the ground and returned fire. He put round after round on target, ripping through the open driver's-side door.

In one fluid motion, he depressed his pistol's magazine release and flicked the empty magazine out of the butt of the weapon. Before it had even clattered onto the pavement several yards away, he had inserted a fresh mag, snapped the slide back to chamber his first round, and was firing yet again.

As he did, he came up on his feet and rushed the Town Car. The driver didn't return fire.

Coming up on the open door, Harvath saw the man's legs first. Then he saw the rest of him, slumped over the armrest, half onto the passenger side.

"Hands!" Harvath yelled. "Let me see your hands!"

Moving more to his left, Harvath got a better view into the car. The driver's empty pistol, with its slide locked back, lay on the floor. But there was something else in the driver's hand and seeing it, Harvath's blood turned to ice.

Harvath's first shot blew the man's thumb completely off. He put the next four into the driver's head. Even then, he still wasn't sure and shot the man five more times.

Tentatively, Harvath crawled into the Town Car and retrieved the cell phone the driver had been fumbling with. There was a number on the screen that Harvath was certain corresponded to a cell phone detonator somewhere inside the Town Car. Had the man been able to hit Send, the car would have exploded.

Harvath carefully removed the battery from the phone, set both pieces on the dash, and crawled back out of the car.

Popping the trunk of one of the patrol cars, he extracted a medical kit and rushed to the fallen law enforcement officers. Two of them were already dead and several more were badly injured. Gunfire continued to rage across the airport. It was like being in a war zone.

"You, you, and you!" shouted Harvath to a group of onlookers who had taken cover nearby. "These men need your help."

The civilians came over as he ripped open multiple vacuum-sealed packets. He rapidly applied pressure dressings and Israeli bandages, as well as two tourniquets, and sent an additional onlooker to the other patrol car for more medical supplies.

Explaining how to keep the officers stable, he left the onlookers in charge and called in "Officers down" over one of the police radios, giving the location and range of injuries.

That was all he could do for them. He needed to get back in the fight. Running back to the Escalade, he picked up his wallet, got inside, and quickly drove away.

CHAPTER 56

As Harvath raced toward the Tom Bradley Terminal, Nicholas informed him that the fight was over. The LAPD and DHS operators had been able to neutralize the other VBIEDs. All of the terrorists were dead. All, that is, except for Tariq Sarhan, who was still unconscious in the Escalade's backseat.

The word had also already gone out to airports across the country to expect similar attacks. Two had already been uncovered and prevented. Nicholas had been right when he had stated that the attacks they had stopped only months before were just the precursor to a tidal wave set to crash down on the United States. Every time they faced down an attack, more popped up. Where would it end?

Harvath returned to the parking structure and located his rental car. After wrapping Sarhan's knee in a hillbilly bandage, he dumped him in the trunk. As he got into his car, he told Nicholas to make sure to erase any of the airport's CCTV footage of him.

As he drove out of the airport, a tidal wave of emergency vehicles rushed past him going in the opposite direction. They served as a reminder of the need to arrange for transport for himself and Sarhan. He asked Nicholas to get Carlton on the line. When he came on, Harvath said, "How soon until we can get a Sentinel jet out here to pick us up?"

"I'll look into it now," replied the Old Man. "How bad is his condition?"

"He tried to suck on a cigarette lighter and also managed to Tase himself before shooting himself in the knee, but he'll live."

"Understood. We'll figure out how close the nearest aircraft is and then we'll decide on an airport. LAX has been shut down and probably won't reopen for a few days."

"We're also going to need someone to sanitize the house I was using," said Harvath. "I left all the surveillance gear in there."

"We'll have someone handle it."

"You should have a team go through Sarhan's house as well."

"We'll get on that, too," replied Carlton, who then shifted gears. "In the meantime, I'm assuming you took an unattributable phone with you?"

"Of course I did. Why?"

"You've had two urgent calls from a man named Hank McBride."

Harvath recognized the name immediately. Hank had been one of his father's SEAL team buddies who used to come by the house and check on things when Harvath was a kid and his father was deployed.

He was still very close with Harvath's mom and his call could only mean one thing. "Did he say what it was about?"

"Negative. He just left a number and asked you to call him as soon as possible."

Harvath took the number, told Carlton he would call him back, and made for the entrance to the 405 freeway headed south. His mother still lived on Coronado Island across the bay from San Diego.

Speeding through an intersection and a light that had already turned red, Harvath narrowly missed being hit by two cars as he dialed Hank McBride's number.

"This is Hank," the old SEAL said as he answered the call.

"Hank, it's Scot," Harvath replied. "What's going on with my mom?"

"Your mom's fine, relax."

"What happened?"

"Nothing, I didn't call about your mom. I need a favor."

Harvath backed off his speed. "Mom's okay?"

"She's fine," insisted McBride. "I saw her a couple of days ago when I was down her way. Actually, she looks great."

Thank God, he thought as his heart rate began to lower. "Hank, I'm in the middle of an assignment right now. I'm going to have to call you back."

"When?"

"I don't know," said Harvath. "I'll get back to you."

The old SEAL wasn't going to take no for an answer. "Scot, I wouldn't have tracked you down and left two messages at your office if it wasn't important."

Already navigating the freeway on ramp, Harvath decided to give him until the next exit to explain what he wanted. "What do you need, Hank?"

"It's not for me. It's for a friend of mine."

Having worked for a prior president, Harvath was used to people reaching out to him for help with things in D.C. "I can save you some time. I've got no pull with the current administration."

"That's not what this is about."

"I don't want to be rude, Hank, but you need to get to the point. I'm really busy right now."

Hank didn't waste any more time. "Do you know who Larry Salomon is?"

"The movie producer? Of course I do."

"Someone sent a Spetsnaz team to whack him."

"When?" replied Harvath.

"The night before last," said Hank. "It was all over the news. At least it was until those fuckers blew up all of those theaters. My God, what are they going to do next?"

"Turn on your TV. They just hit LAX."

"They *what*?"

"That's part of why I'm so busy right now, Hank. So is Salomon dead?"

The old SEAL, who hesitated as he tried to flip his TV on in the background, finally said, "The technical adviser on all his films is a former Unit guy named Luke Ralston. He's a pal of mine and he was with Salomon when he came home and found those guys. The two of them killed the entire Spetsnaz team."

"Salomon and the guy from the Unit?"

"Yeah, it's a long story."

"Which they probably ought to be telling the police."

"That's just it," said Hank. "They can't. At least not yet. But here's the good part. Ralston knows who helped coordinate the hit."

"And he's not talking to the police?" replied Harvath. "Hank, let me give you a piece of advice. Steer clear of this entire thing. If they can't take this to the cops, there's something very wrong."

"That's why I'm trying to help them, Junior."

Harvath hadn't had McBride call him Junior since he was a kid and had gotten in trouble for fighting back when he was in school. The tone no longer intimidated him, but it did catch his attention.

"So what is it you want from me?" asked Harvath.

"All my contacts, and all Luke's, for that matter, are pretty much in the Special Operations community. We don't know many secret squirrel types, at least none that we trust. You, on the other hand, are very well plugged in."

"I know some people in Russian intelligence, if that would help, but it's going to have to wait until—"

"No," interrupted McBride. "We already crossed that bridge. The man who brought the talent into L.A. for the hit was a former FSB operative based here. The man who ordered the hit, though, was British intelligence."

"British intelligence?"

"MI5, to be exact."

Hank had to have gotten his facts wrong. "Why would somebody from Britain's domestic intelligence service want to splash a Hollywood movie producer?"

"That's what we need to figure out. Do you have any contacts you could reach out to?"

Harvath did. In fact he'd just helped MI5 and Scotland Yard take down a large terror cell in London and prevent a massive attack. "I've got a guy I can ask. What's the name of this MI5 operative you think was behind the attack?"

When McBride said the name Harvath couldn't believe his ears.

There was such a long pause, the old SEAL thought they might have gotten cut off. "Are you still there?"

"I'm still here," replied Harvath.

"Can you help with this Robert Ashford character or what?"

"This is a very serious accusation. You're going to need proof. Lots of it."

"We've got proof," said Hank. "You sound different all of a sudden. Why?"

Harvath ignored the question. "I want to see the proof you have."

"You're welcome to it. But it's not something I can just put in the mail."

"You don't need to. I'll come to you."

"You're here?" said McBride. "California?"

"I'm on the 405 right now. I don't have my regular cell with me, so give me your address again."

Hank did, and after Harvath told him to sit tight, not to move, and not to talk to anyone else, he ended the call and picked up his speed once more.

He thought about calling the Old Man. Carlton, after all, was the one who had introduced him to Ashford. But as quickly as the idea had materialized in Harvath's mind, he dismissed it.

Robert Ashford had been read into their operational plans in Yemen. The Old Man had done it as a courtesy. Aazim Aleem was a British citizen and Ashford had been especially helpful to the Carlton Group in London.

Harvath was beginning to wonder, though, if Ashford could have been the reason the Yemen op had gone sideways. And until he had a firm handle on what the hell was going on, he wasn't going to be making any phone calls.

CHAPTER 57

Harvath backed into Hank McBride's driveway and parked underneath the carport near the kitchen door.

"Thanks for coming," said the old SEAL, giving him a hug.

"No problem," replied Harvath. "You look good."

"Must be all my healthy habits."

Harvath knew what a hard drinker and terrible eater Hank was known to be and he smiled.

"C'mon inside," said McBride. "Luke and Salomon are looking forward to meeting you."

"I need your help getting something out of the trunk first."

Hank looked at him. "*Something* or someone?"

Harvath directed him to the rear of the car and popped the lid.

"Who the hell is he?" the old SEAL asked.

"He was never here. You never saw him."

"Did he have something to do with what just happened at LAX?"

"I don't want to get into it," said Harvath.

"Son of a—" said McBride. He pulled back his fist and punched Tariq Sarhan in the head before Harvath could stop him.

"For fuck's sake, Hank. Knock it off."

"So what? Tell them he slipped getting out of the car."

"Are you going to help me or not?" asked Harvath.

"Just leave him in there," said the old SEAL. "What do you need to bring him into the house for?"

"Ever heard of *sudden in-custody death syndrome*?"

"As in you've got some wiseass and you decide to throw him off a bridge?"

"If you leave a suspect duct-taped in a confined space for too long he can die," said Harvath.

"The whole country's going soft," replied McBride. "We used to leave shitbags like this in trunks for days at a time. I always found it made them a lot more cooperative."

Harvath ignored him. "I need a pole. Something that'll support a lot of weight and won't break. A sheet, too."

McBride shook his head, walked into the house, and reappeared a couple of minutes later.

After making sure there was nobody who could see them from the street, they pulled Sarhan from the trunk and laid him down on the concrete apron on his stomach. They slid the pole under his duct-taped ankles and then beneath his FlexCuff'd wrists, which Harvath had reinforced with more tape. Throwing the sheet over the pole, they lifted him like a couple of Bushmen returning to their village with a fresh hog and moved him inside.

Once safely into the kitchen, Hank let go of his side of the pole. "Woops," he said.

Harvath lowered his end, withdrew the pole, and pulled off the sheet.

"Where do you want to put him?" asked McBride.

"We can leave him right there."

"You don't care who he sees or what he hears?"

Normally, Harvath wouldn't have cared, but he had no idea where Sarhan was going to end up. The less he knew about everything, the better.

"Do you have someplace we can put him?" asked Harvath.

Hank shook his head. "I should start charging rent," he said as he motioned for Harvath to follow him.

Harvath grabbed Sarhan by the back of his shirt and dragged him across the linoleum floor and down a short hallway to McBride's laundry cum hobby room. He knocked and the door was opened by another man, who Harvath assumed was Ralston. Sitting next to the old SEAL's workbench was Larry Salomon. Harvath had seen his picture many times before.

On the floor, and also restrained with duct tape, was a man about Hank's age with greasy black hair and a pug face.

"Sorry we're late," said Harvath as he let go of Sarhan.

"Another piñata," replied Ralston. "Now things are getting interesting."

"If you gentlemen want to use the kitchen to talk," said Hank, "I'll keep an eye on these two."

Harvath thanked him and followed Ralston and Salomon out. As he was leaving, he reminded the old SEAL not to abuse his prisoner. Hank picked up a ball-peen hammer from the workbench and told him he wouldn't dream of it. Shaking his head, Harvath joined the other men in the kitchen.

Ralston introduced himself and then Salomon.

"I'm a big fan," Harvath said to the producer.

"Thank you. We appreciate your coming."

"Why don't you tell me what's going on," said Harvath as he motioned at the kitchen table for the men to sit. He saw that Hank had a pot of coffee made and helped himself. He offered to pour for the other two men, but they politely refused.

Sitting down at the table he listened as Luke laid out what had happened and Salomon filled in some of the details.

Twenty minutes and an additional cup of coffee later, Ralston finished by saying, "That's when Hank called you and here we are."

It was an amazing story. Harvath leaned back in his chair, processing what he had heard. "For what it's worth, you were smart not to kill Yatsko."

"I gave my word," replied Ralston. "That said, I probably ruptured his eardrum, discharging the weapon so close to his head."

"He deserves to pay," said Salomon.

Harvath nodded in agreement. "You both did the right thing, though." Changing gears, he asked, "What happened to the homeless guy in his trunk?"

"After I dumped Yatsko here, I drove the car back up to L.A., wiped all of my prints off it, and left it in his garage."

"Where's the hard drive?"

Ralston reached under the table where it had been taped, removed it, and handed it across to Harvath. He then gave him the code the Russian had revealed out in the desert.

"You haven't tried to open it, have you?"

Ralston shook his head. "He was bargaining for his life, so I think he was being straight with me. But I've dealt with this stuff enough to know that he could have given me a kill code. I didn't want to type in that password only to have it fry the entire drive."

"Smart," replied Harvath. "We've got somebody back east that should be able to get into it and see what's there. What about Project Green Ramp? You said it was a plan to weaken the United States and then collapse it via a black swan event? Do you have any idea what kind of black swan? Could that be what's behind all of these terrorist attacks?"

"You probably shouldn't rule anything out," Ralston replied with a shrug, "but I don't see Standing as the terrorism type. He's a financial guy who buys influence and messes with currencies and economies."

"Who may have used an active MI5 operative as a cutout to hire a Russian wet work team to kill Mr. Salomon."

"I guess when you put it that way, anything is possible."

It was definitely possible. In fact, having the *unrestricted warfare* piece of the puzzle, Harvath now saw Standing as highly likely to be behind the entire thing. He had the financial means. He also, from what Harvath knew, had the ideology and hadn't been shy in his public calls for the American system to be replaced with something else.

"If Ashford is dirty," asked Salomon, "will you be able to link him to Standing?"

"We'll definitely try. But it would be helpful to have copies of the material you were working on. Did you back it up offsite or does the LAPD have all of it now as part of their investigation?"

"Everything was in my home office at the time of the attack."

"So, no backup, then."

"No," said Salomon. "There's a backup. I just don't know how you can get to it."

"Let me worry about that," replied Harvath, figuring the Old Man could put together a team to take care of the job. "Where is it?"

"Back at the house. I have a stack of high-capacity portable drives in a locked cage hidden in the basement. My entire life is backed up on those things, including the rough cut, or at least as far as we had gotten on it, of the *Well Endowed* documentary. If you can get someone past the police and into the house, I can tell them how to find the cage and access the drives."

As Ralston and Salomon began to sketch out a map of the house and the surrounding property in Coldwater Canyon, Harvath stepped outside to make a phone call.

He needed to bring the Old Man up to speed on what he had learned, but more important, he needed to lay the groundwork for what they had to do next. Reed wasn't going to like it, but they were going to have to go after Robert Ashford.

CHAPTER 58

A civilian Lockheed L-100 Hercules was waiting for Harvath at the Los Alamitos Joint Forces Training Center, forty-five minutes south of Hank McBride's home in Hermosa Beach.

Also waiting was a SEAL team contingent who had been choppered up from Naval Amphibious Base Coronado. As Harvath was transferring both Sarhan and Yatsko back to the East Coast, the Old Man wanted to make sure he had all the additional manpower he might need.

The guards at the base gate were expecting Harvath and waved him through. The L-100 was parked on the tarmac outside Hangar Three with its rear cargo ramp down.

Upon seeing Harvath, one of the young SEALs at the base of the ramp shouted into the plane. Moments later, Harvath and his vehicle were guided right up into the belly of the enormous aircraft.

As this was a black flight with no records, the SEALs were dressed in civilian clothes. Only first names were used. Harvath introduced himself as Bob. It wasn't that he didn't trust them. On the contrary, these were his brothers. He knew that it was better for them if they knew zero about him.

Once his vehicle was secured, the cargo ramp was closed and the crew instructed everyone to prepare for takeoff. The men took their seats as the four massive turboprop engines were started.

Slowly, the enormous bird began to roll forward and taxi out to the runway. Harvath was exhausted and allowed himself a few minutes to lean back and close his eyes. This was not going to be a relaxing flight. There were still dots all over Nicholas's map in Reston representing further terrorist attacks. Back at LAX he had wanted Sarhan to tell him what he knew about that immediate attack. Now, he wanted to know about everything else. He figured the man wasn't going to be any more cooperative than he had been at LAX.

When the plane leveled out, Harvath opened his eyes and nodded to the SEAL in charge. He in turn signaled his men, who all produced black balaclavas and rolled them down over their faces.

Harvath opened the trunk and three of the SEALs shined bright flashlights into the faces of the two captives. Two other SEALs reached down and yanked out Tariq Sarhan, after which Harvath slammed the lid back down. Yatsko would get his turn, but for the time being, Harvath wanted him as disoriented and as frightened as possible.

A heavy steel cable, complete with a metal hook, had been thrown over one of the cargo area's upper supports. It ran to a winch covered with chipped yellow paint.

The two SEALs held Sarhan upright under his arms as Harvath removed his knife and cut through the tape and FlexCuffs binding his wrists. The sense of relief the terrorist felt at having his hands cut free was short-lived as one of the other SEALs forced his wrists together in front of his body and resecured them again with tape.

The hook was then slipped beneath the tape, and the SEAL manning the winch was instructed to take up the slack. The cable grew taut and Sarhan's arms were lifted above his head. The winch kept cranking until the terrorist was forced to stand on tiptoe and Harvath signaled for it to stop.

Reaching up for the piece of duct tape he had placed across Sarhan's mouth, Harvath ripped it away along with the crust of dried blood that had formed around his badly burned and blistered upper lip. His scream was so loud it could be heard well above the roar of the aircraft noise.

The man was cursing in Arabic, and Harvath gave him an open-handed slap to the side of the face to get him to shut up.

"Tariq, you're in a lot of trouble, my friend," said Harvath. "Do you know where we're going?"

Sarhan didn't answer, and Harvath hadn't expected him to.

"We're on our way to visit some friends of mine in Cairo," he told his prisoner. "The Mukhabarat are very interested in your visit."

The terrorist looked at him with contempt. "You lie," he hissed.

"There is no more Mukhabarat. The Egyptian secret police were thrown out after the revolution."

"Unfortunately for you, that isn't the case. You see, the new government needs the Mukhabarat even more than the old government. And let's face it, what would Egypt be without its secret police?

"Maybe the name will change, but their methods will still be the same. By the way, they wanted me to ask you if you had any family members you'd like them to contact for you. Actually, don't bother answering that. I'm sure they're already busy tracking them down."

If Sarhan was troubled by the threat, he didn't show it.

"Here's the thing, though, Tariq. I don't want to go to Cairo. That's too long for me to wait to get the answers I need. Too many Americans have died for me to risk a single life more. So you and I are going to have a very intimate conversation. Right here. And you're going to tell me every single thing, no matter how small or unimportant you think it may be, and you're going to tell me right now."

Tariq Sarhan had his answer ready. Once again he attempted to spit at Harvath and missed.

"Bad choice," said Harvath as he nodded to the SEAL operating the winch to tighten the cable up even further.

For the next three hours, Harvath worked on Sarhan. After the third time the terrorist passed out, Harvath had him taken down. Sarhan knew very little beyond his own operation. There were bits and pieces that Harvath would include with his debrief, but he doubted they'd be of much help. This network had been very careful to keep things as compartmentalized as possible. Sarhan had no idea how many other attacks were planned, who was involved, when they would happen, or how to stop them.

Harvath was beginning to believe that it would take a major mistake by the terrorists before they could be completely taken down. He hoped that mistake, though, had already been made and that it was Robert Ashford.

No sooner had Harvath gotten Yaroslav Yatsko out of the trunk and prepped for his interrogation than one of the Marines informed him that the crew, who, per orders, had remained in the cockpit for the duration of the flight, was ready to make their approach into Dulles.

Harvath and the SEALs quickly outfitted the two prisoners with black goggles, sensory deprivation headsets, surgical masks to prevent them from picking up olfactory cues, and blackout hoods, then shackled their wrists and ankles and covered their hands with heavy canvas mittens.

They were then laid back in the trunk of Harvath's car on their stomachs and had their ankle shackles connected to their wrist shackles via a short chain.

When the L-100 landed it taxied to the cargo services area of the airport, where Reed Carlton had two teams waiting.

When the cargo ramp was lowered, one of the teams boarded the plane and traded keys with Harvath. The car with the two trunked prisoners was backed down the ramp and was met on the tarmac by a heavily armored black Suburban. The Carlton Group kept a fortified safe house in Maryland. As the two vehicles disappeared from the airport, Harvath figured that was where they were most likely headed.

After thanking the SEALs, he walked down the ramp and disappeared himself. He found the car that had been left for him and climbed in. He wanted to get Yatsko's hard drive to the office as quickly as possible so the IT team could get to work on it. He also wanted to go over his plans with the Old Man in person. Carlton had been friends with Robert Ashford for many years, but Harvath had to know if Ashford had been the one who had compromised the Yemen operation. He needed to look the Old Man in the face and see for himself that he was all in and willing to do whatever needed to be done.

Starting the car, he rolled down the windows and shifted into drive. America was reeling from yet another attack. People across the nation were mad as hell, but they were also terrified. They had no idea where or when the next attack would come. All they knew was that they wanted it stopped.

After it was stopped, they would want revenge. Harvath was already one step ahead.

CHAPTER 59

A cross the country, families, friends, and neighbors huddled around television sets. They watched over and over the repeated horrors of the last two days. Many asked *Why?* Many more asked *Could it have been prevented?* Even more asked *Would it happen again?* For all its strength, for all its greatness, much of America was paralyzed. *Much,* but not all.

As Harvath passed through security and into the Carlton Group offices, they were alive with an activity he had never seen before. Shifts and hours had been tossed out the window. All hands were on deck. The entire twenty-fifth floor was teeming with activity.

Harvath made his way to Digital Ops, punched his code into the door that guarded Nicholas's domain, and when the lock released, slid the door open and stepped in.

His tiny friend looked like hell, but before Harvath could even comment, he was preempted. "There's some body spray around here somewhere," he said. "If I need it, let me know. Other than that, I don't want to hear about how I look, okay? I haven't been out of the SCIF much in the last seventy-two hours. Carlton has had someone walking the dogs for me."

There were times when Harvath was stunned by the man's ability to practically read his mind. Bending over to quickly scratch both of the dogs behind the ears, he replied, "Everyone's stretched to the max."

"True," said Nicholas, who snapped his fingers and held out his hand. "Drive."

Harvath removed the device from his pocket and handed it to him.

Nicholas studied it for several minutes and then connected one of the many hydra-headed cables near his work station to it.

"What did the Russian say the password was?" he asked.

Harvath repeated it to him and Nicholas rolled his chair over to another keyboard and punched it in.

"Do you mind?" asked Harvath, gesturing at the minifridge.

"Help yourself."

Opening the door, he reached inside and withdrew an energy drink. Popping the top, he grabbed a chair and sat down. "How many other airport attacks were there?"

"Based on LAX, they were able to prevent attacks at Denver, Miami, JFK, DFW, Boston, and San Francisco. The FAA and the White House have shut down the entire commercial air system. United, Delta, Southwest, American, none of the airlines will be flying tomorrow. Not until a new set of security procedures is developed."

Harvath had long been worried about how vulnerable Americans were in airports. They were incredibly soft targets. It was only a matter of time before the terrorists zeroed in on them. In fact, they already had, and the one thing everyone in the antiterrorism communities knew was that today's terrorists learned from yesterday's mistakes. No one responsible for airport security could claim they didn't see this coming. There had been more than enough warnings.

The 1972 attack by the Japanese Red Army at the airport in Tel Aviv had killed two dozen people and wounded seventy-eight others. That should have been the wakeup call. The only people who woke up were the Israelis. The rest of the world stayed asleep.

Then came the Rome and Vienna airport attacks by Muslim terrorists in 1985. In 2002, an Egyptian-born, green-card-carrying gunman, employed as a limousine driver, and living in the United States for ten years, opened fire at the El Al ticket counter at LAX. In 2007, a Muslim doctor and a Muslim engineer tried to drive a bomb-laden Jeep Cherokee into one of the terminals at Glasgow International Airport. Would America wake up now?

Harvath had no idea. What he did know was that when Muslim doctors, Muslim engineers, as well as Muslim green card holders in the most prosperous nation in the history of the world committed acts of terrorism, it wasn't because of economics. It was because of ideology.

What Harvath also knew was that airline travel was going to become even more of an aggravation than it already was. With each terrorist attack on U.S. soil, Americans gave up more of their rights. Harvath was reminded of the line, paraphrasing Benjamin Franklin, that those who trade some of their liberty for a little temporary security deserve neither and will lose both. The wisdom of the founders never ceased to amaze him.

Nicholas pointed to a stack of reports on the foiled attacks and Harvath wheeled himself over to them.

As he sifted through them, he asked, "Any progress with Mansoor in Iceland yet?"

Nicholas shook his head. "He's not bouncing back as fast as they would have liked. Riley's last report says they're afraid that they may have to take him back into surgery, or that he does have some low-level brain damage that they can't nail down. It's been very slow going."

"We're also going to need to look into James Standing, the hedge fund guy. When you're done with the drive, put him in that TIP program along with Ashford and see what you can find, okay?"

"I'll add it to my list," the little man replied, without looking up from what he was doing.

Harvath could tell he was distracting his friend, so he stopped talking and paged through the rest of the reports. DHS, TSA, and law enforcement at every airport across the country had gone on high alert. Based on the information they had been supplied from the attack at LAX, they had known what to look for and had been able to move quickly to take the terrorists down. It was a win for the United States, one it desperately needed. It had also saved thousands of lives.

Setting aside the last report, Harvath leaned back and watched Nicholas work. Regardless of how rapidly his fingers moved across his keyboard or how many times he clicked and double-clicked his mouse, the man's expression was tranquil.

In this he resembled the multitudes of counterterrorism operatives Harvath had worked with over the years. No matter how dangerous the situation, they approached each mission with an icy resolve. Though they all felt strongly about what they were doing, it was as if they were completely devoid of emotion, which was probably true. As things heated up, they calmed down and became completely focused. Essentially, each was in his or her own particular *zone*. That was exactly what he saw in Nicholas at the moment.

Ten minutes passed. Then twenty. Half an hour after he had begun, Nicholas turned from his computer. His expression reminded Harvath of that of a doctor stepping out of a difficult surgery to update an awaiting family.

"There's a lot here," he said.

"If you're talking about loan sharking and racketeering, I'm not interested. We can leave that for the Feds. Is there anything damning on Ashford or not?"

The little man tilted his head to the side. "By name, no. Everything so far is coded. Everyone appears to have a different designator. It's filled with random strings of letters and numbers."

Harvath wasn't surprised. Yatsko had been a professional spy, and some old habits died very hard. "So we've got nothing."

"Not exactly," said Nicholas. "There's one remaining file. I think it's a Rosetta stone that might explain all the other data, but it's heavily encrypted."

"Can you crack it?"

"Given enough time, I can crack anything. But all things consid ered, why don't we just crack Yatsko instead."

"I think they took him to the house in Maryland. I'll have the Old Man call the interrogators."

"The Old Man is Yatsko's interrogator," said Nicholas.

"Reed? Really?"

"*Really.* I think the two of them have a history. Don't ask me what it is. Reed Carlton has more secrets than anyone I've ever met."

Harvath didn't know if he should like the sound of that. From what Ralston had said, Yatsko was a tough son of a bitch. The Old Man, though, was the toughest son of a bitch Harvath had ever met. If the two men had a history, it could result in a very successful inter-rogation. There was also a flip side. History could also result in an extremely regrettable interrogation.

"Did they take Yatsko to the farm in Maryland?"

"*Maryland?*" replied Nicholas. "Why bother? They wanted to get started right away, so they brought him and Sarhan here."

"They brought them *here*?"

"Yeah, Carlton has them downstairs on twenty-four."

•   •   •

There was a stairwell near Nicholas's SCIF that Harvath knew led to the twenty-fourth floor. Access was via a keypad next to the door. Harvath punched in his code and waited. The tiny light above the pad remained red.

He tried it again. *Nothing.*

"Damn it," he muttered.

Finally, Harvath decided to try the code he'd seen the Old Man use on multiple occasions. He punched the numbers into the keypad and watched as the little light turned green and he heard the sound of the locks releasing.

Pulling open the door, he stepped into the stairwell and headed down to twenty-four. It had always been characterized as "empty office space" to him. It was a buffer between their offices and the rest of the building. It had also been explained as future space that the Carlton Group could grow into. As Harvath descended the stairs, though, he wondered if maybe he hadn't been told the whole truth.

In fact, as he neared the landing for twenty-four he was reminded of something Robert Ashford had told him the first time they had met. The MI5 man had picked Harvath up at the airport, and after whisking him through customs and passport control, he had inquired as to the Old Man's well-being. Of course, as they were about the same age, he hadn't referred to him as the Old Man. That was what his employees referred to him as. But Ashford hadn't referred to him as Reed or Carlton either. He had called him *Peaches.*

When Harvath had jokingly asked if it was because his boss was so sweet, Ashford had laughed and flatly stated, "No."

The two men had worked together many times over the years and Ashford explained that Carlton was anything *but* sweet. No matter how unsavory a tactic the enemy employed, Carlton would always one-up them. According to Ashford, the Old Man had never shied away from doing whatever needed to be done. He was apparently a very aggressive interrogator. *Bloody ruthless,* in Ashford's words. Hence the nickname *Peaches*—the antithesis of the man's operating style.

Ashford was one of the few people Harvath had met who had worked with the Old Man in the field. He found his stories about Carlton fascinating. He also found some of them very disturbing. Allegedly, he had pushed a handful of interrogations way too far. Prisoners had died, or so the rumors went.

Though the Old Man had never been charged, some of the whispers cited his tactics as a prime reason he and the CIA had parted company.

Harvath knew not to put a lot of stock in rumors, especially Washington rumors, but nevertheless, as he plugged Reed Carlton's code into the keypad at the door for twenty-four, he couldn't help but wonder what he would find on the other side.

There was a particularly nasty rumor about the Old Man's beating a prisoner with an electrical cord. Harvath had overheard several staffers talking about it when he first came on board at the Carlton Group. He'd made the mistake of asking the Old Man about it and had been put firmly in his place. Harvath hadn't asked him again.

As he stepped onto twenty-four, he didn't know what he would find, but when it came to Carlton and his reputation, he figured nothing would surprise him. Harvath's mind, though, was about to be changed.

CHAPTER 60

Harvath moved from one empty office and conference room to the next. Finally, on the west side of the building, he located Reed Carlton and his "prisoner."

They were in a small suite of tastefully decorated rooms that looked as if they had been plucked right out of the Four Seasons. Propped up on a hospital-style bed was Yaroslav Yatsko. His wounds had been cleaned and dressed, and an IV had been started. Each of his legs was in a straight-leg brace with a large ice pack atop each knee. Sitting in a chair next to him, drinking a glass of wine, was Reed Carlton.

The Old Man looked up when Harvath stuck his head into the room. "What are you doing down here?" he asked.

"I heard the housekeepers forgot the mints for the pillows," replied Harvath.

The Old Man set his glass on the table and stood up. "I'll be right back," he said to Yatsko and motioned for Harvath to follow him into the hall.

Once they were in the hall and the door to the suite of rooms was closed, Harvath asked, "What's all of that in there? Extra-extraordinary rendition?"

"Yaroslav is an old acquaintance."

"That's a pretty nice room you've got him in. Do we have a spa around here, too, that I don't know about?"

"Relax," said the Old Man. "We rented a hospital bed and put it in one of the old executive offices for him."

"Why?"

"Because Yatsko needs to be protected."

Harvath looked at him. "From what I hear, it's everybody else that needs to be protected from Yatsko. How do you know this guy? And why are we taking care of him?"

"First of all, we're not taking care of him. We're *using* him, the same way he and the Russians would use us. And as to how I know him, let's just say we crossed paths many times in the old days."

"Reed, this guy sent a wet work team to smoke Larry Salomon. Yatsko's Spetsnaz guys killed two filmmakers. Two *American* filmmakers. How the hell was he even able to sneak into the country in the first place?"

"He didn't sneak in," said Carlton.

Harvath looked at his boss. "We've actually known all along that he's been here?"

"From what I hear, he's been helpful."

"*Helpful* how?" asked Harvath. "Helpful thinning the ranks of Hollywood producers?"

The Old Man shook his head. "He's been a good source of intelligence for the CIA in Mexico. Facilitating the hit on Salomon, though, crossed the line. The Agency should have yanked his leash a long time ago."

"So why didn't they?"

"If I had to guess, it's because much of what he's been doing south of the border has been beneficial to the U.S. In exchange, Langley has been looking the other way, and that includes his criminal endeavors stateside. Murder for hire of American citizens, though, was a big mistake. It's unforgivable and he knows it. He got too greedy."

"What's going to happen to him then?"

"At best, he'll be persona non grata in the United States."

"And at worst?" Harvath asked.

"He'll stand trial for murder."

"You think they're actually going to give him a choice?"

"No," replied Carlton. "We are."

"What's he going to do for us?"

"He's going to help us nail Robert Ashford. And once we've taken care of Ashford, we're going to settle America's account with James Standing."

"So you believe Ashford and Standing are connected to the terrorist attacks?" asked Harvath. "You think they were the ones who stole the unrestricted warfare plans from the Chinese?"

The Old Man took a moment to gather his thoughts. "I think we've got a lot of questions that need answering."

"Well, we should start with your pal Yatsko. The password he gave back in California didn't unlock his entire drive."

"I know," replied Carlton as he removed a piece of paper from his pocket and handed it to Harvath. "It was his insurance policy. Give this to Nicholas. It should unlock the remaining file."

Harvath took the piece of paper. "The fact that he's cooperating doesn't mean we should trust him."

The Old Man smiled. "Believe me, I know. It's one of the hardest things about our business. You always have to assume that everyone is running an angle."

"Even Robert Ashford."

"Even Robert Ashford," the Old Man agreed.

"So how are we going to get to him?" asked Harvath.

"We're not. We're going to have him come to us."

"Why would he come to us?"

"Because he doesn't know what he doesn't know and that's the sort of thing that bothers a man like Robert Ashford."

"I'm not exactly following you," said Harvath.

"There's a reason Ashford hasn't retired. He lives for the intelligence game, and the intelligence game is all about gathering information. The more you have, the more powerful you are.

"Right now, Ashford's going nuts because he doesn't know how much or how little we know about the Aleem network."

"How can you be so sure?" asked Harvath.

"Because shortly after Uppsala he contacted me. He said he had some information he thought might be helpful to us and wanted to compare notes."

"Wait a second. He knew we were behind Uppsala?"

"No. He was fishing."

"What did you tell him?"

"I told him," said the Old Man, "that I was busy and would get back to him."

"Do you think you can lure him over here?"

"I think so. In fact, I think we have to. It'd be too difficult right now to launch an operation in his backyard. I'd rather we do it in ours, where he's out of his element and we have control."

"In addition, Ashford has no idea that we know anything about Yatsko, much less that we have him in our custody."

The Old Man smiled. "And that's how we're going to bring down Robert Ashford."

CHAPTER 61

It was early Monday morning and Robert Ashford was taking his breakfast at his tidy little row house at number 22 Portobello Road in London's Notting Hill. Like many people around the world, he had his television on and was watching scenes from the terrorist attacks that had taken place in America over the last couple of days. Spread out on the dining table in front of him was a cross-section of domestic and international newspapers, along with reports from MI5 and MI6.

When his phone rang, he figured it was yet another call from his office. He had come home only long enough to shower, change, and get something to eat, but the calls had kept coming. Both MI5 and MI6 were desperate to make sure that what had happened in the United States didn't happen in Britain.

Of course Ashford knew they didn't have anything to worry about, at least not from the group pulling off all the attacks in the United States, but he had to play along and appear distraught and quite concerned that the United Kingdom could very well be next.

He was surprised when the voice on the other end of the phone didn't belong to someone from his office at all, but to Reed Carlton back in the U.S.A.

"I'm very sorry for what has happened," said Ashford, who then moved the receiver away from his mouth so he could take a bite of toast.

"Thank you, Robert. The attacks have been devastating to our country. I'm sure it's all over the TVs there, but you have no idea what it's like over here."

Ashford remembered the 7/7 attacks in London and tried to recollect his feelings from that day to stir up some convincing sympathy for the Americans. "Terrible, terrible business, all of this," he said. "I understand the prime minister has been in touch with your president and has given our condolences and pledge of support."

"He has, and I'm sure it was very much appreciated. That's actually why I'm calling," replied Carlton.

Ashford was about to take a sip of tea, but, his interest piqued, he changed his mind and set the cup back down. "You know, if there's anything at all we can do for you . . ."

"I'm hoping there is. The only problem is that it's kind of delicate."

"*Delicate* in what fashion?" the MI5 man asked warily.

"We have some leads independent of the FBI and CIA back here that we're running down and it would help us tremendously if we could liaise with your office in a somewhat unofficial capacity."

"That hasn't been a problem before. We have a relationship with your organization and if there are any connections to what happened in America and British interests or British citizens, then I can very much guarantee that any resources we have would be at your disposal."

"Thank you, Robert," replied Carlton. "That's good to hear. Especially right now. Between you and me, things are in absolute turmoil here."

"I can only imagine." Ashford waited a moment and then said, "Were you calling just to put us on notice that some requests may be coming or was there something specific you needed?"

"Both, actually. I know before the most recent attacks happened, you said you had some information we might find useful and wanted to see what we had been able to compile, particularly as it had to do with Aazim Aleem."

"And that offer still stands."

Carlton decided it was time to bait the hook. "Were you aware that Aazim had a nephew?"

"Really? I didn't know that, but these people do often come from large families, so it isn't too much of a shock to discover. Was the nephew a British citizen as well?"

"Unfortunately, he is."

"Why do I get the feeling I'm not going to like this?" asked Ashford.

"There's a good part and a bad part. I'll give you the bad news first," said the Old Man. "The nephew ran all of his uncle's IT operations, and he did so from London."

"Past tense," noted the MI5 man. "Does that mean he's no longer among the living?"

"No, and that's my good news. We have him."

"Really?" said Ashford, trying to sound calm. "You know, it's not going to play well if it gets out that you ran your own little operation and snatched a British citizen from British soil."

"We didn't grab him in Britain."

Even though the MI5 man already knew that, he asked, "Where was he when you took him? Pakistan?"

"Someplace a lot blonder, but I'd rather not get into the details over the phone."

"Of course not."

"Our problem is that he had a preexisting heart condition and there was a complication when we began his interrogation."

"What kind of complication?" said Ashford.

"He had a heart attack."

"What's his prognosis?"

Carlton was honest with him. "We think he'll be okay, eventually. But in the meantime, our hands are somewhat tied, as you can understandably appreciate, as to how forceful we can be in our interrogation. If we're not careful, the concern is we could cause him to have another heart attack and he could die."

"You are in a bind, aren't you?"

"That's where we were hoping you could help. I'm sure the Security Service has you busy, but if they could see fit to part with you for a few days we'd like to have you come assist us in the interrogation as well as making sense of some of the backgrounds of the terrorists involved in the recent attacks," said Carlton, adding, "I have to be honest with you, Robert. We are completely in the dark."

Ashford smiled, lifted his cup, and took a sip of tea. "I'll call the director general right now."

"Thank you, Robert. I really appreciate this."

"Not at all, Peaches. You know I'd do anything for you. After all, we're allies, aren't we?"

• • •

The men spoke for a few more minutes about the trip. Carlton explained that because commercial air travel had been suspended, he'd be glad to send a plane for Ashford. The MI5 man appreciated the gesture and thought it was a good idea as it would demonstrate to the director general how seriously the Americans needed Ashford's help.

After the rough details were hammered out, they said good-bye and Ashford hung up the phone. Walking to his study, he removed the encrypted phone he used to contact James Standing and dialed his number. Despite the very late hour back in the States, the billionaire was wide awake.

"I have good news," said Ashford.

"It can only improve your situation. What is it?"

Standing was still very upset that not only had the LAX attack been nearly completely foiled, none of the other airport attacks had succeeded either. Upon hearing the news, he had called Ashford and chewed him out.

"Reed Carlton has asked me to come over and assist with the investigation in the attacks."

"Well, you can pack light. He'll soon learn how useless you are and send you home."

Ashford fought to keep his anger under control. "For your information, I just learned that it was the Carlton Group who took down the rabbit hutch."

Standing was silent for a moment. "Finally, you've produced something useful. A little bit late, but still useful."

"You're welcome."

"Don't be a smartass with me, Ashford. If you want attaboys, join a cricket team. I'm paying you for results. So Carlton is dumb enough to think you can somehow help with their investigations. Was there anything else you wanted to waste my time with?"

"They have Oxford's nephew in custody."

"Why should we care?"

"Because according to Carlton, Oxford put his nephew in charge of his IT operations."

"Who the fuck told that hook-handed simpleton that he could do that?" Standing demanded.

Aazim's handicap should have concerned them from the beginning. In hindsight it wasn't unthinkable that he would take someone into his confidence to help him with computer-related things, especially a young family member. Believing that the terrorist leader, with nothing but time on his proverbial hands, gladly sat around typing out messages, hunting and pecking on his keyboard with the steel tips of his prosthetic hooks, had been a mistake.

"The good news is that so far, they haven't been able to get any information out of the nephew. Apparently, he had some sort of heart attack shortly after they took him into custody."

"And how the hell did they pull that off? I'm assuming the nephew was a Brit. Or was he some backwards-ass relation living in a mud hut in some Arab country?" said Standing.

"He's British," replied Ashford, "but to quote Carlton, they grabbed him someplace *blond*."

"Uppsala."

"I think maybe now we know who was seen being laid down in the back of that car and driven away."

"You'd better make sure the nephew has another heart attack. Do you understand me? I want him silenced."

"I'll take care of it," said Ashford. "Don't worry."

"Fuck you, *don't worry*. I am worried. Do you have any idea how close we are?"

Ashford had no idea if the question was rhetorical, but knowing Standing, it probably was, so he didn't bother to reply.

"We're buying oranges tomorrow," said the billionaire.

Ashford couldn't believe it. "So soon?"

"I'm not waiting any longer. I have everything I need in place and that's all that matters."

The MI5 man knew that the orange attacks were paired with another color-coded attack, and it reminded him of a nursery rhyme from his youth:

Oranges and lemons,
Say the bells of St. Clement's.

Bull's eyes and targets,
Say the bells of St. Marg'ret's.

Here comes a candle to light you to bed,
And here comes a chopper to chop off your head.

"We'll need lemons," said Ashford, pausing. "According to the recipe, that's the next ingredient. Should I contact our grocer?"

"No," replied Standing. "I'll contact him. You go handle things with the Carlton people."

"I will. I'll make sure everything is taken care of."

"You'd better," said the billionaire. "And one other thing, Robert."

"What's that?"

"When the next wedge of black swans sails into their pond, try to look surprised."

Before Ashford could say anything in return, Standing had once again hung up on him.

CHAPTER 62

NEW YORK CITY

Technology amazed James Standing. Setting his laptop on his living-room table, he marveled at what an incredible instrument it was. With it, he could move markets. He could fund startup companies. He could create political organizations. He could change public perception. He could sow peace. He could bring war. All of it could be done from anywhere he found himself on the planet and it all could be done clandestinely. It was indeed a tool fit for a god.

Yet what did most people do with their computers? They played video games, wasted themselves on so-called social media, or consumed pornography. His contempt for the intellectual lethargy of mankind ran as deep as his belief in mankind's boundless potential. The planet and its inhabitants could be so much more than they were, but they would never even come close if left to their own devices. They would always choose their narrow self-interest over everything else.

They would never realize how miserable they truly were and how they could transcend that misery. You could paint the most glorious picture of what awaited, but they wouldn't grasp it. Some might, but the majority, the masses, truly were asses. The only way they would become better people and society would be improved was through force. They couldn't be led to a better life, they had to be dragged there by the state like the dumb beasts they were.

There would be those whom even force would not be able to persuade. There was only one solution for that problem. The world would be a better place without people who wanted to cling to the status quo. For mankind to survive, for mankind to reach its brilliant potential, not only must there be progress, but all resistance to that progress must be stripped away and destroyed.

What awaited mankind was an earthly paradise of gleaming, golden cities; a perfect socio-politico-legal system in harmony with nature.

What Julia Winston, the young *Financial Times* reporter, called socialism was actually opportunity. Though it was beaten back repeatedly by small minds, it continued to outstretch its warm and generous hand, waiting to take mankind and civilization forward. Attempts to take mankind into this land of promise had indeed failed in the past, but now it would be different, for one very specific reason. This time, those leading the world forward had an advantage those before them did not—they had technology. Technology was what would allow the enlightened to shift the paradigm and move human beings to the next stage in their evolution.

Powering up his laptop, Standing engaged two more pieces of technology that amazed him, Skype and an absolutely fluid translation platform that made him appear the perfect Arabic speaker.

As salam Alaikum, Mustafa Karami typed when he saw his benefactor had logged on to speak with him. *Peace be upon you.*

Wa 'alaykumu s-sal•mu wa rahmatu l-l•hi wa barak•tuh, Standing replied, using the formal response he thought befitting his Sheikh from Qatar persona, *May Allah's blessings be upon you.*

Karami was quick to accentuate the positive of the past two days.

Allahu Akbar. We rejoice for the brothers who have gone to paradise.

Allahu Akbar, Standing typed. **Inna Lillaahi Wa Inna Ilayhi Rajiun.** God is great. To Allah we belong and to Allah we return.

Robert Ashford didn't like it that Karami got his marching orders from two different sources. Standing didn't care what he thought. Sometimes, he liked to delegate the job to Ashford, sometimes he liked to pull the figurative trigger himself. He also liked to convey the impression to Karami and the others that they were part of a very large organization, which they were.

We stand ready to serve in Allah's great and just cause, wrote Karami.

I bet you do, thought Standing. **Why was I not told about the Mufti's nephew?** The Mufti of Jihad was the pen name Aazim Aleem had been known by throughout the Muslim world for his sermons on jihad.

It took Karami a moment to type his response. To his credit, he didn't lie. **You should have been told.**

You're damn right I should have been, was what Standing wanted to say, but instead he wrote, **Where is the nephew now?**

We do not know.

If the authorities have him, how much of a danger will he be to our operation?

That we also do not know.

Standing was further tempted to ask what the hell they did know, but then Karami added to his last transmission saying, **We must assume he knows everything the Mufti himself knew.**

So, Karami wasn't a complete fool after all. **I agree,** typed Standing.

We stand ready, the terrorist stated again.

Standing typed the words **Orange** and **Yellow,** then hit Send.

When?

Orange is to happen Monday, replied Standing, who had been wrestling with the timing for the follow-up. He needed the orange attacks to get extensive, deep coverage before the next attack. It was a gamble, though. If Aazim's nephew knew everything the uncle did and the Carlton Group broke him, he'd be lucky to see any more attacks.

And yellow? Karami asked.

Wait forty-eight hours after the orange events have been reported. Then you may launch yellow.

Insha'Allah, we will be much more successful this time.

Insha'Allah, Standing agreed before ending the conversation and exiting Skype.

The Chinese seemed almost to have designed this next wave of attacks with him in mind. Not only would it help further push the United States into a state of incredibly disruptive chaos, but he had even found a way to profit by it. America was indeed an incredible country.

CHAPTER 63

NORTHERN VIRGINIA

After leaving the Carlton Group offices, Harvath had driven straight home, taken a quick shower, shaved, and fallen into bed. He wasn't going to be any good to anyone if he didn't get some rest.

When his phone rang, it drew him out of a very deep sleep. Fumbling blindly over the nightstand, he felt around until he found his BlackBerry. Without opening his eyes, he activated the call and brought the device to his ear.

"Scot, it's Nicholas," said the little man from up in Reston. "I think I found something."

"Have you been to sleep at all?"

"No. Listen, you asked me to look into connections between Standing, Ashford, and the attacks."

"What did you find?" asked Harvath.

"Remember the bomber in Chicago, the one who blew himself up several weeks ago before he could take down that building above the Amtrak tracks?"

"One hundred North Riverside Plaza. Yeah, I remember."

"Well, I was looking at all of the dots on the map again, trying to figure out what they all meant. Then I threw Standing into the mix and that's where I think I found something."

Harvath continued to lie there with his eyes closed. "Keep going."

"The unrestricted warfare plan calls for terrorist attacks that not only sow fear and cause massive loss of life and property damage, but also do dramatic economic damage, right?"

"Right."

"James Standing has also called for economic damage to the United States. In fact, he has been quite vocal about it. That got me thinking. If he's the driving force behind all of this, the guy who put up the money to finance hijacking the blueprint from the Chinese, would he be bold enough to try to turn a profit from all of this?"

"I don't think Standing got rich by being stupid."

"You obviously haven't had much exposure to bankers," said Nicholas. "I have."

"You're saying they're stupid?"

"No, not stupid, they're aggressive; very aggressive, and they're smart as hell. They're risk-takers to the nth degree, and James Standing is no different. It's well-informed gambling in most cases, and in some it's counting cards and dealing from the bottom of the deck."

"Cheating," mumbled Harvath.

"Yes."

"So what did you find?"

"I looked at all the color-coded dots on our map again, but this time from a financial perspective. I asked myself how I would try to make money out of these attacks, and that's when it hit.

"I don't think the failed bomber in Chicago was targeting 100 North Riverside Plaza because it was built above the train tracks. That might have been part of it, but if so, it was secondary."

"What was the primary reason, then?"

"It was home to Boeing's corporate headquarters," said Nicholas.

"You think the bomber wanted to bring down the entire building just to get to Boeing?"

"I do," replied the little man, "and it's not just Boeing. I think this is what the orange dots are all about. The one thing they have in common is that they're in cities from Fairfield, Connecticut, to Palo Alto, California, that are home to the corporate headquarters of all the companies that make up the Dow Jones Industrial Average. Can you imagine taking out all thirty headquarters at once? Do you have any idea the economic chaos that would cause, especially if you timed it so that most, if not all, of the senior management was present when the buildings came down?"

Harvath's eyes were wide open now and he propped himself up in bed. "That would be huge."

"It wouldn't just be huge, it would be game over. Let's set aside for a moment that the Dow is basically a BS indicator—"

"What do you mean? The Dow is the financial indicator *everyone* looks at."

"No," Nicholas clarified, "it's the indicator that *retail investors* look at. Since 1910 it has been on an upward trajectory. The funny thing is that only one of the thirty companies that make up the Dow has been there over the last hundred years and that's GE. It's a massive psychological operation. If a company does poorly, it gets yanked, so the Dow can keep climbing."

"So if it's all BS, what difference does it make if it takes a hit?"

"Regardless of what you think of the index, the companies on it are currently some of the best-performing in the United States. A massive, coordinated terrorist attack, wiping out just the top twenty-five people in each company, in effect their intellectual horsepower, could absolutely devastate their stock and, in turn, the financial markets."

"If your goal was to collapse the United States," said Harvath, "why not go right for the Dow attack then?"

"To soften the battlefield. I'd want to sow as much chaos and panic as possible. I think it's brilliant. Make people across the country feel that they aren't physically safe anywhere and then take all their money away in a financial crisis, and they'll beg for a return to normalcy. Start throwing in more attacks after that, and they'll give up anything and stand behind anyone who promises to return things to the way they were. At that point, America, as its citizens know it, is over and is never coming back."

Having studied history, Harvath knew that once people gave up their freedom in order to restore order, that freedom was never returned. He didn't even want to consider that this was possible, but he knew that it was and he knew that they had to figure out a way to prevent it from happening. "You're sure that's what the orange dots represent?"

"As sure as I can be," he replied. "But it's not just because of the locations. I found something else, and it's exactly what I would do if I were James Standing and thought I was smarter than everyone else and wouldn't get caught."

"What is it?"

"Beginning six weeks ago, significant bets were placed that all thirty companies making up the Dow were going to drastically lose value over the subsequent three months."

"You mean someone is shorting them?"

"That's the way it looks," said Nicholas. "Very much in the same way options were purchased against United and American Airlines stocks right before 9/11."

"Is it Standing?" Harvath asked.

"I said people like Standing were aggressive, not stupid. The shorts lead back to a series of holding companies, most of them offshore. I'm trying to use the TIP to pierce them. In the meantime, though, what should we do about my hypothesis?"

"If you were going to try to take out the senior management of all these companies, when would you do it?"

Nicholas thought about it for a moment. "Maybe at a corporate retreat or a shareholders' or board of directors' meeting."

"I'm talking about all thirty companies at once and at a time when as many of those people would likely be at their corporate headquarters."

"If you're speaking Monday through Friday, then I would say definitely do it on a Monday."

Harvath looked at his watch. It was technically already Monday. "DuPont Chemical is up in Wilmington, Delaware. They're still part of the Dow, right?"

"Yes. Why? What are you thinking?"

"I think we need to check out your hypothesis."

"You only want to check out DuPont?" asked Nicholas. "Why not warn all of them?"

"Because, in light of the attacks we've just suffered, everything is already on edge. If word got out that we thought these companies were targets, it would create a panic that could be just as bad as if they were attacked."

Harvath had a good point. "You're right," agreed Nicholas. "What do you want to do?"

"Have you called the Old Man yet?"

"No, I wanted to talk to you first."

"Anything out of Iceland?"

"Nothing yet."

Harvath had already gotten out of bed. "Okay," he stated. "I'll call Reed. You keep working on things there."

"You're going up to DuPont, aren't you?"

"I am."

"Well, you're going to need help," said Nicholas. "I'm looking at pictures of the building their headquarters is in right now. It takes up an entire city block and is thirteen stories tall. You can't possibly search the entire thing by yourself."

"I won't be going by myself," replied Harvath. "I'm going to bring a few friends with me."

CHAPTER 64

The massive, eight-bladed, three-engine Sikorsky CH-53 Sea Stallion helicopter thundered over the Atlantic Ocean, straight up the East Coast. Inside, Harvath sat with members of the U.S. Navy's Explosive Ordnance Disposal (EOD) Group Two out of Naval Amphibious Base, Little Creek, Virginia.

Multiple, rapid-deployment U.S. Army Chemical, Biological, Nuclear, Radiological and high-yield Explosive Enhanced Response Force Package teams, also known as CERFP teams, were already en route to Wilmington via Blackhawk helicopters from Fort Meade and Andrews Air Force Base. Rodney Square, directly across the street from the DuPont building, was the designated landing zone and had already been secured by the Wilmington Police Department.

The building was composed of a hotel, theater, bank, retail shops, DuPont's corporate headquarters, and other general-purpose office space. The hotel was at 30 percent occupancy and its guests were sleeping when the first of the helicopters landed.

The concrete corridors of Wilmington's downtown business district reverberated with earsplitting thunder as one after another, the large birds flared, then touched down and quickly disgorged their teams and equipment, before lifting back off again and disappearing.

DuPont's executive director in charge of corporate security, Ron Lamat, was one of the most experienced executive protection specialists in the country. A former Baltimore County Police major, he had trained with the Secret Service and was a graduate of the FBI's National Executive Institute. When he wasn't keeping DuPont's hierarchy and their families safe, he was teaching other executive protection specialists how to do the same for their clients. In a crisis, Harvath couldn't have hoped to have liaised with a more competent or professional chief of security.

Lamat met Harvath and his team outside at the LZ and led them into the building. Schematics had been laid on hastily erected tables in the lobby. Building engineers, roused from their beds and rushed to the scene, stood by ready to answer any questions or provide access to any of the common or private areas. Rows of radios stood in charging stations plugged into outlets along one wall in case the teams needed a uniform means of communication. Lined up near the radios were four of Lamat's best men, ready to assist in any way they were needed.

Harvath stood aside talking with the security chief while the EOD and CERFP team leaders discussed how to divvy up the search. As soon as they had come to an agreement, they established a communications protocol and split up.

Based on the failed Chicago bombing of the Boeing building, they began their search focused on the DuPont building's structural supports.

Even with the large amount of manpower and technology they had, they moved excruciatingly slowly. The first floor alone took more than a half hour to clear.

As they moved up to the second floor, Ron Lamat pulled Harvath aside.

"Do you mind if I make a suggestion?" he said.

"I'm all ears," replied Harvath.

"I know you wanted to keep this quiet, but you kind of blew that with the helicopters and by using the local PD to secure your LZ. I think we need more searchers or we're still going to be working our way through this building come lunchtime."

"What do you have in mind?"

"I can make a couple of phone calls," said Lamat, "and have fifteen bomb-sniffing dogs here within half an hour. We use one per floor and we can be done here real quick."

Harvath had wanted to keep things as quiet as possible, but Lamat was right. The dogs could move a lot faster. "Okay, do it," he replied, "but tell them we need this kept as quiet as possible."

As the teams had deployed C-Guard RF manpack IED jammers around the perimeter of the building to prevent remote detonation, Lamat's cell phone couldn't get a signal and he had to retreat upstairs to his office, where he made the calls via his landline.

• • •

Forty-five minutes later, the dogs and their handlers had joined the search and were sweeping throughout the offices on every floor.

When a Belgian shepherd named Gina stopped at a section of drywall in an office on the fourth floor, sat down on her haunches, and looked up at her handler, word went out that they had a hit.

A nearby CERFP team rushed to the office and conducted its own methodical search. Ten minutes later, the team confirmed what the dog had alerted them to. A large amount of explosives had been secreted behind the drywall at a support column.

With Harvath's approval, Ron Lamat made the decision to evacuate the building, starting with the hotel, while the search continued.

Gina ended up getting hits on every single support column on the fourth floor. After the rest of the building was checked and no other explosives were found, the dogs and handlers were released. The EOD/CERFP teams then moved from support column to support column on the fourth floor, using portable X-ray devices to see exactly what they were dealing with. Insulation had been removed and shape charges made of C4 had been affixed directly to the beams along with remote detonators and extra power packs. There were enough explosives in place to bring the building down three times over. Harvath needed to let Carlton know so the other Dow Jones corporations could be warned.

Using the landline phone in Lamat's office, Harvath called the Old

Man, who was now in the TOC in Reston, and gave him a full situation report.

"Do we have any idea how the explosives got in there or how long they've been there?" Carlton asked.

"At this point, we don't know," replied Harvath. "Ron is putting an email together right now with a full list of tenants and anything else he thinks might be helpful."

"Have him send it directly to me."

"Will do. Anything else?"

"No," said Carlton. "You've done all you can do there. Let the teams handle the explosives. I need you back here. Ashford's plane is going to be landing soon."

CHAPTER 65

By the time Robert Ashford's jet touched down at Dulles, Harvath was already at the Landmark Aviation FBO waiting for him. Customs and Immigration had been alerted to the MI5 operative's arrival and processed him quickly and professionally right at the plane. Harvath met him on the tarmac.

"I don't suppose they have any bottled water inside?" Ashford asked after the pair shook hands. "Bloody caterer forgot to load any beverages for the flight."

Harvath wanted to rip the guy's face off right there, but he kept his anger under control and tried to act as normal as possible, given the situation. "I think I may have some water in my truck," he replied as he steered the man toward the parking area.

After a quick search inside his armrest, Harvath apologized and asked if Ashford could hold on for just a few minutes longer. The Brit nodded, Harvath put his car in gear, and they drove out of the airport.

"Reed would have come out to meet you himself," Harvath said as he headed for the Dulles Toll Road, "but as you can imagine, things have been very chaotic back at the office."

"Of course. In fact, you didn't have to come all the way out to get me. I could have taken a cab," replied Ashford.

Despite flecks of spittle at the corners, the Brit's mouth was bone-dry. He was obviously dehydrated. And though he tried to hide it, Harvath could see that he was also on edge.

"It's ten minutes each way," said Harvath. "It's not a big deal. We appreciate your dropping everything to come help us."

"How's your investigation going?"

"Not good," he stated as he got onto the toll road.

"That's what I was told. I hope that there's some way we can help. The loss of life your country has suffered is nothing short of tragic."

Harvath nodded and changed the subject. "We've got a room reserved for you at a hotel in Reston, but the boss was hoping you wouldn't mind coming straight into the office. We want to get you up to speed and then someone can drive you back to the hotel. Would that be okay?"

"Of course," he replied. Then, changing the subject back, he asked, "Any change in the status of Aazim Aleem's nephew? What was his name again?"

"Mansoor Aleem? No change, but we're all hopeful."

"You picked him up where? Somewhere in Scandinavia, I'm assuming."

"Sweden, actually," replied Harvath.

"So you all were behind that bit of unpleasantness in Uppsala then. You know the Swedes think it was the French."

"That's what the boss wanted them to think."

"He's a very clever man, that Peaches," said Ashford.

"He is indeed," said Harvath.

"What was Mansoor Aleem getting up to in Uppsala, of all places?"

"From what we have been able to put together, after Aazim was killed in Yemen, a new commander in the network was promoted.

His name is Mustafa Karami and he was based in Uppsala. Karami brought Mansoor to Sweden because he wanted to know more about someone they referred to as the Sheikh from Qatar. Ring any bells?"

Harvath tried to study the Brit's face, but it was too dark in the SUV.

"I can't say I'm familiar with any Sheikh from Qatar, but that doesn't mean we don't have something in our files. When I get near a computer, I can send a note back to my office and have them begin checking."

"Thank you."

"You're welcome," said Ashford, who then asked, "So Mansoor Aleem is the young Arab that witnesses saw being taken out of that apartment building in Uppsala and driven away?"

"No. That was one of our guys we had managed to infiltrate their cell with."

Harvath didn't need to see the Brit's face. The surprise was evident in his voice when the MI5 man said, "Really?"

"Yes," replied Harvath. "He had infiltrated their Chicago cell, too. That made a big difference in lessening the effect of the attacks they attempted to pull off there. We've been able to learn a lot about the structure of the network."

"Anything that we might find helpful back in the U.K.?"

"Tons."

Ashford listened as Harvath laid out everything they knew about the Chinese, Site 243, and the unrestricted-warfare plan.

Harvath was still talking when they pulled into the underground parking structure beneath the Carlton Group's offices. In the first flash of overhead fluorescent lighting, he was able to catch the look on the Brit's face. It didn't last long, but it lasted long enough. The man was dumbfounded. And it wasn't by the audacious scope of the unrestricted warfare plan, it was by how much Reed Carlton and his group had been able to put together.

Harvath parked his Tahoe and he and Ashford climbed out. "Have you been to the office before?" he asked.

"No. I haven't," replied Asford. "This is my first time. He told me he had a devil of a time finding the right space. He said he made a lot of modifications and that I'd be quite surprised with what he had done to it."

Harvath waved a key fob in front of a reader and opened the glass doors for the main elevator bank. He allowed the MI5 man to step in first and then followed. Reaching over, he pushed the button for the twenty-fourth floor.

"So, a key fob? That's the extent of your security?" Ashford said with a chuckle. "What am I missing?"

Harvath forced a smile. "You know what they say. When it comes to security, it's not necessarily what you see, but what you *don't* see that counts."

"Quite right," the Brit agreed.

On the twenty-fourth floor, Harvath let his guest step into the hallway first and then exited the elevator car behind him. He led him to a large door with gray lettering that read *Parsons, Charrington & O'Brien.*

"Law firm?" the MI5 man asked.

"Accounting firm," said Harvath as he withdrew a set of keys.

"I suppose it has a bit more panache than *Universal Exports,* now, doesn't it?"

Opening the door, Harvath forced another smile and showed his guest in. When the door had closed behind them, he took a step away from Ashford and, gesturing at the small reception area, asked, "So, are you surprised?"

The MI5 man looked around at the empty waiting room, wondering if this was some sort of a joke.

"How about now?" asked Harvath as his fist came sailing forward and nailed the older man right in the stomach.

CHAPTER 66

Harvath would have liked nothing more than to have beaten Ashford to death, but the Old Man had been very specific not only about where he could hit him, but how hard. In case they needed to use him operationally, there were to be no blows to his head, neck, or face.

The punch had completely knocked the wind out of the MI5 operative, and after removing everything from his pockets, Harvath dragged him down a narrow interior hallway to the room that had been set up for the interrogation. It was important that they work fast.

They needed to keep him mentally off-balance. The harder they came at him the harder it would be for him to concoct a story. Kicking open the door, Harvath dragged Ashford inside.

Reed Carlton knew one very important thing about the MI5 operative. It was the only pressure point he needed to conduct a successful interrogation.

Harvath dropped Ashford into a prisoner restraint chair that looked as if it had been designed for Hannibal Lecter.

"What the hell are you doing?" the man wheezed, as the air began to rush back into his lungs.

He struggled, but Harvath struck him again, this time in the solar plexus, almost knocking back out what little air he had recovered.

When he ceased struggling, Harvath worked quickly to strap him in. When he was finished, the MI5 operative's torso, limbs, and head were completely immobilized.

On a table in the corner was a large black bag. Harvath removed a small handful of what looked like pieces of candy, dropped them in his pocket, and walked back over to Ashford.

"Why are you doing this?" the man demanded once more.

Harvath removed one of the ammonia inhalant ampules from his pocket, and placing it under Ashford's nose, cracked it open.

The Brit's eyes shot open wide and he tried to twist his head to get away from the smell, but he couldn't. Harvath waited a moment and then did it again.

"Stop it!" Ashford shouted, but Harvath kept going until he had used up all the ampules he had in his pocket.

"I want Reed here, right now," Ashford demanded.

Harvath ignored him as he retrieved three large strobe lights and, placing them on stands, positioned them about a foot away from the MI5 operative's face.

"Do you have any idea who you're fucking with?" Ashford was now screaming. "Do you know the kind of trouble you're in? Do you?"

Harvath smiled. The Brit was getting nice and worked up. Walking back over to the black duffel, he removed a pair of stereo headphones with an extralong cord. Placing the headphones over Ashford's ears, Harvath then ran the cord back to a large boom box sitting under the table and plugged it in.

It had been Carlton's idea to exacerbate Ashford's propensity for migraines. That's why the plane had taken off from London without beverages. Dehydration was a frequent migraine trigger. Harvath, though, had wanted the man to suffer.

Stress, strong odors, bright strobing lights, and loud music were also migraine triggers. Turning the boom box on and the volume all the way up, Harvath then walked over and activated the strobes.

When Ashford began to scream again, Harvath pulled a roll of duct tape from his bag, tore off a piece, and placed it over the man's mouth.

Fishing a Power Bar and a large bottle of water from the duffel, he stepped outside for his Interrogators Local Union 152–sanctioned break.

• • •

When Harvath stepped back into the room ten minutes later, Ashford's face was wet with tears. Harvath slowly turned off the strobes. He then calmly turned off the music and removed the headphones. Next, he removed the piece of tape from over the man's mouth and dismantled the strobes, putting all of the equipment back near the table. Moments later, Reed Carlton walked into the room carrying a red file folder in his left hand.

"Hello, Robert," he quietly said as he approached his old friend.

"Why are you doing this?" the MI5 man stammered.

"How do you feel, Robert?"

"How do you think I feel, you bastard?"

Carlton motioned for Harvath to bring him a chair, which he placed several feet in front of Ashford.

"He doesn't need to have his head restrained like that," said the Old Man.

Harvath walked behind him and released the strap.

"Does that feel better, Robert?" Carlton asked.

"Up yours."

The Old Man ignored the insult. "Robert, I believe you know how this works. I have a series of questions that I will ask you once and only once. If you lie to me, it's all over. Do we understand each other?"

"May I have some water?"

"Answer my questions and I'll be happy to give you some water. I'll also be happy to give you one of those," he said, pointing at the bottle of pills sitting on the table that Harvath had removed when cleaning out the man's pockets.

"And then what? You hand me over to the authorities here or back in the U.K.?"

The Old Man shook his head. "No. That's not an option. You and I go back a long time. You know what I'm capable of, both good and," he paused, "less than good. So, I'm going to give you a choice. If you cooperate, you'll have to leave MI5 and leave the U.K., but I'll resettle you with a new identity. You go into retirement and I never want to hear from you or see you ever again."

"And if I don't cooperate?"

"Then no one will ever see you or hear from you again."

"I'm not leaving the Security Service."

"I'm not here to bargain with you, Robert. You know full well that I can make good on either of the two options I offered you."

Ashford didn't respond. His head was killing him. It felt as if someone had split it wide open with an axe. "I don't know what you want from me."

Carlton opened his folder. "Why don't you start by telling me about the hit on Larry Salomon."

"Who?"

The Old Man shook his head, closed his file, stood up, and began walking away.

Ashford looked at him. "Where are you going?"

"I'm sorry it had to end like this, Robert."

"I told you, I don't know any Larry Salomon. You can't do this. You can't just kill me. You won't kill me."

Carlton walked back to his chair, set his file folder down, and sprang at the MI5 man. Grabbing a fistful of hair, he torqued the man's head back. "Thousands of Americans are dead and you think I'm going to play games with you?"

"I'm not involved with the terrorist attacks! Why are you doing this, Reed? I don't know what you're talking about. Who put you up to this?"

The Old Man bent the Brit's head back even farther. "I know the routine, Robert. Deny, deny, deny, and then launch counter-accusations. It isn't going to work. I've offered you an incredible deal, you son of a bitch. It's better than you deserve. Don't be an idiot. Take it."

"But you don't have a thing on me. I don't know why you're doing this."

Carlton looked at Harvath and said, "Go get him."

"Go get who?" asked Ashford as Harvath left the room.

"Shut up."

"Reed, you and I are friends."

The Old Man wasn't listening to him. "What changed you, Robert? Was it money? Is that what this is all about?"

"I don't know what you're talking about."

"Show a little character, Robert. Show some dignity. I have offered to let you disappear into retirement. Take the offer."

"But I haven't done anything," the MI5 man insisted. "I don't know any Larry Salomon. I'm not involved in these horrible terrorist attacks. All I know is that if you had one shred of proof, you'd produce it."

As the man finished his sentence, Harvath wheeled Yaroslav Yatsko into the room in a wheelchair.

"Hello, Robert," the Russian said.

CHAPTER 67

"You think MI5 would take his word, a former KGB operative's, against mine? The word of a man who admits he's in the murder-for-hire business? You're crazier than he is!"

Carlton opened the file and showed Ashford what he had. "You two go way back. He kept very meticulous records."

"If I did communicate with trash like this," said the Brit, "do you honestly think I'd be stupid enough to do it with an email address that traced back to me?"

"We also have the banking information for the payments made to Mr. Yatsko."

"Again, how stupid do you think I am?"

"And then there's Yemen," said the Old Man.

Suddenly, Ashford's mask slipped. A flash of panic rippled across his face, but was quickly suppressed.

"That's right, asshole. We've got you dead to rights in Yemen," said Harvath.

Carlton closed the file and looked at the MI5 operative. "There's no way out, Robert. There's also no more time left on the clock. We know everything. The only reason we're having this conversation is that I wanted to give you a way out. I'm closing the window, though. Either you accept my offer, or I have a van waiting downstairs with a team that will take you out to the country, put a bullet in your head, and plant you in a very cold and lonely piece of ground."

Harvath had already taken Yatsko back to his room and returned. He was now watching Ashford to see what he would do. They didn't have him dead to rights on Yemen. That had been a bluff. Harvath had been adamant that Ashford believe that the case against him was overwhelming. He lived for his career, and he needed to believe that it was over. They needed to psychologically strip him naked and convince him that the only way out was through the Old Man.

"And you give me your word that you'll relocate me? A new identity? A new life? All of it?" said Ashford.

"The economy being what it is, you may end up recycling boxes at a Walmart, but I give you my word," said the Old Man, who gestured for Harvath to give him some water.

Harvath did as he was instructed.

"I want the person pulling your strings," replied Carlton, as he motioned for Harvath to bring him the vial of pills from the table.

Ashford was quiet for several moments. Finally, he said, "I won't testify. It'd be a death sentence. I'd never live to see any trial."

"You let us worry about the trial."

"I want money, too. If you want my help, it's going to cost."

"I think we should just kill him," said Harvath.

Carlton waved him off. "I'm not changing the terms of my offer, Robert. It is a take-it-or-leave-it deal. You're either going into the brand-new Reed Carlton witness protection program, or you're going into a cornfield in rural New England. It's your call."

Once again, the MI5 operative took several moments before responding. When he did speak, he said, "Give me two of my pain pills. Actually, make it three and I'll tell you anything you want to know."

"I'll consider giving you *one*," said the Old Man, nodding to Harvath that it was okay to prep one, "when you start filling us in on what we want to know."

Ashford looked at the two men. The tears were flowing again. He had given up. He was broken. They had him. "Where do you want me to begin?" he asked.

Harvath stepped in, opened the bottle, and shook out one of the pills. Ashford opened his mouth. Harvath placed the pill on his tongue and then gave him some more water to wash it down.

"Let's start with who you're working for."

"You already know who it is," said Ashford.

"I want to hear you say it."

"James Standing."

"The terror attacks in Europe and Chicago that you helped us work on, who was behind those?"

"James Standing."

"And the attacks on movie theaters across the United States that just happened?"

"James Standing."

"The airport attacks?"

"Standing," Ashford repeated yet again.

"Tell me about the terror network itself," said Carlton.

The MI5 man looked at him. "It was built by the Chinese as part of an asymmetric warfare plan called *unrestricted warfare*. Standing financed and helped arrange for the stealing of the plan from the Chinese military. He then had every person who had been involved in crafting the plan killed."

"How many terror cells are in the United States?"

The Brit had to think for a moment, but then replied, "Hundreds. Easily, hundreds. Your entire country is infested."

"How do you communicate with the cells?"

"I want a guarantee in writing that I am honestly going to get immunity from prosecution."

Harvath leaned forward. "How about instead we dump you outside the Russian Center of Special Operations with a sign around your neck saying you helped get three Spetsnaz soldiers killed?"

Carlton motioned for Harvath to back off. "We're not negotiating anymore, Robert. I gave you my word. Now tell me how you communicate with the cells."

"There is a hierarchy of commanders," Ashford finally stated. "When Aazim Aleem was killed—"

"By *you*," Harvath clarified.

"Yes. By me. After I killed Aazim, a man named Mustafa Karami was promoted. I then relayed commands to him, or Standing did. He then contacted the appropriate cells through emails, chat rooms, coded telephone conversations, and the like. Despite having been set up as a tool of the Chinese, for all intents and purposes it is a fully functioning Islamic terror network."

"Why was Aazim killed?" asked Carlton.

"Isn't it obvious? We couldn't have the CIA interrogating him. That would have been the end of all of it."

"And what was your end game in all of this? What was your goal? Yours and Standing's? Certainly, this isn't just about terror for terror's sake."

Ashford grinned sadly. "It was about making the world a better place."

"By murdering people? Innocent men, women, and children?" demanded Harvath.

"All in pursuit of a greater good."

"In other words, the ends justify the means?"

Ashford nodded and Harvath wanted to beat the Brit to a pulp, *all in pursuit of a greater good*, but the Old Man could see he was getting worked up and signaled again for him to stand down.

"How were these attacks supposed to make the world a better place?" Carlton asked.

"The only hope for the world is the collapse of the narrowly focused nation-state model. The planet is too interconnected, society too complex to be ruled by mob mentalities that only care about what's good for them and don't give a damn about anyone else."

"So the attacks were meant to collapse the concept of the nation-state?"

"They are meant to collapse the United States. Once the U.S. is out of the way, the rest of the world can be led—"

"Into complete and utter darkness," interjected Harvath. "Without America, there's no peace. Without peace, there's no prosperity."

The Brit shook his head slowly. "Without America, there is justice."

Carlton studied his former friend. "How did you go from fighting communists to becoming one?"

"I opened my eyes, Reed. I saw the incredible suffering in the world. Then I opened my mind and went looking for answers."

"You have no idea," said Harvath, "what the world would be like without America."

"We'll see soon enough."

"Really? And who'll govern this new world order? Some elite ruling class of intellectuals? Americans will never stand for the overthrow of their government."

Ashford smiled again. "Of course they will. It's already happening."

"Trust me, your attacks will only bring the American people closer together."

"I'm not talking about the terrorist attacks. Those are simply part of the final phase. The overthrow of America has been going on for decades. If someone tried to collapse the United States overnight, of course the American people would revolt. That's why it had to be done slowly, quietly. It has been aided from both the outside and the inside. All of the massive problems besetting your nation, all of the economic, political, and social turmoil, hasn't suddenly picked up speed by accident. It's all by design and it all has a singular, overriding purpose."

The man was insane. "And just so I don't miss this glorious new dawn of global governance when it happens, what should I be on the lookout for?" asked Harvath. "Blue-helmeted United Nations soldiers marching up Main Street, U.S.A.? Or will it be more subtle than that?"

"You don't have to look for anything," replied Ashford. "It's already here. It's all around you. You've been looking right at it for years without knowing. You still have your name. You still have your flag. You still believe you have your freedoms, though in reality they have been slowly siphoned away. You still believe you have a Republic when, day-by-day, what you are being left with is merely the illusion of a Republic. Your entire house, as it were, has been rebuilt one brick at a time and no one has even noticed. No one has done a single thing about it."

"How do we stop it?" asked Carlton.

"I don't think you can," replied Ashford.

"Standing wants to push the nation over the edge. He has some vision in mind of how to push us past the point of no return. How does he do that? How many more attacks are coming?"

"At this point, I only know of two that have definitely been activated, but there's literally thousands of options he can choose from. The unrestricted warfare plan is as deep as it is broad."

"What are the two?" said Carlton, eager to ascertain whether Ashford was telling them the truth.

"All of the attacks are color-coded. The next two attacks are orange and yellow. Orange will be attacks on the corporate headquarters of the companies listed on the Dow Industrial Average.

Some of the companies are in regular office buildings, others are on campuses. Provisions have been made to collapse some buildings entirely and in other cases to have explosives detonate in the offices, boardrooms, and executive dining rooms of senior management."

So far, it appeared to Carlton that Ashford was telling the truth. "And when are those attacks supposed to happen?"

"Today."

"What are the yellow attacks?" Harvath asked.

"The yellow attacks are a follow-on. They target the major news outlets, the idea being that if they can be taken out, national news will essentially cease to exist. Local news will continue, but there won't be anyone to truly connect and expose the dots on a national level."

"That's it?"

Ashford shook his head. "Not exactly. Standing is worried that the network has been compromised. He rushed the Dow attack forward because he wanted to create financial chaos. He wanted to really hit people where they'd feel it in order to add to their panic.

"If he can, I think he'll activate one additional attack. He's particularly enamored of a final attack on the nation's infrastructure."

"What part?"

"Standing has always been interested in taking down the Internet and as much of the power grid as possible. He wants everything to grind to a halt and to plunge the country into literal darkness. It's kind of the coup de grâce for him."

"When? How soon?"

"When we discussed it, he said the best timing would be before all of the crops could be harvested. With no fuel being delivered to power tractors or trucks, food would rot in the field and never make it to market. Millions would starve and millions more would freeze to death over the winter."

Harvath looked at Carlton and gestured toward the hallway. They left Ashford strapped to the chair and stepped out of the room, closing the door behind them.

"We're going to need a complete map of that terror network. Names, pictures, telephone numbers, addresses, means of contact, all of it," said Harvath. "Then somebody's going to have to figure out how to take down all of the cell members, all at the same time, all across the country, without any word leaking out."

"That's going to mean an extremely well-coordinated law enforcement effort," replied Carlton.

Harvath nodded. "We also need to get our hands on that unrestricted warfare plan. If Ashford has a copy, and we should assume he does, we need to get it ASAP. The more we know about what's in that playbook, the better defense *and* offense we can mount."

"Which brings us to James Standing."

Harvath took a moment as he tried to be certain he had put all of the pieces together correctly. "If Ashford and Standing control the network and we have Ashford, then the only one left calling the shots is Standing."

"Correct."

"At some point, though, when he's unable to make contact with Ashford, he's going to know that something is up. In fact, when the Dow attacks don't happen, he'll know he's been penetrated."

"And could go for broke and activate all the remaining attacks."

"Which is why we need to get to the network's current commander, this Karami guy, as well as Standing, right away," said Harvath. "If we can do that, we might be able to short-circuit the network and render it inert until all its members can be rounded up."

"There's just one thing," said Carlton. "Taking out some foreign terrorist like Karami is one thing. Dealing with a politically connected billionaire American philanthropist like James Standing is something totally different."

"I agree," replied Harvath. "And I know exactly how we should handle it."

CHAPTER 68

Robert Ashford had provided Harvath with the rough layout of James Standing's New York City apartment. He had also provided an accurate picture of the billionaire's personal security detail.

For the overnight shift, only four men were kept on duty. One was positioned in the lobby with the doorman, while another was at the receiving entrance. A third man remained in the apartment in a small security room located off the kitchen, monitoring the building's closed-circuit camera feed. The fourth agent operated as a "floater," moving from position to position, relieving the other men when it was time for their respective breaks and filling in as an impromptu driver when needed.

Harvath had gained access to the building via the roof of an adjacent structure. He made his way down the interior security stairs to the back door of Standing's apartment, underneath which he slid a fiber-optic surveillance camera. Cupping the scope to his eye, he slowly scanned the interior of the kitchen.

Because of the angle, he couldn't see into the security room, but he had little doubt that the agent watching the CCTV feeds was there. Retracting the camera, Harvath put it back in his pack and removed a short aluminum cylinder wrapped in clear tubing, as well as a full-face respirator.

Placing the respirator over his head, he made sure the seal around his face was tight and then unwound the tubing from the cylinder and fed it beneath the door.

There was a barely perceptible hiss as he opened the valve and began to pump the contents of the cylinder into the kitchen.

Three-Methylfentanyl, or 3-MF as it was known, was an opioid analgesic that ranged anywhere from four hundred to six thousand times more powerful than morphine, depending upon what type of isomer it was combined with. Harvath was using a cis isomer, which pushed the gas being emitted from the tube beneath the kitchen door to its most effective range.

It was the same substance used by the Russians in the Moscow theater hostage crisis in 2002 and was extremely tricky to work with. Minimum exposure could knock a person out for hours. Anything more than minimum exposure and the chances of overdose and death rose exponentially. The common temptation to believe that if a little bit was good then a lot was better had to be avoided at all costs. The Russians had overadministered the substance in Moscow and had ended up killing not only the hostage-takers, but the hostages as well.

Harvath kept a close eye on his watch and then reached down and shut off the gas.

He pulled the hose from under the door, wrapped it around the cylinder, and tucked the device back into his pack. He then removed his lock-pick gun and went to work opening the door. A few clicks of the gun and a slight turn of the tensioning wrench later and he was in. Shouldering his pack, he drew a suppressed Glock and crept inside.

The door swung noiselessly on its well-oiled hinges and Harvath made sure to close and quietly lock it behind him. The only illumination in the kitchen came from dim undercabinet lighting. It took a moment for his eyes to adjust to the semidarkness.

Around the corner he could see the glow of television monitors spilling into a narrow corridor. Cautiously, Harvath made his way forward.

He found Standing's agent slumped over a small desk in the tiny security room that had likely functioned as a maid's quarters at some point. Reaching down with his latex-gloved hand, Harvath felt for a pulse. The security man was still alive. Glancing up, he checked the monitors and located Standing's three other security men, all of whom were still downstairs.

Leaving the security room, Harvath passed through the kitchen, pausing only long enough to open a window, drop a piece of maroon foil from the top of an expensive Bordeaux in the trash, and locate a wineglass. Once he had taken care of those, he headed for the master bedroom.

Harvath estimated the apartment had to be at least ten thousand square feet. Once a safe distance from the kitchen, he removed his respirator.

At the end of a long hallway carpeted with Persian rugs, its walls lined with silk tapestries, was the door to James Standing's bedroom. Harvath slid his fiber-optic camera underneath the door and took another long, slow look around.

Satisfied that Standing was in bed, alone, and still asleep, Harvath tucked the device into his pack and carefully opened the door.

His objective was approximately thirty feet away from Standing on the other side of the billionaire's enormous bed. Harvath had no doubt that somewhere near the bed there was a panic button, so he crossed the room as quickly and as quietly as he could.

Slipping into the master bathroom, he set down his pack and organized his materials. When he was ready, he closed the drain and turned on the water in the tub.

• • •

James Standing awoke to the sound of running water. At first, he thought it had been a dream, but the longer the sound persisted, the more he became convinced that it was in fact real and that it was coming from his bathroom.

But why would his bath be running? Still half-asleep, he threw back his bedcovers and swung his feet out of bed.

Sliding his feet into his Stubbs & Woottons, he ignored his robe and padded across the bedroom to figure out what the hell was going on.

As he got closer to the bathroom, the sound of running water got louder and he picked up his pace.

Pushing open the door, he clicked on the lights and sure enough, his bath was running. *How the hell was that possible?*

Walking across the polished marble floor, he arrived at the tub and reached for the handle. As he did, he heard a voice from behind say, "Let it fill up."

The voice so startled him that his heart nearly burst from his chest. Spinning around, he saw a man completely dressed in black holding a suppressed pistol, which was pointed right at him.

"Who are you?" the billionaire demanded. "What the hell are you doing in my apartment?"

"Robert Ashford sent me," said Harvath, as he watched the fear etched on Standing's face deepen.

"All I have to do is shout and my security team will be in."

"Who? The three men downstairs or the one near the kitchen I already took care of?"

The financier didn't reply.

"You can shout if you want to, but nobody is going to hear you."

Standing looked as if he was thinking about doing just that, but quickly decided not to. "What do you want? Are you here to arrest me?"

Harvath pulled a vial of pills from his pocket and tossed it to him. "Eat."

"*Eat?* What the hell are these?"

"Laxatives."

"Why the hell would I want to take a bottle full of laxatives?"

"Because you're about to go on a very long trip with no bathroom breaks," said Harvath.

"What are you doing? Kidnapping me? Did that idiot Ashford put you up to this?"

"I'm doing you a favor. Start chewing."

Standing opened the bottle and dumped several of the pills into his hand. He looked down and then threw the entire handful at Harvath. "Fuck you."

Harvath smiled and tucked his pistol away at the small of his back. Reaching above the toilet, he took down one of Standing's mono-grammed bath towels and started walking forward.

Instinctively, the billionaire began backing away from him. The moment he did, Harvath sprung.

Twisting the towel tightly around Standing's head, he used it to pull him off-balance. As the older man fell, Harvath steered him toward the tub, where he landed with a splash.

As soon as he hit the water, Harvath had him under it, careful to do everything with even pressure across the towel so as not to leave any marks.

Standing was strong for his age and struggled wildly. After a few more seconds, Harvath let him up. As his head broke the surface, he sucked in huge gasps of air.

"Let me make this very clear," said Harvath. "You're going to take those pills. Understand me?"

Standing didn't respond, but he was visibly shaken by the explosion of violence that had just occurred. The tub was almost full and Har-vath turned off the water.

In his fall, the billionaire had spilled the rest of the pills. Harvath scooped up a handful, gave them to him, and repeated his order. "Eat."

This time, Standing did as he was told. As the man sat soaking in his pajamas, Harvath removed an opened bottle of wine from his pack and pulled out the cork. After filling the glass, he walked over to the tub and handed it to Standing. "Drink," he said. "Red wine speeds up the process."

He hesitantly accepted the glass as if he was suddenly beginning to grasp that maybe he was being lied to.

"Drink," Harvath repeated. "All of it."

As the man tilted it back, rivulets of wine ran down his chin and dripped into the water.

When the billionaire had drained the glass, Harvath refilled it. The man didn't need to have the order repeated. He knew he was supposed to drink.

He had consumed about half of the second glass when Harvath told him to stop. He could see the man's eyes were starting to have trouble focusing. He needed to say what he was going to say now, before the man could no longer grasp what was happening.

Harvath sat down on the edge of the tub and leaned in so James Standing could hear everything he was about to say.

"Listen to me very closely, you son of a bitch. Those weren't laxatives. Right now, your heart is rapidly slowing down, unable to pump blood through your body. In about a minute, you're going to find your lungs suddenly can't seem to get enough air and you're going to gasp for breaths that just won't come.

"Before you die, I want you to know that everything you have spent your entire life working for has been completely undone. Every organization, every company, every foundation you have ever created, all of it. You're going to be known the world over for the monster you are. Your name will forever be synonymous with evil."

Standing tried to speak, to say something in response, but he couldn't. The words wouldn't come.

"Every family who lost someone in the attacks you financed will sue your estate and they will drain it of every last single penny. People who once held you in high esteem will mock your memory or recoil in horror at the mention of your name.

"All the money in the world can't prevent what's about to happen to you. On behalf of every one of your victims, I hope you rot in hell."

Standing up, Harvath took the wineglass from Standing and set it on the side of the tub along with the half-empty bottle. He took the billionaire's weakening fingers and pressed them against a straight razor, which he dropped into the water along with the towel.

After mopping up the floor with a shammy he'd brought in his pack, Harvath gathered up his belongings and exited the bathroom.

Passing through the bedroom, he stopped at a large flat-screen TV. Ejecting the tray of the DVD player beneath, he inserted the disc Nicholas had given him and turned everything on.

Back in the kitchen, the gas had dissipated. Closing the window, he gave the security monitors one last check before leaving the apartment and the building the same way he had come in.

He could see the sun just beginning to come up as he crossed Central Park. Removing his cell phone, he plugged in his earbuds, and called Carlton.

When the Old Man answered, he simply said, "It's done."

"Good," Carlton replied. "Come home."

CHAPTER 69

ONE WEEK LATER

The story of James Standing's "suicide" made headlines around the world. The question from Hong Kong to Hartford, though, was *Why?* Why would a man who had everything end his own life?

That question was answered days later when the *New York Post* ran a front-page story about documents and photos that had been sent to one of its Page Six gossip editors. The story, presumed to have been leaked by an NYPD detective or forensics investigator, detailed how Standing had consumed a combination of wine and sleeping pills and climbed into his bathtub to slit his wrists. Before he could do so, he succumbed to the overdose. The razor was found after the tub had been drained.

The motivation for his death was said to be a DVD the police found in his bedroom. It was a rough cut of a documentary entitled

Well Endowed. The film detailed how Standing had funneled profits from several of his hedge fund clients into a grand plan designed to collapse the U.S. government called Project Green Ramp. The film also included interrogation footage of two men, both of whom had had their faces blurred. One of the men, whom the *Post* claimed spoke English with a heavy Russian accent, could be seen admitting to having been hired to kill the film's creative team, executive producer Larry Salomon, director Chip Marcus, and associate producer Jeremy Andrews. The mere suggestion that James Standing might be connected to the multiple homicides in Los Angeles set the media on fire.

The real bombshell in the *Post* story came from the interrogation of the second subject, a British man, who claimed that James Standing had financed and planned the devastating wave of terrorist attacks that had killed so many innocent Americans.

Within hours of the *New York Post* story, the Department of Justice launched a formal investigation.

Based on information provided by Robert Ashford and corroborated by Mansoor Aleem in Iceland, a detailed list of U.S. cells within the unrestricted warfare terror network was developed and delivered to the FBI, which, in conjunction with the U.S. Marshals Service and local law enforcement agencies, orchestrated an amazing nationwide roundup of all of the terrorist suspects.

Sean Chase and Pat Murphy flew from Iceland back to Sweden and found Mustafa Karami and Sabah right where Ashford told them they would, in a small apartment in Stockholm's red-light district. Chase was forced to use his left hand but dispatched Karami with exceptional precision. Pat Murphy, on behalf of his teammates, made Sabah suffer. He shot him in the knees and worked his way slowly upward until he decided to end it and put his last round in the giant's forehead and the man's lifeless corpse slumped to the ground.

Back in Los Angeles, Martin Sevan accompanied Larry Salomon and Luke Ralston to a quiet meeting with LAPD detectives and the

Los Angeles County district attorney. They were no longer active suspects in the murders that had taken place at Larry Salomon's home.

Martin Sevan wanted the entire thing put to bed. Both of his clients wanted to get on with their lives. With all of the buzz *Well Endowed* had received in the press, Larry Salomon was eager to complete the film's postproduction.

At first, he'd had no idea how James Standing had gotten hold of a rough cut of the film. But when he heard it included interrogation footage and that one of the men being interrogated was a Russian, he realized Scot Harvath must have been behind it.

Though he wasn't officially asked to keep quiet about Harvath's involvement, he knew it was the right thing to do. Thanks to him, everyone was clamoring to see *Well Endowed*. Several prestigious film festivals even offered to host, sight unseen, the premiere.

Salomon, though, had a different idea. If the communities would have him, he wanted to screen the film in the cities and towns whose movie theaters had been attacked. His plan was to show the film in outdoor venues. It seemed only right that those who had been attacked get the first look at the documentary.

All the cities and towns had to say was *yes.* Salomon didn't want anything else from them. He would cover all the screening costs. He wanted to be part of helping people to heal.

And in a way, maybe it would help him heal. After the screening tour, Salomon planned to travel to Israel. He needed to make peace. He needed to make peace with himself and with what had happened to Rachael. He no longer wanted to be the man he was. He wanted to go back to being the man he had been before Rachael's death. To do that, he needed to let go of a lot of things. He hoped the screenings and time away would allow him to do that.

Under Martin Sevan's counsel, they went through the formality of answering a final round of questions for the authorities and were then allowed to leave.

When Luke Ralston stepped outside, he saw Ali Sevan waiting for him. He exchanged a few words with Larry and Martin, who walked off to their cars as he walked over to talk with Ali.

"Case closed?" she asked.

"Case closed," he replied. He was surprised to see her and also surprised that her father hadn't even batted an eye when he saw her outside waiting for all of them. "What are you doing here?"

"I thought maybe we could have lunch."

"Lunch?"

"There are some things we should talk about."

Ralston was unsure what to make of her offer. "Does Brent know you're here?" he asked, referring to her husband.

"That's one of the things I want to talk about," she replied, holding up her left hand.

He must have missed it on the beach, but she wasn't wearing a wedding ring.

Reading the look on his face, she said, "We've been divorced for about six months."

"When I asked you about him, you said he was fine."

Ali smiled. "I was telling you the truth. As a lawyer, I'm professionally forbidden to lie."

Ralston smiled back. "We'll have to take your car," he said. "Mine's going to be in the shop for a long time."

•   •   •

While the rest of the loose ends were being tied up, the Old Man had sent Harvath to Paris for a meeting. Reed Carlton had always had a good relationship with Israeli intelligence. Harvath's assignment was to see that it continued.

He carried with him a file that detailed how James Standing had intended to turn his sights on bringing down Israel, one of the world's few other true democracies, once the United States had been collapsed.

The billionaire had planned to draw Israel into a war with its neighbors. But on top of that, he had developed a means to ensure that America would not come to her aid.

When Israel most needed America, Standing planned to release documents that would make it appear that Israel had created the Aleem terror network, a ruse to make Americans believe that the Israelis had ordered the terrorist attacks on the United States in order to manipulate public opinion and national policy. The documents would allege that Israel had dreamed up the elaborate plot in order to con America into rushing to Israel's aid because the same common enemy was attacking both nations.

The Israeli intelligence officer Harvath met with was grateful for the information.

As their meeting ended at the La Closerie des Lilas bar in Montparnasse, the Israeli slid an envelope across the small table.

Harvath was confused. "What's this?" he asked as the man stood up to leave.

"I was told to give it to you when we were finished."

As the man walked out of the bar, Harvath opened the small envelope. Inside was a piece of paper with an address in the Sixth Arrondissement. It was written in the Old Man's hand.

Carlton had told him there was something else he wanted him to do in Paris, but he hadn't elaborated. Most likely, the address was for the Carlton Group's new Parisian safe house and there'd be further instructions waiting for him there.

Carlton could often be cryptic like that. He compartmentalized everything, revealing only as much as he felt you needed to know. Robert Ashford could have had no clue about the nature of the new life and identity the Old Man had promised him in exchange for his cooperation. The Brit had made the mistake of referring to James Standing as the "world's deadliest catch," and that cemented his fate.

Ashford was quite distraught once he learned that he was being relocated to Alaska. Harvath could only imagine the look on the MI5 man's face once he discovered that his new career was nowhere near as pedestrian as recycling boxes at the Fairbanks Walmart.

Rawhide was a ninety-two-foot crab-fishing boat out of the Aleutian Islands port of Dutch Harbor in Unalaska. Robert Ashford was her newest deckhand.

The Old Man had kept his word, but he had simultaneously sentenced Ashford to a life of hard labor. Carlton had made it very clear that, if Ashford tried to run, there was an open kill order for him and Harvath would fill it personally.

The Old Man then turned Yaroslav Yatsko over to the CIA. Though they might very well kick him out of the country and turn him loose, the Carlton Group needed to purchase a modicum of goodwill with the Agency. Harvath wanted to see the man tried for setting up the murders of the filmmakers and the attempted murder of Larry Salomon, but the Old Man had his mind made up. He did, though, make sure the CIA intervened with the L.A. County authorities on behalf of Ralston and Salomon, and for that, Harvath was grateful.

• • •

Stepping out of the bar, he turned up the collar of his coat. It was a chilly night, but Harvath decided to walk anyway and headed north.

Unlike Venice, Paris was a city that could be romantic and still not make you feel self-conscious about walking its streets alone.

As he walked, he remembered the last time he had been in Paris. He had been sitting in a café, ready to propose to a woman with whom he thought he could spend the rest of his life and leave his career behind, when his career had reappeared and sucked him back in.

It hadn't been that long ago, but it seemed like a lifetime. So much had happened since. So much had changed.

Couples passed by on the sidewalk. They seemed oblivious to his presence, too wrapped up in each other to even notice him. Harvath shook his head and moved on.

He wondered where he was going and why the Old Man had transmitted the address through the Israeli.

Entering the Sixth Arrondissement, he conducted another round of SDRs. Finally, he arrived at the address.

He stood outside looking up at the limestone façade of the building with its black, wrought-iron balconettes. The ground floor consisted of a patisserie and a wine shop separated by a security door that likely provided entrance to the dwellings above.

Harvath studied the note again. There wasn't any name, just the address.

As he removed his cell phone to call the Old Man, it vibrated with a text message. Harvath clicked on it. It was from Carlton. All it said was *Ring #7*.

Harvath approached the buzzers. Number 7 was listed under the name Bonduelle. He pressed the button.

Moments later the door clicked open.

Harvath stepped into the eighteenth-century lobby. A gilded, cage-style elevator was surrounded by a stained marble staircase.

Not a fan of tiny elevators, Harvath opted for the stairs and began climbing.

Stepping onto the landing, he found the light switch timer and depressed it to give him enough light to navigate the hallway.

As he walked past the old, scarred doors, he wondered what his next assignment would be.

The sounds of French programming could be heard from each apartment he passed until he reached number 7. From behind the large, wooden door, he could hear music playing. It sounded like Pavarotti.

Reaching out, he twisted the brass handle, which rang the bell inside, and then he waited.

The music turned down. There was the sound of footfalls approaching the door and then a pause as someone gazed out the peephole.

The metal clacking of an old lock sounded and the old door creaked as it was slowly pulled open.

Inside stood a woman in jeans and a white button-down shirt. Her reddish-brown hair fell past her shoulders. Even in the half-light of the hall, her blue eyes shone. Harvath was taken completely by surprise.

Her lips spread into a smile. "Hello, Scot," she said softly.

He was about to lean forward and kiss her, when he noticed movement at the stairs.

"Gun!" he yelled, and knocked Riley Turner back into the apartment just as a hail of bullets splintered the door frame.

ACKNOWLEDGMENTS

Writing the acknowledgments is always enjoyable, as it means the book is finished and I get to thank all the people who made it possible. For me, the most important people to thank are you, the **readers.** Whether you have been with me from *The Lions of Lucerne*, are brand-new to my novels, or fall somewhere in between, I thank you for your support.

My thanks also go out to all of the fantastic **booksellers** around the world who continue to turn so many people on to my work.

James Ryan, Ronald Moore, Sean Fischer, and **Rodney Cox**—all great friends—were once again indispensable to my writing. Been-there-done-that-and-have-got-the-empty shell-casings-to-prove-it doesn't even begin to sum up the knowledge I am able to tap with these gentlemen. Thank you.

I also want to thank my good friends **Scott F. Hill, PhD,** and **Steve Tuttle** for all of their help with the novel as well.

There were several additional people who also contributed, but asked that their names not be used. Each of you knows how much I appreciate not only what you have done for me, but what you continue to do for our country. Thank you.

A novel's success is directly proportional to the quality of the people on its team, and I am lucky enough to be working with some of the absolute best. My thanks to everyone at Atria and Pocket Books, including: my exceptional editor, **Emily Bestler;** my wonderful publishers, **Carolyn Reidy, Judith Curr**, and **Louise Burke**; my fantastic publicist, **David Brown**; the terrific **Atria/Pocket sales staff, art, and production departments**, and **audio division**, as well as the incomparable **Michael Selleck, Kate Cetrulo, Sarah Branham, Irene Lipsky, Ariele Fredman**, and **Lisa Keim**.

I also wish to thank my remarkable literary agent, **Heide Lange**, of Sanford J. Greenburger Associates, Inc., as well as the unparalleled **Jennifer Linnan** and **Rachael Dillon Fried** for all that they do for me.

In Hollywood, my outstanding entertainment attorney, **Scott Schwimer,** continues not only to be my guide, but also my very good friend. Thanks, Scottie.

I always save the best thank-you for last. The most critical members of my team are my wonderful **family**. Without them, there would be no book. They are my inspiration. I love you all and am particularly indebted to my beautiful wife, **Trish,** who keeps the world at bay so I can write. Thank you, honey. I love you.

Turn the page to enjoy an exclusive excerpt from
Brad Thor's next pulse-pounding thriller

BLACK ICE

PROLOGUE

Helicopters, it was said, didn't fly—they merely beat the air into submission. But halfway between continental Norway and the North Pole, it felt as if the air were winning.

As sleet slammed against the exterior, another sixty-plus-mile-per-hour gust rocked the airframe. The rotors groaned in protest. There was only so much the helo could handle. They were pushing it beyond its limits.

Scot Harvath didn't need to see the water to know the slate-gray ocean was roiling with whitecaps. This far above the arctic circle, where moisture from the south collided with icy, polar winds, massive depressions formed, unleashing nightmare weather.

If anything went wrong, there would be no rescue. No one back at the U.S. Embassy in Oslo, much less anyone at the White House, would acknowledge him, nor the mission he was on.

He glanced at the cracked face of his watch, blood crusted atop its bezel. *Just a little farther*, he thought to himself. *We're almost there*.

Ignoring the pain in his ribs, he reached for his pack and opened it. Everything was still in place. *Take care of your gear and your gear will take care of you*. It was a mantra that had saved his life again and again.

Under his mountaineering jacket, he felt the cold press of metal against his skin. No one knew if the odd-shaped key, hanging from a piece of paracord, would even work—not after all this time.

If it didn't, all of the danger, all of the risk, would be for nothing, and the consequences would be deadly. Failure, though, wasn't an option.

That was the world he lived in. He wasn't interested in easy tasks. In fact, he had always chosen the most difficult, the most perilous assignments.

It was how he was wired. No matter how bleak the scenario, he would never give up. Success was the only outcome he would entertain.

But as yet another gale-force blast of frigid air convulsed the 0helicopter, causing it to swing violently from side to side, he began to have his doubts.

Moments later, an alarm began shrieking from the cockpit, and Harvath knew they were in trouble.

The pilots, though, were able to regain control. The bird was still swaying, but nowhere near as badly as before. It looked like everything was going to be okay.

Then there was an ear-splitting crack. It sounded as if the helo had been hit by lightning. It was followed by the tail rotor completely shearing off. And as it did, the helicopter began to spiral.

They were going down.

CHAPTER 1

There was only one problem with summer in Norway—it was too short.

Sitting at his favorite outdoor café, Harvath raised his face to the sun. The warmth felt good. *He* felt good. Better than he had in a long time. The last two months had been exactly what he had needed.

He and Sølvi had bounced between her apartment in the city and the cottage he had rented out on the fjord. It depended on her schedule. As one of the newest deputy directors at the Norwegian Intelligence Service, or NIS for short, she had been pretty busy.

Because the commute was easier from the apartment, they usually stayed in Oslo during the week and headed for the fjord on Fridays. That was fine by Harvath. He had enjoyed getting to know the city. There were plenty of museums and cultural sights, not to mention great bars, restaurants, and cafés.

Most mornings, if Sølvi didn't have to leave too early, they would go for a run. The lush Akerselva River Trail was a favorite, as was the Ekeberg Sculpture Park. For safety, they always mixed things up, never frequenting the same location two days in a row.

In addition to running, Harvath had joined a neighborhood gym. When they were at the cottage, he would swim—a lot.

The physical activity had been restorative. He had put back on the weight he had lost and had returned to his full level of fitness. And while he still consumed alcohol, it wasn't like before. A half-empty bottle of wine could sit in the fridge for days before they finished it off.

In a word, he was happy. *Really* happy. Sølvi was an amazing woman. She was not only beautiful, but smart and talented as hell. To be honest, she was probably smarter and more talented than he was. The only realm in which he was confident that he had her beat was experience. But even then, it was only because she was several years younger.

Despite the age difference, though, they shared something very powerful, something that went beyond their physical attraction to each other. Her past was as dark and troubled as his own. They had both been shattered but, in coming together, had found a way to glue their pieces into something better, stronger.

Ultimately, what he loved most about her was her sense of humor. It was a sign of how intelligent she was.

It was also a coping mechanism. The espionage business could be exceptionally brutal—a fact he knew all too well.

Devoid of meaningful relationships, spies often became disillusioned, cynical. Many checked out via booze or other vices—another fact he knew all too well. He was determined not to allow that to happen to either of them again.

He wanted to make Sølvi happy—as happy as she had made him. Second chances were exceedingly rare in life. He was determined not to screw this up. Which was why mapping out their next step was proving to be difficult.

It was one of the best summers he'd ever had. They had squeezed every drop out of it. The cottage had come with a boat, and they had gotten out on the water as often as they could. A few mornings, he had even used it to drive Sølvi to work, dropping her at the dock adjacent to The Thief hotel where she'd catch a ride to the office.

There had been barbecues and beach parties. A rotating mix of friends from NIS and the CIA's Oslo Station had drifted in and out of their lives—both in the city and out on the fjord. It was rare to see a weekend where they weren't hosting some sort of get-together, or attending someone else's. It had been wall-to-wall fun, and it was no surprise that no one wanted it to end. But at some point, it had to.

He had burned through all of his sick leave, as well as his vacation days. To say the office was eager for him to return was an understatement. In fact, his boss had told him in no uncertain terms that if he wasn't back the following week, he would be "cashiered."

It was a dramatic term to have used. Not *fired*. Not the more genteel *let go*. But *cashiered*—the public humiliation of having one's military insignia ripped away and their sword snapped in front of their comrades.

It was an old-school term. *Really* old school. Yet it was perfectly in keeping with the Cold War–era warrior he reported to.

He couldn't blame the man for wanting him back. Had their situations been reversed, he would have wanted the same. In fact, he was surprised he had been allowed to stay away as long as he had. That's where his next steps with Sølvi got tricky.

There was no telling where he would be sent next, much less for how long. On the whole, his were quick, in-and-out jobs. What they weren't was predictable.

In an attempt to give their relationship some structure, something for the two of them to look forward to, he had printed out a calendar.

The idea was to ink specific dates they felt certain they could be together. The additional hope was that in between his assignments, he could swing through Oslo to see her. With her promotion, she was wedded to headquarters. Any hope of tagging up with him on an assignment expense account in a hotel room in some far-flung, exotic locale was out of the question. Their best chance of seeing each other was in Norway.

It would be tough, but not impossible. He was committed to making it work. And when he set his mind to something, he made it happen.

With the clock ticking down, he wanted their remaining time together to be special. They had been eating a ton of takeout lately, so tonight he decided he'd cook a real American dinner. Something for just the two of them. It would be a night he could freeze in his memory and replay until he returned and they were together again.

He finished the last sip of his kokekaffe—a popular Norwegian afternoon coffee served black and slightly cooled. Standing up, he put on his sunglasses and strolled across the cobbles of Christiania Square, headed toward his favorite butcher shop.

Though it was a bit of a walk to the food hall in Mathallen, it was worth it. *Annis Pølsemakeri* had the best meats in town.

Out at the cottage, there had been an old smoker that he had made his mission to get up and running again. Once he had, he decided to throw a Texas-style barbeque. When he asked friends where he could get the absolute best brisket, ribs, and pork butt, everyone had said *"Annis's."* So that's where he had gone.

The staff had been so friendly that he had gone back again and again—even just to pick up ground beef for burgers. They were an amusing bunch and tried to upsell him into horsemeat or beef tongue, trying good-naturedly to see if they could gross out their American customer. They had no idea that over the course of his career, he had eaten much, much worse.

After buying a couple of T-bones at *Annis*, he would hit *Vulkan Frukt og Grønt AS* for fresh vegetables. He figured it was a safe bet that they'd have potatoes and salad fixings. Hopefully, they'd have fresh ears of corn as well.

Once those items were taken care of, the next thing on his list would need to be a nice bottle of wine.

Not far from the food hall was a *Vinmonopolet*. He'd probably have to pay through the nose for a good California red, but if they had one, he planned on ignoring the price tag. He wanted their dinner to be as American as possible.

All that was left was to figure out dessert. Apple pie felt a bit too on the nose. What's more, while he could grill or smoke up a storm, he was no baker.

Since Sølvi was a big fan of dark chocolate, Harvath figured that's where he would focus. There was a stall in the food hall called *Sebas-*

tienBruno that sold chocolates, but what she really liked were Belgian chocolates. He made a mental note to keep his eyes peeled for any along the way.

After dinner, if there was time, they could stream a movie. Her passion for classic Hollywood films was bottomless. So far, they had watched *Casablanca*, *Lawrence of Arabia*, *Psycho*, *The Godfather*, *On the Waterfront*, *North by Northwest*, and *Citizen Kane* together. Tonight, he wanted to introduce her to *The Night of the Hunter* from 1955. It was unsettling, but a classic nonetheless.

A few blocks from the food hall, he spotted a small boutique that looked promising for quality chocolate. But when he was fifty yards away, a taxi pulled up and disgorged a ghost.

The sight of the man stopped Harvath dead in his tracks. His eyes had to have been playing tricks on him. The man he was looking at was dead.

Harvath had killed him himself.